"Did you decide to marry me next week?" Mitch asked.

"Next week? Things are moving right along," Perri said, reaching across the table to pat his lean forearm. She wouldn't mention again that he had to accept the Lord's sacrifice for him. No one can be forced into a sincere commitment. She shook her blond head. "I may as well be frank with you. The only thing I'd like better is to be married tomorrow. But it would be a big mistake. I'd rather never marry than to find myself in Kaima's position."

Mitch took a long drink. "Don't you know me better than that? I'd never hurt you, Seabrook. Never."

"I know you wouldn't want to, Mitch. I wouldn't want to hurt you either. But aside from our differences when it comes to God, you might end up finding it very painful being married not only to me but to my four boys. Living in constant bedlam? Never having a moment for your nerves to settle down? Having your most private moments subject to interruption?"

"I try not to think about it," he said after a moment's hesitation.

"I rest my case. I could never marry you until you do think about it—a lot.

VERALEE WIGGINS is the author of many novels, including *Llama Lady* and *Heartbreak Trail* which were voted top favorites by **Heartsong Presents** club members.

Books by VeraLee Wiggins

HEARTSONG PRESENTS

HP17—Llama Lady
HP33—Sweet Shelter
HP76—Heartbreak Trail
HP83—Martha My Own
HP92—Abram My Love
HP128—Misplaced Angel
HP149—Llama Land
HP183—A New Love

Tomorrow's Rainbow

VeraLee Wiggins

Heartsong Presents

For you, Perri. With my very dearest love.
May God shine on you forever
and give you your very own Rainbow—tomorrow.

ISBN 1-57748-045-7

TOMORROW'S RAINBOW

Cover illustration by Jeanne Brandt.

PRINTED IN THE U.S.A.

one

Perri Seabrook sat at the red light, tapping her fingers impatiently on the steering wheel of her beat-up station wagon. As the light turned green, she glanced at her watch, then stepped on the gas and surged forward. Eight-thirty-eight. Why, when she finally had gotten an interview for this fantastic position, did she have to be so late?

She pulled into the parking garage, grabbed the yellow ticket from the attendant, and anxiously scanned the rows of cars for an empty space. Finding nothing in the two lower levels, she checked her watch once more and bit her lip. Eight-forty-five. On the third level, she sighted a parking spot and breathed a sigh of relief. If she ran all the way, she could still reach the insurance building in time.

But as she slowed to turn in, a rusty and dented convertible backed out in front of her. Its ratty-looking top began to wiggle and shake. Perri sucked in an impatient breath; why didn't the guy just get out of her way? She checked her watch again. Eight-fifty. Ten minutes to reach the bottom of the parking arcade, run the block to the building, and locate the correct office. The convertible's white top jerked halfway down, back up, then shuddered back and forth.

Perri saw her perfect job disappearing even before she had the interview. "Forgive me, Lord," she breathed—and leaned on the horn.

Before she lifted her hand, a curly dark head popped through the rotten top, and black eyes bored into hers. Then two large hands clawed frantically at the mouldy fabric.

Perri leaned out the window. "Could you please hurry and get out of my way?" she called. "I'm late for an appointment."

The head disappeared, and a moment later a man in an expensive suit tumbled from the old car. The man waved wildly, pointing at the ruined top.

"Please move it," Perri pleaded. "I'm in a hurry."

The man trotted to Perri's window, his lips moving and his face dark. "See what you did?" he bellowed.

"You did it," Perri retorted, louder than necessary. "Now please move that thing so I can park." The man glared at her.

His car blocked the passage so she could neither park in the vacant spot nor move around it. "Please, won't you move your car?" she implored. "I have to be somewhere right now."

The man glared at her another moment, then slammed back into his car and jerked it ahead ten feet. Perri quickly parked and raced to the stairs, bypassing the elevator.

Five minutes later and puffing hard, she found a wide door with black-edged gold lettering that read: *Mitchell Winfield Insurance Agency*.

Throwing her shoulders back, she took five controlled breaths, then reached for her compact mirror. Her blond hair curled softly around her shoulders. Her eye makeup looked fine, nearly invisible, yet still emphasizing her large, bright blue eyes. Her cheeks blazed from the unaccustomed run, but that didn't hurt her appearance. She glanced down at her crisp light-blue linen suit and matching sandals. Everything seemed all right. She counted slowly to twenty-five and stepped through the door.

The clock on the wall said 9:05, and her heart sank. The receptionist gave Perri a smile. "May I help you?"

"Yes, I'm Perri Seabrook," she said breathlessly. "I have an appointment with Mitchell Winfield." Her voice quavered, and she hated herself for being so visibly nervous. She'd never held a job in her life and this was her first interview since her recent graduation from the University of Oregon. The experience in the parking arcade hadn't helped her nerves, either.

The receptionist looked at the clock. "Mr. Winfield will see you in a few minutes. Won't you have a seat?"

Perri sank into a bright orange plastic chair and snatched up a magazine, which she read with her eyes while her mind jumped to the frightening prospect ahead. Ten minutes later she looked up to find the receptionist gazing at her. The girl shrugged and smiled apologetically.

All this hurry for nothing. She might as well have been patient while that poor jerk tried to control his convertible top. A smile touched her lips as she remembered the sight of that old canvas top jerking back and forth. And then the black head popping through—just like a jack-in-the-box.

"Mr. Winfield will see you now, Miss Seabrook," the receptionist said, pointing to a door behind her desk.

Well, this is it. Look confident, wear a relaxed smile, agree to anything he says. She thanked the receptionist and opened the door.

As Perri stepped into the room, she inhaled a combination of after-shave and soap. Mmmm. The dark-headed man behind the desk stood to greet her. Both their mouths dropped open.

She faced the owner of the ruined convertible. After a long moment, the man jerked his gaze from hers and sat down at his desk. He shuffled papers for another long moment. Perri's stomach clenched.

"Is it all right if I leave now?" she finally asked softly.

"Not yet," he answered without looking up. He continued rearranging papers, writing on some, moving others.

Five more ageless minutes passed and several more papers passed through the man's hands.

At 9:35 Perri came to herself. Why was she standing here? She had important things to do at home if she wasn't getting a job. "I'm sorry this turned out badly, but I must go." The man stood. "I'm also sorry I honked at you," she continued. "Not only because it cost me the interview but because it wasn't nice." She bit her lip to hide a shame-faced smile. "I knew God wouldn't want me to honk my horn like that," she murmured. "So I guess this serves me right."

She turned to go but as she reached for the doorknob his voice stopped her. "Miss Seabrook, I'm not through with you yet."

She turned to face him. "Should I make another appointment?"

"That's not what I had in mind. Would you please sit down?" He indicated a large brown leather chair beside his desk.

What did he want? For her to pay for the top of that old car? She sat down. So did he—and then turned his attention back to the papers on his desk.

Several more minutes passed. She felt red streaks burn their way up her neck to her face, and her breath came short and fast. Nowhere did the Bible say she had to take this! She jumped up. "I'm sorry, Mr. Winfield, but I have to go."

He stood up too. His black hair curled in loose ringlets around his face. Any softness they might have given his face was counteracted, however, by his straight narrow nose, wide mouth, and jutting chin. The expression in his dark eyes told her he was used to being in control. She thought he also probably took his own attractiveness for granted.

The man's face suddenly softened, and he nodded, his black eyes gleaming. "I'm Mitchell Winfield." He glanced at the note pad on his desk. "And you're Perri Seabrook. Now that we have our names all figured out should we sit down and talk about this opening I have?" Perri dropped back into the comfortable chair with a sigh. He settled back and arranged his elbows on the polished desk.

"I thought we said it all in the arcade." Perri said.

He smiled. "We said a lot, but there may be something left."

"Are we talking about the car top?" she asked.

Mitchell Winfield leaned back in his chair and laughed. "No, not the car top. I didn't realize how rotten that top was." He thought a moment. "You'll have to admit it was pretty funny. Okay, this is your chance to tell me about your experience in the insurance field."

Of course. The first thing he asks for is experience. She lifted her chin. "I just graduated from the U. I'm ready for a position in business administration and saw your ad in the paper. So here I am."

"What do you know about your field of work?"

"I know how to make a business go. Believe me, I'm well-trained. I graduated at the top of my class."

"Did you have any education specifically in the insurance field?"

"Is it all that different from other businesses?"

"Can you write business letters?"

"I graduated with honors," she reminded him.

"Why do you want the job?"

"Wait a minute! Why does anyone want a job?"

He shook his head and his wide mouth opened into a friendly smile. "I don't know. Money? Prestige? Satisfaction? Fulfillment?"

Perri began to relax a little. This guy was being pretty nice considering she'd made him wreck his car. She flashed a smile and her wide blue eyes crinkled. "All of the above, I guess. With particular emphasis on money."

He laughed. "Isn't it always? But tell me, what do you know about insurance?"

"I always use it. On my car and also my house."

The flippant answer slipped out before she thought, and her face burned, but the man's eyes sparkled. He smiled again and stood to his feet. "I'd like to give you a try. When can you start?"

Perri hardly believed her ears. He'd barely mentioned the earlier incident. He'd barely even interviewed her. "Would now be all right?" she asked, surprised at her own daring.

"You bet. Come, I'll show you to your office, Miss Seabrook."

Perri stopped short. "Wait a minute, please, Mr. Winfield. I prefer to be called Ms. Seabrook."

"Are you married?"

She hesitated a moment, then shook her head. "No."

"Okay, Miss Seabrook, let's find your office."

A few minutes later Perri sat alone behind a walnut desk in a sunlit office. Good amateur paintings on the walls made the room feel homey. Another door led into Mr. Winfield's private office. She opened all her desk drawers, one by one, and found them empty except the deep one on the right side. Red hanging files held blank insurance forms.

"Miss Seabrook," a deep voice crackled over the intercom.

"Yes, Mr. Winfield?"

"Would you bring your pad into my office please? I'd like to dictate a couple of letters."

What did he think he'd hired anyway, a secretary? Perri looked around frantically for a pad. She didn't even have a pencil! After a moment of futilé searching, she jerked a three by five note-pad and short ballpoint pen from her purse and tore into her employer's office.

Dashing for the leather chair beside the large desk, she threw herself into it as if it were a refuge. After she caught her breath she arranged her tiny pad on her lap and clicked out the point of the three inch pen. Then she looked into the amused eyes of Mitchell Winfield.

"There's a large stack of yellow pads in the closet in your office and several dozen long pencils. Or are these tiny things a fetish?"

"N-no sir, I didn't see anything else to use. Just a moment, I'll get some." She jumped up, ran to her office and found the supply closet, then hurried back to Winfield's office with a pad and pencil.

"Ready?" he asked, his black eyes laughing at her.

Perri nodded and the man started rattling words off so fast he'd reached the third paragraph before she could tell him her pencil hadn't been sharpened.

"Mr. Winfield—"

He kept going, covering another paragraph.

"Please stop, Mr. Winfield. My pencil isn't sharpened."

He stopped.

"May I sharpen it please?"

"Please do."

Where? Perri looked frantically around the room.

Winfield took the pencil and pushed it into an electric sharpener on his desk. "Now, are you ready?"

Perri nodded and he took off again, speaking so fast she understood fewer than one word in five. After a few attempts to get it down she sat back and waited for an opening. Finally he stopped to take a breath.

"Mr. Winfield," Perri said firmly. "I do take shorthand, although it's not a prerequisite for the job you've hired me to do. It was not my understanding that this was a secretarial position. However, I'd be glad to take this letter if you could speak in our native tongue."

Winfield chuckled. "How much did you get?"

Perri shook her head. "None." She suspected that her job would end right here.

"Miss Seabrook!" His deep voice made her jump. "I think it's time we dispensed with the last names. You call me Mitch and I'll call you—Perri, is it?"

"Yes." Her voice sounded small and meek, and mentally she shook her head at herself. She had the feeling that she was caught in a nightmare, that none of this was really happening after all. She sucked in a long, shaky breath, trying to calm herself.

"All right, Perri." He peered at her. "Are you frightened?"

She straightened up and cleared her throat. She'd better show some initiative here, she decided. "Of course I'm not frightened." Her voice came out high and dry, and turned into a sharp squeak on the last word.

"Would it help if I tell you I never fire anyone until they've been with me at least two months?"

Perri forced herself to take some deep breaths before she spoke. "I'm ready to try the dictation again, Mr. Winfield."

The dark man leaned back in his chair and clasped his hands behind his shiny hair. She readied her pencil over the pad, and met his eyes, trying to appear unflappable. She understood every word of his next attempt.

"I can have this ready for your signature in a few minutes," she informed him, then hurried back to her own office.

Her fingers flew over the computer keys as she transcribed her neat notes. When she finished, she relaxed a moment before facing her employer again. He'd purposely been unintelligible in that first try at dictation. Why? Was he testing her? Or maybe retaliating for the morning encounter? She sighed and carried the letter and the addressed envelope into his office.

Winfield glanced at the letter and signed it. "Beautiful work. You needn't be nervous." He pointed at the brown chair again. "Sit. Now let's see, you trained to be a business administrator, right?"

She eased herself into the soft leather. "Yes, sir."

"But you know nothing about the insurance business?"

"No, just general business. I learn quickly, though. Do you have a book I could study?"

He considered her suggestion. "I may be able to find something. Would you really do that?"

Perri's blue eyes brightened and her lips turned into the first real smile since she'd arrived. "I'll study every night until I know everything about insurance."

"Good." Winfield got up. She noticed that he had nice shoulders, lean hips, and a flat stomach. Her stomach gave another little twist, but she didn't think it was nerves this time.

"Just a moment, Perri. I'm taking you to lunch so we can talk a little more about the business and get acquainted."

Perri froze, then shook her head. "I couldn't eat a thing, Mr. Winfield. I'll stay here and get settled a bit. I'd like to explore the place and be prepared to work more efficiently this afternoon. Thanks, anyway."

"I don't care whether you're prepared. I want to eat with you."

"Well, the truth is, Mr.—"

"Mitch!" he corrected.

"Oh. Well, the truth is I never go out with men. Never."

"Oh." She couldn't believe the disappointment she thought she heard in his voice. A moment later his black eyes met hers again. "Would you mind telling me why?"

She shrugged, still standing. "I don't have time."

He pointed at the chair again. "Sit," he commanded in a no-nonsense voice. She sat. "Do you have anything against men?" he asked.

She shook her head. "No, I just don't go with them."

His eyes drilled into hers. "Are you a lesbian?"

She laughed, a tinkly laugh that echoed with real amusement. "No, I'm just too busy." She giggled again. She had several perfectly good reasons for not going out with men but they really weren't his business. She'd tell him the truth when she was ready—if ever.

two

He relaxed visibly. "Is the situation likely to change? Will you presumably go out with men someday?"

She gazed out the window a moment before answering. "It's possible, I suppose. Yes, I probably will. Someday."

Seemingly satisfied with the turn of the conversation, he bid her good-bye and left the office. Returning to her own office, Perri snooped through the supply closet and stocked her desk with paper, tape, staplers, pencils, pens, markers, paper fasteners, and some of everything else that looked interesting. She sharpened several pencils with the sharpener she discovered on her own desk. Now she'd be ready for anything.

After tapping lightly on Perri's door, the receptionist came in. "So you managed to get on the payroll."

Perri smiled, eager for a friend. "At least for the moment. I'm Perri Seabrook—and I'm scared to death."

The girl returned her smile. "I'm Trish Trenton. Welcome aboard, and you needn't be frightened. Mr. Winfield's nice."

The girl's friendliness sent a sense of relief flooding through Perri. "Thanks, Trish. I needed some reassurance. Are we the only two employees?"

The younger woman shook her short brown curls. "He keeps two typists busy." She pointed toward the open door. "Their office is on the other side of the reception room. I'll introduce you when they get back from lunch. I'm on my way to brown-bag it," she said, moving toward the door. "Are you going out to lunch?"

"No, I'm not hungry." Perri patted her flat stomach. "Too many butterflies in here." The statement wasn't strictly true, but buying even one lunch would knock her budget into an outer galaxy. She'd live without a meal.

Trish reached the door, then turned back to Perri. "If you decide to bring your lunch tomorrow we could eat together."

"I'll be bringing my lunch every day, Trish. I have four places for every dollar I get my hands on."

Trish brightened, waved, and went back to her desk.

A little later she called Perri out to meet the typists. Erika Williams, young, pretty, and plump, had red hair, green eyes, and a few freckles across her nose. She smiled and welcomed Perri to the office. Then Perri met Jessica Stone, about forty. Her dress looked straight from Paris and not a platinum hair dared be out of place. "I hope you know what you're doing," Jessica said. "Mr. Winfield doesn't mess around with duds."

"I don't know much yet," Perri admitted. "But I'm a fast learner."

Jessica sniffed. "You'd better learn before he figures out you don't know what you're doing."

"Come on, Jessica," Trish said laughing. "Mr. Winfield hired Perri, after all. I'm sure he has a good sense of her abilities. Give her a chance."

"I will," Jessica said. "I just hope he will. And don't go trying to get personal with him. That's the quickest way out. He never socializes with his employees." Her voice was frosty.

Trish walked back to Perri's office with her. "Don't mind Jessica. She wanted desperately to be Mr. Winfield's new assistant. She did everything including beg for the job. But she'll simmer down."

"I hope so," Perri said. "I don't want to start off with an

enemy. Tell me one thing, Trish. Is it true that Mr. Winfield doesn't harass his female employees?"

Trish nodded. "Right. Some of us wish he would."

"Not me," Perri said. "I don't go out with men and it will be much more pleasant working with someone who doesn't care."

Trish laughed and shook her head. "You can't mean that. Have you looked at him? He has two-inch eyelashes, and everything to go with them."

"I've looked. But I really don't go out. He's all yours—and Jessica's."

"Mine and Erika's," Trish said quietly. "Jessica's married, thank God. I'm just as glad she doesn't want Mr. Winfield—because she usually gets whatever she wants."

Mitchell Winfield stuck his head through the door. "Who's this lucky person who gets whatever she wants?" he asked.

No one answered for a moment. "I'm going to be that lucky person if I last longer than two months," Perri finally said.

"Ask Trish when I've ever fired anyone." He backed through the door and disappeared. Trish followed him, and Perri settled down to read blank insurance forms. As she read, she thought about the ease with which she'd acquired this job. She never even showed the man her diploma or high grades or—oh well, she had the job.

About fifteen minutes later, Winfield poked his head into her office again. "Busy?" he asked quietly.

Perri's silvery laugh tinkled. "How could I be busy when I don't know what to do?"

He perched on the edge of her desk. "Dinner tonight?" he asked.

"Mr. Winfield—" Perri began.

"Mitch," Winfield corrected.

Perri pushed two pencils to the other side of her desk, opened the drawer, and rolled them in. Then her blue eyes met his black ones. "The girls just told me you never socialize with your employees."

"Never have before. Never had the urge." He grinned. "How about dinner? I'll teach you everything I know about insurance."

A smile turned up the corners of Perri's mouth. "If you can teach me everything you know in an evening, I'll soon know more than you."

He grinned, then asked, "Do you mind if I ask your age?"

"I mind," Perri said. "I mind a lot but I'll tell you anyway. Twenty-nine."

Winfield's black eyebrows shot up and he shook his head vigorously. "No way! What are you really, twenty-three?"

"Thank you, I think. But I'm twenty-nine. Last April."

"Not only do you look six years younger, but isn't twenty-nine a little old to be graduating from the university?" He grinned again. "Maybe you're slower than I figured." Sliding off her desk, he settled into a chair beside hers.

She watched him warily as he arranged himself. *Trish is right—he is good-looking. But so what? I'm here to do a job and that's it.* She lifted her chin. "How old are you and when did *you* graduate? Or do you mind my asking?" She mimicked his voice.

Winfield leaned back and crossed his right ankle over his left knee. "I don't mind. You're allowed anything to ask anything you want. I'm thirty-three, and graduated from Lane Community College—no big university degree for me, I'm afraid. But I did manage to graduate before I turned twenty. After that, I worked for a large insurance company for two years, then formed my own agency, which has been growing ever since. So," he lifted an eyebrow, "do we agree that I've been a little busier in the last ten years than you?"

Perri hesitated. "Maybe." She really didn't agree at all. She'd definitely been much busier than Mitchell Winfield the last ten years. "Now," she continued, "why don't you teach me everything you know about insurance?"

The dark head turned slowly back and forth. "Tonight. Over steaks."

Perri's full lips narrowed into a thin, straight line. "Please don't press me, Mr. Winfield."

"Mitch!"

Perri nodded. "Whatever. But I meant what I said when I told you I don't go out with men. I don't. Ever. So could you please not ask me anymore? I'll do my very best for you at the office and I'll take home anything you want me to study. Fair?"

"Okay. For now." He spent the next two hours explaining insurance. She took everything down in shorthand and after he left she transcribed her work onto the computer and printed it. That information, together with a pile of blank forms, gave her plenty to study later.

That night in bed, as soon as she closed her eyes, she saw a strong square face with a jutting chin. She forced him from her mind and asked the Lord to help her with her new job and especially to help her remember all the things she'd just studied. She thanked God for opening this door for her. Then she slept.

She felt much more confident the next morning when she settled behind her desk.

"Perri, could you take a letter, please?" her intercom asked.

"Be right there." She gathered up two sharp pencils and a legal-sized pad. If he wanted her to be his private secretary—well, he was the boss.

Mitch's black eyes gleamed when Perri walked into his office. His eyes slid over her white cotton dress with red ruffles and lace, but he said nothing. Perri settled into the chair beside his desk, crossed her knees, and looked up expectantly, pencil poised over the pad. "I'm ready, Mr. Winfield."

"Mitch! I'm beginning to understand why it took you ten years to get through the university. You don't learn very fast, do you?"

She couldn't resist explaining. "I finished in three years, Mr.—uh—Mitch, with a grade point average of 3.92."

He nodded, obviously not listening. "Sounds nice," he murmured absently, his eyes focused on her shining hair. Then his gaze snapped back to hers. "Of course." He dictated the letter in clear concise sentences. "Now," he said, "after we get you going, I won't be doing much dictation. I'll simply tell you to write the letters. In fact, I probably won't even need to tell you. You'll know and take care of the correspondence. You'll meet and care for clients too. Before you know it you'll be my full-fledged assistant."

"What?" she asked in mock distress. "After all the hours I've practiced shorthand? And here I thought I was going to be your personal secretary."

The corner of his mouth lifted. "I think you'll prefer the salary that goes with being my assistant."

Perri settled back. "Right." She tossed the pencil over her shoulder onto the deep carpet. "Who cares about dictation, anyway."

As the days passed, Perri became comfortable with her work and extremely efficient. But every day Mitch asked her out—and every day she refused. Each night she took something home to learn. And sometimes in the night Mitch's ebony eyes laughed at her from her darkened ceiling.

One afternoon he called her into his office. "How can I help you, sir?" she asked lightly.

"I just wondered, what do you think about the Ronsen fire?"

She didn't hesitate a second. "Arson. A lovely new home, no one living in it, and the owner four months behind on the mortgage payments."

Mitch nodded. "Good work."

She sat up with new eagerness. "You learned something?"

"Yep. Kerosene soaked rags in the furnace room."

Perri laughed. "See? I may be slow, but I do learn."

Mitch's eyes devoured her. "Let's celebrate with dinner at Shoji's. They prepare and cook the meal right at your table." He watched for a response but received none. "Please?" he asked softly.

Perri sighed. "How many times have you asked me out?"

Mitch shrugged. "I lost count long ago," he admitted. "But however many times you've refused is the number of times I've asked."

"Can you remember the reason I refused?"

"Oh yes. I know it by heart. 'I don't have time to go out with anyone, ever,'" he mimicked in a falsetto voice that made them both laugh. "Can't you make an exception just this once?"

"I can't, Mitch."

He got up and walked away from the desk. "I've never met anyone I wanted to take out as badly as I do you," he said, looking out the window.

She walked over and stood beside him, watching the cars pass in the street below. "It's only because I won't go," she murmured. "I'm sure I'm the only person ever who didn't jump to accept your invitation. Except for that one thing, I'm totally ordinary."

He turned to look at her, his eyes bleak. "I don't think so."

"You'd quickly find out I was right if I ever did go out with you."

"Then why don't we try it and find out?" He smiled, but his gaze was still sober.

Perri shook her head and returned to her office.

She wrote several letters to would-be clients before the intercom crackled to life. "I'm begging you to go to dinner with me tonight. Please?" After a moment's silence he went on. "Can't you see I'm on my knees?"

Perri slipped to the connecting door, inched it open, and tiptoed in behind him. "How can you say no?" he asked pitifully into his intercom.

"Because you aren't really on your knees," she said, laughing. "But mostly because I don't go out."

Mitch swiveled his chair to face her, dropped to his knees, and reached for her hand. She snatched it away.

"Know what?" he asked, settling back into his chair. "I'm not going to eat until you agree to go out with me. I'm serious about this, Perri. After all, it worked for Ghandi, didn't it?"

Perri groaned. "Most people can well afford to lose a few pounds, but you look almost perfect." Oops, she hadn't meant to say that. "What I mean," she corrected, "is have a good fast. Perhaps you'll find it's a spiritual experience." She walked back to her own office.

The next morning she thought he looked a little pale, but

she said nothing. About mid-morning he called her on the intercom.

"Everything all right?" she asked, lowering herself into the soft leather seat.

"Do I look all right?"

She shook her head. "You look tired."

"I look hungry."

Her blue eyes opened wide. "Don't tell me you're really doing it."

"They say starving to death isn't so painful after the first few days."

The next day he looked worse. "Please don't tell me you still haven't eaten," she said when he walked in.

"They're right, it's getting better. I'm guessing it'll be smooth sailing now, until I die."

"Why don't you go comb your hair and straighten your tie?"

"I'm conserving my energy. You wouldn't believe how weak a person gets if he doesn't eat."

The next day he didn't look any better. "If you don't have dinner with me tonight, I won't be able to come into the office tomorrow," he told her.

As she worked, the solution to the entire problem popped into her head. She strode briskly into Mitch's office.

"I finally figured how I could go out," she said, her lips quirking into a mischievous smile. "But I guarantee you'll be sorry."

Mitch jumped from his chair as if it were connected to electricity. "I knew you wouldn't let me die," he said gratefully.

That evening Perri checked herself in the hall mirror, then opened the door. "Okay," she said, "this is it!"

Mitch stepped inside and Perri drew in her breath. He

didn't look starving now, his broad shoulders holding a dark jacket to perfection. His hair waved carelessly, drooping over the tops of his ears, and his large black eyes gleamed in his square clean-shaven face.

"Is this the man, Mommy?" a small voice asked.

Perri watched eagerly as Mitch's startled eyes took in four boys, all dressed in clean jeans and white shirts, standing backlit in the living room doorway.

three

Mitch's eyes widened as the four boys smiled at him shyly. "Wha—What's—Who are those guys?" he finally stammered.

"Mitch, I want you to meet my four sons—Judd, who's ten, Hugh, eight, Scott, six, and my baby, Tad, who just turned four." She watched Mitch carefully. His face had turned hard, and his lips pressed tight together.

Tears welled up in the smallest boy's big blue eyes. "He doesn't like us, Mommy," he cried, his lips trembling. "I don't like him either."

After a long, long silence, Perri's laugh filled the room. "Well, Mitch, you're looking at the four reasons I don't go out."

Mitch cleared his throat twice, looking as if he'd choke to death any second. "I see," he finally managed.

"Won't you come in for a minute?" she asked, taking pity on him. She took Mitch's arm and gently steered him through the gray-carpeted living room. Gently pushing him into the soft depths of the love seat, she settled on the couch where she could see him.

"Are you all right?" she asked softly.

Mitch swallowed loudly. "Sure, I'm all right," he said, his voice husky. "Why didn't you tell me?"

Perri tipped her hands in an outward motion and shrugged. "I don't know. At first I thought you wouldn't hire an old woman with four kids. And maybe I enjoyed having someone find me attractive after all these years." A mischievous smile danced on her lips. "Maybe I thought it would be interesting to see your reaction to the scene we just had." She looked into his eyes. "You must admit I didn't encourage you. Not even a little."

Mitch nodded. "Where is he?" he asked. His voice was harsh.

"He?" Perri repeated. "Oh. You mean Jerry. He died in a construction accident before Tad was born."

He met her eyes. "And that's why you graduated from the university at twenty-nine."

"Yes. I married at eighteen and had Judd the following year. Then another little boy came along every two years until Jerry—until I found it necessary to get an education."

"I see." Mitch looked at his shoes. "I see lots of things," he whispered, as if to himself.

"Mommy—" Tad began.

Mitch jumped up. "Come on, guys, we're going out to eat."

"Are you sure?" Perri asked. "All of a sudden, it doesn't feel nearly as good as I thought it would."

"Of course I'm sure. Did I or didn't I force you into this?" He strode to the wide front door and held it open. "Everybody out," he called. The four boys ran under his arm through the door, followed by Perri.

"Hey, this car won't hold us all," ten-year-old Judd said, standing beside a low red sports car.

Mitch shook his head and smiled wryly at Perri. "He's right. I'll go home and get another car."

"No, let's take the wagon."

Everyone ran toward the garage except six-year-old Scott. "I want to ride with Mr. Windshield," he wailed.

Mitch ruffled Scott's red hair. "I'm riding in the wagon, sport. I could take you for a spin when we come back, though."

When the maitre d' greeted them, Mitch explained that there would be six in the party rather than two. After a moment of confusion, the man led them to a large table at the back of the restaurant. As soon as they all settled into their chairs to await the meal, six-year-old Scott leaned across to Tad. "You don't get any supper," he announced loudly.

Tad dropped off his chair into a heap on the soft carpet, screaming at the top of his lungs. Perri picked up the broken-hearted little boy and comforted him. "You'll get a great big supper," she crooned, putting him back onto his chair. "Don't do that again," she hissed at Scott.

A moment later she heard a tiny whisper. "You don't get any pie."

Tad landed on the floor again, screaming, and Perri felt certain folks heard him from outside the restaurant. Snatching him up again, she assured him he'd get as much dessert as Scott. She put him back in his chair and brushed the damp blond curls from his flushed face.

She turned venomous eyes to Scott. "If you say one more word before we're served, I'll take you outside and wallop you."

Scott smiled innocently into his mother's eyes before lowering his reddish orange lashes. A moment later Perri saw Tad gazing spellbound into his big brother's eyes. Scott didn't say a word, but shook his head slowly.

The little bomb hit the floor with a thud and screams split the quiet air once more. Perri snatched Tad and ran for the front door. When she returned five minutes later, leading a smiling Tad, Mitch stood and greeted her with a tense smile. He helped Tad onto his chair and held Perri's for her.

"There won't be any more trouble," he said, lowering

himself into his chair. Perri looked at Scott, who nodded agreement with a happy smile.

At that moment, a waiter brought bowls of green soup, several kinds of crackers, and a dish of rolls. Five seconds later eight-year-old Hugh shook his brown head violently. Noisily, he spewed a large mouthful of soup back into his bowl. "I don't like that stuff," he said loudly. "What's in it, turtles?"

Immediately six-year-old Scott and baby Tad spat their soup back into their bowls with enough racket to cause people several tables away to look toward the commotion.

"It's not turtle, Hugh," Perri whispered, ducking her head with embarrassment. "It's broccoli soup, and it's delicious."

"I want good food, Mommy!" Scott yelled.

A few minutes later a waiter placed freshly tossed salads before everyone. Mitch sat quietly, trying to eat, while each of the boys explained in a loud voice why he couldn't stand the salad.

"How come you brought us to a dumb place like this?" Hugh asked. "Why can't we have hamburgers or hot dogs?"

"I want hot dogs. I want hot dogs," Tad and Scott bellowed in unison.

Perri met Mitch's eyes and shrugged. "I didn't say it would be easy."

The main course finally arrived. Steaks, mashed potatoes with gravy, and peas with pearl onions. And more hot rolls.

"Ah," Mitch said, sniffing, as he looked at his large steaming plate. "Everyone will like this."

Perri enjoyed a few minutes of blessed silence as she started making inroads on the delicious food.

Then, "This bread tastes awful!" from Scott.

"The 'tatoes are mushy," Hugh added.

Perri swallowed a bite of fluffy mashed potatoes. "Hush,

boys," she whispered, "it's yummy."

A moment later half a thickly buttered roll sailed across the table and smacked ten-year-old Judd on the forehead, butter side first.

"You creep," Judd said, and threw it back at Scott, who caught it with no damage done.

"Settle down, boys," Mitch said amiably. "Eat your steak. It's good."

Baby Tad, unwilling to miss any excitement, picked up an unbuttered roll and threw it across the table, hitting Hugh in his left eye.

The eight-year-old's brown eyes grew bright with anger. He scooped up his whole serving of mashed potatoes and gravy and threw it murderously at Tad. It missed and splashed over the entire front of Mitch's face and shirt.

Mitch calmly wiped himself off as best he could with his napkin, and stood up. "This meal is finished," he said firmly.

Perri soon turned the station wagon into her driveway and climbed wearily out. "I get to ride in Windshield's car," four-year-old Tad said.

"Not tonight you don't," Perri said. She grasped his hand and propelled him toward the house. The others followed and Mitch brought up the rear.

A half hour later, after a Bible story and a short prayer, Perri tucked the boys in bed. Five minutes later, she tucked two of them in again. She brought a drink to Scott. She assured Tad that Jesus would not let the bogeyman get him. She told Scott to stop telling Tad stories about the bogeyman. She tucked three of them in yet again. She told them all that she loved them.

At last, she went downstairs and dropped to the couch. "Now I remember why I don't go out," she said.

"I understand, but why don't you get a sitter?"

"I can't afford to. Jill, my sister, stayed with the kids while I went to school and now while I work. I didn't pay her anything before I started working, and not as much as I should now. No way could I ask her any more than necessary."

Mitch settled back on the love seat and put his feet on the coffee table. "I suppose being left with the job of supporting four children was tough."

"Yes." Perri wondered how much to tell him. Oh, well, why not? She felt good having someone to talk to. "It really was. In more ways than one. But money isn't the only reason I don't go out. The kids and I have clung together for comfort and strength. When something like—what happened to their father—well, when that happens, you don't accept it right away. It's been more than four years and I'm barely beginning to admit that I'm single. But back to the money. I collected fifty thousand dollars from the insurance company and spent almost the entire amount in the three years I went to school. I'll also collect Social Security until the kids grow up. I couldn't have gone to school without that."

Mitch sat silently thinking for a few seconds. "What happened?" he finally asked.

"To Jerry?" She swallowed. She still had trouble talking about the horrible experience. "He worked for a commercial construction company and one day he stood in several inches of water in a ditch, laying pipe along with two other guys. An excavator knocked a high voltage power line into the ditch." She tried to swallow the lump that had lodged in her throat. "All three died," she concluded in a hoarse whisper.

Mitch looked into her eyes. When he reached for her, she melted into his arms, breathing hard, tears streaming down her cheeks. She couldn't believe how good she felt having someone comfort her for a change.

"Does it still hurt so very much?" he asked, massaging her back gently.

She reached for a tissue. After tossing it into a basket, she shook her head. "Mostly I'm used to it, but when I think how horrible it was, it still gets to me." She got up and went to the kitchen. Mitch followed.

"Would you like a cup of Roma?" she asked. "It's sort of a fake coffee."

After dawdling over the hot drinks, Mitch got up. "You go to bed, little mother, and have sweet dreams." He closed the door softly behind him.

Well—Mitch had finally met her boys, and what an initiation they'd given him! But she had been glad to have a man to talk to. She'd been lonely the last few years, in spite of all the support and physical help Mom, Dad, and Jill had provided. She picked up the phone and called Mom, telling her about the disastrous evening. Then the two women laughed together.

The next morning, Perri wrote three letters to delinquent accounts before Mitch arrived. He wore shirt sleeves and he looked windblown.

She pursed her lips and nodded. "I know what you've been up to. You drove that rattle-trap convertible to work, didn't you?"

A smile flitted across his mouth before he answered. "Do you know what that 'rattle-trap convertible' is?"

Perri shook her head slowly. "Haven't the foggiest. Would it matter?"

"It might. It's a '59 Edsel Citation. Does that mean anything to you?"

She shrugged, then grinned. "Just that it's older even than my car."

"Perri," Mitch said, brushing his flyaway black hair back

with his hand, "the Edsel was Ford's 'big mistake.' They only made it for a few years and not many of them. Its price is soaring and I'm hoping it will be worth a lot of money someday. I'm restoring the Edsel, and no, I didn't drive it this morning."

"Why did you happen to drive it the morning we—uh—met?" she asked. "And why is it painted that horrible neon aqua color?"

"I'd just taken possession of the car that morning." He laughed at the memory. "My trouble didn't end with you. I had a horrible time getting it home." He shook his head. "It's not going anywhere again until it learns who's boss." He glanced at his watch. "Now that you've had your morning lesson in ancient automobiles, we'd better get to work. Oh yes, I have no idea why the aqua color—but I'll restore it to its original color when I have time to dig through all the coats of paint to find out what that is."

Perri worked efficiently for the rest of the day. Late in the afternoon, he called her into his office. "I need to talk to you, sort of clear the air," he said.

Perri plopped into the soft leather chair that she'd started calling hers.

"No, I mean some place private," he said. "Since I know all your secrets now, could you go to dinner with me?" When she started to object, he continued, "Just this once. I need to apologize and a few other things."

"I'm the one who needs to apologize. Honestly, the boys don't always act like that." After a moment of silence her silvery laugh warmed the room. "Sometimes they're worse." Mitch joined her laughter. "But I still don't go out," she continued. "I'd invite you to my place, but you can imagine how private that would be. What's the matter with here?"

Mitch picked up a paper fastener and busied himself straightening the fine wire. "No, I want to have time to really talk, not just say my piece and be through. I owe it to you." He thought a moment, then snapped his fingers. "When do the kids hit the sheets?"

"Do you mean the first time, or the fifth, or the tenth?"

"I mean at night. What do you mean?"

"I mean kids, Mitch. You put them to bed each night. Then it's a game to see which one can think of the most reasons to get up. You saw what it was like last night."

He grinned knowingly. "Got it. I mean the last time. What time do they go to bed for the last time?"

"You could come for supper, and wait them out."

"Well," he said slowly. "I sort of promised the boys a ride in the Ferrari. . ."

Much later Perri and Mitch sat side by side on the love seat. Mitch outlined the pink and maroon flowers with his right index finger. "Do you think they're all through getting up?" he asked.

Perri nodded, her chin pointed up in a determined way. "I threatened them with yard duty tomorrow if they get up once more. And it's been a while since we heard from them. So what's the big secret? Have you decided you can't have the mother of four savage animals for your assistant?"

"Do you read Bible stories and pray with the kids every night?"

"Yes. We cut it a little short last night and tonight though, so we wouldn't waste your time."

"Well, I want to apologize for forcing you to go out with me. And I need to confess that I lied to you about not eating."

Perri nodded in agreement. "I knew that," she said philosophically, "and you had to find out about the kids sometime."

"That's really what I'm here to talk about," he said. "I've been giving those kids a lot of thought." He stopped a moment, sighed audibly, then went on. "I'm not sure you realized it, but I really felt something for you. You seemed to be exactly what I'd been looking for—for a long time." He stood to his feet and walked to the window. Gazing thoughtfully out, he thrust his hands deep into his front pockets.

four

Perri swallowed. "I notice you're speaking in the past tense," she said. "I guess I have too many men in my life already, right?"

He ran his hand through his hair and settled back down beside her. "It's not exactly like that," he said. "It's just—well—I don't think it would be wise for us to get involved." He got up and began pacing again.

"Relax," she said. "I'll live. If they weren't my flesh and blood, I probably couldn't handle them, either. Oops, a poor choice of words. I guess you think I don't handle them very well."

He swung around and dropped beside her. "It isn't that, though they do sort of overwhelm a person." He cleared his throat. "I just wanted you to understand how it is with me. The thought of four kids blows my mind. All that responsibility." He grinned wryly. "I may as well be totally honest. The thought of four kids pretty much knocks me dead."

"Are you a Christian?" she asked softly.

He shook his head. "I don't know. I used to go to Sunday school when I was a kid. I gather you are."

"Yes, and I take it very seriously, so don't go away feeling bad. I wouldn't have allowed our relationship to continue anyway, not when we feel differently about God. You and I—it couldn't have come to anything, anyway." She hesitated. "But I hope I can retain my job. I'd really appreciate that."

He assured her the job wasn't in jeopardy, and then he

35

quickly made an excuse to leave.

❧

At work the next day Mitch was friendly but impersonal. Before the day ended, she felt lower than a fallen leaf. She went home and spent a turbulent evening with the boys. They seemed ten times worse than usual, and she had no patience to deal with their shenanigans.

When they were at last in bed, she had a talk with herself. Were the boys really all that bad tonight? No, they merely reflected her bad mood. What caused the bad mood?

She wasn't sure. Could she care more for Mitch than she'd realized? Was she, in spite of herself, disappointed that he'd stopped pestering her? Maybe she enjoyed having a man around for once. Had she been taking her disappointment out on the kids?

She got in bed, turned over, and had her evening talk with God. "Thank You for loving me so much," she whispered. "I love You too, Father. Help me treat the kids better tomorrow. And help me not to give Mitch another thought. I know if you want me to marry again, you'll have a kind Christian man, who loves kids, waiting for me when the time's right. Thank You, Father, in Jesus' precious name. Good night," she murmured and fell asleep.

The next morning Perri immersed herself in paperwork. At noon she joined Trish for their usual brown bag lunch. After they finished and were talking, Jessica stopped by the desk where they sat. Perri's guard snapped to attention because Jessica usually strutted past without glancing her way.

"I see you had to learn the hard way."

"I'm sorry," Perri replied. "I'm afraid I don't know what you mean."

"I mean the way Mr. Winfield had to put you in your

place. It always happens when someone forces herself on him." Jessica's ringed hand smoothed an imaginary stray hair, and her smile held more animosity than sympathy.

"I still don't understand what you're saying."

"Everyone in the office saw the big play you made for him. Don't be surprised if you find yourself occupying a less prestigious position in this firm." She lifted her chin and marched through the door to the typing room.

Perri turned shocked eyes to Trish. "What was that all about?"

"Forget it," Trish said kindly. "Don't you know there's an overgrown grapevine in any office staff of three people or more?"

"What are they saying? And where do they get their information? I haven't been after Mitch!"

Trish nodded. "For starters, everyone hears you calling him Mitch. The rest of us would never think of using his first name."

"Oh." Perri didn't mention that Mitch had forced her into that. "Well, I'll call him Mr. Winfield. Will that fix it?"

"I don't know. The talk is that he dumped you."

"That should make everyone happy. But I only went out with him once—and I took my four kids."

Trish's eyebrows shot almost to her hairline. "Four kids!" She jumped up, prancing like a race horse. "I have to see someone. See you later, Perri."

Perri smiled as Trish rushed into the typing room. "So much for that friend," she told herself out loud. "She couldn't wait to spread the word that I have four kids. And that Mitch took me out only once."

❧

The days crept slowly past, one by one, and summer warmed the mild Oregon days. Perri called him Mitch only when no one else could overhear, and he called her Mrs. Seabrook when they weren't alone. Whether or not they were alone, he treated her kindly and with respect—and impersonally.

Late one Friday afternoon he rushed into her office. "Edwin and Frances Miller have been in a car accident. Could you file a claim for them?"

"Sure, I'll do it right away. Just leave the info."

Perri left the office long after everyone else, feeling she'd done a good day's work. The feeling compensated somewhat for having to be away from her boys for so long when she'd planned to spend the afternoon home with them.

After supper, Mitch called, the first time he'd called her at home. "I wondered if you'd like to ride out tomorrow to Detering's for some early peaches," he asked, his voice velvet smooth. "Just as friends, of course."

Perri's heart thudded against her chest. Why did she suddenly feel so light-headed? And breathless? Not because she'd get peaches. She knew where the vast Detering Orchards were. In fact she'd been there many times, and as much as she loved peaches, they had never before made her dizzy and out of breath.

"I'd love to," she said, forcing her voice to be coolly casual. "Fresh fruit sounds fantastic but I couldn't leave the kids even for that long."

A long loud sigh crept into Perri's ears, and then after an awkwardly long moment, Mitch said, "Bring them. What can they do in an orchard?"

"What can't they do?" She thought a moment, really eager to see him again. "Well, I guess we can try it. We can take the station wagon."

"Okay. I'd take the pickup but that wouldn't work with the kids."

They set a time and Perri felt strangely exhilarated as she

had her private time with God. Strangely, in her Bible reading that night, she happened on the verse that said not to be unequally yoked with unbelievers. Her exhilaration melted away like an ice cube in hot tea. "I knew that, Lord," she said aloud. "But thanks for reminding me anyway. I also know that when the time's right you'll have someone for me to share my life with. Someone who'll share my faith. The right someone." She smiled. "I hope You won't make me wait until my wild kids are grown, Lord. I try not to think about it, but I do get lonely." She fell asleep satisfied to do the Lord's will.

The next morning Perri dressed her boys in their best jeans and clean sweatshirts. Mitch arrived promptly on time and they all piled into the old station wagon. At the busy orchard, they were directed to the U-Pick trees.

"Do you want the boys to pick?" Mitch asked as he leaned a long ladder against a heavily laden tree.

"No, they'd pick the peaches whether they were ripe or not. And besides they'd probably fall off the ladder."

"Okay, you pick from this ladder and I'll put mine on the other side of the tree."

Perri hung the bucket over her arm and clambered up the ladder. The peaches hung thick and ripe, their cheeks a warm strawberry pink. She filled her bucket in less than ten minutes and emptied it, peach by peach, so she wouldn't bruise the tender fruit, into one of the boxes they'd brought.

"Can we eat one, Mommy?" Tad asked.

Perri watched Mitch jump down his ladder, graceful as a large cat, and asked him if the peaches were safe to eat.

He shook his head. "They're heavily sprayed, guys, but we'll be through and home before you know it. Can you wait just a little while?"

Perri's next bucket filled the box to capacity. She scrambled back up the ladder to help Mitch finish his.

"Get out of there!" Judd yelled, from the bottom of the tree.

"Leave me alone," Scott answered.

A moment later Scott's screams brought Perri down the ladder two steps at a time. She rushed to the six-year-old and picked him up. "What happened?" she asked. "Did you get stung?"

"Judd knocked me off the box."

Perri looked around with a sinking feeling in her stomach. Then she noticed sticky yellow-orange juice drenching Scott's feet past his sneakers and halfway up his socks. Her eyes fell on the peaches which only half-filled the box and were completely smashed. Juice ran from the soft wet cardboard.

"What were you doing in the peach box?" she asked.

"I smashed them down so you could get more into the box," he explained.

"You ruined them, Scott." She heard her voice rising high, and she pressed her lips together to keep back her anger.

The racket brought Mitch down from his ladder and he dropped an arm over Perri's shoulder. "Come on," he said quietly, "we can refill it."

"But I'm not going to. Scott's going to learn a lesson by doing without."

Mitch tugged Perri away from the boys. "Help me fill my box, then," he said as they moved away. When the boys couldn't hear anymore, he turned his bucket upside down and sat on it. "Why don't you overlook it?" he said, looking into her blue eyes. "He didn't intend to ruin those peaches. Did you see how he looked at the smashed fruit? Let's pick some more and forget all about this little incident, okay?"

He touched her chin with a large thumb. "Relax, Perri. A few squashed peaches aren't the end of the world. Honest."

Perri took a deep breath. She felt her anger draining from her as she returned Mitch's smile.

In less than fifteen minutes the hot and dusty little group drove back to the weighing shed. The young man weighed Perri's large box. "Forty-two pounds," he announced in a monotone voice.

When Perri handed him her check he looked at it, then back at her. "I said the peaches weighed forty-two pounds," he repeated.

Perri smiled and nodded. "We accidentally smashed the first box. So I figure we owe you for about eighty-four pounds."

The man counted change into Perri's hand. "People often steal fruit from us, but you're the first who's ever offered to pay for stuff they didn't take home. Thanks, but no."

Back at the house, Mitch carried Perri's box into the utility room, then took four peaches to the kitchen and washed them thoroughly. He handed one to each boy. "Take them outside under a shade tree and enjoy," he ordered.

"Well, Perri," he said a few minutes later, peach juice running down his chin, "I'll never doubt your integrity again. Not that I ever did."

"Thanks, Mitch. I had a good time today, in spite of Scott's misadventure." She shook her head, remembering. "Can you believe kids?"

"I can," he said laughing, "but it isn't easy." He finished his peach and dropped the pit into the trash.

Perri had barely started her peach when the boys trooped back in. Mitch washed four more peaches and told them to eat the fruit outside.

Perri pulled her baby onto her lap. "I love you, sweetie,"

she whispered. Dropping a kiss on the top of his yellow curls, she set him on his feet. "Go eat your peach, then play with Scotty for a while."

After Tad slammed the door behind him, Mitch smiled at her. "You made a beautiful picture holding that child. He looks so much like you."

Perri felt her face redden. "Thank you," she said quietly.

"What did he look like?" Mitch asked.

"Who?"

"Your husband. You have brown-headed kids, a red head, and a blond."

"Jerry had brown hair and eyes. Darker than the boys', but not nearly as dark as yours. I guess our combination made the red."

After a silence Mitch muttered something she didn't quite understand.

"What did you say?" she asked.

"What?" Mitch looked confused. "Nothing, I guess. Just rambling."

Later that night Perri tumbled into bed worn out from the busy day. As she lay waiting for sleep's sweet release, she saw Mitch's strong dark features. He laughed and his white teeth sparkled in his wide mouth. "Wonder what kind of kid we'd make," he said clearly.

She jerked upright in bed. That's what she'd thought he'd said. Why would he say a thing like that? She said her prayers and dropped off to sleep.

❧

The next day she was busily working at the computer when Mitch flung open the door, rushed to her side, and dropped into a chair.

She finished her sentence, then looked up into his eyes. "What's up?"

"Remember the Miller accident?"

"Yes, late last week. What about it?"

"The policy was never renewed."

Perri's heart skipped a beat before she remembered. "Yes, it was," she said with assurance. "I took care of it myself."

Mitch heaved a sigh of relief, then the worried look returned. "I just talked to the company in Maine, Perri. They never received the renewal—or the check."

Perri thought a moment. "I remember taking the information into the typing room. Or did I give it to Trish? Maybe three months ago?"

"That's about the right time, but what could have happened to it?"

Perri turned to her computer and began scrolling. "Yep, here it is." She brought up the account and found where she'd entered the name, date, and amount. She got up. "Let's go through the checkbook."

"Well, that's interesting," Mitch said a few minutes later. "The Millers' check was deposited into our account, but no corresponding check or renewal papers sent to the company."

five

What could have happened? A lump the size of an iceberg accumulated in Perri's throat. "I hope the accident was a fender bender," she said grimly.

"It didn't amount to much, but we'd better get to the bottom of this. Something like this can ruin an insurance agency."

"I suppose I'm to blame," Perri said, "but I did enter it into my computer and I remember giving it to one of the girls to type."

"Which one?"

Perri shook her head. "I remember taking it in there."

Mitch got up. "Don't worry about it, Perri. You're the most conscientious worker I've ever had."

She stared at the wall until he returned. Flipping his leg across the chair he sat down. "All three deny seeing the renewal forms. They say they remember all the names, but I doubt it."

"I guess the buck stops with me," she said softly. "Could you take it out of my check in payments?"

Mitch snorted. "Hardly. You're the only one who has proof you attended to the matter. I have no idea what accounts are covered in the checks I write to the different companies. And besides, the buck stops with me."

Perri emitted a sigh of relief. "Thanks. This afternoon I'll balance the last three months' outgoing checks with the accounts."

A smile spread across Mitch's wide mouth. "Need some help?"

"Thanks, but it won't take very long," Perri said, then noticed a cloud move across his face. "Of course, if you have time, it would go faster," she amended, her heart beating a little faster.

A smile spread over the angular features once more. "Sure, I have time. Let's shoot for two o'clock."

"I'll be ready. Let's hope we don't find any more problems."

Why was she looking forward to this afternoon almost as though it were a date? Perri wondered as she prepared for the afternoon's work.

At lunch time, Trish couldn't wait to discuss the incident. "Someone really goofed up," she said, unwrapping her tuna sandwich. "Or could someone have embezzled the money?" She took a huge bite and swallowed it almost whole.

Perri choked on her half-chewed carrot stick. "I'm sure it was just an oversight," she said. "No one around here would steal from anyone, let alone Mr. Winfield." She stuck the rest of the carrot into her mouth, hoping Trish would be content to find another subject now.

"Erika thinks Mr. Winfield suspects her," Trish offered.

Perri started to deny that, then nibbled on her cookie, saying nothing.

At two o'clock, she readied her computer and all the corresponding hard records for Mitch's arrival. Rushing into the rest room she double-checked her hair and makeup. Back in her comfortable chair, she asked herself why she'd done that.

Finally Mitch came in, checkbook in hand and a smile on his face, as though he too were looking forward to the afternoon's labors.

"You don't have the appearance of a man who's looking for an embezzler," Perri said, motioning for him to sit in the chair she'd pulled alongside hers.

Mitch laughed. "Embezzler? You've been seeing too many movies. I'm sure this was an isolated mistake that will never happen again."

But they discovered three more accounts had lapsed—one car insurance and two home-owner's policies. In each case the renewal check had been deposited into the company account, but no record existed of the transaction after it left Perri's desk. Mitch wrote the checks immediately and she filled out the papers so the policies could be mailed before the day ended.

After they had the policies ready to go, he looked at her and shook his head. "What do you think now?" he asked, his voice husky.

A small silence followed. "It's not an accident," she finally said.

"I agree. Once, yes. Two, possibly. Four times, never."

"Nothing like this ever happened before you hired me, right?"

Mitch nodded. "That's right. So?"

"Since I've taken over all the renewals, it makes me either very careless—or downright dishonest."

"No way! I saw you try to pay for some smashed peaches, remember?"

Perri bit her lower lip. "What then?"

A light turned on in his eyes. "Someone's making you look guilty!"

She sucked in a deep breath. "I agree! I'm going to write down everything I pass to the girls and check each night to see what comes out of that office."

"Good. And don't explain anything to anyone. Not even that we found any more problems." Mitch glanced at his watch and then back to Perri's concerned face. "Don't look so worried. I think we should celebrate. Just think what would have happened if one of those houses had burned while it wasn't covered. Or, God forbid, if there'd been a bad automobile accident, with major medical expenses." He made a throat-slitting motion with his index finger. "We'd have been dead."

"For sure. I hope you don't think I could possibly be that careless."

Mitch shook his head violently. "You're the most meticulous person I know. I have absolute faith that you'll find the problem. Now—let's go find something to eat. I'm not sure about you, but I need it, after this."

A smile flitted across Perri's face. "Sorry to remind you, but I still have a houseful of kids. And we're visiting my folks in Veneta tonight."

Mitch reached for her hand. "Could you visit the grandparents tomorrow night? I'll pay for a sitter."

Electricity raced from Perri's fingers to her shoulder, then throughout her body, causing every nerve to sing. She pulled her hand away.

"I'd love to, Mitch. I really would. But I don't even know a sitter, let alone one I'd trust with my animals." Her voice wavered. "I wish I could."

Mitch's ebony eyes bore into her sapphire ones. "Do you mean that?"

"I do, but kids aren't something you have around just when it's convenient. They're a full-time commitment."

He got up and walked to the door. "I'll see what I can do."

A half hour later he returned, his eyes shining. "I found a sitter," he said. "One I'll personally guarantee."

Perri's heart sped up. "How did you manage that?"

"Easy. It's my brother, Brock. He's an animal lover from

way back." He gave Perri a sideways grin. "I figure he'll do just fine with your four."

"I couldn't ask that of your brother, Mitch. I have to find a sitter who's not a relative."

"What's wrong with relatives? My relatives have always been my favorite people. At least some of them."

Perri sighed. "You know what I mean. A sitter does it for the money. A relative does it because he's been had. Right?"

The light dimmed in Mitch's eyes. "Well, maybe," he agreed, "but Brock's agreed to do it this once. Let's not waste it."

Perri thought a moment. "A lot of people would be very disappointed if I didn't go to my folks tonight." She shook her head. "I don't think I'd better go with you, Mitch."

His eyes narrowed. "Okay, I'll find someone else who likes to eat out." His voice was cool.

Lying in bed that night, Perri wondered if Mitch really had taken someone else out—or if he'd only said he was going to because he was hurt and angry. He *should* go out with someone else, she knew—but she hoped he hadn't. Yet how could she wish him to spend every evening alone just because she did?

The next day Mitch laughed and joked as usual. He didn't mention his activities the previous night.

❧

After a week of careful watching, Perri found another account that derailed somewhere between her desk and Mitch's. According to her records Trish had taken it from her office to the typing room. Perri worked up the papers immediately and Mitch made out the check.

"I'm going to fire the lot of them," Mitch said when they finished. "They aren't so valuable they can't be replaced."

Perri shook her head. "Wouldn't that be overkill? I was

the most likely suspect when the problem surfaced, but I'd have felt awful if you'd fired me."

Neither said anything to anyone, but she decided to deliver the papers to the typing room herself from now on so she'd know who did them.

かわ

Leaving the office together one evening, Mitch and Perri opened the outside door to a sheet of rain. Not unusual for Eugene, but rather unexpected in July. As they stood under the porch they watched the downpour. People scurried to find the nearest shelter, and the gutters filled in a matter of minutes. Water washed from the street over the sidewalk and the few people attempting to cross the street found themselves wading in water nearly to their knees.

"You wait here," Mitch instructed Perri. "I'll get my car and take you home. We'll pick up the station wagon later."

A few minutes later his red Ferrari pulled up to the curb, splashing dirty water over its shiny sides. Perri ran through the drenching rain and climbed into the warm car.

He laughed at the rain beating down. "This is amazing," he said. "I've never seen a downpour like this, even in winter."

"Your lovely car's a mess," Perri said. "We should have used the wagon."

He shrugged. "It'll dry out."

They rode in companionable silence as the windshield wipers went squish-squish-squish, futilely attempting to clear the glass. The rain lessened as they neared Perri's place and visibility improved. Finally they turned into her driveway.

"Thanks a lot," she said. "This was going beyond the call of duty." She opened the door and started to step out.

"Wait," he said, grasping her arm. "Let's go get hamburgers."

She shook her head and stepped out. "You've done too much already. Thanks again. See you tomorrow."

He rolled down his window. "Don't make dinner," he called. "I'll be back with hamburgers."

"If you insist, how about vegetable pizza instead?" she called. He nodded and water sprayed ten feet behind the car as he sped away.

Perri barely had time to thank Jill for sitting, shower, and change into dry jeans and sweater before Mitch returned, wearing dark brown cords and a cream sweater, his hair still soaked. He carried two large bags and two pizza boxes.

They unwrapped two large pizzas and filled two bowls with french fries. "I knew better than to get salads," he said, sheepishly pulling six candy bars from another bag, then six large milkshakes. He wadded up the bags. "That's all, folks," he announced to the boys, who eagerly crowded around the table.

Perri distributed the food. "Can you drink all of this big milkshake?" she asked Tad.

He nodded energetically. "I can eat everything." Then he gazed at the tiny slices of green pepper. "Scotty," he asked gazing at his hero, his role model, his mentor, and chief tormentor, "do we like green pepper?"

Scotty's head started to swing but Mitch dropped an arm over his shoulder. "Of course, you like green pepper," he said. "I heard a guy at the pizza place say how lucky we are that the rain kept the rabbits from eating all of them so we could have some."

Perri watched the look Scotty sent up at Mitch's face, and she saw Mitch's answering grin. Scotty nestled ever so slightly against the large arm that gripped his shoulders, and Perri's heart turned over inside her chest.

Sitting in the rocking chair that night while everyone

slept, Perri went over the evening's activities. Mitch had stayed and played with the boys until their bedtime. He'd sat attentively through their Bible story too, though she had no idea what he'd thought.

His wide smile played on her mental VCR. Long lashes dropped across his inky eyes. His fingers gripped the steering wheel of his car. His beautiful long narrow hands.

What's happening to me? she wondered. *Am I falling in love again? Did the thought of Jerry used to affect me this way?*

"Oh, Jerry," she cried aloud, "I can't see your face in my mind!" Jumping from the rocker, she pulled down the photo album and flipped it open. Oh yes, there he was, standing beside her, holding Scotty in his arms. She gazed at her tall smiling husband, looking so much alive. *Why did you have to leave me, Jerry?* Then with a guilty start she realized that for the first time she didn't really mean it. He was a precious part of her past but that's where he would remain forever. In the past.

What she wanted now was Mitchell Winfield. She, Perri Seabrook, had fallen in love with Mitch! Head over heels, wild and crazy love! And they could never be together for she'd never ever be unequally yoked with an unbeliever.

six

Anyway, he wasn't interested in instant fatherhood—especially to four wild and unpredictable boys. She locked the doors, turned out the lights, and crept into bed.

"Please help me get over my feelings for Mitch," she whispered to God. "He's my boss and nothing more. A nice boss, but that's it. Help me do it, Father. Thank You." But despite her prayer, she tossed and turned for a very long time.

The next morning she thought about Mitch as she booted up her computer. She mustn't be aloof with him, just friendly. She could do it, she told herself. Then he walked in.

Her face tightened and hot streaks rushed from her neck to her hairline. When another man followed him through the doorway, she sighed with relief.

Mitch grinned and jerked a thumb over his shoulder at the other man. "I tried to keep him out. This is my brother, Brock. He insisted on meeting the mother of the kids he didn't baby-sit the other night."

Perri extended her hand to the handsome man. He looked a little like Mitch, though not as dark, and probably younger. "I'm glad to meet you, Brock," she said. "I probably wouldn't be brave enough to say that if you had sat for me."

"Well, well, well," Brock said slowly. "The teenager with four kids."

Mitch laughed. "I said she *looks* like a teenager. Was I right or what?"

Brock nodded, frankly looking Perri up and down. "Yep, you were right—about everything." He turned back to Perri. "Since you wouldn't let me sit while you went out with Mitch, how about letting him sit while we go out?"

Perri smiled. "I always take my boys. Ask Mitch."

"Don't ask," Mitch retorted.

"Well, I'd better clear out of here," Brock said. "Bye, Perri. Any time you need a sitter call me. Better yet, call when you need a date."

When the door closed, Mitch settled into a chair beside her desk. "That's my kid brother," he said. His eyes searched her face, and he shifted uncomfortably. "I should have realized that as soon as he met you he wouldn't be willing to play baby sitter for your kids. Brock has always—well, when he sees something—or someone—he likes, he makes sure he gets what he wants. One way or another." He cleared his throat and studied the toe of his shoe. "What did you think of him?"

"He seems nice," Perri said. "But I'm not planning to start going out, and I couldn't take advantage of him."

Mitch looked startled. "What do you mean?"

"I wouldn't want to ask him to baby-sit my kids, just because he's your brother. I wouldn't feel right about it."

"Neither would I at this point," Mitch muttered. "But you do deserve one night out." He reached for her hand, and fireworks shot through her. "Just one night," Mitch added.

She pulled her hand away. No good would come from feeding the already-raging fire in her heart. "I have to be away from my kids to work, but otherwise, I spend my time with them. Thanks, anyway."

Tears gathered in her eyes, Unwilling for Mitch to see, she excused herself and bolted for the rest room. After blowing her nose, she washed her face with cold water, applied fresh makeup, brushed her hair, and returned to her office with red-rimmed eyes to find Mitch gone. Sitting down to her computer, she discovered a message on the screen: *What could make a pretty girl cry? Sorry if I did it. Double sorry if you're feeling lonely for your husband. Come out with me and I'll make you laugh.*

She should have known he'd recognize the tears. Well, she couldn't go out with him.

🙢

During the usual wild affair she called supper, Perri answered the phone to Brock's voice. "Just checking to see if you need a sitter," he said in a voice so like Mitch's it gave her goose bumps.

"Really," Perri said, "I don't go out, but thanks."

"How would you like some company?"

"You wouldn't like it here. It's bedlam—and that's no exaggeration."

"Oh, come on. I like kids. Give me your address."

Should she? Why not? She was lonely for an adult to talk to, and she knew she was in no danger of falling in love with Mitch's brother. She and Mitch could be only friends, but she felt safer with his brother than she did with Mitch. "Sure, why not?"

🙢

Driving to work the next morning, Perri thought about Brock's visit the night before. He had looked and sounded like Mitch, but the resemblance ended there. Where Mitch had never said anything even remotely sexual to her, Brock had been quick to openly proposition her. She doubted she ever did manage to convince him that she planned on being celibate, even after having been married. The idea that God's ways are always best seemed totally beyond his experience. Brock finally left, disappointed but assuring her he'd be back.

She turned into the arcade and parked. Well, she still believed the Bible and the way she read it, keeping pure wasn't old-fashioned. She locked the car and hurried down the street, enjoying the warm summer sunshine.

❧

Brock appeared on her doorstep soon after she arrived home that night. "Hi," she greeted him. "I thought you got enough of us last night."

"Oh, no. I had a good time." Without waiting for an invitation, he stepped through the door.

She said nothing, but began making spaghetti sauce and cutting vegetables for salad. Brock sat on Tad's high stool and talked to her, but he didn't offer to help. He told her about graduating from the University of Oregon.

"Where are you working now?" Perri asked, dropping a cup of chopped onion into the sauce and stirring it with a wooden spoon.

"Well," he said, "I'm not working right now."

"Oh? Where have you been working?" she asked, concentrating on the spaghetti sauce she'd just tasted. Pretty good. Maybe just a touch more oregano. Tossing the spoon into the sink, she reached for a clean one.

He muttered something about not working yet.

That caught her attention. "When did you graduate?"

"A few years ago," he mumbled.

"Shame on you. I just graduated this spring and I'm trying hard to make my education pay off," she said. "Mitch doesn't even have a degree and look what he's done."

Brock looked uncomfortable. "Yeah, but he's had more breaks than I. He has so much money now, he doesn't even need help from Dad."

"I should hope not. You two are big boys. By the way,

how come you two haven't married?"

"Never met the right girls, I guess."

Everything was ready, so Perri called the boys. Receiving no response, she went to the window. Her mouth opened in shock. Somehow the boys had wrestled a small tree onto its side and placed a stubby stick upright on a limb. When the boys released the tree, it snapped up; the stick flew like an arrow across the lawn, smacking the garden house with a whack. Four young voices screamed approval.

Brock, who'd moved to Perri's side, laughed out loud. "All right!"

The boys jumped onto the tree and wrestled it down again, laying Tad's brown teddy bear on the leafy top. It flew like a cannon ball, slamming into the aluminum side of the shed exactly as the stick had.

"That did it! That's bear abuse," Perri said, heading for the door. But Brock grabbed her wrist and pulled her back beside him.

"Let's wait and see what they do next. Watch."

Soon the tree top touched the ground again, but this time the boys hustled Tad into position high in the top.

Perri jerked free. "Let me go!" she yelled. "They'll kill him."

Brock grabbed her again. "They're just playing." He laughed at her frantic struggles.

Terrified for Tad's safety, Perri kicked Brock hard on the shin, but he held fast. As she slammed her hand against his face, she saw Mitch run across the lawn, snatch Tad into his arms, and head for the house. The other boys followed. The treetop whipped back and forth.

Mitch opened the door and walked in. "You'd never believe what I found the animals doing," he said, putting Tad into Perri's arms.

"We saw," Brock said, laughing. "Quite a bunch of kids, aren't they?"

Mitch whirled to face his brother. "Quite of bunch of kids? They could have killed him." He turned to the three boys. "Go to your rooms until dinner's ready—and think about how badly you could have hurt Tad."

After the boys disappeared, Mitch turned back to Perri. "Were you standing there watching them turn Tad into a cannonball?"

Perri dropped her eyes to his shoes.

"Maybe you were so involved with each other you didn't see it. Much as I hate that idea, it's better than the last one." He stormed out the door, slamming it behind him.

"You go too, Brock," Perri said, her voice cool.

Brock fingered his bruised cheek. "I was just playing with you," he said. "I haven't had experience with a bunch of kids the way you have."

Perri opened the door. "Go. I'm too upset to be good company—and I don't enjoy people who force their will on me, anyway."

Perri called the boys to supper. As they inhaled the spaghetti and sauce she asked them whom they liked better, Mitch or Brock.

"Mitch," Scott yelled. "He plays with us."

"Mitch," Hugh repeated. "He buys pizza."

"Mitch," Judd said quietly. "He cares about us."

"I don't like Mitch," Tad said, his blue eyes meeting Perri's. "He wrecked our game. I was going to fly like a bird."

"No, you weren't, my love; you were going to get hurt."

After putting the boys to bed, she called her folks and told Dad about Tad's near accident. He actually laughed, then told her to forgive herself, that God did, and to be sure to thank Him for sending Mitch to save Tad.

❧

The next morning Perri could have sworn she felt frost an inch deep in the office. After lunch she tapped on Mitch's door, then went in and sank into her chair. "Why don't we just talk about it?" she asked. "We'll both feel better."

He leaned back, looking into her eyes. "Know what?" he asked. "I thought you were the best little mother in the world. I can't tell you how much you impressed me with that my-kids-come-first routine."

Her eyes never left his. "Now I'm the worst mother?"

His eyes finally dropped. "Why don't you tell me what you were doing while the boys prepared to fire Tad away?"

She wanted desperately to tell him about Brock, but after all, they were brothers. He wouldn't believe her. She shook her head.

"I'll bet you and Brock were all wrapped up in each other!" he muttered.

Perri almost smiled. He was close. "Why don't you ask Brock?" she suggested. "I'd much rather he told you."

"I'm not asking Brock anything. You tell me—or this conversation is concluded."

For some reason a giggle escaped Perri's lips. "Will this affect our working relationship?" she asked in a tiny voice.

"It won't affect mine," Mitch said tightly, opening the door leading into her office. She barely made it through before it crashed shut.

What on earth was that all about? Perri wondered, dropping to her own desk. *How would he be so incredibly upset because he didn't like the way I handled my kids?* She grasped her head between her hands. What was she saying? From his perspective, she had been negligent, a careless mother who pursued her own pleasures at the expense of her children's safety. But he seemed to have taken the incident so personally. She hadn't thought he cared so much about the boys.

&

Mitch's face floated above her as she tossed and turned that night, unable to sleep. He looked at her reproachfully, his black eyes sad. *Mitch,* she thought, *people make mistakes, and thanks to you no harm came to Tad. Can't you forgive me?* Then it hit her. She sat bolt upright in the bed, staring into the darkness.

Mitch was jealous!

seven

Perri jumped out of bed, threw on a robe, and ran to the kitchen. She leaned against the table; she had to think about this. If Mitch wasn't interested in having a relationship with her, why would he be jealous of Brock? He'd told her explicitly that he didn't want to pursue anything with her, because of the boys. Maybe, though, his heart didn't listen to his head. Or maybe he'd learned to care for her since he told her no.

And maybe he wasn't jealous!

How did life get so complicated? She liked her job; she liked her boss, too—but complications like this could be the end of her job. And anyway, whether Mitch was attracted to her or not, she knew what God wanted her to do: forget her personal feelings and be the perfect assistant to Mitch. Unless he was committed to God the way she was, a relationship between them would only lead to heartache. She drank a glass of cold milk and went to bed.

❧

The first thing the next morning Mitch called her into his office. "You're right," he said looking tired and rumpled. "We have to talk."

"You don't look so great," Perri said.

He pushed a black wave away from his forehead, then leaned his square chin on his hand. "I have to know what you and Brock were doing the night Tad nearly became extinct."

"Please forget it," she pleaded. "It was a bad scene and

60

not what you think. But it's all over and thanks to you, no one got hurt."

"I want to know."

"I want you to know, too, but I can't be the one to tell you."

"I asked Brock, Perri, and he insinuated you were doing something quite pleasant. If that's true and you're embarrassed to talk about it, I'll understand."

Red streaks burned up from Perri's neck across her face. Her breath came in short puffs. "What happened was neither pleasant nor sexual. When I saw what the boys were doing, I tried to run out to stop them. For some reason Brock physically held me inside. I punched him and kicked him. I know I hurt him, but he wouldn't let me go." She drew in a few short breaths. "That's the whole rotten story."

Mitch fell back in his chair and the strained look disappeared from his face. For a moment Perri thought he started to reach for her, but he didn't. "I see," he said slowly at last. He fiddled with a pen on his desk, sliding it back and forth, then looked up at her. "Think we could see each other socially? I mean I want to spend time with you." His eyes implored Perri to accept his offer.

She shook her head, while her heart sank; was he more like his brother than she had thought? "You made it clear you aren't interested in anything permanent. Therefore I assume you're suggesting a sexual relationship." She swallowed. "I believe that God intended sex to be a special gift between a husband and a wife, not something to be engaged in casually or selfishly. I haven't been with anyone—like that, not since Jerry died, and I won't unless I remarry someday. As far as I'm concerned, a lifetime love with someone who loves God the way I do is something I hope for—but I know I may not ever have that sort of love again. I guess it's a little like waiting for tomorrow's rainbow. If it doesn't happen—" she shrugged. "Well, I always have the kids."

Mitch's fingers whitened as he grasped a yellow pencil. Perri watched, expecting the pencil to snap. Finally his eyes met hers. "It doesn't have to be sexual," he said. "That wasn't what I meant. I meant—" He shrugged, and looked away. "Could we at least be friends?"

Perri's heart perked up. What could it hurt to spend time together, now that he understood the rules? She'd never marry someone who didn't put God first, but she could use a friend. She'd just control her heart and not get involved. Surely she could do that.

Her wide mouth curved into a smile. "I'd like that. How'd you like to go out to Perkins Point with us this weekend? We'll take a picnic lunch, swim in the lake, and be lazy."

He nodded his dark head. "Sounds great. What can I bring?"

"Not necessary. You can help another time. Now, Mr. Winfield, if you don't get out of my office I'll be in trouble with my boss for dallying away the day."

Mitch jumped up. "I'm on my way." He held his hand to Perri, who grasped it in a firm shake. "Thanks a lot," he said quietly.

Perri fell into her work with verve, having left several things undone the previous night. As she rushed along, Trish knocked on her door. "Excuse me, Mrs. Seabrook, your ten o'clock appointment is here."

Perri shoved the papers into a drawer in a jumble, smoothed her blond curls, and walked into the reception room with Trish, where a young woman was waiting. After Trish introduced them, Perri led the woman to her office and settled her into a soft chair. After visiting a few minutes, Perri helped the woman decide which policy fit her needs.

Then they chatted for a little while before concluding the appointment.

She discovered Kaima Kingston was twenty-four years old and had a three-year-old daughter, Merry. She also discovered she really liked the bright and friendly young woman. When she found the family lived only two blocks from her, she smiled into Kaima's gray eyes. "Howdy, neighbor," she said, reaching for Kaima's hand. "We should get together some time. It would be a shame to waste all that nearness."

Kaima agreed, and Perri wrote herself a note to drop some goody at the Kingston home soon. Then she gave the papers to Trish to deliver to the typing room.

"Are you busy, Mrs. Seabrook?" her intercom asked.

"Just finished, Mr. Winfield, I'll be right in." After straightening the papers she'd dumped into her desk, she picked up her pad and pencil, then opened Mitch's door.

He looked up with a silly grin on his face. "I guess you wouldn't want to leave the kids with Brock."

"I guess you could say that," she murmured. "The man's a certifiable maniac."

He nodded. "Just checking."

"Just testing, you mean, don't you?"

"No. I really want you to find someone to stay with the kids so we can do some grown-up things."

"I'll work on it." She positioned her pencil over the pad, looking hopefully at him.

He laughed. "You know I don't do that anymore. You know more about this business than I do. I keep waiting for you to start paying me."

She grinned impishly. "You're wasting my time, huh? Well, I just sold an insurance policy to someone who seemed special."

He studied her a moment. "Is he better looking than I?"

Perri thought a moment. "She probably is. It's a hard call, though. You're no slouch in the looks department."

Plainly pleased, Mitch grinned. "Thanks. Hurt you to say it, though, didn't it? Okay, you met a woman. What of it?"

"She lives two blocks from me and she's a bright, smart girl. I'd like to get to know her."

Mitch leaned back, lacing his fingers behind his head. "Why don't you invite her and her family on our weekend outing?"

"That sounds nice—but you and I would see less of each other."

He shrugged. "I know. Friends don't mind."

•

The day dawned clear and sunny. Perri had everything ready at nine o'clock and waited eagerly for ten-thirty, when Mitch planned to arrive.

But Brock beat Mitch, swinging his sleek blue-gray convertible into Perri's driveway at ten o'clock. Perri wondered what to tell him. The boys would no doubt tell all, anyway.

"Well, sounds as though you have a day planned," Brock drawled, dumping himself onto the sofa.

"Yep."

"Who all's going?"

Was this a trap? What had the kids told him? "Well, some people I just met are going along."

"Is that all?"

She couldn't come right out and lie, not even to Brock. "I really don't feel you have the right to ask," she said, adding a smile to soften the words.

"That's all right," he said. "I just wondered who'd be there besides Mitch." So he had known all along that his brother was going. Perri gave him an annoyed sideways glance.

Just then Mitch walked in. After a little verbal sparring, he invited Brock on the outing; Perri's heart sank.

The Kingstons were driving their own car and meeting them later, Mitch rode with Perri and the boys, and Brock drove the ten miles to the lake alone. "At least we're here to see that he doesn't drown anyone," Mitch said.

In a little while bright quilts covered the ground and the boys ran down the gravelly beach into the cool water, opaque with wind-blown silt. Perri put her beach towel down and eased herself onto it.

"Hey, you can't do that," Mitch said. "This is a swimming party."

Perri nodded at the four whirlwinds tearing into the water. "Watching that bunch is a full-time job. Anything could happen if I tried to swim, too."

"I see. Do you trust me?"

"Of course."

"Good, then we can take turns swimming and watching."

Perri shook her head. "Wouldn't that be taking advantage of our new friendship? Besides, the boys will be tired pretty soon. Then I'll get to swim."

"Okay." Mitch ran down the beach and flopped into the water. Perri laughed out loud as her three larger boys shoved him under the water. He might not be ready for the boys, but she'd never seen anyone so good with them, including her own father.

"Hi, gorgeous, mind if I sit down?"

Intrigued with the action at the water, Perri hadn't seen Brock approaching. "Sure. You can watch the swimmers," she said.

"Why would I watch a bunch of idiots splashing around

in dirty water when I can look at you?"

"Dirty water?" she repeated, grasping at anything to change the subject. "You may not realize it, Brock," she continued, keeping her eyes on the figures in the water, "but this lake tests out the cleanest in the state."

He dropped to his knees beside her. "I don't care if the water has blue dye in it. I have some fantastic sun screen here. Want me to rub you down?"

She'd rather burn up than have Brock touch her. Come to think of it, she might burn up at that: she'd forgotten to protect her fair skin from the warm sun. "Nope," she said anyway. "I'm fine."

The Kingstons' arrival saved her further hassle for the moment. Kaima wore a bright yellow one-piece suit that set off her coloring beautifully. Her husband and baby, both red heads, wore yellow swimwear too.

"Perri," Kaima said, "meet my husband, Rob."

Perri extended a hand. "I've been waiting to meet Kaima's lucky husband," she said. "She's quite a girl."

"You can say that again," Rob said laughing, giving his wife an appreciative glance.

"She's quite a girl," Brock repeated suggestively.

"This is Mitch's lecherous brother, Brock," Perri said. "Watch out for him, Kaima."

Brock sent a reproachful look Perri's way, but the Kingstons took the remark for a joke.

As baby Merry toddled toward the lake, Rob snatched her up and splashed into the water, then turned on his back, set Merry on his stomach, and swam around inside the ropes. Kaima watched, her eyes loving and proud.

"You have a darling family," Perri said.

Kaima nodded in agreement. "Yes. Rob's a fantastic father."

Brock moved to Kaima's side. "You're starting to look like a lobster," he said. "Let me put on some sun screen."

Kaima twisted her head to examine her shoulders. "I don't see anything—oh well, it can't hurt. Thanks."

Brock shot Perri a who-needs-you? smile, unscrewed the cap, and poured some of the milky liquid into his palm. Then he started massaging it into Kaima's shoulders, arms, and back. The heavy coconut fragrance made Perri feel nauseous.

"Ummm, that feels good," Kaima purred.

"I'm good at massages," Brock answered.

Perri simply had to get away from that guy before she beat him to a pulp. "I'm going into the water for a while," she said.

No one answered, so she ran to the lake. All four of her boys and Mitch gave her a shower that induced her to drop into the water at once.

"Glad to see you," Mitch said. "Don't you think we can swim if we both watch the boys? I'll watch Judd and Hugh and you take Scott and Tad."

"Sure, let's try it for a while." She showed Scott how to put his hands on the bottom, kick his legs, and crawl toward shore. And she held Tad's hands while he tried to kick the entire lake onto the rocky beach.

Rob swam to Perri, with Merry still riding his stomach. "What's with Kaima?" he asked. "I thought she'd be in the water before I parked."

Perri felt anger for Brock well up in her again. "I guess she's trying to tan a little," she answered.

"I'll go get her." Pulling his strong body upright, he handed Merry to Perri and loped off toward the two sitting so close together on the beach.

eight

"Why the scowl?" Mitch asked. "You look prettier wearing a smile."

Perri smiled briefly, but then the scowl returned. "Your brother's doing his best to cause domestic trouble and it irritates me."

"I want in the water," Merry said, wiggling in Perri's arms.

"Okay, love, in you go." Perri dangled Merry's legs in the cool water.

"Stop!" Mitch yelled.

Perri jerked Merry up and turned in time to see Mitch retrieve Tad from Scott and Hugh. Mitch's lips quirked into a grin. "The boys were throwing Tad over the floats into the deep water." He raised his voice and called, "Hugh and Scott, come here."

A moment later they stood before him. "Did you boys stop to think that Tad can't swim and neither can you? What did you plan to do after you threw him into the deep water?"

Scott shrugged and looked up at his eight-year-old brother for an answer. Hugh shrugged too, then met Mitch's black eyes. "You swim great, Mitch. We knew you'd get him."

"You also know he's afraid of deep water. You wouldn't like it if I tossed you into deep water, would you?"

With promises to be more careful, the boys went back to their play, and Perri smiled. "I can't believe how good you are with the kids."

He gave her an embarrassed grin and then yelled, "Okay, all out for lunch." All four boys raced away, leaving Perri, still carrying Merry, and Mitch to walk back more slowly.

When they neared the picnic area, Perri heard harsh voices, but both Kingstons flashed tight smiles when Mitch and Perri appeared. Brock had disappeared. For good, Perri hoped, handing Merry to Kaima.

As they were finishing their meal, however, Brock returned. Kaima and Rob tensed.

"How about an hour's rest for everyone?" Mitch suggested as they put the food away.

Surprisingly, the boys settled quietly onto the quilts in the shade of the big trees. Merry fell asleep, and the grownups spent the time quietly getting acquainted. The Kingstons had been separated from their relatives and friends since their move to Eugene. They seemed eager to make ties in their new home.

"We'll have to get together often," Perri said eagerly.

Kaima flashed a furtive glance toward Brock, but she nodded her dark head.

❧

That night Perri put her tired little family to bed after a quick Bible story and prayer. Mitch helped. Although she wasn't about to get involved with him, she wished she could think of a way to teach him about God's love. After all, Christ wanted her to witness to His love to everyone.

They'd barely started a game of Scrabble when the phone interrupted. "Hi, gorgeous," Brock's smooth voice intoned. "Got that wild bunch in bed yet?"

Perri swallowed a nasty retort. "Sure do. Everything's quiet. Mitch is busy trouncing me in a game of Scrabble."

The long silence made Perri wonder if Brock were still there. "Well," he finally said, "I just wanted to say thanks for a nice day. See you later."

Mitch raised his eyebrow in a silent question as she hung

up the phone. "Brock," Perri answered.

Mitch's black eyes smoldered. "I'm telling him to stop bothering you."

Perri's heart did a triple somersault in her chest. Firmly, she informed the foolish organ that Mitch was simply looking out for her welfare, the way he would for any friend. "While you're about it, tell him to stay away from Kaima Kingston," she said, her voice not quite steady. "Did you see how unhappy Rob was with him?"

❧

Early the next morning Kaima called and asked if Perri and Mitch liked to play Pictionary. "Mitch and I are just friends," Perri told the younger girl. "New friends at that. But I'll find out."

"One more thing," Kaima said, "we wondered if you'd like to trade baby-sitting once in a while."

Would she! Kaima was the answer to Perri's prayers. "Yes, but I'll sit four times for every time you sit. That's the only way it would be fair."

Kaima laughed. "Let's just say we'll sit when the other needs it and see how it works out, okay? And be sure to check about Pictionary. Rob and I love to play and that's something we could do at home."

❧

The following week, when Perri checked the accounts, she discovered the Kingston account hadn't returned from the typing room.

"I'll just do it myself and be sure it gets done," she told Mitch.

Mitch nodded. "And write up a policy for yourself," he said. "I'll discount my commission, so it'll save you a bundle."

Perri whirled to face him. "Thanks, but you've been in

my house. It's due to go up in flames any minute. You'd better stay clear of that place."

Mitch shrugged. "I did see the condition of your house. That's the reason I want you protected with a good policy."

"Well, my insurance is due early in September, so I'll think about it. And thanks. It feels good to have someone thinking about my welfare. Oh, by the way, have you ever played Pictionary?"

"Yeah, a few times. But it takes more than two people."

Perri nodded. "I know. The Kingstons would like to play sometime."

Mitch's black eyes bore into Perri's. "Do you get mad at your partner?"

"Of course not. It's just a game."

"I had a girlfriend once who used to rip up my drawings and throw them in my face." He grimaced. "So be warned. I'm not much of an artist."

☙

Two nights later the Kingstons came to Perri's house after the boys had been put to bed. Mitch had come for supper and rough-housed with the kids until they were all tired—including Mitch.

Rob snapped at Kaima for her drawing before they had finished the first round. Mitch raised his eyebrows ever so slightly at Perri.

After the first game Perri pushed her chair back. "Come help me fix a snack, Kaima."

As she laid out slices of cheese and whole wheat crackers, Kaima apologized for Rob's temper. "He really isn't like that," she said quietly. "He's unhappy with me because Brock keeps coming over when he's at work."

"Why do you let Brock?" Perri asked.

Kaima shook her head slowly. "I don't know how to stop

him," she said sadly. "He doesn't do any harm, and I'm not a rude person."

"Look, Kaima," Perri said patiently. "If he's causing strife between you two, he's doing harm. Send him packing. I won't let him hang around here."

Perri picked up the tray and Kaima brought the hot chocolate. "Rob's ordered him off the place," Kaima whispered in Perri's ear. "Maybe he'll stay away now."

Rob blew wide open during the second game. "You don't even try to draw pictures I can recognize!" he yelled at Kaima. "Anyone with half a brain would have drawn a rabbit. Hair—hare."

"I'm sorry," Kaima said, "I guess I wasn't thinking."

"You were dreaming about that rich bum again!" he yelled.

Kaima didn't answer. After a long silence she cleared her throat. "He's talking about Brock," she said in a flat voice. "He doesn't think a man and woman can have a platonic relationship."

"He's right, Kaima," Mitch said with a loud sigh. "Chase Brock off."

Perri couldn't let that pass. "I couldn't agree more about Brock," she said, "but a platonic relationship describes us perfectly, Mitch."

A smile pushed Mitch's lips into a crescent. "Don't change the subject—but since you did, can you say you've never had a romantic thought about me?"

Perri's face burned. Her breath caught in her throat. After swallowing twice, she cleared her throat. "Of course, I can," she croaked. Three pairs of eyes burned into hers. She giggled and leaned her mouth against her hand. "But it wouldn't be true."

Mitch threw back his head and laughed. "She's human!"

he shouted at the ceiling.

"She's human, all right," Rob growled.

"Shut up," Kaima said out of the side of her mouth.

The laughter died on Mitch's face. He sat up straight in his chair and glared at Rob. "What's that supposed to mean?"

Rob glanced at Kaima and said nothing.

Mitch's voice rose. "I said, what did that remark mean?"

Rob half rose from his chair. "Let's go home," he said to Kaima.

Mitch hooked a large hand over Rob's shoulder and shoved him back down. "I want to know what you meant by that snide remark about Perri."

"Go ask your brother. He knows all about your platonic friend."

Mitch's face turned livid and the cords in his neck stood out. He jerked Rob to his feet, holding him by the shoulders, then shoved him back into his chair.

"I'm asking you, not my brother," Mitch whispered. "Tell me what you're talking about. Now."

Rob shook his head.

"I'll tell you," Kaima finally said. "Brock told us that Perri has been more than friendly with him. I told Rob it wasn't true, but he went into orbit over it. He thinks Brock's trying to make a statistic out of me now."

Mitch dropped into his chair and made a tiny sound. Seeing the pain in his eyes, Perri put her arms around his sagging shoulders. "Mitch, she said softly, "you know it isn't true."

She turned to the other two. "Brock has said this kind of thing before. This is his response to rejection."

Mitch recovered somewhat and stood beside her, draping an arm over her shoulders. He grinned sheepishly at Rob.

"You thought Kaima got you into some wild bunch, didn't you? Let me assure you it's the furthest thing from the truth. Perri would never fool around with my brother. I'm just a little—" He shrugged and ran his hand through his hair. "I'm just a little crazy when it comes to Perri. She's the most honest person I know, and she has something special with God, something I've never seen before. My brother would like to drag everybody down to his own level—but Perri's too certain of what she believes for Brock to influence her." He gave Rob a sympathetic look. "I know he's my brother, but he also can be a real jerk. I'm sorry now I ever introduced him to Perri. And I'm sorry he's been annoying you and Kaima. Please believe me."

Mitch thrust his hand out and Rob accepted it. "I believe you," Rob said. "But that—that jerk has been in my house for the last time." He looked sternly at Kaima. "Do I have your cooperation?"

Kaima nodded. "If I see him coming I won't answer the door."

"All right." Rob gathered up the sleeping Merry, and the Kingstons left.

Mitch smiled at Perri. "So much for games with our new friends."

Perri picked up the scratch paper they had used for drawing. "The worst flop of any party I ever gave," she said.

"I'm sorry for my part in ruining it." Mitch ran his fingers through his rumpled hair. "I don't know how I could let that—my brother—throw me, even for a second."

Perri's gaze met his for a moment. "It's possible that you could learn something from this horrible night," she said softly.

"And what could that be?"

"Well, for starters, assuming you believe me, you must

realize what a jerk your brother is. You said it yourself."

A smile flicked across Mitch's face. "I realize it—more than you even know," he said. "I've tried to believe in him but he hasn't worked a day since his fancy education, a master's degree from the big U. And I'm partially supporting him. Me, with an associate degree from a community college!"

"Aha. That's why you said he owes you, when you offered his sitting services."

Perri walked him to the door. He stood on the porch, looking at her in a way he hadn't before. "I guess I'd better go," he said, making no move to leave.

"What's wrong, Mitch?" Perri finally asked.

"Do you really have romantic thoughts about me?" he whispered.

Perri backed away, tossing a laugh into the night air. "Only when you put your head through car tops."

"Oh." He stood, transfixed, still gazing at her, as though searching for something. "In that case—" he leaned down and gave Perri the most gentle kiss she'd ever received. When his lips touched hers, they felt soft and yet firm. She longed to lean toward him and wrap her arms around him, she longed to feel his arms around her.

Alarm bells drowned out her longings, and she jumped away. What was she doing, anyway?

nine

He stood for a moment, transfixed. "I've imagined kissing you but—" He shook his head. Before she could move, he kissed her again twice, so gently she wondered if he really touched her. Then he turned and ran to his car.

Perri stumbled to her bedroom and into her bed. "Dear Father," she prayed, "I know You don't want me mixed up with an unbeliever and I know it'll only bring me unhappiness. Please help me teach him about You—and if he can't love You, give me the strength to follow You. Even if I have to change jobs. I'm getting in too deep, Father. I really need Your help."

&

The next morning she didn't know what to expect when she faced Mitch. "Good morning, friend," he said softly, pulling out a sheaf of papers. "I'd like to spend the morning checking the company's growth for the last two years."

"Great." She inched her chair closer to the desk.

Later she checked her watch and gasped. "I didn't realize it was so late." She noticed Mitch's grin. "Since we've just discovered you're one of the fastest rising young executives in the country, I'm taking you to lunch."

His eyebrows shot up. "You are? We're having lunch together? Well, grab your money, Seabrook, and let's get out of here."

At the restaurant, Mitch ordered the most expensive meal on the menu. *Oh well, who cares?* Perri told herself, ordering the same. They'd never be celebrating his 115 percent growth rate again.

"I can't believe how we've grown," he said as they waited for dessert, "but I have a pretty efficient crew."

Perri nodded. "Yes, except for a few accounts that get lost."

He slapped his forehead with the heel of his hand. "I forgot all about that. You've been covering it so well, it completely left my mind. Do you have any idea who's doing it?"

Perri shook her head. "I thought it must be Jessica because she's never made any pretense of liking me. But she seems to be doing her job."

"Who, then?"

"I have no more idea than I did in the beginning. I can't believe it's Trish but she's hard to check out."

Mitch rubbed his chin thoughtfully. "I always ask Trish to run my accounts to the girls."

"I know. Maybe I really am the one, Mitch. Maybe I'm just a careless slob and don't know it. After all, I've been with you only three months. We didn't check your growth— or loss—for the last three months."

He smiled. "Want to do that this afternoon?"

The dessert came and they forgot all about the office. When they were done, Mitch quietly picked up the tab. He grinned at Perri's protests. "I'm good for it, remember?"

❧

Late that afternoon, Mitch heaved a sigh. They'd checked the growth rate of the business for every three month period for the last two years. "Are you satisfied?" he asked.

She sighed with relief. "I guess I'm not a liability. I sure would have been, though, if we'd had a major fire or accident before we discovered the problem." Perri hurried toward her office door.

Mitch followed her in and sat down beside her desk.

"Let's not think about business now," he said. "Are we continuing our celebration tonight?"

Perri's heart lurched in her chest and her mouth went dry. *Father, give me strength.* "I'm sorry, friend," she said, "but I can't. You remember how much you don't care for wild kids. And I couldn't be happy with anyone who loved God less than I."

He leaned back in his chair. "What's He ever done to make you like Him more than you do me?"

She sat up straighter. Here was the opportunity she'd been waiting for praying for. *Help me do it right, God,* she prayed silently. "He died for me," she said softly.

"I'd die for you—but then I wouldn't be around to enjoy the reward."

She returned his smile, then turned serious. "He didn't do it for any reward. He did it because He loved me so much He couldn't bear for me to die." He looked interested so she continued. "He died for you too, Mitch."

"Yeah? I hear people saying that kind of stuff, but it sounds like a bunch of mumbo jumbo. Does anyone know what it means?"

"Yes. Suppose I'm embezzling the money from the policies that are turning up missing and I get caught. After a trial the judge sentences me to ten years. Well, you tell the judge I have four kids depending on me and that you'll serve my time for me. How do you think I'd feel?"

Mitch leaned forward, vitally interested. "In debt to me forever, I hope. Maybe you'd even love me."

"Right. And that's exactly what Jesus did, Mitch. God told Adam and Eve they'd die if they disobeyed, which is sin. And sure enough they did. But Jesus loved us so much He died our death for us, so that after our bodies die our spirits will live with God forever. And that's only the beginning. If we stay close to Him, He gives us happiness here and now that you can't imagine." She smiled at Mitch and added softly, "He's real, Mitch. Believe me. And He's the most important Person in my life."

He leaned back in his chair and looked into her eyes. Neither said a word for a moment, then he got up. "Whew! That was quite an earful." He thought another moment. "I guess you still won't help me celebrate tonight?"

She shook her head. "I have to spend the evening with my kids. But how'd you like to go to church with us this weekend?"

He considered a moment, then shook his head. "I can't this Sunday. I have to visit my parents. Another time, though. Good night, friend. Thanks for the sermon." Without warning he leaned down and fluttered the gentlest of kisses against her lips.

The door opening brought Perri to her senses. What was she doing? And in her office!

"I'm sorry," Trish said, "I had no idea." She turned and hurried back to the reception room, slamming the door behind her.

Mitch grinned into her eyes. "How soon will everyone know?"

Perri sighed. "It'll be close to instantaneous."

"I'm sure. Well, if you won't have dinner with me, I'll see you tomorrow." He winked and disappeared, quietly closing the door behind him.

❧

"What do you want for supper, boys?" she asked later that afternoon after she'd changed into jeans and tank top.

"Pizza!" Scott yelled.

"Mushroom pizza!" Hugh screamed.

"Tomato and green pepper pizza," Judd said quietly.

Tad slid from her lap and jumped up and down. "Let's have everything." He ran to his biggest brother. "Judd, I'm eating three whole pizzas."

"Sure you aren't," Judd said. "You won't even eat one piece."

Tad broke into genuine tears. "Mommy, Judd says I won't eat anything."

"Sure you will," Perri said. "You'll eat until your tummy's stuffed." She pulled the ingredients from the refrigerator and went to work.

Just as everyone had a big piece of gooey pizza on his plate, the phone rang. "I wondered if you'd watch Merry for a few hours tonight," Kaima Kingston said. "I know it's short notice, but Rob insists he has a surprise for me and he wants to go in a half hour. I know you're a busy person—and I know I'm gushing." She laughed and Perri did too.

"We aren't doing a thing," Perri said. "Bring her any time."

"You have to promise to let me watch the boys soon, okay?"

Perri smiled to herself. She wasn't sure she'd ever go any-where again. "Sure. Just bring her over. We'll love having her."

She hung up the phone. "Now remember, she's a girl and lots smaller than you," she said, meeting each boy's eyes.

All the boys played with her for a while, taking turns car-rying her around while Perri folded several loads of shirts and jeans. Finally she finished and flopped onto the couch to think.

Merry! She hadn't heard a thing from any of the kids for quite some time. "Judd," she called stepping onto the front porch. Seeing no one, she called again. A moment later Judd stuck his head in from the back door.

"Hi, honey, what's going on?" Perri asked.

"Nothing, I'm trying to put Scott's bicycle chain back on." He disappeared and Perri followed. Scott stood beside Judd, waiting for his bike to be fixed. Hugh had his bike upside down doing something to it too.

"Where are Tad and Merry?" Perri asked.

"I dunno." Three heads returned to their work.

She went back into the still house. This time she heard voices and she followed them to the bathroom. "Tad," she screamed, "what do you think you're doing?"

Tad and Merry sat in the bathtub, fully clothed, in several inches of water. Eight flat tubes, obviously from the medicine cabinet, lay on the floor, and miles of pink, blue, green, and white stuff ran in shimmering ribbons through the water and around the kids.

"What's in your hair, Merry?" Perri asked, picking up the tubes. Toothpaste, shampoo, first aid cream, athlete's foot medicine, hair conditioner, facial cleanser, and hair remover. Hair remover! She snatched the shocked child from the water and smelled her hair. Strong mint. Whew! Relieved, she set Merry on the counter, her clothes dripping onto the floor. Slimy water sloshed from her tennies, and her arms and legs felt as slippery as butter. She set Tad on the other side of the sink.

"Tad," she said patiently, "why does Merry have toothpaste in her hair?"

"Cause she got dirt in her hair."

"Why did you squeeze everything out of all those tubes?"

"I was trying to find the shampoo."

"And you finally found it, huh?"

He nodded again.

Supporting Merry's little head over the sink, Perri began rinsing the sticky red curls. The more she rinsed the slimier it became. Eventually, though, Merry's hair squeaked so Perri turned her attention to first Tad and then the tub. After spraying the long ribbons down the drain, she took off the kids' scummy clothes and put them back in the tub. Then she sprayed them squeaky clean, dried them, pulled two sets of clothes from Tad's drawer, and put them on the tots. Then she threw the clothes into the washer and cleaned up the bathroom. Later she put Merry's things back on her and tucked all the kids into bed. At last, Perri poured herself a glass of diet pop and relaxed on the front porch swing, feeling she'd done a day's work in the last two hours.

When the Kingstons came to pick up their daughter late that night, Perri didn't mention the bathroom incident to them. "Promise you'll let us return the favor soon," Kaima said as they went out to their car. Perri only smiled. If Tad and Merry could get into so much trouble while she watched them, what would happen if she trusted her four to someone as innocent as Kaima?

❧

The next morning Perri found a note on her desk instructing all employees to meet in Mitch's office at eleven o'clock. Curious, she hurried to get her morning work out of the way.

Cracking open the connecting door, Perri peeked into Mitch's office at exactly eleven, to see the three other girls sitting on the couch in the back of the room, talking and giggling.

She marched in holding her shoulders back and her head high, carrying a yellow pad and pencil. Mitch wasn't there so, after speaking to the girls, she took the chair beside the desk.

"What's this meeting about?" Trish asked.

Perri shrugged. "I don't know. I just found a note on my desk."

"Where's Mr. Winfield?" Erika asked.

Perri smiled and shook her head. "I haven't seen or spoken to him since I left the office last night."

All three girls burst into loud laughter. "Sure." "I'll bet." "We know."

The door opened and Mitch came in and sat at his desk. His wide shoulders in his crisp gray summer suit made Perri's breath come short and hard. Then the fragrance of spicy cologne and soap washed over her. His intense look made her heart pound.

"I've called you here to discuss a recurring problem of some importance." He intertwined his long fingers on his desk and the mere sight of his strong hands raised goose bumps on Perri's arms.

"A small percentage of the policies aren't getting to my desk for completion. I don't know where the foul-up is, but if a major accident or fire occurred while a policy was lost, it would ruin me. I'd have to cover it myself, and if it should be more than I could raise I'd face a criminal charge. I trust none of you wish that." He paused expectantly, waiting for comments.

No one said a word, but three faces turned to Perri. She burned as the familiar red streaks blended together to cover her face. "Are you three accusing me?" she asked quietly.

ten

Jessica shrugged daintily. "How long has this been going on?"

"A couple of months, I'd say," Mitch replied. "Does that tell you anything?"

"No, but the rest of us have been here much longer. Could Perri be overlooking some of her policies?"

Mitch hesitated, then continued. "I didn't call you here to accuse anyone. If we're all aware of the problem, we can be extra careful and even help each other." His wide mouth broke into a smile. "I guess we all live or die together. Otherwise, the business is doing well, and I think we'll live together a long time."

He stood up, signify the meeting had concluded. "Thanks to each of you for coming to this meeting and for your faithful work."

Perri darted into her office before the others moved. She dropped into her chair and put her head on her arms on the desk, feeling exhausted.

"Well, Seabrook, you look a little worse for wear."

Perri jerked her head up to find Mitch seated on the edge of her desk.

"Now the question of the day," he said. "Who's buying lunch?"

Perri swallowed. "I wouldn't know, boss. I tried to yesterday."

They ate in a small restaurant on Broadway. "When are we going out at night?" Mitch asked as they left the restaurant.

He took her hand and led her through a small park.

Perri turned toward the fountain at the center of the park, watching the silvery spouts of water. She stepped up onto the wide stone circle that enclosed the fountain and lifted her face to the cool spray. "I baby-sat for Kaima last night," she said at last, against her better judgment, "and she wants to return the favor soon." She bit her lip as soon as she said the words.

"Yahoo!" Mitch yelled. He leapt onto the stones beside her, and grasping her in his arms, he started to swing her— but before he made a quarter-turn, his right foot struck a slippery spot at the edge of the fountain. Although desperately gripping Perri's hands, he slid until he sat down in two feet of water. His unexpected weight forced her to her knees, then onto her back and into the water.

"Mitch, it's cold," she screamed, her head across his thrashing legs. Before she could figure how to get out of the fountain, the heavy spray pulsed upward and fell over her head, the only part of her that had eluded the pool.

After several attempts, Mitch managed to scramble up the slippery side of the shallow pool. Then he helped Perri work her way up the slimy incline. Finally she stood beside the pool and laughed.

He wiped the water from his face and made a face. Then he took her hand and they headed toward the office, all four shoes sloshing at every step. "Hush, woman," he said, laughing too. "And don't ever remind me of this unfortunate incident."

Perri felt warmer as they walked in the sunshine. She looked down at her grayish linen dress that until a few minutes ago had been lime green. "Do I have to work in this outfit all afternoon?"

Mitch extended his arms, coat sleeves dripping. "Only if

I have to work in this." People on the sidewalk turned to watch the soaking-wet pair. He alternately hunched and straightened his shoulders a few times. "Seabrook, I have to get this stuff off."

"It's time to be back at work now. How do you like facing your employees looking like an overcooked noodle?"

Mitch looked down at the wet mess beside him, then stopped and ruffled her hair, spraying drops of water over their faces. "That's for your impudence. Now, who's going up to tell Trish we'll be late?"

"Not me. I'll work wet first." But Perri couldn't imagine what the girls would say if they saw her in her present condition.

They arrived at the building and several people turned to stare. "I guess that leaves me," Mitch said. "Wait here. I'll be back in five minutes." He stepped into the elevator and disappeared.

As Perri waited in the building's foyer, Brock pushed the door open and hurried inside. He saw Perri, nodded distantly, and continued toward the elevator. Halfway there, he stopped, turned around, and stared. Shaking his head, he went on.

She'd barely recovered from that when the outer door opened again, and Erika and Jessica stepped through. Jessica caught sight of Perri and stopped short. When both girls had a good look, they approached her laughing.

"Must have been hotter than I thought," Jessica said to Erika.

"Yes, couldn't you wait until after work to go swimming?" Erika laughed. "Or is that sweat?"

"She never worked up a sweat in her life," Jessica said. "Honestly, Perri, I've never seen you looking so nice. At least you're coordinated, head to foot for the first time ever."

"All right girls, better get to work," Mitch said pleasantly, coming up from behind. "Perri and I will be just a little late. For obvious reasons."

Seeing how well Mitch matched Perri, Jessica and Erika burst into wild laughter and darted for the elevator.

"Brock laughed too until I refused another advance on his allowance," Mitch said as they walked to his car.

On the way to her house Perri told Mitch about Tad and Merry flattening all the tubes in the house, then climbing into the tub.

"They must have looked like us now," Mitch said. "That reminds me. When are we going to use that baby-sitting coupon you have?"

"Truthfully, I'm terrified to leave the boys with unsuspecting Kaima." She knew she shouldn't go out with him, not on a real date.

"She'll do all right. She outweighs you by several pounds."

Mitch pulled up before Perri's house and walked her to the door. He tweaked a lock of her limp hair. "See if you can do something with that hair, won't you, Seabrook?" He grinned.

❧

Early Saturday afternoon Mitch called and told Perri to get everyone ready for a swim. He had a surprise.

"What is it, Mommy?" Scott asked. "Does he have a swimming pool?"

"I don't know, love," Perri said. "I've never been to his house."

"Nah, he's taking us to the Y," Hugh said.

Everyone was waiting outside when Mitch finally pulled into the driveway. He drove a white pickup with bright blue trim, and pulled a big white boat with royal blue and red trim.

Mitch jumped out and scooped Tad into his arms, holding the child high in the air. "Who wants to go boating?" he asked.

"I'm going with Mr. Winfield," Judd announced.

"Me, too," Hugh repeated, followed by echoes from Scott and Tad.

"Who's riding with me?" Perri asked, knowing Mitch couldn't haul all four.

"I'll take Judd and Hugh," Mitch said. "The little guys can ride with you."

When they pulled into Orchard Point Park, Scott and Tad jumped out of the car and landed running toward the boat dock where Mitch slowly backed the boat trailer into the water. He stopped. "Think you can back this thing up?" he asked Perri. "I'll get the boat off the trailer and we'll be ready to go." He closed the truck door and ran back to the boat.

Although fearful, she slowly backed into deeper water until the boat floated free and Mitch did something, then signalled her forward. She drove the pickup and trailer to a double-length parking spot beside her wagon and raced back to the water. Mitch and the kids all sat in the boat, parked against the dock. Taking her hand, Mitch helped her in.

"Here, let me help you with this vest," he said, slipping Perri's arms through a orange life jacket and fastening it carefully all the way to the top.

"I see the boys are wearing vests, too," Perri said. "What a relief. Knowing my kids, someone will be in the water before the day ends."

Mitch nodded. "Everyone wears vests in my boat. Who knows? That someone who ends up in the water may be you. Or even me. Knowing our luck."

He sat down at the steering wheel and slowly turned the

boat around in the deep muddy water, then shoved his foot to the floor. The motor roared too loudly for them to talk, so they all silently enjoyed the swift ride across the rough water.

Perri sat beside Mitch, the wind in her face. A moment later Tad quietly climbed into her lap and sat contentedly. Mitch drove around Fern Ridge Lake, a large man-made body of water, for an hour or so, pointing out the large dam, Richardson Point State Park, and several other points of interest, including Perkins Point where they'd been on their last visit to the lake. Finally he stopped the boat in the middle of the lake. "I brought some lunch," he said. "Shall we eat now, or would you like to take a turn at the wheel?"

In response to the hungry wails, Mitch pulled into Zumwalt Park, where they all scrambled from the boat onto the grassy beach. After a lunch of peanut butter sandwiches, chips, cookies, watermelon, and pop, Mitch brought out a monstrous bag of caramel corn.

He winked at Perri over the boys' heads. "We have plenty of pop in the cooler. Otherwise I'd have kept that stuff hidden."

Hugh ate two large handfuls and reached for more. "I'm sure glad my tooth isn't aching," he said, stuffing another wad into his eager mouth.

"Hey, sport, you been having trouble with a tooth?" Mitch asked.

Hugh shook his head. "Nope." He shoved in the rest of his thickly candied corn and ran to the faucet to wash his hands.

Mitch looked at Perri, who shrugged. "Don't ask me," she said, laughing.

They rested for a while, then Mitch struggled to his feet and held a hand to Perri. "You drive this afternoon," he said a few minutes later, backing the boat away from the bank.

Perri didn't take long to learn, and she thoroughly enjoyed piloting her little crew around the lake. Scott sat beside her most of the time, watching every move she made. "Can I drive, Mommy?" he asked several times. Mitch let all four boys steer while sitting on his lap.

Later Perri took a nap in the back of the boat. She awoke from her doze to hear Mitch say softly to the boys, ". . .throw her in and jump in behind her. You guys wait in the boat. Don't jump in now. You'll get to swim later."

As Perri came to life she saw four heads nodding wildly and four smiles traveling from ear to ear. Then Mitch approached her, wearing a smile of his own. She jumped up and braced herself. "Oh, no, you don't!" she yelled.

Mitch didn't say a word, but picked her up as easily as though she were Tad—and dumped her over the side of the boat. She grabbed a deep breath before she hit the water, not having any idea how deep it was and how long it would take her to surface, but her vest popped her to the top of the water long before she needed air.

Then a large splash three feet from her sent the water surging over her head again. Before she got her bearings she felt arms around her. Mitch wiped the water from her face and hair. They both were treading water, although the vests supported them sufficiently.

"I've been wanting to do this all day," he said. "It's a perfect day for—"

The boat roared to life, gave a giant jerk, and took off through the water as though an enemy sub were after it! A tiny splash about fifty feet from Perri and Mitch made their hearts leap with fear. Someone had fallen from the boat into the water! And the boat raced across the lake with only small children inside it!

eleven

"Somebody's in the water," Mitch said. "Thank God for the life vest." He headed in the direction of the splash, using long powerful strokes.

Perri followed as quickly as she could, watching the place she'd seen the splash, praying as she went. She couldn't hear the boat motor anymore. No telling where the other boys were by now. Something small and green popped to the top of the water. An empty life vest. "Oh Lord," she breathed, "watch over my babies. All of them."

Mitch had removed his vest, which bobbed ominously beside the small one in the gentle waves. He dove beneath the water, then surfaced and looked at her with frantic, anguished eyes. "Tad," he choked. "Pray." He disappeared again under the murky water. Perri jerked off her vest too and dove down, unable to see more than a foot in the gray-green water. *Father, help us find him!* she pleaded, popping up to take in some much needed air. Plunging down, she strained her eyes through the watery shadows, looking for a small blond boy who meant more than life to her. She searched the empty water, feeling as if she were the only person in the world. Surfacing again, she found Mitch six feet from her, treading water. Tad was in his arms, lying very still.

"Quick," he said. "Bring his vest."

Perri, exhausted from her efforts, felt strength pour into her muscles as she stroked after the small vest that had been too large to stay on Tad. Mitch threaded the small arms into the vest and fastened it securely, then started mouth to mouth resuscitation.

"Do you know how to do the Heimlich maneuver?" Perri squeaked.

Mitch pulled his mouth from Tad's. "Yes." He started breathing into the small mouth once more.

"Try it, Mitch. It works to get water out of the lungs."

Mitch turned Tad sideways in the water and gave a quick squeeze on his body, just below his chest. Water squirted from Tad's mouth, so Mitch repeated the maneuver. This time only a small amount trickled down the child's chin.

"Get our vests and put yours on," Mitch instructed, lowering his mouth over Tad once more.

Before Perri reached the vests, she heard Tad choking and Mitch comforting him. "Thank You, Lord," she murmured, unable to believe how beautiful a little boy's painful choking could sound. "Oh, thank You, Father. I love You!"

When she reached them again, Tad's arms stretched toward her. Mitch held his small body firmly. "Put on your vest," he commanded Perri. Perri slipped it on, fastened it securely, and then Mitch relinquished the child and put on his own vest.

In a few moments Tad stopped choking and relaxed, allowing Perri and his vest to support him in the cool water. "I want to go home," he said, his voice hoarse.

No boats appeared in the large lake, only gently lapping water and small whitecaps as far as the eye could see. Following Tad's eyes, Perri wondered if he felt as small and alone as she. "We'll go home, honey, as soon as the boys come back after us," she said, feigning a cheerfulness she far from felt.

"Or someone else," Mitch said with confidence. "Those kids couldn't have gone far without attracting attention."

After a moment's silence, he turned to Tad. "Did you notice who drove the boat, sport?"

The small blond curls waved back and forth as the little boy shook his head. "I fell in the water."

Perri held him closer. "You sure did, but you're okay, now. I'm going to hold you tight until a boat comes."

The small body began to tremble with cold, but before Perri could decide how to warm him, a boat appeared, coming toward them.

"Give me the boy," a smiling man in khakis said, bringing the boat to a clean stop beside the little group. He wore a shield with engraved lettering: Lane County Sheriff. Perri gladly handed the shaking child up into the boat. A moment later all three sat in the boat with blankets around their shoulders.

"Where are the others?" Mitch asked as they rode across the large lake.

The big blond man smiled. "We towed them to Perkins Point. After the youngest boy started the engine and took off, the oldest one turned the motor off and jerked the keys out. When we found them they were floating. He directed us back here after you."

ಶಿ

Later that night Mitch put the boys to bed. Judd grinned up at him from his pillow. "You're a mature and dependable young man," Mitch said. "If you hadn't stopped the boat it would have rammed another boat, a lake bank somewhere, or even the dock. Your quick action saved the boat from damage—and saved you boys from getting hurt."

"Mature and dependable" Judd put his arms around Mitch's neck and gave him a childish hug. Then he turned away, embarrassed. "Yeah, well, thanks," he muttered. "Good night."

Mitch ran down the stairs into the kitchen where Perri was drying the last pan. "All's well that ends well," he said, breathing a big sigh. "Judd knows he did well and Scott knows he could have killed Tad." He walked quietly to her and wrapped his long arms around her.

Perri drew in a quick breath. *Why does the sight of those dark eyes make my heart ache?*

A moment later he pushed her back and looked into her eyes. "Do we need to reassess our relationship?"

Perri nodded. "We have too many problems. I still have all my kids and you still aren't a Christian." She laughed softly. "But how come you ordered me to pray this afternoon? That was my line."

He moved away and shook his head. "Desperation, I guess. And now that I'm getting acquainted with your kids, I—I like them. But I still can't picture myself with so much going on all the time."

Perri saw real pain in his eyes. "But—but you're so good with them. You act as though you really care about them."

"I do care about them." He dropped into a chair, holding his head in his hands.

She lowered herself into a chair across the table and watched him intently. "I guess it's me you can't handle," she said quietly, her eyes twinkling.

He reached across the table to take her hand in his. "You're something else, Seabrook, you know?"

Perri nodded. "Only something else would dare to have four kids."

"Right. And only something else would have been so kind about the afternoon's events. You could have yelled at me for leaving the kids alone in the boat. I should have known better than to leave four boys unsupervised on a motor boat. You could have beaten Scott within an inch of his life for dumping Tad into the water. I have to say this thing you have with God impresses me—a lot."

Why should relief pour throughout her body? He hadn't become an instant Christian. And he'd made it abundantly clear that he wasn't about to take on a ready-made family. She forced herself to pull her hand away, and a small crooked smile tipped up the corners of her lips. "Well, thanks, friend. Maybe some day my Best Friend will be yours too." After a moment, she extended her hand again, and he enclosed it in his much larger one.

When the sound of the doorbell interrupted the quiet, Perri glanced at the stove clock—10:50.

Mitch got up. "Kind of late for company," he said, opening the door.

Kaima Kingston stood on the porch with Merry sleeping in her arms. Red-rimmed swollen eyes and tear stains emphasized her pale cheeks.

"Come in, Kaima," Perri said, pushing open the screen door.

"Am I interrupting anything?" Kaima asked, looking from Mitch to Perri.

"Not a thing," he assured her. "I was just leaving." He gave Perri an impersonal peck on the cheek and stepped past Kaima.

Perri forced a smile to her lips. "I'll fix a bed on the couch for Merry, then make some hot chocolate."

Kaima sniffled and tightened her grip on the sleeping girl. "I wondered if we could spend the night."

"Of course. You can have Tad's room, but can you put her down while we put clean sheets on the bed?"

In ten minutes Tad slept peacefully in Perri's queen bed and Merry slept in Tad's double bed. Perri smiled into Kaima's troubled eyes. "How's that for playing musical beds without waking anyone? Let's hit the kitchen."

Kaima sat at the table, sniffing quietly while Perri made the hot drink. "Now tell me what's wrong," Perri said, sliding a large mug to Kaima. "Judging from the time of day and your appearance, I gather it isn't good."

Kaima hiccuped and took a sip of chocolate. "I'm pregnant," she whimpered, choking on the words.

That was absolutely the last thing Perri had expected her to say. "Well, why aren't you celebrating? That's great news. At least I always thought so."

Tears poured from Kaima's swollen eyes. "I'd love to be celebrating," she choked, "but Rob kicked us out."

"What! Why would he do that?"

Kaima gestured mutely toward her stomach.

"Because you're pregnant?"

The dark head nodded once, and Perri had never seen such pain. She led Kaima into the living room and pushed her gently down onto the couch, then hugged her close. "Could you tell me about it?"

"I told him I suspected two weeks ago, but he wouldn't believe me," Kaima began, her voice low and shaky. Perri waited for the girl to gain control. "I went to the doctor today," she sniffed, "and the test confirmed it." She put her face in her hands and her shoulders shook. Then with a great shudder she repeated the words, "I'm pregnant."

"But this doesn't make sense," Perri said. "Why should Rob be so upset? After all, he had something to do with your getting pregnant."

Kaima sobbed again, then cleared her throat. "He really didn't want Merry, but this time he went berserk." She looked into Perri's sympathetic blue eyes and nodded. "He shoved me out the door. At ten o'clock at night! But I couldn't leave my baby in the house with a madman so I pounded on the door and screamed for her." She shook her head slowly. "Finally he opened the door and threw her into my arms. I started walking and ended up here."

Perri tried to take in the incredible story. "I can't believe this," she said. "He threw you out: no clothes, no money, no place to go?"

Kaima nodded and sniffled once more. "I really appreciate your hospitality tonight. Tomorrow I'll find something."

Perri's mind still worked at unscrambling Kaima's plight. "Do you think this is forever?"

Kaima nodded. "He said to come back when there are only two of us." Tears pushed into her eyes again. "He wants me—he wants me to put Merry up for adoption. That's just ridiculous of course, but he also wants me to have an abortion. I couldn't kill my little baby."

"Of course you couldn't." Perri looked at the large gold and glass wall clock. Midnight. "We really should get to bed. We can talk more tomorrow. Don't worry about finding another place. You're welcome here."

After a warm bath, Perri crawled between the sheets and pulled clean, sweet-smelling Tad into her arms. "I'm so very thankful your daddy loved each of you as much as I do," she whispered to the sleeping child, nuzzling his soft blond curls. And she could have lost him at the lake today. "Thank You, Father," she whispered into the dark. Then she asked Him to be close to Kaima and bless her. Lastly she asked her precious Lord to watch over Mitch—and not let her do anything she'd be sorry for. "Please help me to leave my relationship with Mitch in Your hands."

The next morning Kaima and Merry joined Perri at the breakfast table. Kaima looked much better. "Who watches the boys?" she asked, spreading strawberry jam on Merry's toast.

"My sister, Jill. She'll be here in about a half hour. Hey, she won't need to come if you're here!"

Kaima wiped Merry's chin with a napkin and gestured to the phone. "Right. Call her."

Forty-five minutes later, Perri sat down at her desk at Mitchell Winfield Insurance Agency, read through the mail, then glanced over her appointments. Mitch came in and dropped into the chair beside her desk. "Was Kaima's visit last night as disastrous as it looked?"

His nearness made Perri's heart pound against her ribs. She picked up the stapler and turned it idly in her hands, forcing her thoughts to Kaima. "Yes, even more so."

He leaned back in the comfortable chair and clasped his hands behind his head. His apricot silk shirt rippled across his chest. He'd rolled up his sleeves two turns and his forearms looked muscular and tan. A gentle breeze from the window wafted spicy whiffs of aftershave her way. She swallowed and looked away.

"Let me guess," he said, his deep voice soft. "They got into a fight over Brock and she walked out."

"He threw her out because she's pregnant."

Mitch whistled softly. "Rob doesn't want another child?"

"Right. And I have an appointment in less than fifteen minutes, so if you'll move your carcass into your own office I'll get ready."

After her clients had gone and she'd given the information to Jessica, Perri leaned back in her chair and thought. Rob kicked Kaima out because he couldn't handle two kids. His own two kids. Maybe Mitch was wise to seriously consider whether he could live with four kids that weren't his.

"Come on, woman, I'm famished," he called from the doorway.

At the restaurant, they enjoyed each other's company until they had nearly finished their platter-sized chef salads. Then they both looked up and met each other's eyes. "Perri," "Mitch," they said in unison, then laughed together.

He pointed at her. "You go first."

"You're sure?" she asked. "I'm going to ruin our good lunch."

"In that case, let me go first. I wanted to talk a little more about Rob and Kaima. Do you know what she plans to do?"

Perri looked thoughtfully into her milk glass, absently swishing the foamy liquid around. "She's going to be at my house for a while. Then—who knows? Maybe they'll get back together. I can't believe Rob would be so stupid as to throw away his wife and child—children. He needs to see a counselor."

Mitch took the glass from her hand and set it on the table, then took her hand in his. "How can you take Kaima and Merry in with the crowd you already have?"

She smiled. "How can I not take them in?"

"This got something to do with your religion?"

She giggled out loud. "Maybe. Remember God loved them enough to let His only Son die for them. He'd have died for you, Mitch, if you'd been the only person who'd sinned. That's how much He loves Mitch Winfield. As for Kaima and Merry, the Bible says if we do something for the least person, we really do it for Jesus." She shrugged. "But all the preaching aside—I just did it because they need help."

He nodded. "You did it because of this thing you have with God." The long look he gave her made her feel uncomfortable. "But I've been thinking about Rob," he finally added. "The way he doesn't want to have to cope with a couple of kids. Sounds pretty selfish, doesn't it? But does he remind you of anyone else?"

A smile touched the corners of her mouth, and her blue eyes filled with love. "That's what I wanted to talk to you about."

"Oh. Me, too." His dark eyes searched hers a moment. He rolled a napkin, then shredded it. "Rob looks pretty small and mean, doesn't he?"

She nodded. "Yes, but that's not what reminds me of you."

Mitch swallowed loudly, his Adam's apple jerking up and down. "What then?" he asked, his voice hoarse and choked. He took a sip of water.

"Well, those kids are Rob's own flesh and blood. If he can't handle his own two, why should we be surprised that you can't take on four you barely know?"

"Maybe I could," he croaked.

Perri shook her blond head. "Maybe you couldn't. Maybe if you tried, it would end up like Rob and Kaima. It would be lots more likely to fail, because they aren't yours. And I do realize they're difficult kids."

His eyes looked like those of an injured animal. "So, what are you suggesting?"

"I don't know. You know I'd never marry outside of my faith, and you can't magically change your feelings about the boys. We'd better cool it before we get more involved."

His black eyes drilled into hers. "Is that what you want?"

"No, I'm already emotionally involved. A lot. But it would be easier to break it off now than to spend a lifetime knowing I'd done the wrong thing." A tear ran down Perri's cheek. She brushed it away impatiently. "That doesn't excuse Rob Kingston, though. Those are his kids and his responsibility."

Mitch pushed his plate away. "You were right. You spoiled the mood." A moment of silence swelled into several minutes. "Well," he finally suggested, "let's head for the office."

A subdued pair walked back to the large building. "Would you like to take the afternoon off?" he asked kindly, before they entered the elevator.

"No, I have a lot of work to do."

They rode silently up to their floor. When the elevator stopped, Mitch dropped an unexpected kiss on her lips. "This isn't settled yet." Putting his hand behind her back, he steered her through the reception room, into her office.

"Thanks," she whispered. "Trish took a good look."

❧

Perri crept into the reception room after work that afternoon, hoping to avoid Mitch.

"Mr. Winfield's out with a client, checking out a house," Trish sang out. "He's with a gorgeous female."

"Hope he makes a sale," Perri said, ignoring the inference. She walked out with her head high and a big smile on her face.

"How'd it go today?" she called, walking into her house.

Kaima lay on the couch with a wet towel across her forehead. "Not well. And I have a splitting headache."

Perri lowered herself into a rocker. "What did the boys do?"

"I haven't been able to think of anything except Rob, and Merry spent the day asking for him." She pulled the towel from her forehead and raised on one elbow. "What am I supposed to do?" she asked fretfully.

Perri's mind snapped into gear. "We're going over to your place and march right up to the door. Do you have a key?"

Kaima shook her head.

"In that case we'll wait until Rob's home. I don't know what will happen, but at least we'll get clothes for you and Merry."

After supper they all piled into the station wagon and drove the two blocks to the Kingston place. Judd watched the kids while they played outside.

Kaima led the way onto the back porch, and finding the door unlocked walked in. Perri followed.

"What do you think you're doing in my house?" Rob yelled, then showed embarrassment when he realized Kaima wasn't alone.

"You can't do this to me, Rob," Kaima whined, sinking into a chair.

"Kaima," Rob began, in an entirely different tone, "we can't carry on a private conversation with a third party present."

"We can't carry on a conversation, anyway," Kaima screamed into his face. "But she knows, Rob. I told her. I told her what a rotten person you are."

Rob shrugged. "It's impossible to talk to Kaima," he said. "She's always having fits."

Kaima started yelling again and reached for a cup on the table. Perri snatched it as Kaima drew back to hurl it at Rob. Suddenly, Perri didn't know for sure what was going on. Maybe Kaima wasn't quite okay. Maybe both she and Rob were in desperate need of some professional counseling.

She held Kaima, gently patting her back. Her eyes met Rob's. "Did you kick her out because she's pregnant?" she asked quietly.

"I told her before we married that I didn't want children. She was supposed to take care of it."

"So you kicked her out."

Silence.

"And you told her she could come back only if she came alone, right?"

Rob's head hung a moment, then he straightened up and spoke in a firm voice. "I let her get away with it one time. We'll keep Merry—I was just angry when I said I wanted to put her up for adoption. But this time Kaima's doing it my way."

"Do you wish you hadn't had Merry?"

"I love my little girl. But having a kid around is a lot of bother. I'm not having another."

"I think you are, Rob. Why don't you start getting used to the idea? Come on, Kaima, let's get your clothes."

In a few minutes the two women walked through the front door, each carrying a large box of clothes.

"You're welcome to use this room as long as you need to," Perri said a little later, dropping her box on Tad's bedroom floor.

Tears welled up in Kaima's eyes. "What would I do without you?"

"Do you know God?" Perri asked.

"A little bit."

"Well, can you take hold of His hand and believe He loves you and will make this all turn out for the best?"

Kaima nodded. "I'll try," she whispered.

They barely got downstairs when Mitch called. "Did Rob and Kaima get straightened out?"

"No, but we got their clothes."

After a long pause, Mitch took a deep breath. "Do you think Rob and I are alike?" he finally asked.

"Not in the least. Don't give it another thought."

"Are the boys in bed yet?"

"No." She laughed. "We have wall-to-wall kids. You might not think one more would show, but it does."

Mitch cleared his throat loudly. "Could I come over later?"

Perri shook her blond head. "Better not."

Let him come, you crazy girl! her heart screamed.

No! her head answered. *Everytime you see him you care more than the last time.*

"I need to talk to you," he pleaded. "I promise to leave in an hour."

That's not asking much, her heart said. *You owe him more than that.*

I know, her head told her heart coldly, *but you're trying to take over, and you won't like it too much if you get all smashed up.*

"Sure, come on over," she said aloud. "Whenever you want."

Perri rushed the kids to bed a little faster than usual that night, amid loud singing from her heart and dire threats from her head—and strong worries from her spirit that she wasn't following God's will.

"Shall I go to bed, too?" Kaima asked when Perri appeared dressed in a light green sundress, freshly combed, and made up.

"No, I'm just going to tell him we can't see each other anymore," Perri said. "We have the same problem you and Rob do, only worse."

"Oh my goodness, what could be worse?" Kaima asked in a hushed voice.

"I have four boys that blow Mitch away. Add to that, my Bible tells me not to marry an unbeliever."

The doorbell interrupted their conversation. After greeting Perri, Mitch turned to Kaima. "How are you? Or should I ask?"

Kaima smiled slightly. "We're both fine, aren't we, Perri?"

"You bet. We're just A-okay. Want to sit down, Mitch?"

Mitch glanced at Kaima, comfortably ensconced on the sofa, then back to Perri. "I thought we might take a little drive."

Maybe they did need some privacy, Perri thought, agreeing to go. "At least you have an instant baby-sitter," Mitch said, helping Perri into the car.

They did not speak as he wove deftly through the evening traffic and onto the highway. Soon he made a right turn, climbed a quarter-mile incline, pulled off the road and turned off the engine.

"Hey, we're at Perkins Point," Perri said amazed. "I didn't even notice."

Mitch opened her door. "Let's watch the moon rise from the dock."

She strolled hand in hand with him, her heart bursting with joy, and her mind knowing full well she was acting the fool.

twelve

Mitch led Perri through the darkness, down the hill to the edge of the water and onto the floating dock. They walked to the end, then stood enjoying the quiet night sounds, frogs singing in chorus nearby and the water lapping softly against the worn boards.

A large night bird, disturbed by their voices, lifted from the shallow water nearby, gave one loud squawk, and disappeared into the shadows of the park, leaving the added sound of water splashing and settling down.

"Oops, we're frightening the rightful owners of this place," Perri whispered. The slight rocking of the dock as it floated on the quiet water soothed her nerves and nearly made her forget her fears and resolves. She sat on the dock, pulling Mitch down with her.

"Do you think we could take off our shoes and let our feet hang in the water?" he asked in a hushed voice.

"Sure." In a moment four shoes sat in the middle of the dock and four feet slipped silently into the water. "It feels good," Perri whispered. "Did you have something special to talk about?"

"Yes, but we can't talk yet."

"Why not?"

"I just want to wait a little while. Do you have time?"

For answer, she scooped up a handful of water and dribbled it over his head. He snatched the wet hand, brought it to his lips, and kissed each finger.

"What was that all about?" she whispered in surprise.

"Because I. . ." Suddenly he turned her head toward the east, where a golden glow appeared over the treetops. "Shhh," he whispered. "Just watch."

They didn't have to wait long before the huge orange moon peeked over the trees and sent a shimmering reflection across the water.

"I call that cooperation," he said quietly.

"It's gorgeous. It's just beautiful," Perri said, watching the moon rise higher into the glittering black velvet sky. "It almost makes me forget the problems of life."

"That's what it's supposed to do," Mitch said.

Perri could see Mitch's face clearly now, dark and silvery in the moonlight.

"I want to marry you."

She jumped with surprise. "What!" Before she recovered her equilibrium, she felt herself sliding off the dock. Then cool water gently closed over her head.

Even before she surfaced, she heard a soft splash and felt strong arms buoying her up. After spitting out the water and pushing her dripping hair from her eyes, Perri broke into a joyful laugh. "It's glorious," she said. "Not even cold."

"I love swimming," he said, "but not at what I'd hoped would be an irresistibly romantic moment."

He put his arms around her, cradling her gently against his chest, treading water. She relaxed, letting the water hold her. He kissed her softly, gently. They dipped lower and lower in the water until once again the small cool waves closed over their heads.

"We'd better get out of here before we drown ourselves," he whispered into her ear when they surfaced.

After he helped her back to the dock, Perri laughed. "We don't look quite as beautiful as we did a few minutes ago."

They tried to squeeze the water from their dripping clothes and hair.

"I'm sure I don't," Mitch said, "but you look positively radiant, with the moon turning your beautiful hair silvery soft and your face angelic. You look about sixteen years old." He brushed her hair away from her face, so very gently. "Are you in there, Seabrook?" he whispered. "What are you thinking?"

Perri tried hard to jerk herself back to reality. Mitch had just asked her to marry him! He really had! She felt like a young girl in the throes of her first love, floating so high she couldn't feel the gentle rocking of the dock anymore. She wanted to reach her arms around him and scream, "Yes! Yes, let's get married tomorrow, before you change your mind."

But she couldn't. Never would she marry anyone who loved her heavenly Father less than she. Why was she messing around with Mitch like this anyway? Pretty soon she'd think up some good reason why she could be the exception, why her marriage would work when millions of others didn't. It was time to put a stop to this.

Before she could speak, Mitch lovingly gathered her into his arms and dropped a feather-light kiss on the top of her wet head. "What are you thinking?"

She jerked herself to attention. "I'm sorry, Mitch. A million scenes just played in my mind. They reminded me that I still have four rowdy kids." She didn't mention his not being a Christian. The thought of the kids would calm him down. He had to find God in his own way in his own time if his conversion was to be sincere. She didn't want to pressure him.

He put his arm over her dripping wet shoulders to guide her back to the car. When they stepped off the dock onto the lush grass, he turned them around for a last look at the perfectly round moon, considerably higher in the glittering sky and silver now rather than gold, but still sending its shimmering trail across the still water.

"Thank you for bringing me here," Perri said, leaning her dripping head against his cold, wet shoulder. "I've never been to the lake at night."

Mitch sighed. "I brought you here hoping you'd forget all our problems in the moon's magic light."

"I almost did," she murmured.

He turned on the heater as they silently drove the ten miles back to Perri's house. When he backed into the driveway, she found herself again looking at the silvery disk, now floating high in a blue-black sky.

"Now we're warm again, we can continue our conversation," he said.

"Okay, why do you think we should get married?"

"Haven't you noticed the sparks flying when we get near each other?"

She shook her head. "Mitch, you're not a kid. You know sparks last hardly any time at all. Even fires go out sooner or later."

"Don't you care for me, Seabrook?"

"I do care for you, Mitch." He'd never said he cared for her. Ever.

The moon disappeared over the top of the car and Mitch's handsome face melted into the darkness. A gloom settled over her. She knew he felt something for her. Was it only physical attraction?

He swallowed loudly, then settled against the seat. A moment later he cleared his throat. Then he coughed. "I care, too," he murmured. "I care a whole lot. Enough to take on the boys. In fact, I care for them, too."

Perri heard a heart pounding violently and wondered if Mitch really cared that much, then realized it was her own. "Thank you," she said, her eyes shining with still unproclaimed love. To her, caring and loving weren't synonymous. "Thank you, Mitch," she repeated against his cheek. "I better go in. Let's forget this evening happened while we sort things out."

Mitch dropped his hands to his knees but said nothing and made no move to leave the car.

"Don't feel bad," Perri pleaded. "Tonight's been the most beautiful night of my life. And things will work out as they should if we only give them time."

He opened his door and a moment later hers. "Come on out, my wet little moon angel," he said, laughing. "Maybe it turned out all right, after all." They walked arm in arm to the porch where he kissed her tenderly, pushed her away, and ran to his car.

Kaima had gone to bed, so Perri took a shower and fell into bed, too. "Please, Father," she murmured, "help me do the right thing. And help me live in a way that will help him know You."

Perri woke the next morning with a heavy cold. Her throat felt fiery and her voice sounded like someone who'd smoked for three hundred years.

"Don't come near me," she warned Kaima and the kids when she staggered downstairs in her warm but faded terrycloth robe.

"Want me to call the office?" Judd asked.

Perri took a glass of orange juice and settled into the rocking chair. "Thank you, Judd," she rasped.

Kaima offered to watch the kids, and Perri's aching head encouraged her to return to bed.

Sometime later a slamming door aroused her, then Mitch's

voice thundered over her. She sat up and looked around, having slept so soundly she didn't know whether it was day or night. Mitch stood beside the bed, looking mad. Why would he be angry? Why was he in her bedroom?

"Whatever it is," he yelled, "I'd rather you'd just come out and say it."

Perri pulled the quilt higher over her shoulders. "Say what?" she tried to ask. It came out in an unidentifiable croak.

"What did you say?" he asked.

Perri glanced at the clock. Ten-thirty. Bright daylight flooded the room so it must not be night. Hey! She was supposed to be at work. That's why Mitch was mad. She started to jump out of bed, but the room revolved around her. She fell back onto the pillows, finally meeting Mitch's eyes.

He leaned over her and put his hand on her forehead. "Maybe you don't feel so good," he said gently.

"I have a cold," she croaked. "Judd said he'd call."

Mitch sank onto the edge of the bed and drew her into his arms. "You're burning up, Seabrook, and it's all my fault."

"How could it be your fault?" she asked in a hoarse voice.

"You know. The swim?"

Perri laughed. Or cackled. "Don't be silly. Getting cold doesn't cause colds. Germs do. I must have been coming down with it last night. Maybe I gave it to you." She felt breathless and her throat ached.

Mitch held her left hand in both of his. "I thought you stayed home to avoid me. Kaima insisted you were sick but I wouldn't believe her."

He stayed a few more minutes, then left, telling her to take as long as she needed but not another minute more because he missed her.

She slept most of the next two days, then watched game

shows for two more, thankful for Kaima's care. Two large bouquets of red roses arrived, each bearing a "missing you" card from Mitch.

"What's going on between you and Rob?" Perri asked a couple of evenings later as the two women played Rack-O.

Kaima's clear gray eyes clouded. "Nothing. I guess he doesn't want to talk to me." Kaima's voice caught on a sob. "I should be thinking of making some permanent living arrangements."

"Do you have money?"

Kaima bit her bottom lip and shook her head. "No," she admitted, "and I can't very well find a job while I'm pregnant. I don't know how to do anything, anyway. I'm not smart like you."

"It has nothing to do with smart, Kaima," Perri said. "I didn't know how to do anything, either, until after Jerry died. Why don't you just stay on here for a while until you see what Rob's going to do?"

Kaima's eyes filled with tears. "Thanks, Perri. I thank God every day for you, my only really truly friend."

"God's a better Friend then I, Kaima. Just think, He died for our sins so we could live forever with Him. And He's making beautiful homes for us where no one will throw us out. Just love Him, Kaima, as He loves you." She reached for her phone book. "I have the number of a Christian counselor who might help you sort through your troubles. Who knows? Maybe Rob would even talk with her too. Why don't you give her a call?"

❧

Several days later Perri felt strong enough to drive to the office. Her desk, which she'd expected to be piled high, looked surprisingly bare.

Trish stuck her head in the door. "Glad to have you back,"

she said, "but Mr. Winfield discovered he can get along without you."

Perri smiled at the small barb. "No one's indispensable, Trish, not even the president. But I'll try to make myself useful in some small way."

Within a half-hour Mitch came in, bearing more roses and smiling as though it were Christmas and his birthday, all rolled into one happy package.

"Welcome back, Seabrook, and don't ever do it again."

"Why not? I just heard that you learned to get along without me."

Mitch shook his head. "Don't believe everything you hear—make that anything you hear. What I learned is that I can't get along without you. Take that any way you choose and you'll be right."

"Okay, I will. What's happened while I malingered at home?"

Mitch turned to the business at hand and they spent a pleasant morning going over recent transactions.

"Well, what do you think? Are we doing all right?" Mitch asked as he put everything away.

"I think Trish is right. You don't need an assistant."

"Oh, but I do. And I don't mean only in the office." His black eyes had never looked so sincere—or so pleading. "You've monopolized my mind day and night since our trip to the lake. And before." He pulled her to her feet. "Come on, let's go fill out the hollows in your cheeks."

They walked hand in hand past the fountain to the same little restaurant and sat at the same table that saw their last unhappy meal. "Did you decide to marry me next week?" Mitch asked as they sipped tall glasses of lemonade, waiting for their lunch.

"Next week? Things are moving right along," Perri said,

reaching across the table to pat his lean forearm. She wouldn't mention again that he had to accept the Lord's sacrifice for him. No one could be forced into a sincere commitment. She shook her blond head. "I may as well be frank with you. The only thing I'd like better is to be married tomorrow. But it would be a big mistake. I'd rather never marry than to find myself in Kaima's position."

Mitch took a long drink. "Don't you know me better than that? I'd never hurt you, Seabrook. Never."

"I know you wouldn't want to, Mitch. I wouldn't want to hurt you either. But aside from our differences when it comes to God, you might end up finding it very painful being married not only to me but to my four boys. Living in constant bedlam? Never having a moment for your nerves to settle down? Having your most private moments subject to interruption?"

"I try not to think about it," he said after a moment's hesitation.

"I rest my case. I could never marry you until you do think about it—a lot. And you'd have to not only feel that you could bear it but enjoy it. Enjoy the kids for themselves, not merely put up with them."

The meal came and they ate silently and sparingly, until they walked out into the cheering sunshine. He took her hand and smiled into her eyes. "You're right, of course," he said. "Tell me, oh wise one, what's the solution?"

"I don't claim to be wise, but the answer seems plain. We go back to being friends again. You're welcome at my place any time. Maybe you could learn to know the boys individually, rather than seeing them as a crazy bunch."

He shook his dark head and pushed the elevator button. "I'd like to get to know the boys better, but go back to being friends with you? Never."

🎜

"Daddy came!" Merry screamed in delight when Perri stepped into the house that evening.

Kaima nodded in agreement, then turned to Merry. "Could you go see what the boys are doing, sweetie?" She waited until Merry closed the door before continuing. "He demanded that Merry and I return home," she said, breathing a loud sigh that didn't show much joy.

"Isn't that what you want?"

"He said he had an appointment for me next week at a clinic."

"Oh. He can't make you do anything you don't want to, you know."

"I know. I'll never have an abortion. How could I ever live with myself if I murdered someone? Especially my own helpless child. My child that God has entrusted to my care. I'd better stay here. I know God would never forgive me if I gave in and had an abortion."

"He'd forgive you for any sin you could commit, if you truly repented, but don't do it. How come Merry's so excited?"

A smile swept across Kaima's face, remembering. "He's crazy about that kid, Perri. He adores her and she feels the same about him. It's the one thing about him that gives me hope." She paused in the doorway to the kitchen. "By the way, your sister stayed with the kids earlier today while I talked to that counselor you told me about. Some of the things she said made a lot of sense. I'm going to see her again next week. I asked Rob to come with me." She hesitated. "Please pray that he'll come."

Perri smiled. "Let's pray together right now." They sat down around the kitchen table and put the welfare of Kaima's marriage into God's loving hands.

Mitch dropped by a little later. "Taking you up on your offer of permanent open house," he said.

Perri told him about Rob's visit as they drank root beer in the kitchen.

"He'll come around," Mitch surmised. "If they're going for counseling together that should help. I'd advise her to go home, but only if she's strong enough to stick to her principles."

"That's what I thought, but I don't want her feeling pushed out."

"Right! And think how great it is to have a built-in baby-sitter."

Later Perri walked Mitch to his car. "Thanks. I enjoyed the visit."

He started the motor. "I enjoyed it too, but it wasn't the dock at Perkins Point." He drove away into the night.

How can I teach Mitch about God's love? Perri wondered as she brushed her hair into a light shining mass before she went to bed. *Is it possible that if he learned to love God that I could find as much happiness as I once had with Jerry? Could Mitch learn to love the boys as much I do? And what about Kaima?* After dropping all her problems in her Lord's lap, she fell asleep.

❧

"September's nearly here," Mitch said the next week while they cleared away their work for the day and filed it in the steel cabinet.

Perri looked up and laughed into his long-lashed eyes. "I know, I know," she said. "What with school starting up soon, that means something to me, but how come you're waiting for it?"

"Your homeowner's policy runs out in September, as I remember, and I'm ready to write a policy for you."

"Oh." She shoved the last file into the cabinet and dropped into her chair. "You never stop working, do you?"

"So what's so great about school starting?"

"The kids will all be gone all day, except Tad. That means fewer kids to be baby-sat. Although actually it's been working out pretty well having Kaima baby-sit. We've sort of traded baby-sitting for food and lodging."

"Maybe she'll stay on."

"Maybe."

Mitch sat on Perri's desk. "Could you go out for dinner tonight?"

"I'd like to if all's well at home."

But when Perri arrived home, she found Kaima upset nearly to the point of tears. "Rob came over and had a giant fit," she choked.

"Brock almost hit him," Hugh said.

Perri's mouth went dry. "What was Brock doing here?"

"He comes all the time," Scott said, nodding his head importantly. "He even brings us candy."

Perri ignored Scott and forced Kaima to meet her eyes. Kaima nodded. Her thick lashes dropped over her eyes, then she gazed into Perri's troubled blue ones again. "I get lonely, Perri. Don't you know?"

"I know. I get lonely, too—but Kaima, you're married and pregnant."

"We just talk or play games. But you should have heard Rob. You'd have thought it was a federal offense."

Perri called Mitch, canceled their dinner date, prepared supper for her enlarged family, did up the laundry for Kaima and Merry as well as her own family, put the kids to bed, and dropped between her own sheets, exhausted. "Good night, Mitch," she whispered into the moonlight that streamed through the open window. "Good night, dear heavenly Father. Stay close, Father, and guide my every step. I know I'm being foolish—but I promise I'll never marry an unbeliever. Help me do Your will, God. I love You."

Kaima felt nauseated the next morning, couldn't eat breakfast, and felt unable to watch the kids, so Perri called Jill to come take care of everyone.

Finally at the office, a discouraged Perri leaned her elbows on the desk. Mitch crept in and kissed her ear. "I'm not the guy who kept you up too late last night, Seabrook," he said in a light tone.

Perri sat up and smiled into the strong masculine face. He looked so good and smelled so nice. "It was my six kids plus the laundry."

He nodded. "You said Brock had something to do with it?"

"Rob didn't feel too pleased to find his wife entertaining another man."

Mitch rubbed his hand over his shadowed chin. "What were they doing?"

Perri raised her eyebrows and shrugged. "Talking or playing games. I believe it, Mitch. Five kids run around there all the time."

Mitch pursed his mouth. "Right. Well, maybe I can keep him away."

"What could you do?"

"Cut off his allowance. Haven't you heard? Money talks. Hey! Are we on for tonight?"

"Afraid not. Kaima seems to be having morning sickness, so I had to get Jill to take care of her and the kids."

"I see." He started to leave, then stuck his head back through the door. "I planned to take you to see the Eugene Emeralds trounce the Spokane Indians. Think the boys would like to go instead?"

"Are you sure you want to do this?"

"Sure. It's a great way to get acquainted. All guys love baseball."

Mitch called, and all four boys eagerly agreed to go, though they'd barely played softball with the neighborhood kids, let alone gone to a real game. Perri hurried home and made sure the boys were bathed, brushed, and wore clean jeans.

"Will we get to play, Mommy?" Tad asked, his blue eyes shining.

"No, you'll watch some big men play," Perri answered, smoothing down his collar.

"Are we taking our lunch?" Scott asked, watching Kaima and Merry eating corn on the cob.

"No," Perri said, "Mitch is buying food at the baseball game. That's part of the fun. You'll have lots of good things."

The boys fairly bounced up and down with excitement. Perri walked to the car and kissed each one as he climbed in.

"I get one, too," Mitch said after the boys belted themselves in.

She leaned into the window and pecked him lightly on the lips. "Have fun," she said. "I'll be waiting to hear all about the game."

thirteen

"What a mess," Perri said much later as the boys arrived, covered with mustard, Coke, frosting, cotton candy, chocolate, and catsup. "You must have had a wonderful time." Then she noticed brown stains covering Mitch's clothes. She grinned. "I wouldn't even expect that of Tad."

"Well, expect it of Tad," Mitch replied. "It wasn't my root beer."

"I don't feel very good," Judd said, dropping to the carpet.

"Me, too," three small voices echoed.

"I think I'm going while I can," Mitch said.

"Thanks for the great ball game," Judd said. "I really had fun."

"Me, too," three small voices echoed. Hugh ran to Mitch, pulled his head down, and before Mitch could retreat, kissed him on the lips. "I had more fun than I ever did in my whole life. I love you."

The next morning Perri couldn't wait to see Mitch. To hear the boys tell it, the evening must have been fantastic from the beginning to end. She almost felt left out, but knowing her five favorite people in the world had enjoyed an evening together made her totally happy.

"The Emeralds must have won last night," she sang out when Mitch breezed into her office looking clean and smelling spicy.

He grinned sheepishly. "I have no idea."

"Mitch! How are you going to teach the boys to enjoy a baseball game if you don't even know who won?"

He grinned again. "They taught me the fundamentals of watching a baseball game with kids. In one easy lesson." He stopped and shook his head remembering. "I didn't see one play in the entire game and neither did they. You saw all the stuff they had to eat—on their clothes. Besides that they all had to go to the rest room, one at a time, of course. And the best trick they pulled was their disappearing act. When Tad dumped his pop on me we came home." They laughed together, then returned to their work.

Late in the afternoon she heard loud voices in Mitch's office. "You can't do this to me," a familiar voice yelled.

"I told you I will and I mean it," Mitch said loudly. "You go near Seabrook's house once more and you'll see what I can do."

Brock! Mitch and Brock were fighting!

"I wonder what the folks'll think about it," Brock shouted.

"I suppose you'll tell Mommy on me," Mitch bellowed. "That won't work anymore. I'm through covering for you."

"Someday you'll find out who's so righteous," Brock yelled. A door slammed and silence filled every crevice of the building.

Perri's office door opened and Mitch came in. "Let's write up that home owner's policy for you," he said quietly.

"All right," she whispered, fearful of breaking the calm.

He took her hand. "You heard."

Perri nodded. "Everyone in the office heard. Maybe everyone in the building."

"I don't care. And I want everyone at your house to have strict instructions to report any sightings of my slick brother. Got it? We may as well give Rob and Kaima the best possible shot at a reconciliation."

"You bet. Now let's write up the policy."

Perri passed on Mitch's instructions but didn't worry too

much about Brock because Kaima still felt queasy much of the time. Perri figured she was just to sick to entertain an admirer.

The next Monday, Perri took Judd, Hugh, and Scott to school and made certain they were all happy before reporting to work.

"It must be our turn for an outing," Mitch said as they left the office in the afternoon. "Could we go to the concert in the park tonight after you put the boys in bed?"

"Sure, I'd like that. Why don't you come for supper? The boys would love to see you, and Kaima will, too."

Mitch went and the boys monopolized him, telling him about their first day at school, until he tucked them all in. Tad pulled Mitch down to the bed and kissed him on the cheek. "I love you, Mitch," he said.

"I love you, too," Mitch said, surprising Perri. And she felt even more shocked when she caught a glimpse of his expression. He meant it.

"You'll be all right, won't you, Kaima?" Perri asked before they left.

"Yes, I feel pretty good, and I won't have anything to do, except be here. I'll probably read or watch TV."

After the concert Mitch put Perri in his car and started the engine. Perri glanced across at him, Schubert's beautiful "Serenade" still filling her soul. She stared at his straight nose and strong chin.

"Do you, Perri?"

She came to. "Do I what?"

"Do you have to go straight home?"

"I guess not. Why?"

"Great. Let's go up on Skinner's Butte and look at the city lights." He turned the car north and began climbing the steep hill. A moment later he pulled to the edge of the parking lot and turned off his lights.

"Eugene's really pretty from here," she said.

"So are you."

Perri laughed softly. "You can't even see me."

"Yes, I can. Every time I shut my eyes there you are, beautiful and pure as an angel."

That made Perri warm and happy. "You know what? It's the same with me. I see you the last thing at night and the first thing in the morning."

She felt his lips touch hers as a butterfly must touch a rose, so lightly she barely felt him. "I love you, Perri," he whispered, his lips still against hers. "I love you so much I can't think of anything else."

"I love you, too, Mitch," she murmured. "So much it hurts. But I have to think about something else. Four of them."

He pushed her away. "What it comes down to is that you love the kids so much you really can't see anyone else. Is that it?"

She shook her head, knowing he couldn't see in the dark. "No, that isn't it at all. But the kids are helpless—and my responsibility. That's why they have to come first."

Mitch sighed heavily with relief. "I don't see the problem, then. I'm willing to marry the kids, too."

"Better start thinking how it will be listening to their trivial problems when you're involved with real ones. Are you ready to have things being spilled on you as a way of life? What about refereeing their constant battles?"

The long pause became unbearable. "I'll get used to it," he finally answered. "I love you enough to make the sacrifice. Really I do."

"That's the point, Mitch. You can't spend the rest of your life sacrificing. It'll get old long before we do."

He tried to pull her back into his arms, but she resisted.

"I like the kids, Perri," he protested. He sighed. "I guess we'd better go home," he said after a moment of quiet. "We can take this up another night."

When they pulled into the driveway, Perri noticed a car parked in the street in front of her house. "Wonder who that is."

"My brother," Mitch said. "I'm going in."

He burst in like a cop on a drug bust. Perri followed and found Brock and Kaima deep in a Rummy-cube game, numbers all over the table.

Brock looked up and grinned sheepishly. "Caught in the act," he said. Then to Kaima, "I'm going out." He put out two more numbers and turned his tile holder over.

Mitch pointed toward the door. "You sure are," he shouted. "And now."

Brock raised his right hand in a smart salute and walked through the door. "See you later," he said to Kaima just before shutting it.

Mitch turned his attention to Kaima. "Do you want to get back with Rob or not?" He went on without waiting for an answer. "And you know Brock isn't to come around here. Either you obey the house rules or you'll have to leave. Understand?"

Kaima put her head in her hands and began crying. "Of course I want to get my family back together, but I'm lonely. Can't you understand?"

Perri pulled a chair beside Kaima's and put an arm around the girl. "We understand, but you mustn't antagonize Rob. You're going through a really bad time, but you're a married woman and have two babies to make a home for. And I don't want Brock in my house again. I don't want him around my own children."

Kaima sniffed. And swallowed. "I know. I won't let him

come anymore." She got up and ran upstairs to the bedroom she shared with Merry.

"If I can't find anyone else to yell at, I may as well go home," Mitch said, with a wry smile.

Perri walked to the car, leaned through the window, and touched his lips with hers. "You taste like wild honey," he said, shoving the car into reverse.

In bed Perri again asked the Lord to help her teach Mitch about Him—and strength to accept it if he didn't learn.

The next morning when Perri arrived at work, she found all the girls talking in the reception room. "Good morning, fellow slaves," she said cheerily.

"'Fellow slaves,' she says," Jessica said to the others with a sneer. "I ask you, fellow slaves, is a concubine a slave?"

Perri whirled around and retraced her steps to Trish's desk. "Don't you dare put that label on me," she said shaking her finger in Jessica's face. "Especially when you don't know what you're talking about. I'm not anyone's concubine." She started for her door again, then turned back to the startled group. "And I never will be. Why would I possibly want to risk my relationship with God over some man—no matter how I felt about him?" She snapped the door open and spurted through.

I don't know why I even try to be friends with that bunch, she said to herself, jerking files out and slamming them onto her desk. Since she had started lunching with Mitch, even Trish had defected.

Mitch came for supper that night and helped celebrate Hugh's birthday. Perri had forgotten to buy matches, and he helped her light the candles by igniting a napkin on a hot stove burner. He even asked for a second slice of the lop-sided cake Perri had made. After the excitement had died down and the kids were busy playing with Hugh's new toys, the grownups set up a game of Scrabble.

"I appreciate this," Kaima said with a sweet smile. "I need to be baby-sat myself once in a while." She laid out all seven tiles across the pink center square to form the word, *fighter.*

"Hey, hey," Mitch said, "I see we're in for a real fight."

Almost as if the word *fight* were a signal, Hugh and Scott started screaming at each other, fists swinging and feet kicking. The boys fell to the floor, rolling and writhing, trying their best to injure each other.

Almost before Perri knew what happened, Mitch dropped to the floor and snatched each boy in an arm hold. Then, roaring like a lion, he rolled across the carpet, holding his elbows stiff to protect the boys from his weight as his body passed over them.

The boys forgot all about their disagreement, laughing loudly as they bumped around the room. Finally Mitch stopped, and Tad piled into the fray. Mitch released the boys, turned to his stomach to get his feet under him, but instantly three little boys straddled his back screaming for him to giddap.

After a romp around the room, the horse's feet and arms gave way and everyone tumbled off, roaring with laughter. Mitch lay on the floor panting and breathless. After a few moments he climbed slowly back into his chair. "Well, they aren't fighting, anymore," he said, laughing sheepishly.

❧

"He's so clean and good," Perri told her heavenly Father later. "But help me remember I can't have him until he has You. Make me strong and help me not to get more involved."

"How would you like to go to the coast this weekend?" Mitch asked one evening after the boys were in bed.

"I don't know if Kaima could watch the boys that long."

"We'll take the boys. And maybe Rob and Kaima. What

do you think?"

"Fantastic. We'll do a little matchmaking."

Rob agreed to go, and the next Saturday morning Perri's old Ford station wagon set off on Route F, creaking with its load. Mitch and Perri sat in the front seat, with Tad strapped in between them. Kaima and Rob shared the back seat with Merry's car seat and Scott. Judd and Hugh rode in the third seat that faced toward the back of the wagon. A large picnic lunch was squeezed in between their feet.

"Want to go to Heceta Beach or Devil's Elbow?" Mitch asked anyone who could hear.

"Devil's Elbow," Rob said with certainty. "It's protected from the wind. Neither of my girls need to be blown around right now."

Perri glanced at Mitch and raised her eyebrows. *Sounds good, so far,* she read in his expressive eyes.

An hour later he signalled a left turn, pulled off the coast highway, and drove slowly down the steep hill to the small beach. The boys burst from the car and raced to the ocean.

"Those guys don't like the ocean much, do they?" Rob asked after he'd helped Kaima and Merry out of the car. He gathered up the quilt he'd brought and held Merry's hand as the three walked toward the large rocks at the north end of the beach.

"And then there were two," Perri said just before Mitch's mouth settled on hers. The kiss was soft but meaningful, and her heart felt as light and joyful as the frothy bubbles on the ocean waves.

"Let's go join the boys," Mitch said. "Can't let them have all the fun."

He held her hand tightly as they climbed over the drift-wood, through the dry sand, to the ocean where the boys splashed in water up to their knees. He pulled her into the icy water as it foamed onto the beach, and Hugh began splashing them both. Mitch dropped Perri's hand and tore across the incoming wave after Hugh, who almost walked on the water in his haste to escape.

A minute later Mitch returned to Perri, with Hugh writhing on his shoulder. "Here it is," he said, laughing. "What shall we do with it?"

"Feed it to the seagulls," Perri said, looking overhead at the screeching gray and white birds.

He deposited Hugh on the sand, fifty feet from the ocean, then raced the boy back to the water. Perri sat down in the wet sand and watched the boys frolic with Mitch, feeling all her troubles washing away with the tide.

"I'm hungry, Mommy," Scott said later, dropping beside her. A multitude of goose bumps ineffectively tried to warm him.

"Okay, you call the others and I'll go after Rob and Kaima."

After calling the Kingstons, Perri went to the car and began carrying baskets and coolers of food to the picnic area above the beach. Before they had the lunch spread out on the table, a group of speckled seagulls landed on the lawn, squawking for food. They took bread, chips, or anything Scott held out to them.

"I think they're young birds," Rob said. "There are a couple of the gray and white ones, but notice how they hang back." His face was lit with interest and Perri smiled at him, pleased to see another side of him.

Scott finally left the table and began following the large flock of birds. They retreated just out of reach but didn't fly. "I'm going to catch one and take it home," he told Perri.

"Oh, Scott, think how sad it would be, away from its family and friends."

He thought a moment. "Okay, I'll just play with it a while, then let it go." But, though the birds seemed friendly, he didn't catch any.

After lunch Perri asked if they'd like to play a game.

"Brock likes to play games with Kaima," Tad said.

Rob catapulted off the quilt he'd been sharing with Kaima and Merry. He grabbed the front of Tad's shirt. "What did you say?" he yelled at the frightened child.

Tad's big blue eyes grew round and doubled in size as he attempted to draw away from the angry man. Immediately Mitch arrived on the scene with a chop to Rob's arm that released the small boy. "All right, Kingston, let's not kill the messenger." He lifted Tad in his arms and took him to Perri. "You stay here," he said quietly and turned back to face Rob.

"What's the kid saying?" Rob yelled. "What do you know about it?" He backed away from Mitch and turned to Kaima. "Are you playing games again with that—jerk?"

Kaima cowered next to Merry on the quilt. "I'm not playing games with anyone, Rob," she whined.

He whirled to face Perri. "Are you providing a nice little nest for my wife and her boyfriend's games?"

"Be quiet!" Perri yelled into his face. "Just shut up and listen." She couldn't believe it when Rob shut up, but she took advantage of his silence. "Nothing's going on. Brock did come over to play board games with Kaima a few times—but Mitch has told Brock to keep away from my house. We haven't seen him in weeks."

Rob's red face turned chalk white and he turned back to Kaima. "Is that your story, too?" he whispered.

She nodded.

He sneered. "So that's what you expect me to believe, is it?" He looked from face to face. He started toward Tad again, but the boy darted behind Mitch, who reached behind and lifted the child into his arms.

Rob's face began to redden again. "Let me talk to the kid," he roared. "He's the only one who'll tell the truth."

"And you've alienated yourself from him," Mitch said, holding Tad close. "You aren't getting near any of these boys, Rob, until you calm down."

Rob gave Kaima a look that would have wilted a rock. "All right, take me home—right now!" he bellowed at Mitch.

Mitch glanced at Perri and barely shook his head. "We came for the day, Kingston, and we're not ready to leave yet. Why don't you just apologize to your wife and spend the afternoon planning your family's future? Come on, guys, let's go build a castle."

A subdued group plodded back to the ocean and built a monstrous sand castle. But the carefree atmosphere had disappeared. "Let's dig a moat around our castle," Perri said, starting the ditch herself. As they dug into the sand, the little ditch filled with water.

"We have a real moat, Mommy," Judd said, excitement starting to show in his voice again.

They played in the ocean some more until Mitch took Perri's hand. "It's almost time for the sun to set. I want to watch it drop into the ocean from Rhododendron Park, so we'd better be going."

Love shone from his black eyes. *Maybe we can salvage something from this trip yet,* Perri thought, herding everyone toward the car.

"Come see the sunset, guys. It's going to be a nice one," Perri called to Rob and Kaima. Kaima shuffled to the car, sniffling. Rob stomped across the pavement with Merry in his arms. The little girl looked worried.

The car remained unbelievably quiet while Mitch drove

the ten miles back to the park and stopped. "Okay, we'll go over behind these trees," Mitch said. "They'll protect us from the wind and we can watch the ocean."

"Blue!" Merry yelled. "Blue water."

"She just learned her colors," Kaima explained.

Rob didn't get out of the car. The others watched quietly as the large red orb settled into the restless waves. The sky and also the ocean turned a deep crimson-gold. Mitch held Tad on his lap and with his other arm kept Perri close. "How does that compare with a moonrise?" he whispered into her ear.

"It's nice," she whispered in return, "but the ambiance is gone. I can handle confusion, kids fighting, traffic snarls, and even seagulls. But grown-up battles do me in."

Mitch nodded. "Right. Okay, back to the car, everyone."

After they had been on the road a little while, Mitch started singing, "We're fifty-five miles from home, boys. We're fifty-five miles from home. We drive a mile and catch a smile, and we're fifty-four miles from home."

As he continued the song with fifty-four miles from home, everyone joined in. They nearly made the sides of the old wagon bulge with their volume until they reached forty-nine miles.

"All right, you idiots, enough!" Rob yelled.

Merry started to cry, but Rob got his wish. No one sang another word. No one said a word either, and the trip seemed to last forever.

When the car stopped in Perri's driveway, the boys exploded from it, leaving the grown-ups to straggle out, tired and sandy. Rob walked to his car, climbed in, and roared off down the street.

Mitch shook his head and unlocked the door. After letting the kids and Kaima in, he pulled the door shut and led

Perri to the porch swing. "What a flop," he said giving a push with his foot.

Perri leaned against his chest. "I liked it. I enjoyed your company."

Mitch turned her around so she faced him and looked deep into her eyes. "You can have my company forever, you know."

Her arms wrapped themselves around his neck and her hands rifled through his windblown hair, scattering sand in her face. A moment of love-filled silence passed. "I enjoyed the boys," he finally said. "They're pretty neat kids."

Perri nodded happily. "I couldn't agree more."

She fed everyone sandwiches, then had worship with the boys and put them to bed. When she had said good-bye to Mitch, she swept and vacuumed sand. After she finished, she showered and shampooed, wondering if she could do anything more to show Mitch God's love.

Hungry for a cup of hot chocolate, she ran downstairs to make it. Passing through the dark living room, she heard quiet sobs. Kaima. Sorrow for Kaima made her feel guilty. She'd almost ignored the girl all day, but Rob had been there. She hadn't wanted to intrude on them—but being with her husband all day, in the mood he was in, had probably been worse for Kaima than being with no one.

Perri flicked on a lamp and sat down beside her. "Was it really awful?" she asked, pulling the crying girl to her side.

The sobs increased, and Perri sat quietly stroking Kaima's hair, letting her cry it out. After fifteen minutes the sobs stopped and Kaima lay quietly, breathing deeply.

"Would it help to talk about it?" Perri whispered.

Kaima nodded and rubbed the tears from her eyes. She sat up facing Perri and sniffled once more. "He's taking Merry from me."

fourteen

Perri's mouth went dry as she held Kaima. "He said he didn't care about the new one," Kaima continued, "but he couldn't let me corrupt Merry."

"Don't worry, Kaima," Perri said. "I can almost guarantee you he didn't mean it. He was hurt and jealous about Brock, and he was trying to hurt you back. He knew losing Merry would hurt you more than anything else. But if it came down to actually going to court, I for one will testify that you're a good mother."

After a while Perri helped the worried girl to bed and dropped into her own, forgetting all about the hot chocolate.

❧

Mitch showed up the following Sunday dressed in an immaculate suit. "I thought I'd finally check out your church," he said. "See if that's what makes you so nice."

At first delighted, Perri agonized over every word spoken. What if someone said something to drive Mitch away? But things went smoothly as usual, with the minister giving an exceptionally encouraging sermon about God being our Father. Our perfect Father who loves us many times more than the very best earthly father or mother could.

"I like your church," Mitch said at lunch. He grinned. "Everyone said exactly the same things you told me. Makes a guy think it could be true."

"It is true," she said.

Tell him how to be commit his life to Me, a still small

voice whispered into her ear. *But he didn't say anything about wanting to make a commitment,* she thought. *Tell him how,* the voice repeated.

She swallowed. "I'll tell you how to approach God in case you ever should want to accept His sacrifice for you," Perri said, her voice trembling with apprehension.

He jerked erect. "All right!"

She swallowed. "Well, you just thank Him—however you want, in whatever words you want—for loving you so much He gave His only Son to die your death. Say that you want to accept His great sacrifice for you. Ask Him to forgive your sins, and ask Him to send the Holy Spirit to teach you His ways. Open yourself to His love."

"Wow! Sounds pretty complicated."

Perri shook her head. "No. Just thank Him, accept His sacrifice, ask forgiveness, and then open yourself up to the Holy Spirit."

He asked her a few more questions, and they talked quietly until he left.

Mitch came for supper several times that week. He played with the boys, and both he and Perri did their best to keep Kaima cheered. Neither Brock nor Rob came around.

Friday night Mitch took Perri out for dinner. "Do you have to go straight home?" he asked as they left the restaurant.

"I think Kaima could handle it a little while."

"Good. How about a moonlight boat ride?"

"Will you order up a moon?"

"Yes, I've ordered a full moon. Would you believe it's been a month since we took our moonlight swim off the dock?"

In a little while Perri sat beside Mitch in his boat, gliding slowly and almost silently through the water. The sun had set nearly an hour ago, and stars glittered in the darkening sky. The soft calls of redwings, mixed with cooing doves, cried a quiet good night to the watery world.

"The lake's so full we'll have to duck as we go under the bridges," Mitch said quietly.

Perri felt his strength as he expertly steered the boat through the still water. What more could she ever ask, than to be with this quiet man, gentle yet strong enough to guide her and her boys through life's tumultuous streams? *You could ask for a man who loves and follows Me,* a silent voice told her heart. *Oh, Lord,* she answered, *You know I'd never marry anyone who didn't love You. Never.*

After Mitch had negotiated the highway bridge, then the railroad bridge, he turned his attention to Perri. "We'll go slowly and as quietly as we can. We may see something interesting."

As they idled up the twenty-foot-wide stream, the slapping of the water against the boat's bow soothed Perri almost into lethargy. The occasional splash as small creatures sought the safety of the water and the beginning frog chorus magnified the feeling of isolation, as though they were the only inhabitants in a quiet and lovely world.

Mitch stopped the boat, pointing over the trees to the east. "Our moon is beginning to lighten the sky."

They sat quietly rocking, as a large creamy moon rose above the trees to sit on the silhouetted branches. Perri felt the strength of the big man at the wheel, at peace with the tranquil world that whispered around them.

"Seabrook, have you any idea how gorgeous you look in the moonlight?" Mitch whispered, leaning toward her.

When a sharp beam flashed on them, they jerked apart as though caught stealing diamonds. "You guys all right?" a rough voice called, shattering the mood they'd shared.

"We're okay. Something wrong?" Mitch called huskily.

"Yeah. A boat needs a tow and we don't have a line. Do you?"

"Sure do." Mitch sighed heavily and started his engine. He threaded his way back down the narrow stream, under the railroad and highway bridges into the large body of water. "Those guys must have seen us go under the bridges," Mitch said, accelerating to keep the other boat's small headlamp in sight.

Finally a boat half again as large as Mitch's appeared, silhouetted in the moonlight, rocking silently in the center of the large lake. Mitch pulled alongside and Perri made out three figures huddled together on the backseat. The man who had steered Mitch and Perri to the crippled craft gave a little honk, shoved the throttle down, and took off with a roar.

"You guys need some help?" Mitch asked, cutting his engine.

A slight feminine figure stood up. "Yes, our engine stalled. Could you pull us to Orchard Point?"

"Sure." Mitch hooked a strong yellow cord to the ring in the back of his boat and tossed the other end to the woman who'd spoken to them.

Back in the driver's seat, Mitch slowly turned the two boats toward the large dock on the north side of the lake. Fifteen minutes later the shoreline came into view and he led the other boat to the paved launching ramp. When he had the boat as close as he could tow it, he jumped into the water, grabbed the back of the other boat, and pushed with all his strength. Very slowly, the boat turned and headed for the launching spot. "One of you will have to get your trailer," he said to the quiet women aboard the dead boat. "Then I'll help you load it."

The good deed completed, Mitch shoved the pedal to the floorboards and his boat hit the water as though racing. The bow raised and lowered gently as it slapped the waves at top speed. Ten minutes later they backed into position to load their own boat, tired but knowing they'd helped some people who really needed them.

The moon, now nearly overhead, cast a silvery glow on the world around them as they climbed into the pickup and drove east on West Eleventh Avenue toward home.

"Wish you'd gone straight home?" Mitch asked.

Perri shook her head in the dark. "No way. I always pray to do God's will and He led us to the lake tonight," she added. "Those women would have sat in the middle of the lake until morning if we hadn't helped them."

Mitch nodded as he flipped on the pass signal. "I did it for 'the least of them,'" he said, grinning. He sobered. "I mean that, Seabrook. I could almost feel God whispering in my ear out there. It was—" He broke off and pointed northeast. "Could that be a fire?"

"It could be," Perri said, seeing the orange glow over the edge of Eugene. Then she turned to Mitch with a small laugh. "Don't tell me you want to chase a fire, after all we've been through tonight. Is God whispering in your ear again?" She spoke lightly, but the words filled her with happiness. Obviously, Mitch was already opening himself to the Holy Spirit.

He gave her a sheepish grin. "Nope, I don't hear anything this time. I'm ready to quit. Probably a field burning, anyway. Fires are like rainbows, a lot farther away than they look."

But as they drove, the glow brightened. Mitch took Perri's hand in his. "It seems to be in town—and close." He smiled down at her. "We may have to swing by and check it out after all."

As he turned into the streets leading to her house, the fire stayed in front of them, and they began to smell smoke. They stopped talking, and Perri decided the fire was close.

As they pulled into Perri's street she saw several fire trucks with flashing lights a couple of blocks down, and police cars blocked the street. Flames leaped into the air from a house on the west side of the street. She lived on the west side! Mitch stopped and a uniformed policeman stepped to his window. "Sorry, sir, but you can't go through." He pointed in the direction from which they'd come. "Just back around the corner and you can bypass this block."

Perri's mouth felt dry and a knot accumulated in her throat. She leaned forward to see the officer. "But I live on this street," she choked.

fifteen

"Which house is it, officer," Mitch asked. "Do you know?"

The officer looked down the street. "No. Why don't you just ease on down. Stay back from the fire site, though."

Perri wanted desperately to close her eyes as the car moved into the block where the fire raged, the block in which she lived. Mitch stopped. Her house was the one burning.

She jumped from the car, running toward her house. "Hey, stay away from there," a policewoman called, then forcefully stopped her.

"My children are in there," she screamed, fighting desperately to free herself from the strong arms.

"No one's in the house," the large woman said. Perri continued flailing her arms in an attempt to escape. "NO ONE'S IN THE HOUSE!" the officer yelled. "Somebody took them away a half hour ago."

Finally the words penetrated. The kids were safe. She felt Mitch's arm slide over her shoulders and pull her close. "She said the kids are all right," he said into her ear. "Shall we go find them?"

"Yes. No, I have to get some of my things out." Perri broke away from Mitch and ran again toward the fiercely burning house.

He caught her before she'd gone ten feet and held her tightly. "Perri, get hold of yourself. The house is gone!"

The fire chief stepped to their side. "Mrs. Perri Seabrook?"

Perri nodded.

"Sorry to bother you right now, but I need to know you where you've been for the last two hours."

"Boating at Fern Ridge Lake."

The fireman nodded and put his pencil in a pocket. "All right. Thanks." He motioned toward the house. "Sorry about this."

"Thank you," Mitch said. "Could you tell us where the kids are?"

The soot-covered man shook his head. "Check with friends, I guess." He started to walk away, then came back. "Do you happen to know if the place was insured?"

Mitch gave Perri a quick squeeze. "Yes, thank God the building and contents are completely covered."

"Good." The man walked back toward a group of firemen.

Mitch squeezed Perri again. "I'm thankful you're covered with our own policy," he said quietly. "You'll be able to collect in a hurry."

Perri could think only about all the things she was losing in the blazing inferno before them. A lifetime of treasures. All of her mementos of her life with Jerry. Maybe later she'd be happy about the insurance but now she could feel only horrible grief. She felt as though her past had just been erased.

"Let's try to find the kids," Mitch said, pulling her toward the group the chief had joined.

But no one had any idea where Kaima had taken the boys.

"Call your mother," Mitch suggested. Perri was crying too hard so he did, but the shocked woman hadn't heard a thing and could barely communicate after hearing the news.

"Let's go to my place," Mitch suggested after watching the blazing destruction another half hour.

Perri sniffed, unmindful that black ash now covered her

and the clothes she'd chosen so carefully for her special evening with Mitch.

"I can't go away when I don't know where the boys are," she whimpered.

A car approached from the direction Mitch and Perri had come, and her parents jumped out and ran to her. They both enclosed her in their arms, and her mother kissed her blackened face.

"I'm so sorry, baby," she whispered. "You didn't need this. A person can take only so much."

Perri felt strength flow into her body as her mother held her. "I'm all right," she said bravely. "Mom, Dad, this is Mitch."

They greeted him and invited him to their place too. "Perri's told us so much about you, we feel we already know you," Mom added. Mitch grinned. "I should know you folks too then, but right now we better find the boys. Kaima's taken them somewhere."

Perri's dad brushed his mat of gray hair from his face. "She'd take them to her house."

Perri looked at Mitch with her mouth wide open. "Of course. Let's go see!"

"Just a minute, pumpkin," her dad called. "I'm taking Mom home so we can get the house ready for you. You come whenever you're ready."

"Thanks, Dad." Perri realized how good she felt to have her parents looking after her.

"This scares me a lot," Perri said as Mitch rang the Kinsgstons' doorbell. Lights glowed from several windows, but the silence screamed into her ears.

After an eon, a porch light snapped on and Rob opened the door. When he recognized Mitch and Perri he opened the door wide. "Come in, everyone's fine."

Relieved, Perri stepped inside and saw all four of her boys sitting at the dining room table eating frosted cinnamon rolls and drinking hot chocolate. She snatched the closest, Hugh, into her arms and began crying all over again. The other three boys threw themselves at her and they all sank to the carpet, laughing, crying, and hugging.

Mitch dropped to the floor and hugged the boys, too. Then Perri threw herself into his arms. "We're all right," she whispered.

After a few minutes Perri noticed Rob's arm around Kaima. He kept it there, no matter what, and his eyes held a special glow.

All things work together for good to them that love God. The words echoed in her head. Well, at the moment she failed to see any good in the loss of her home, but if it helped Rob and Kaima that was something.

"Where's Merry?" Mitch asked.

"In bed, sleeping it off," the happy-looking Rob replied. "It didn't seem to affect her as much as the boys. Maybe because they're older. Maybe because it was their house."

"You must stay here tonight," Kaima said. "Sort of returning a favor. I don't exactly know where everyone will sleep, but we'll figure out something."

Perri shook her head. "My folks are getting ready for us." She looked from the smiling Kaima to Rob's happy face. "I think you two need to be alone, anyway."

Perri and Mitch gathered up the four boys and headed out West Eleventh Avenue again, stacked two-deep in his pickup. "Well, at least something good came from the fire," Mitch said. "Did you ever see anyone as happy as Rob?"

Perri shook her head. "I hope it's for real." After a moment of silence she cleared her throat. "It seems I should be taking clothes if we're spending the night," she said in a hushed voice as the enormity of the loss flooded over her. How could they ever gather the things they'd need to run a home? She looked at her ash-covered blue silk dress. Her entire wardrobe consisted of the clothes she had on! And the boys had only the dirty play clothes they wore.

"Oh Mitch," she said, "I'm not sure I can handle this. We don't have a home, or anything to put in a home. We don't even have any clothes."

Mitch's eyes tightened a little as they followed the beam of his lights on the road. "Try not to think about it," he grunted. "It'll be hard, but you'll all end up with nicer things than you lost."

His hand snaked into her lap and stroked her trembling hand. "Your God will help you handle this. You know He will." He smiled tenderly at her in the dark. "And I know a nice place just waiting for a family."

Perri looked at him questioningly.

"My place."

She didn't reply, but she savored his loving thought. In a little while he turned in to her parents' ranch-style home, and unloaded the sleepy boys. He cradled Tad in his arms and followed Perri to the front door.

Mr. and Mrs. Roman helped Perri and Mitch care for the boys and put them to bed, then they went to bed too. Perri collapsed in the large wooden rocker she'd loved since childhood. Mitch sat on the hassock at her feet.

"Do you think the kids are all right?" he asked.

"I think so. Of course they haven't yet begun to realize."

Mitch nodded and reached for her hand. "They looked cute in your dad's T-shirts, didn't they?"

Perri smiled, remembering her sweet smelling, freshly bathed boys in Dad's red, blue, yellow, and green shirts. Tad's nearly reached his feet, and each of the others got a little shorter. "Yeah. They've been wearing them for pajamas when they visit my parents ever since they got out of diapers, so they feel right at home in them." A tear rolled out of her eye and down her cheek. "Until morning when they don't have anything to put on."

"Can you remember back to our moonlight boat ride?" Mitch asked.

"Barely." Her lips turned up in a small smile. "It seems a long time ago."

He nodded. "It was special, though. I keep remembering that sense I had of God's presence. I can't believe He would have been looking out for those women on that boat and have forgotten about you. He must know what He's doing. Just hold on to your faith, Perri." He dropped her hand and stood up. "I'd better go. Don't think about coming in to work," he said. "I'll go long enough to turn in the claim, then come back out here. I'll take you clothes shopping if you'd like."

"I'm too tired to think right now. Call me—or come on out."

He leaned over the rocker, kissed her on the forehead, and left.

Perri showered, shampooed, and fell into bed at 4:30 in the morning. She slept soundly until she felt a small body climbing into bed with her. Rolling over, she gathered him close and fell back to sleep.

She next opened her eyes at 9:00 and jumped out of bed as though she had to hurry to work. She put on a pair of Mom's worn jeans and a bright yellow shirt, but what could the boys wear?

Mom met her with a firm hug. "I didn't expect you to be up so early," she said, wearing the same ready smile that Perri always flashed.

"Scott crowded me out of bed. Oh, but it felt good to have him close. Your clothes are great for me, Mom, but I don't know what the kids are going to wear this morning."

Mom pointed at the couch. "No problem. I stuck them in the washer." Four small piles of clean clothes lay waiting to be slipped into.

"Dad and I thought we'd take the boys shopping this morning, if you don't mind," Mom said, obviously looking forward to the expedition. "They need to be back in school tomorrow."

"Sure. I'll just cash a check. Oh, no! My checkbook burned."

Mom scurried around in the kitchen, making breakfast for Perri and the boys. "That won't be any problem; you can get more checks, but Dad and I are writing the checks for this." She raised her eyebrows at Perri. "You didn't tell us how handsome Mitch is. Dad and I both think he's nice too."

Perri hugged Mom. "He's almost perfect," she said. "Almost."

Mom and Dad had barely left with their car full of excited boys when Mitch drove in.

"I turned in the claim," he said after a gentle hug and kiss. "Would you like to go to the house this morning?"

How could she face the charred remains of the home she'd seen so much happiness in, and also such heartache? But something drew her, as light draws a moth.

One fire truck remained at the house, spraying water on the remains whenever an occasional puff of smoke erupted. An inspector wearing special equipment sorted through the ashes.

"What's that guy doing?" Perri asked Mitch.

"Probably trying to find the cause of the fire."

"That shouldn't be too hard. The house was sixty years

old and had the original wiring. I've been afraid of this ever since Jerry and I bought it."

Mitch waited while Perri took in the devastation. "Ready to go?" he finally asked.

"Sure. Where?"

"To the clothing stores, Seabrook. You have to get back to work."

He helped her pick out four pairs of jeans and eight tops, dress pants and blouses, dresses, shoes, then walked away while she bought underwear.

"Do you feel better?" he asked, putting the sacks into his trunk.

She smiled. "A lot. I guess shopping is good medicine."

He slid behind the steering wheel and started the car. "Does it help any to know how much I love you?" he asked almost shyly.

She unsnapped her shoulder harness and leaned on his chest, his chin on the top of her head and her cheek against his neck. "Yes," she said quietly, not adding that what meant most to her were the words of faith he had spoken the night before. Would he ever be ready to accept Jesus' sacrifice for his sins?

Late in the afternoon they dropped in at the office to check for any emergencies. The girls surprised Perri by expressing their sympathy with no sarcasm behind their kind words. While Perri told them about the fire, Mitch rushed in, his face red and breathing hard.

"Would someone explain why Perri's policy never reached the home office?" he yelled, casting quick glances from one to another.

Perri felt a rock land in her stomach. Did this mean she wasn't covered? No way could she survive this disaster without insurance.

"I never touched it."

"Neither did I."

"I didn't even know she owned a house."

Mitch listened, as in a daze, then his eyes met Perri's. "Do you know who typed it?"

"I don't remember. Oh, Mitch, things have been going so well, I haven't taken the time to check for a while!"

Perri rode in silence as he took her back to her folks' place. What would she do if she couldn't collect insurance? And why had Kaima let the car burn in the unlocked garage? Mitch walked her to the door, kissed her, and drove away.

The boys eagerly showed Perri their new clothes. "We got more new clothes today than we did when school started," Hugh said, modeling three shirts at once.

Finally the dam broke and Perri slumped into a chair, sobbing brokenheartedly. No one, not even Tad, could reach her until she'd cried it all out. Then she moved to the couch and slept.

As she slept she heard a voice. *I'm still here, Perri. Where's your faith? Don't you know that faith when things go well isn't faith at all? Faith when things go wrong is true faith.* Perri smiled in her sleep. "Thank You, Lord," she heard herself say. "Don't leave me now. And give me a large slice of faith. Thank You, God. I love You."

"Come, try to eat, pumpkin." Perri felt herself being shaken and opened her eyes. "You've slept for four hours," Dad said, his eyes shining with love.

Perri dragged herself to the table and ate, although the food tasted like cotton balls.

After Perri tucked the boys safely into bed, she told Mom and Dad about the unfiled insurance policy. Mom voiced her sympathy to Perri, but Dad sat quietly. Finally Mom ran out of words. "Have you thought of the largest implication, pumpkin?" Dad asked softly.

"I don't know," Perri answered. "It looks pretty bad. I don't have a home for my kids, and not even a car to drive to work."

"There's more," Dad said. He sat down beside Perri and put his arm tightly around her shoulders. "Brace yourself, Perri, this one's rough. You're still responsible for the mortgage on the house."

The color drained from Perri's face and her wide eyes looked blank. She couldn't seem to feel anything. What did it matter? What did anything matter? She began laughing and couldn't stop.

Mom put a cold cloth against Perri's face and wiped gently. "Honey, stop!" she said sharply. "You're hysterical."

Then Mitch arrived from somewhere and shook her. "Perri, we'll handle it. God will give you the strength." He pulled her into his arms and sat on the couch rocking her gently. She leaned against his crisp light gray shirt and inhaled his clean spicy smell. What was the matter with her? She still had the kids—and God. Of course they'd be all right!

"I'm sorry," she said wiping her face with a tissue Mitch provided. She looked around and noticed her folks had disappeared. "I'm thoroughly ashamed of myself. Could you wait while I wash my face?"

She returned fifteen minutes later in new jeans and a soft blue top, her face freshly made up and eyes bright. Mitch met her at the hall doorway. "Now you look like my princess."

He led her through the door onto the back porch where an unrelated assembly of furniture lived. When they sat on a rattan love seat she turned her face up for his kiss. His lips touched hers gently, not as a taker, but a giver. Her heart didn't race, and her breath didn't stop. Instead, she felt secure and loved. Her spirits lifted, and the moon peeped from behind the clouds.

"Our moon's been hiding its face, but now things are going to be all right," he said tenderly. His hands brushed her long soft hair from her face as they leaned back together and relaxed.

A moment later she heard his breath coming regularly. He'd fallen asleep. She snuggled close, watching the moon move higher overhead. Things would be all right. She knew they would with God leading.

After a while Mitch awakened and left. Perri offered to go to the office in the morning but he told her to rest another day.

The next morning Dad drove to Eugene to take the boys to school. "I'll have to get a place in Eugene so they can catch the school bus," she told him. "Two trips a day is too much."

"Maybe we should transfer them to the school out here," Mom said.

"Changing schools wouldn't be good for them right now. Besides, you've already raised your family and it isn't fair that you should raise mine, too."

Dad tweaked her hair. "You know you're welcome to stay as long as you please. But things look pretty serious between you and Mitch. Do you want to tell us anything about that?"

Perri laughed, then flushed. "Nothing new. He still wants to marry me, but he's still not a Christian. I'm also hesitating because of the boys."

"What about the boys?" Mom asked in surprise. "They need a father."

"I know that, Mom, but can Mitch walk into a nest of

half-grown boys and survive? I have to know before I jump into marriage."

"He seems to think a lot of the boys," Mom mused.

Perri nodded. "He really does, and I think he's about to accept Jesus' sacrifice for him too. If he does, I suspect we'll be married."

A little later the doorbell chimed and Mitch walked in, a horrified look on his face. "I just got the report from the fire inspector," he said in a choked voice. "The boys started the fire playing with matches." He looked like an animal caught in a steel trap. "I've learned to care a lot for your boys, Perri," he whispered. "I think I can honestly say I love them. And I love you more than life itself." He cleared his throat twice. "But I'm just not sure I can handle the things they do." He wiped his eyes with the back of his hand and stepped through the front door, closing it softly behind him.

sixteen

Perri stared, wide-eyed at the closed door. Her mother slid her arm around her neck. "He'll be all right, honey."

Perri moved to the old rocker and lowered herself into the curved seat. "The kids set the fire," she mumbled, then sat still, her eyes blank. "The kids set the fire. The kids set the fire." She leaned her head on the tall back of the rocker. "The kids set the fire."

She sat for a few more minutes, then jumped to her feet, ran to her mother and began shaking her arm. "The kids did *not* set the fire!" she cried.

Mrs. Roman gently dislodged Perri's fingers and stepped backward a few feet. "It's all right, dear. Kids sometimes do play with fire, you know. It would have been an accident."

"Mom," Perri cried, "they didn't set the fire. I know they didn't."

Dad put his arm around Perri and steered her out the front door. "Come on, pumpkin, let's sit out here and talk. It won't seem so terrible after you get used to it." He guided her to the wicker love seat, and sat beside her. His gray eyes smiled into hers. "And don't you worry about Mitch. I've seen how he looks at you. He didn't mean what he said. He'll be back before the day's over."

Perri shook her head. "Couldn't you see how much it hurt him to tell me? No, Dad, he knew exactly what he was doing. What it boils down to is that he dreads four wild boys more than he loves me. But the boys didn't start the

151

fire. Judd is much too reliable, and the others are scared to death of fire."

Mom stepped onto the porch, distributed three hot drinks, and lowered herself into the old rocker. "The fire inspector called. He wants to talk to you and the boys, Perri." She leaned over and patted Perri's knee. "Don't worry, honey, Dad and I'll be with you."

Perri sipped her drink. How quickly a world could crumble. Last week at this time her life had seemed fantastic.

The arrival of the bright red fire chief's car interrupted Perri's chain of thought. Two men, dressed in dark business suits, strode toward the porch. Dad stood up and took the few steps to greet them.

"Good morning, Mr. Roman, I'm Eugene's fire chief, Jason Hall," the tall thin one said, reaching for Dad's hand. "This is Thomas Mullen, the state fire inspector." He turned to Perri. "Sorry about your fire, Mrs. Seabrook."

Mullen, a big burly man with thick gray hair, accepted Dad's proffered hand, but his bright blue eyes looked as hard as diamonds and his thin lips set in a straight line. His attention turned immediately to Perri. "Mrs. Seabrook? May we speak to you, please?"

Perri motioned to the battered couch across the porch. "Sure, sit down."

The fire inspector stepped to the couch and sat down, but looked pointedly at Perri's parents.

"They're staying," Perri said.

Mullen grunted and dropped to the couch beside Hall. "The fire started in the garage, Mrs. Seabrook." Perri nodded. At least she understood now why Kaima couldn't have saved the car. Mullen continued, "We found a carton of safety matches beside the work bench. Three of the folders had matches missing. Some oily rags ignited almost immediately—and as they say, the rest is history." His steely blue eyes bore into Perri's pained ones. "Someone set that fire, Mrs. Seabrook, and we've concluded your boys did it accidentally, playing with the matches."

Perri jumped up and faced the men. "Your conclusions are wrong," she said, her face white, the veins on her neck standing out. "My boys are scared to death of fire, even a birthday candle."

"I can agree they were frightened. They may have lit the match accidentally, then dropped it because they were scared." He stood up and turned to go. "I'd like to talk to the boys. I understand they're in school in Eugene."

Perri backed away from the big man. "Yes, they are."

"I want to talk to them before you do, so we'll be at the school at dismissal time."

Norman Roman stood up and extended his hand to the serious-faced man. "We'll be there to support the boys, Inspector."

When Perri, Tad, and her folks arrived at the school, the fire inspector had already arranged to use a small room. Perri and the Romans waited with the fire chief and inspector until the boys walked in, looking frightened.

"Don't be afraid," Fire Chief Hall said, motioning them to chairs. "This is Thomas Mullen, the state fire inspector. He'll talk to you about the fire."

Three serious faces nodded.

"We've discovered that some of you were playing with matches," the inspector said in a surprisingly soft voice.

All three sets of young eyes opened wide as the boys looked at each other. No one said a word. Everyone watched the boys. The inspector's soft voice broke the silence. "You aren't in any trouble, boys. We just need the information to close the investigation." He looked at each boy again. The boys looked at each other again, waiting for the others to speak.

The burly inspector stood to his six-foot height. "This isn't a game, boys," he growled. "You can go home when we get this all straightened out."

Judd shrunk three inches lower into his chair. Still no one spoke.

The inspector jumped in front of Judd and pointed a finger into his face. "All right, son, tell me about the fire." He waited a few seconds, during which the room became so quiet you could have heard a match burning. He leaned down until his face nearly touched Judd's. "Now!" he bellowed.

Norman Roman stepped to the inspector's side. "That'll be all for today, Inspector. I can't see bullying a child." Silently, he gathered up the boys and herded them from the room, down the hall, and to the car.

༆

Mitch appeared at the door that evening, pale and drawn. Mary Roman put a root beer in his hand, and then the Romans took the boys for a walk.

Perri sat on the couch beside Mitch. "You don't look so great," she said.

He reached for her hand, but she gently retrieved it. "I still love you," he whispered, his voice hoarse with emotion.

"I'm sorry. It would be a lot less painful if we could push a button and turn off our feelings like a TV, wouldn't it?"

He sat silently looking at her. Her heart ached for the hurt she saw in his soft eyes. *Whoa*, she told herself, *let him take care of himself. You have enough pain of your own to handle.*

But she couldn't turn away from the anguish she saw. A

tear trickled from his left eye to his cheek. "Have you talked to the kids?" he asked, ignoring the drop of water sliding down his face.

Perri nodded. "The state fire inspector bullied them until Dad intervened. They didn't do it, Mitch."

Mitch thought that over for a moment. "Oh, Perri, I wish I could believe that. But they have pretty sophisticated methods of investigating these things."

"I don't doubt that. I believe everything they said. But someone else did it. Maybe Merry. The thing is, my boys aren't very old. What if they had done it? Parents have to forgive their kids, and be there for them. They may do something worse before they grow up. I won't be turning my back on them and giving up."

Mitch reached for her, but she moved away. "I don't blame you," she said. "Not at all. They aren't your flesh and blood and you have no reason to feel responsible for them." She felt a lump growing in her throat and tears threatening to overflow. She smiled weakly. "It would be easier if it didn't hurt so much, though."

A suffocating silence filled the room for several minutes. Finally Mitch cleared his throat. "I don't know what to say. I know I'm wrong, and I don't even know how I feel. Sometimes, even now, I think we can make it. And I'm sure I hurt as much as you do."

Perri smiled. "Let's try it again in—say about twenty years?" She tried to laugh but it turned into a choke.

ᔬ

The next day Perri visited Kaima and asked Merry if she'd been playing with matches. Merry barely knew what matches were, and Perri realized she would could hardly have carried them to the garage without anyone noticing.

Kaima fairly glowed as she explained that Rob wanted

her and Merry to stay with him and that he'd been treating her like a queen. He hadn't mentioned the new baby, so she was just taking a day at a time. He had finally promised her he would go with her to talk with the counselor who had already helped Kaima so much.

Back to square one, Perri thought, as she headed her folks' Honda out West Eleventh to their house.

She dropped the boys off at school the next morning and went to work. Trish spoke pleasantly to her when she passed through to her office. Perri sat in her comfortable chair and leaned her head on her hands, a multitude of feelings pouring through her, clamoring for primacy.

"Good to see you, Seabrook." Mitch's velvet voice poured over her like whipped cream, wonderful to the senses—bad for the health.

She raised her head and shock rippled through her. Dark circles beneath his eyes accented the gauntness of his white cheeks. What had happened to his magnificent tan? His smooth shave and neatly pressed suit ineffectively tried to hide his unhappiness.

She forced a smile. "I'm ready to work. Just tell me what to do."

"May I sit down and talk to you?"

Perri shrugged. "It's your office."

He sat and leaned on her desk, folding his hands. "I've been trying to get to the bottom of your missing insurance policy." His eyebrows rose slightly into his lined forehead. "I feel like firing the lot of them."

"Unless they worked together, that wouldn't be fair, would it?"

"That's why they're still here. But look at it this way. It never happened before you came, then it stopped until your policy went through."

Perri shook her head. "Sounds to me as though you'd be better off without me. Probably be a lot less painful for you, too."

His hand dropped onto hers on the desk top. "Don't even think it. I have to see you."

That hand felt so good on Perri's she could hardly bear to withdraw hers—but she did. "I've heard the best way to kick a habit is cold turkey," she whispered.

꒰ꞈ

Mitch appeared on the Romans' doorstep that night with the boat. "A moonlight boat ride might make everything right again," he said hopefully.

Perri invited him in and got two sodas from the refrigerator. "Haven't you been watching, Mitch?" she asked with a quivering smile. "The moon is only a shadow of its former self."

"Kind of like you," he said.

Perri took a long drink. "I'm all right, and no one bothered the kids today, so I suspect they've concluded the investigation. Conclusion: *Some or all of the Seabrook boys accidentally set the fire while playing with matches in the garage.*"

Mitch leaned forward and ran a finger around the top of his untouched glass. "And you still don't believe it?"

Perri laughed, a dry, humorless laugh. "I'm still the typical mother. Thank God my folks support me—and the kids—in my faith."

Mitch glanced out the window at the darkening sky. "No boat ride?"

"No. And I may as well tell you I'm turning in my resignation tomorrow—effective as soon as possible." His stricken face made her wince inside. "I'm sorry, Mitch, but we'll both heal faster if we aren't thrown together every day."

A heavy sound like a sob escaped his trembling lips. "I don't see it that way, Seabrook."

"I don't either, but we both know it's true." She waited a moment for her throbbing heart to settle down so she could breathe. "How soon can you release me, Mitch?"

He set his untouched pop on the coffee table and struggled to his feet. "You don't have to come back anymore," he whispered hoarsely. He sniffed and brushed the back of his hand under his nose. "I'll send you a check for a month's severance pay." Glancing at her, he rushed out the door.

Perri sat stunned as he drove away. *This is the way it has to be, she told herself. Face it, life isn't a candy bar; it's only the wrapper. Eternity is the candy bar.*

After she put the boys to bed she told her folks what she'd done. "Who knows?" she added. "Maybe God sent the fire to save me from something worse—marrying an unbeliever."

Mom nodded sympathetically. "You've lost almost everything a person can lose, your husband, your home, and now your new love and job. But you did the right thing."

"No, Mother, she didn't," Dad said emphatically. "Mitch just needs a little time, and she's only making it harder for him. I'm convinced that boy is on the very edge of making a commitment—both to God and to you. And you pushed him away."

"I did the right thing, Dad," Perri said with a long sigh. "I couldn't marry Mitch now, even if he wanted to, even if he does accept Christ as his Savior. The boys have to come first. It isn't Mitch's fault that the boys aren't his and he can't force himself to feel as I do about them."

The phone rang sometime after Perri went to bed. Then

Mom knocked softly on her bedroom door. "It's Mitch for you, honey. Are you awake?"

Perri scrambled from her bed.

"I have to talk to you," he said. His voice sounded stronger, somehow. "I'm at the phone booth on the corner."

"What corner?"

"West Eleventh and Ellmaker."

A half mile away! "Why did you bother to call after driving all the way out?" she murmured.

Mitch broke the long pause with a chuckle. "I chickened out."

Perri checked the wall clock. Eleven-thirty. "Come on over. I'll be on the front porch."

They settled into the love seat with a light afghan covering them.

"I can't believe the afghan already," Mitch said. "But it feels good."

"It's almost the end of September," she said. "But you didn't drive all the way out here to talk about the weather."

The crescent moon came from under a cloud and cast its tiny rays on the two. Mitch pointed to it. "That's a sign, my love. Our lives are coming from under a cloud, too."

Perri sighed. "Yes, it just takes time."

"Would you believe I've already been in bed tonight?"

"I'd believe anything, I guess."

"Something popped into my head. When I was twelve and Brock ten, he convinced me to try smoking—in *my* bedroom, of course. Did you notice I said I was twelve? I should have been guiding him, not following him into mischief."

Perri waited for him to continue.

"Well, I got sicker than a pulled-out weed. Vomited all over the bathroom floor—the works. Do you think Brock helped me? No way, he laughed himself hoarse. I cleaned up the mess and sprayed the bedroom and the bathroom with deodorant. Then I crept into bed, hoping I'd die and get it over with. I didn't eat supper that night and worse yet, when my mother came in to check me she smelled tobacco."

"What happened?" Perri whispered, seeing Mitch as a sick little kid.

"Dad grounded me for a month. No TV, no leaving the house except for school, no friends in, no reading, no desserts."

"Wow, some punishment. What about Brock?"

"He remained uninvolved. He'd been smoking for some time so it didn't affect him at all."

"Why didn't you tell?"

"I never told on him for anything, but can't you imagine how they'd have reacted? The older child could hardly blame the younger."

"So, why did you get out of bed to tell me this?"

"I was older than any of your kids. I could have burned the house down. What I did was worse than what they're blaming your kids for."

Perri sat up straight. "I see what you're saying, but the fact still remains that I have a whole parcel of kids and they aren't yours. And try though you may, I don't think you can handle having them around all the time, twenty-four hours every day, seven days every week of the month, twelve months every year."

"I can, Seabrook. I've missed them these last days. I really have. And as time goes by, I find myself believing as you do. They might have done it; any boy might. But those kids wouldn't lie about it. I know they wouldn't. I know them. And—" He shrugged his shoulders. "I love them," he said simply.

Perri settled back in the chair again. He leaned over and rotated her to face him, then turned her chin up. When his lips met hers, soft and questioning, her insides melted.

But she pulled away. "Let's say they did burn the place down, then lied about it. Could you still love and forgive them?"

"I don't care about the house, Seabrook. I love you and I love your kids. How could I not love Scott who forced me to kiss him good night and said he loves me. How could I not love Hugh who snitched a kiss on the lips? How could I not love brave little Tad, who wants to fly like an arrow? And Judd who saved all their lives that day on the boat. They may do all kinds of terrible things. I'll still love them if they burn down the whole town. You just try me."

"That's a mouthful, Mitch." *But have you also learned to love our precious Lord Jesus?*

He got up and tucked the afghan around her. "I'm going home, Seabrook. If you can bring yourself to forgive me for being such a selfish fool you might give me a call." He walked into the darkness, leaving her trying to make sense of her life.

seventeen

Perri sat on the porch for some time, rehashing their conversation. She shivered deliciously, touching the afghan where he'd tucked it around her.

The front door opened and Dad stuck his head out. "Mitch wants you on the phone, pumpkin."

Mitch's voice crackled with excitement. "Remember Hugh's birthday?"

Perri shook her head. What a crazy guy! "Almost always."

"Remember the cake?"

"I made the cake, Mitch. It flopped."

He sighed heavily. "I mean the candles. Remember looking everywhere for matches? Finally I lit a piece of napkin from the electric burner?"

It hit her with the force of a falling tree! She dropped into a chair.

"You there, Seabrook?" Mitch's voice asked from the dangling receiver.

She snatched it back to her ear. "I remember, Mitch. The boys couldn't have done it. We didn't have any matches!"

"Know how I came up with that?"

"I guess not."

"I prayed, Seabrook! I hadn't ever told you—just shy, I guess—but that Sunday after I went to church with you, I gave my life to God the way you said. I've been praying about us ever since—and God always lets me know we belong together. I've been praying about the boys since the fire, asking Him to help me know if they did it. Well, I just went to bed and prayed again. Immediately, Seabrook, exactly right then, I remembered about the birthday cake!

I'm so excited I may not sleep all night."

"I'm happy about it too, Mitch."

"Good night, Seabrook," Mitch whispered. Hearing the dial tone, she gently hung up the phone.

She opened her eyes the next morning to the sound of a robin singing outside her window. The fluffy white clouds made the blue sky look bluer. Tomorrow's rainbow was becoming today's rainbow and growing bright.

Dressing in a hurry, she presented herself at the breakfast table, starved. "Mitch has accepted the Lord! I'm so excited I can't sit still."

Mom set a plate of pancakes on the table and slid back into her chair. "That's wonderful. I suspected he had accepted Christ as soon as I met him. He had that—oh, I don't know how to explain it, but you could tell he'd been touched by the Holy Ghost. When you told me he wasn't a Christian, I thought it must have been my imagination. I'm glad it wasn't."

"He seems to definitely have opened himself to the Spirit's leading. God showed him the boys couldn't have set the fire."

Dad laughed. "I guess the Lord gave him two for one. Now he not only knows the boys didn't do it, he knows the Lord is real and cares about us."

Perri's laughter sounded like a handbell choir. "I can't sit here another minute, Mom. Can you put me to work?"

"I thought you'd never ask." Mom laughed happily and hugged her close.

❧

Perri called Mitch late in the afternoon and invited him for supper. When he arrived she walked into his arms. "You look a thousand percent better than you did last night," she said, noting his clear sparkling eyes with no dark circles under them.

He pushed her away and looked her over carefully. "You look better, too, Seabrook, but it's going to take a while to put all that fat back on you."

He ducked her playful swing. "All that fat?" she asked. "Maybe I won't put it back on."

"Yes, you will, if I have to force-feed you. You almost lost your shape."

"Come on you two," Dad called from the dining room. "If you can hold down the scrapping long enough to eat, it's ready."

After Perri served the dessert, Mitch held up a hand for attention. "I had a colossal idea," he said. "How about you school boys coming to stay with me during the week? Not only will it save someone two long trips each day, but I consider West Eleventh the most dangerous street around. I hate to think of you having to travel it twice every day."

"I won't argue that West Eleventh is dangerous," Perri said. "I'm glad they're finally working on the new highway. But I couldn't let you keep the boys."

"Sure you could. I have fun things planned." He winked at her. "If you're good, we might even include you in some."

"Please, Mommy," Scott pleaded.

"Can we go?" Hugh asked.

"You'd still have Tad," Judd added.

"But I've never been without the kids," Perri said. "And besides, there isn't all that much time for fun when the kids are in school."

"I promise to put them to bed by eight o'clock, and you can repossess them anytime you want."

Perri sighed. "All right, we'll try it for a couple of days." Her eyes twinkled at Mitch. "You'll probably bring them back before morning."

After he left with the older boys, she wandered around the place feeling even lonelier than she'd expected. She had evening Bible study with her folks and Tad, then went to bed. But unable to stay there, she got up and wandered into the boys' room. Somehow she felt closer to them there, so she crawled under the covers with Tad, and after asking

God to bless her helpless little boys, she fell asleep.

The next morning she flew through all the work Mom could find for her and asked for more. She couldn't slow down until the telephone interrupted.

"Thought you might like to hear how the boys did," Mitch said. "We had to use my Bible for stories, but they enjoyed Noah's adventure which I sort of put into my own words. We each took turns praying, and then I gave them cookies and milk and they fell asleep in five minutes."

Perri felt a wave of happiness roll over her. Of course, they'd be all right with Mitch. *Thank You, Father.* Why had she been so worried anyway?

"You still there, Seabrook?"

"I'm here, Mitch. I just thanked our Father in heaven for you—and finally realized the kids are all right with you."

"Of course they're all right with me. I had the best night I've had for years." After a short silence he spoke again. "One more thing. Uh—I really shouldn't tell you this, but I have to. You have to promise never to tell a soul."

"What did they do?"

"Well, I'd just about fallen asleep when someone crawled into my bed."

Perri nodded. "Uh-huh. That would be Scott."

"It turned out to be Judd. He slept with me. He seemed to be having bad dreams. I think he's had to grow up too fast and I intend to see that he gets a little extra attention from now on."

"Wow, I'm surprised. I see why it's secret. I guess I've always taken him a little for granted. Now you bring them home the minute you get tired."

Perri felt only half alive with her three boys gone. She hoped she'd hear from Mitch that evening but he didn't call. She called him at nine o'clock. "Are they homesick yet?" she asked.

He chuckled. "Not that I noticed. We had a picnic at Skinner's Butte Park. You know, where the toys are. Well, I wanted to invite you and Tad but they nixed it. Afraid they'd have to go home."

She slept with Tad again, needing to be with her last child.

She managed to keep busy the next few days and Mitch called in the mornings from work to report things were going better than well.

Thursday Perri wondered how she'd wait until the next afternoon to see her four boys. Yes, four. She'd missed them all so badly she could hardly stand it.

Late that afternoon, responding to the bell, she threw open the door and they mobbed her, all of them hugging and kissing her at the same time. "Well, it looks as though you're glad to be home," she said, choking back tears.

"We aren't home, Mommy," Judd said importantly. "We're here to invite you to a barbecue."

Perri's eyes flew to Mitch's. He nodded. "I have corn in the husk, potatoes cleaned and in aluminum foil, burgers, and hot dogs. Watermelon for dessert. How does that sound?"

"Fantastic. Let me check and see if Mom will keep Tad."

"No!" Hugh yelled. "He's supposed to come."

"How about Mother and me?" Dad asked, walking into the room.

The boys didn't stop telling about their incredible new life until the food disappeared. Perri couldn't stop looking at them all. They looked so happy and cared for that she doubted they'd missed her at all. At seven o'clock Mitch looked at his watch. "Sorry," he announced with a happy twinkle, "but I have to get my kids bathed and in bed. They go to school, you know."

He left the kids in the car while he walked Perri to the door. "This is the only part I don't like about our arrangement. I miss you like crazy." He kissed her lightly and ran down the steps. "Otherwise, I love it, and hope it never ends," he called back.

"We could have some time this weekend," Perri yelled.

Mitch spent the weekend at the Roman house and attended their little church with them. "I want to be baptized as soon as possible," he said at lunch. "I want the whole world to know He's my Savior." He reached across and took her hand. "I owe it all to you, love. What would you think of me being baptized in the little church out here? I felt close to Him today."

The thought of Mitch being baptized enthralled Perri, especially him being baptized in the same church she'd been.

Sunday afternoon Mitch and Perri drove to the coast to be alone for a few hours. She felt warmth and security cuddling in his arms to watch the sun dip into the sparkling Pacific.

"Happy?" Mitch asked, holding her gently.

"I've never been so happy." She squeezed closer under his arm. Then a small cloud hovered in her horizon. "But are you sure about the boys? Four days is hardly a lifetime. Do you think you could handle them forever?"

"I don't want to ever be away from them again," he answered huskily. "In fact I want to adopt them as soon as possible."

"I don't know about that, Mitch. It might mess up their Social Security."

Mitch shoved her back so he could look into her eyes. "You still don't get it do you, Seabrook? Forget the Social Security. I want to support my own kids. Now, are you ready to set a date for our marriage?"

"I'm ready," she answered, her heart so full she felt she couldn't hold all her blessings. *You'd like him, Jerry,* she whispered silently. *You'd want him to be a father to our boys, I know you would.* After a moment she added a final loving *good-bye.* "How about two weeks from today?" she said out loud.

He pulled her into his arms and the kiss they shared was neither light nor quickly over. She felt herself spinning off into space when Mitch pushed her away and started the car.

"What's the matter? Did I do something?"

He winked at her and pulled out of the park and back onto Route F. "You didn't, Seabrook, but I almost did. I'll have to drive like crazy to get my kids into bed by eight."

Perri's joy made her breathless. "I love you, Mitch," she whispered.

"How about one week?" he asked taking a mountain curve as quickly as he dared.

"One week? One week? Oh, you mean we should be married in one week." She shook her blond curls and laughed. "Two weeks isn't much time, Mitch. It'll be gone before you know it. Give me two weeks, okay?"

A resigned look crossed his face. "Two weeks from today, and don't you forget it."

"I'll be there. Scout's honor."

≈

Perri and Mitch talked on the phone each day. One of his favorite topics was how Jesus loved him enough to die on the cross for his sins. His, Mitchell Winfield's. "You once told me He loves me more than any earthly father and mother ever loves their child," he said, awe in his voice. "Now I know He really does."

Thursday afternoon he called with an excited tone in his voice. "I'm coming out right away," he said, "and I won't be alone."

Perri waited anxiously. Who would Mitch bring? She opened the door to discover the fire chief and the inspector with him. Disappointment nearly clogged her throat, but she invited them in.

When they all sat down, the fire inspector spoke. "We've finished our investigation, Mrs. Seabrook, and felt you'd like to hear our conclusions."

She nodded and tried her best to smile.

The burly man leaned forward, his steely eyes looking almost pleasant. "I owe a lot to this young man." He glanced at Mitch. "We'd never have solved the case without him. First he mentioned two people he felt could possibly have started the fire in revenge. Brock Winfield and Rob Kingston. When they checked out clean, he fingered the real perpetrator—Trish Trenton."

"Trish! Why would she do a thing like that?"

Mitch took her hand. "She's the one who sidetracked your insurance papers, Perri, even your own homeowner's policy."

"But why? She was my only friend in the office. And a person would have to be really mad to do something that could kill someone."

"Come to find out, she had an insane crush on Winfield," Mullen explained. "Although I can't understand how anyone could fall for that mug."

"I can," Perri murmured, "but please go on."

"If you remember, she spurned your friendship after you and Winfield became a thing."

Mitch shook his head as though the whole thing were unbelievable. "At first she tried to get you fired. Then she took the stronger approach. She probably didn't intend to kill anyone, but she certainly knew your house wasn't insured. In fact, ditching the policy probably gave her the idea to burn it."

"She'll spend some time incarcerated," Mullen said. He stood up and turned to the other two men. "Ready to go, gentlemen?" At the door he turned to Perri. "Sorry I came down on your kids so hard, Mrs. Seabrook. I sure thought they did it."

"They could have," Perri said.

"Yeah," Mitch added. "No one's perfect. Not even our boys."

❧

The following days flew by in a beautiful haze. Perri made all the preparations for her small wedding as if it were tomorrow's rainbow in which she dared not quite believe.

Mitch took her often to Fern Ridge Lake, though the Corps of Engineers was draining the large lake now for winter flood control.

"It'll always be a magical place for us," Mitch and Perri agreed, as they made plans to build a home on the lake the following summer.

Mitch got so busy at the office, trying to get along without Perri and also Trish, he barely had time to call her.

"Let me come into the office and help," Perri pleaded.

"No way, Seabrook. You get ready for this wedding. Afterwards—we'll see. If you really want to make your mark in the business world, you're welcome. Otherwise, you can just enjoy being a mother—and wife."

Perri thought her dreams complete when Mitch informed her that the insurance company had agreed to cover her fire, as it had occurred between the writing of the policy and its arrival at their office.

As they sat one evening aboard his gently rocking boat, Mitch wrapped his arms around her so tightly she could barely breathe. Her heart bubbled over with happiness.

He nibbled on her cheek and neck. He kissed her ear, making her giggle. Then they looked into each other's eyes, and they both grew serious. "Remember when you told me once that the kind of love God wants between a man and a woman, a committed love that will last for life, was a rainbow you were willing to wait for?"

She nodded, and he continued, "Well, I'm glad you made me wait until our wedding for our own rainbow. It's going to be much more special this way." He stopped, took a couple of breaths, then whispered, "I'm even more thankful God brought us together. Did you know He did? I'm positive He did. In fact, I think He told me so. And one more thing—do you think we could manage one more, Seabrook? I have this crazy desire to see what kind of kid God will give *us*. What do you say. Shall we go for five?"

Perri's kiss was her answer.

A Letter To Our Readers

Dear Reader:

In order that we might better contribute to your reading enjoyment, we would appreciate your taking a few minutes to respond to the following questions. When completed, please return to the following:

Rebecca Germany, Managing Editor
Heartsong Presents
P.O. Box 719
Uhrichsville, Ohio 44683

1. Did you enjoy reading *Tomorrow's Rainbow*?
   ❏ Very much. I would like to see more books
      by this author!
   ❏ Moderately
      I would have enjoyed it more if _____

   _____

2. Are you a member of **Heartsong Presents**? ❏Yes ❏No
   If no, where did you purchase this book?_____

   _____

3. What influenced your decision to purchase this
   book? (Check those that apply.)

   ❏ Cover   ❏ Back cover copy

   ❏ Title   ❏ Friends

   ❏ Publicity   ❏ Other_____

4. How would you rate, on a scale from 1 (poor) to 5
   (superior), the cover design?_____

5. On a scale from 1 (poor) to 10 (superior), please rate the following elements.

___Heroine   ___Plot

___Hero   ___Inspirational theme

___Setting   ___Secondary characters

6. What settings would you like to see covered in **Heartsong Presents** books?_____

_____

_____

7. What are some inspirational themes you would like to see treated in future books?_____

_____

_____

8. Would you be interested in reading other **Heartsong Presents** titles?   ❑ Yes   ❑ No

9. Please check your age range:
   ❑ Under 18   ❑ 18-24   ❑ 25-34
   ❑ 35-45   ❑ 46-55   ❑ Over 55

10. How many hours per week do you read? _____

Name _____

Occupation _____

Address _____

City_____ State_____ Zip_____

101 Ways to Say "I Love You"

How do you say I love you? By sending love notes via overnight delivery. . .by watching the sunrise together. . . by calling in "well" and spending the day together. . .by sharing a candlelight dinner on the beach. . .by praying for the man or woman God has chosen just for you.

When you've found *the one*, you can't do without *one hundred and one ways* to tell them exactly how you feel. Priced to be the perfect subsitute for a birthday card or love note, this book fits neatly into a regular envelope. Buy a bunch and start giving today!

Specially Priced!
Buy 10 for only $9.97!
or 5 for only $4.97!

48 pages, Paperbound, 3½" x 5½"

Send to: Heartsong Presents Reader's Service
P.O. Box 719
Uhrichsville, Ohio 44683

Please send me _____ copies of *101 Ways to Say "I Love You."* I am enclosing $_____ (please add $1.00 to cover postage and handling per order. OH add 6.25% tax. NJ add 6% tax.). Send check or money order, no cash or C.O.D.s, please. **To place a credit card order, call 1-800-847-8270.**

NAME _____

ADDRESS _____

CITY/STATE _____ ZIP _____

Presents

Hearts♥ng Presents
Love Stories Are Rated G!

That's for godly, gratifying, and of course, great! If you love a thrilling love story, but don't appreciate the sordidness of some popular paperback romances, **Heartsong Presents** is for you. In fact, **Heartsong Presents** is the *only inspirational romance book club*, the only one featuring love stories where Christian faith is the primary ingredient in a marriage relationship.

Sign up today to receive your first set of four, never before published Christian romances. Send no money now; you will receive a bill with the first shipment. You may cancel at any time without obligation, and if you aren't completely satisfied with any selection, you may return the books for an immediate refund!

Imagine. . .four new romances every four weeks—two historical, two contemporary—with men and women like you who long to meet the one God has chosen as the love of their lives. . .all for the low price of $9.97 postpaid.

To join, simply complete the coupon below and mail to the address provided. **Heartsong Presents** romances are rated G for another reason: They'll arrive *Godspeed!*

UNDER WESTERN EYES

JOSEPH CONRAD (originally Konrad Korzeniowski) was born in Russian Poland in 1857, and passed his childhood in the shadow of revolution. His parents died when he was quite young. At the age of seventeen he went to Marseilles to become an apprentice in the merchant marine. This began a long period of adventure at sea, Conrad having his share of hardship, shipwreck and other accidents. He became a British subject in 1886. In 1889, at the age of thirty-one, he came to London for a rest after fifteen years at sea. On this short London holiday he began writing a sea novel, *Almayer's Folly* destined to be the first of a long series of novels and stories inspired by his experiences at sea. Some of these, together with his three great novels of revolution and anarchism, *The Secret Agent*, *Under Western Eyes* and *Nostromo*, firmly placed him in the front rank of English literature He died in 1924.

BORIS FORD is the General Editor of the *New Pelican Guide to English Literature* which, in its original form, was launched in 1957. At that time he was Chief Editor and later Director of the Bureau of Current Affairs until it closed down in 1951. After a spell on the Secretariat of the United Nations in New York and Geneva, he became Editor of the *Journal of Education*, and also first Head of Schools Broadcasting with ITV.

Following a period as Education Secretary at the Cambridge University Press, Boris Ford, until he retired in 1982, was Professor of Education at the universities of Sheffield, Bristol and Sussex – where he was also Dean of the School of Cultural and Community Studies. From 1955 to 1986 he edited *Universities Quarterly*. He is now working on a series of inter-disciplinary volumes, *A Guide to the Arts in Britain*.

JOSEPH CONRAD

UNDER
WESTERN EYES

With an Introduction and Notes
by Boris Ford

PENGUIN BOOKS

Penguin Books Ltd, Harmondsworth, Middlesex, England
Viking Penguin Inc., 40 West 23rd Street, New York, New York 10010, U.S.A.
Penguin Books Australia Ltd, Ringwood, Victoria, Australia
Penguin Books Canada Limited, 2801 John Street, Markham, Ontario, Canada L3R 1B4
Penguin Books (N.Z.) Ltd, 182–190 Wairau Road, Auckland 10, New Zealand

First published in Great Britain by Methuen 1911
First published in the U.S.A. by Harper & Brothers 1911
Published in Penguin Books in Great Britain by
arrangement with the Trustees of the Joseph Conrad Estate and
J. M. Dent & Sons Ltd 1957
Published in Penguin Books in the U.S.A. by arrangement
with Doubleday & Company, Inc. 1979
Published in Penguin Classics 1985
Reprinted 1986

Made and printed in Great Britain by
Richard Clay (The Chaucer Press) Ltd,
Bungay, Suffolk
Filmset in 9/11pt Monophoto Photina by
Northumberland Press Ltd, Gateshead
Tyne and Wear

CONTENTS

Introduction by Boris Ford
    Conrad and *Under Western Eyes*   7
    The Themes and Structure of the Novel   22
Select Bibliography   48

Author's Note   49

UNDER WESTERN EYES   53

Notes   350

INTRODUCTION

Conrad and *Under Western Eyes*

'The state of worry in which I am living – and writing – is simply indescribable. It's a constant breaking strain.' In this letter to his friend John Galsworthy, written from Montpellier in May 1907, Conrad goes on to describe how

> It seems to me I have a lump of mud, of slack mud, in my head ... The nervous collapse is considerable. Can't react somehow. I drag about with an arm in a sling, hopeless, spiritless, without a single thought in my head. Borys is coughing a lot and I avow that the sound robs me of the last vestiges of composure.[1]

The Conrads had grounds for distress at this period: Conrad himself suffering a severe attack of gout; his wife Jessie 'cruelly crippled by her leg': and the two boys, Borys aged nine and Jack (named after Galsworthy) still not one, both down with whooping cough. In desperation they moved for the spring to Switzerland and Conrad decided that they should return to Champel, near Geneva, both for its water cure and because he had stayed and worked there before. And it was while they were here that Conrad remembered 'something told me by a man whom I met in Geneva many years ago'.[2] That 'something', and also 'the rubbishy character of stories about Russian revolutionists published in magazines', prompted Conrad to write the novel which he published three years later and which, much of it set in Geneva, he was to call *Under Western Eyes*.

Though nearly fifty, Conrad had published his first novel, *Almayer's Folly*, only twelve years earlier. There had followed, year by year, virtually all the novels and tales linked to the sea and the

7

East which established his reputation as 'a Polish *szlachcic** cased in British tar', as he put it to a fellow countryman. But if they had established his reputation as one of the most compelling and distinctive of contemporary writers, they had not brought him financial success – as he said, 'I was a loss to the Firm' (Blackwood) which published him. Even his visit to Switzerland had to be financed by his literary agent, James B. Pinker. The two novels he had published in the previous three years, *Nostromo* and *The Secret Agent*, which marked such a decisive new development and of which he had such great hopes, were distressing failures, above all financially. As he wrote to the ever-sympathetic Galsworthy about the 'honourable failure' of *The Secret Agent*, 'I own that I am cast down. I suppose I am a fool to have expected anything else. I suppose there is something in me that is unsympathetic to the general public.' And he concluded that this must be his 'foreignness'. It was the novel on which he was now fitfully and laboriously engaged. *Chance*, that was to make him his first modest fortune; and ironically he set this aside for six years in order to write *Under Western Eyes*, which sold even fewer copies than *The Secret Agent*.

The Secret Agent was to have been the third of a group of stories which he began at the end of 1905. The first two, 'produced hastily, carelessly, in a temper of desperation', were entitled *The Informer* and *An Anarchist*. The third, which he envisaged as a 'longish story' and which he started the following year, amid the elegant comforts of Le Peyrou Gardens in Montpellier, was also to be devoted to the theme of militant international anarchy and was entitled *Verloc*. It is hardly surprising that Conrad made very slow progress with this third tale. To Pinker he wrote,

> The conduct of such a story requires no small amount of meditation – not upon questions of style and so on – but simply upon what is fit or unfit to be said. It is easy with a subject like this to produce a totally false impression. Moreover the thing has got to be *kept up as a story* with an ironic intention but a dramatic development.'

That was the novelist's way of putting it. In truth, keeping up *Verloc* as a story must have involved Conrad in a depth of meditation that drew on his earliest boyhood memories, growing up as a Pole

*Land-owning aristocrat.

exiled in Russia. But at the time, as the story protracted itself steadily
if painfully into a full-length novel, 'Conrad kept silent about his
sources and obstinately repudiated not only any political, social or
philosophical motives but even any desire to present the anarchists
in a satirical light.'⁴ However that may, *The Secret Agent* had a
mordant intensity and energy that confirmed the impression that
Conrad was now tapping a new source of inspiration. And so,
apparently, it seemed to him: '... nobody who was "aware" of my
literary existence expected anything like *The Secret Agent*', he wrote
to Pinker early in the new year;⁵ and he went on: 'Well there is more
– and different things too – in me yet.' Different; and yet not so very
different, as he shifted his ironic gaze from the 'Sham' revolutionaries
in the London of *The Secret Agent* to the 'apes of a sinister jungle'
in the Geneva and Russia of *Under Western Eyes*.

He was now writing from England. On returning from Europe, the
Conrads had moved from Pent House, their small rat-infested house
in Kent, with Henry James for a near neighbour, to Bedford, into
'a farmhouse of a rather cosy sort without distinction of any kind,
but quite 500ft above the sea – which is what we both want. Its
name is Someries.'⁶ In the letter to Pinker he had described what
these 'different things' seemed likely to be. He had launched into a
new short story and, though 'a more difficult job than I thought',
it was to be finished within a few weeks. Entitled *Razumov*, his story
was to be 'a contribution to and a reading of the Russian character
... the very essence of things Russian. Not the mere outward
manners and customs but the Russian feeling and thought ... It is
also characteristic of the present time. Nothing of the sort has been
done in English.' And then, offering the opinion that 'the story *is*
effective', he added: 'The subject has long haunted me'. perhaps,
indeed, since his first visit many years before to Champel. Only the
previous day he had written a long letter to Galsworthy, in which he
provides for the first time a glimpse of this story of which he is
already so optimistic:

> I think that I am trying to capture the very soul of things Russian – *Cosas
> de Russia*. It is not an easy work but it may be rather good when it's done ...
> Listen to the theme. The Student Razumov (a natural son of a Prince K.)
> gives up secretly to the police his fellow student, Haldin, who seeks refuge

in his rooms after committing a political crime (supposed to be the murder of de Plehve). First movement in St Petersburg. (Haldin is hanged, of course.)

2nd in Genève. The Student Razumov meeting abroad the mother and sister of Haldin falls in love with that last, marries her, and, after a time, confesses to her the part he played in the arrest of her brother.

The psychological developments leading to Razumov's betrayal of Haldin, to the confession of the fact to his wife and to the death of these people (brought about mainly by the resemblance of their child to the late Haldin), form the real subject of the story.[7]

'And perhaps,' he added, characteristically, 'no magazine will touch it.'

It was in Someries – so Jessie Conrad related in her memoirs *Joseph Conrad As I Knew Him* – that Conrad wrote 'almost all the whole first part of *Under Western Eyes* – the only book which, from a few words which he dropped at different times, I think he regretted having begun at all.' Suffering with his vulnerable health and assailed by his recurrent depressions, Conrad found that he was making slower progress with his story than he had hoped, and that it steadily stretched itself out into novel length. Yet if the impression we have of him at this time is a sombre one (and both he and Jessie were, in their different ways, somewhat unreliable witnesses), Najder reminds us that he continued, in his unfailingly courteous way, to receive guests and visit them, often in London. One of these was an American journalist, Archibald Marshall, who subsequently wrote that

Conrad ... made the deepest impression upon me. His magnificent head, surely one of the handsomest that was ever set on a pair of shoulders, if you are to take into account what a face reflects of the spirit that enlightens it, his dignity, austerity, kindness of heart, even his irritabilities, made him an unforgettable figure. I had no personal experience of those irritabilities, but used to hear enough about them, and they all seemed part of him, for nobody ever took his work as a writer more to heart than he did, and it was because he almost agonized over it that little outside impingements upon his brain annoyed him, like midge bites.[8]

Najder quotes also a reporter who interviewed Conrad:

He is abnormally highly-strung. He is sensitive, intensely susceptible to any slight jarring from outside. His nerves seem to be all on end ... He dislikes certain broad types of people virulently, and says so in a downright fashion. At such times he sloughs his elaborately courteous demeanour he reveals himself as a man of devastating force of character. He grows fierce, passionate violent ... triumphant and obliterating and sweeping away his calculated suavity of speech.[9]

Their portraits complement each other. They are not, as Conrad himself might have hoped, portraits of a Kentish or Bedfordshire gentleman-writer, but of a European Polish 'nobleman' returning, once again, to the political struggles which had surrounded his childhood; and now, nearly a half-century later, engaged in 'earnest meditation' about how 'to strike and sustain [in his new story] the note of scrupulous impartiality' as between 'senseless desperation' and the 'senseless tyranny' which had 'provoked' it.[10]

The Poland in which Konrad Korzeniowski (Joseph Conrad was, of course, his pen name) was born on 3 December 1857 was a country of fiercely liberal sentiments which, sixty years earlier, had been carved up between Russia in the east, Prussia in the west, and the Austrian Empire in the south. Only a comparatively small territory, known as the Kingdom of Poland, remained. As Najder, himself Polish, recounts in his biography of Conrad:

The long years of foreign occupation which followed 1795 were broken at least once in every generation by an insurrection, directed mainly against the most severe oppressor, Russia. The Polish tradition of patriotic conspiracies was almost uninterrupted, and it strengthened the social and cultural role of the heroic virtues of duty, fidelity, and honor. Polish literature took over the functions of suppressed national institutions, and volumes of forbidden poems and dramas were widely circulated, often in handwritten copies, continually reminding their readers of Poland's past glory and their duty to restore the country's independence. In the first half of the nineteenth century many Polish leaders, virtually all of them of *szlachta* origin, coupled demands for national independence with advocacy of democratic political reforms. And as the exhortations to do one's patriotic duty were addressed not only to the traditional arms-bearing class of the *szlachta* but to all inhabitants of the former commonwealth, there followed a peculiar 'democratization' of chivalric ideals: the honor of serving one's country was no longer restricted to the privileged.[11]

Conrad was born in a part of the Ukraine annexed to Russia; and though it had been Polish for 400 years, less than 5 per cent of the population was now Polish. Thus Conrad was born an exile, 'with a profound fear of Russian autocratic power in his blood', as Morton Zabel puts it. For his father, Apollo Korzeniowski, of a *szlachta* family of only modest means, was a poet of strongly radical views and, increasingly, of political activities on behalf of the Polish national cause. Apollo celebrated his son's birth with a poem 'To My Son Born in the 85th Year of Muscovite Oppression'. It begins as a lullaby,

> Baby son, sleep in peace.

but continues as a lament:

> Baby son, tell yourself
> You are without land, without love,
> Without country, without people,
> While Poland – your Mother is entombed.[12]

When Conrad was four, he and his parents moved to Warsaw in the Kingdom of Poland, and here Apollo, now a leading activist, helped to set up the underground Committee of the Movement, which met in his flat. Within days he was in prison and shortly afterwards he and his wife were sentenced to deportation to Vologda, a remote province of Russia, which Apollo described as a 'huge quagmire': 'A winter here has two seasons: white winter and green winter.' He had brought with him from Warsaw a handful of Polish soil, to be strewn after his death over his eyes and heart so that they at least would not be buried in Russian earth.

The following year they received news that the long-planned insurrection had broken out and had been defeated, and that four of Conrad's uncles had been killed or imprisoned. The Korzeni-owskis had now been moved to the milder conditions of the north-east Ukraine. Here Apollo was able to work, translating Dickens and Shakespeare and Hugo to earn his living. But his wife Ewa could not survive the hardships they had suffered and in 1865 she died of consumption. Conrad remained reticent about his mother. In his *A Personal Record* he only mentions the time, his sixth year, in which he begins in retrospect 'to remember my mother with more distinct-ness than a mere loving, wide-browed, silent, protecting presence, whose eyes had a sort of commanding sweetness'. (In *Under Western Eyes*, as in the very title of the novel, Conrad seems to perceive and identify most of his characters through the expression of their eyes.)

So Conrad lived in exile with his deeply grieving father, now sick with tuberculosis. As Apollo wrote at this time to a friend, 'Poor child: he does not know what a contemporary playmate is: he looks at the decrepitude of my sadness, and who knows if that sight does not make his young heart wrinkled or his awakening soul grizzled.'[13] Najder recounts that the 'poor child' seems to have spent most of his early years reading Shakespeare and Polish romantic poetry. And gradually, according to Apollo, 'he begins to look very much like his mother'. But the boy's health seems to have suffered. He was constantly ill. There was mention of kidney trouble, and then of epileptic fits, which Najder assumes were psychosomatic, 'brought on by painful experiences'. Ill health, whether psychosomatic or not, was to dog him for the rest of his life.

In 1867 Apollo and his son were given permission to leave Russia and they moved to Lwow in the Austrian part of Poland. But though everyday life must have become far easier for them, Apollo now found himself assailed by guilt and frustration: guilt for having abandoned his fellow countrymen, and frustration at the lack of revolutionary zeal he found among his countrymen in the west. Najder perceives in him at this time 'the indignation of an idealist and the resignation of dying'. Indeed, he died two years later, 'mortally weary – a vanquished man', Conrad wrote many years after. To the twelve-year-old boy Apollo left

... a formidable psychological legacy: an exceptionally intense emotional life; a rigorous and desperate love of his country, and a spontaneous, instinctive belief in democracy; a hatred of the invaders, particularly Russians; inflexible principles that clashed with his volatile moods; a peculiar approach to life's practical problems that was not based on cool perception but consisted rather of absorbing them as if with sudden spasms of his heart, and viewing them always in the light of ultimate aims; a great love of romantic literature; a solitariness imposed by intractable circumstance; and the bitterness of shattered hopes.[14]

For the next few years Conrad lived under the guardianship of his maternal grandmother and his uncle, Tadeusz Bobrowski.

Bobrowski had little sympathy for either the romantic spirits or the
political ardour of Apollo. He attended to Conrad's education, which
had been at best lop-sided, worried about his health, and reminded
him regularly to try to be 'useful, hard-working, capable and therefore a worthy human being', as he put it in a letter to Conrad shortly
after Apollo's death. Whatever the effects of these injunctions on the
rather enigmatic boy, Conrad suddenly decided at the age of fifteen
to become a sailor. And so, two years later, without having finished
his schooling, he left his adopted home for Marseilles. Contrary to
the many psychological speculations which have been advanced to
explain Conrad's decision to change the course of his life so radic-
ally, Najder insists:

There is no shred of evidence that he or anyone from his immediate circle
regarded the departure to France as a severing of national ties; his uncle
would have considered such an argument as absurd, and in fact Conrad
never dreamt of escaping from European culture. We have to remember that
at the time Poland did not exist on the political map and going abroad for
study, work, or general experience was natural for thousands of young Poles
of a *szlachta* or middle-class background.[15]

What is far more to the point is to ask, as Zabel does, what inheritance the young man took with him to his new life in France:

Thus Conrad brought into his early manhood two strains of his native
inheritance – the patriotic and nationalistic ardor of his father's nature and
the more conservative 'land-tilling gentry' temper of his mother's people, the
Bobrowskis. And while he was to become confirmed in the conservative
leanings of his mother's family, now represented by his uncle Tadeusz
Bobrowski who soon took over the guardianship of the young Conrad, he
carried into his mature life a divided allegiance. One side of his nature was
ardent, excitable, strenuous, adventurous, self-willed, and haunted by the
memory of his father's and his country's dedication – it was the side that
led to his first youthful ventures of bravado, Carlist enthusiasm, amateur
seamanship, and reckless living in France and Spain between 1874 and
1878. The other side of his character was incurably committed to caution
and doubt, a somber pessimism, fearing violence, fanaticism, anarchy and
Slavic instability, all of them symptoms of the autocratic or revolutionary
extremism which both Russia and the Polish nationalist enthusiasm came
to represent in his mind, and which eventually led him to seek his future

in western Europe and finally in the 'sanity and method' of England and her Merchant Service ... Apollo Korzeniowski and Tadeusz Bobrowski conditioned in him a moral character whose divided temper and conflicts of emotion were to remain with him for life.[16]

It was only after the long years in the Merchant Navy, after the solidarities and fidelities of these minute communities at sea, and after the years when, as a writer, he worked over and through these experiences, that Conrad was able to return to the isolation and despair of his childhood years in exile: to meditate on the senseless desperation provoked by senseless tyranny which is one of the major themes in *Under Western Eyes*.

In fact Conrad had returned to these political questions some three years earlier with his essay 'Autocracy and War', first published in the *Fortnightly Review*. This long essay reveals Conrad as profoundly concerned with and disturbed by political developments in Europe, and in particular Russia and Prussia. Writing in 1905, in the year of the Russo-Japanese war and of the abortive revolution, Conrad foresaw the collapse of Russian autocracy in revolution and the danger of Germany's imperialist, vulture-like ambitions. 'Autocracy and War' is notable for its comprehensive denunciation of 'a country held by an evil spell' whose 'worst crime against humanity' is 'the ruthless destruction of innumerable minds': 'from the very inception of her being the brutal destruction of dignity, of truth, of rectitude, of all that is faithful in human nature has been made the imperative condition of her existence.' Through 'the extirpation of every intellectual hope', Conrad saw that the only way out for the Russian people lay in revolution, 'a word of dread as much as of hope'. But he believed gloomily that 'it can never be a revolution fruitful of moral consequences to mankind. It cannot be anything else but a rising of slaves.'

If these were his deeply felt beliefs about Russia, it is perhaps hardly surprising that he continued to make very slow progress with his new novel – for *Razumov* had now grown beyond the scope and scale of a short story. What must also have distracted him was his agreement to write his reminiscences for the *English Review*. Though these reminiscences (later to be published as *A Personal Record*) are predominantly anecdotal and concentrate far more on his uncle Bobrowski than on himself, Conrad claimed that he was 'presenting faithfully the feelings and sensations connected with the writing of my first book and with my first contact with the sea'. Conrad's biographer Baines believes that these were not only the two most important events in Conrad's life but also, because he had been charged with a want of patriotism for leaving Poland, the events

about which he was particularly sensitive because they were bound up with his personal honour. Although honour and dishonour, in their particular aspects of fidelity and betrayal, were constantly recurring themes throughout Conrad's work, it is clear from *Under Western Eyes* and 'The Secret Sharer' that he was specially concerned with them at this time. It is thus not surprising to find that much of *A Personal Record* reads like an *apologia pro vita sua*.[17]

'The Secret Sharer', though quintessentially a Conradian sea story, is strongly linked to *Under Western Eyes* not only, as Baines says, in its preoccupation with fidelity and betrayal but in the very heart of its story. Having killed an insubordinate member of the crew at a critical moment during a storm, the mate Leggatt makes the captain of the ship to which he escapes his 'secret sharer' in his crime and in his further escape to freedom. Unlike the young captain, Razumov tries to deny his secret share in Haldin's fate. But as for Razumov's fate, Conrad was still struggling to bring his novel to a conclusion. The Conrads had now left Someries and returned to Kent, where they lived in a few rooms above a butcher's shop, complete with slaughter house: Conrad's study was a windowless cubicle. Moreover, his gout was particularly troublesome and kept him in bed for much of the first half of 1909, with Jessie doing her uncomplaining best, in spite of her painful knee, to look after him. 'If it wasn't for dear Jess – well I don't know,' he wrote to Galsworthy at the end of the year. At last, by the end of that year, *Under Western Eyes* was finished.

In her book, *Joseph Conrad As I Knew Him*, Jessie Conrad recounts the drama which immediately ensued:

Under Western Eyes was, as it were, the kernel of many happenings. The day Conrad took the pile of manuscript to London marked the beginning of

much misfortune, and was attended by three worrying little episodes. He
started to drive the two miles to the station with our old gardener in a tiny
governess-car. Exasperated and terribly irritable, he drove carelessly over a
bump in the road and broke a spring in the cart; not realizing his nervous
strength, he sat in a big arm-chair at his publishers and forced the back out
of it; and he ended the day by pushing the foot out of the bed in which he
slept that night. This excess of nervous strength brought its usual consequences, added to the fact that in his exasperation he had managed to
quarrel violently, and seriously, with a very old and tried friend. That night
was a very disturbed one, and the next morning it was very plain that
something much more serious was wrong than a passing attack of gout. My
husband's voice, as he gave directions for a doctor to be called at once,
alarmed me by its strangeness, particularly as only a moment before he had
forbidden me to send for our medical man. I followed him into a tiny room
on the top of the stairs, where he had thrown himself on a narrow bed, with
not a little apprehension. Clearly he was very ill, and it behoved me not to
allow my alarm to appear in my face. This was the time for rapid action.
The doctor – he happened not to be the man we usually had, but his partner
– refused to take the responsibility of removing the invalid to another room.
His temperature was very high, but instinct told me I must act at once.
Accordingly I had a bed put in the largest room, where so much of the book
had been written, protected the narrow wooden sides of the fireplace with
some slabs of slate, and with the aid of two farm-labourers carried him into
it. Then began weeks of nursing and anxiety. As usual he rambled all the
time in his native tongue, except when he repeated over and over the Burial
Service, while the bell in the church a few yards away tolled for the passing
of some other troubled soul.[18]

As may be imagined, there has been much speculation about this
severe collapse, from which Conrad did not fully recover for some
four or five months. But it seems to be agreed that his physical
ailments and his depression were greatly aggravated by his inner
struggle with the material of the novel he had at last managed to
complete. There was the natural strain of re-entering, over a long
period, the despotic world he had left as a boy. But there was the
even greater and more complex strain of finding the treatment and
tone which would enable him 'to strike and sustain the note of
scrupulous impartiality' in relation to events about which he felt so
deeply. As he expressed it in his Author's Note, 'I had never been
called before to a greater effort of detachment: detachment from all

passions, prejudices and even from personal memories.' If he achieved a great measure of impartiality as between 'the ferocity and imbecility of an autocratic rule rejecting all legality and basing itself upon complete moral anarchism' on the one hand, and on the other, 'the no less imbecile and atrocious answer of a purely Utopian revolution encompassing destruction by the first means to hand', he certainly did not achieve 'detachment from all passions': or he achieved it only by transmuting them into a work of art. Certainly *Under Western Eyes* is one of the most intense and morally disturbing of Conrad's novels.

'There is the MS complete but uncorrected,' Jessie wrote;[19] 'and his fierce refusal to let even I touch it. It lays on the table at the foot of his bed and he lives mixed up in the scenes and holds converse with the characters.' A few months later, when he had pulled through the crisis, Conrad himself wrote in a letter,[20] 'I begin to see that the horrible nervous tension of the last two years (of which even my wife knows nothing) had to end in something of this sort.' And he added, 'Perhaps it was the only way of relief.' But by May of that year, 1910, he finished working on the manuscript, and Najder's analysis of the alterations he made is interesting:

Three kinds of changes are the most significant: elimination of critical remarks made by the Russians about England and the West generally, about the parliamentary 'tyranny of numbers' and the quiet but soulless life of societies governed democratically (as if the author had tried to adopt a more approving attitude toward the West); omission of all evidence that would betray his personal involvement with presented events; obscuration of the similarities between Razumov's dilemmas and the author's own perplexities.[21]

And so, at long last in December 1910, *Under Western Eyes* began publication in instalments in the *English Review* and simultaneously in the *North American Review*. And in October 1911 it was published as a book in England by Methuen, and in the USA by Harper. It did not sell particularly well: it was, no doubt, too sombre and pessimistic a work to match the relaxed Georgian mood of the public shortly before the war. Baines reports that the novel sold only 4,112 copies in its first two years, compared with 13,200 copies of *Chance* which came out a year later. (It is interesting to note that, in an average year, Penguin Books now sell about twice as many copies of *Under Western Eyes* as of *Chance*.)

Conrad found it hard to accept the notion that he might now be 'drifting unconsciously into the position of a writer for a limited coterie; a position which would have been odious to me as throwing doubt on the soundness of my belief in the solidarity of all mankind in simple ideas and in sincere emotions.'[22] But he had to admit that 'there is no denying the fact that *Under Western Eyes* found no favour in the public eye'.[23]

Yet, as Norman Sherry insists, most reviewers received the novel very favourably; at the least with very great respect. In his book, *Conrad: The Critical Heritage*, he gives lengthy extracts from contemporary reviews, from which the following brief extracts are culled:

Pall Mall Gazette: Keen and merciless in exposure and meticulously searching in analysis, *Under Western Eyes* is a psychological study of remarkable penetration, and, as a novel, is entitled to rank with the best work that Mr Joseph Conrad has given us ... The book startles one by its amazing truth and by the intimate knowledge of the human heart that it reveals in its varied and masterly characterization.

(This anonymous reviewer also saw fit to point out that Conrad 'still confuses the preterite with the perfect and often uses the wrong sign of the future'.)

Morning Post: *Under Western Eyes* is written with that intensity of vision, that complete absorption in and by the subject, and that astonishing mastery of the subtleties of language which have ever distinguished its author's best work. In addition it is constructed with greater ability ... He has never done anything better.

Westminster Gazette: There is the title ... with its suggestion that the Slav is not easily comprehensible to us, Teutons ... *Under Western Eyes* becomes an explanation of the works of Russian novelists; it helps us to understand Turgenev and Dostoyevsky with great clearness; it is a brilliantly successful effort to make the Russian comprehensible to the Westerner.

A number of other reviewers, including Edward Garnett (who with his wife Constance had translated the Russian novelists into English and established their reputation in this country), also referred to

Conrad's affinities with Turgenev and Dostoyevsky. This would have been very mixed praise to Conrad, for whom Turgenev was as superlatively great as Dostoyevsky was unbearable – 'he is too Russian for me'.

What upset Conrad more seriously were the suggestions that he wrote as a Slav; and many, more recent critics have tended to base their interpretations on this assumption. Conrad was a deeply patriotic Polish *szlachic* whose country had been carved up and subjugated by the Slav autocracy of Russia. The last few years had been his most Polish since coming to the West. He had written his reminiscences with their long accounts of his Polish relations. Towards the end of 1910 he had written the story 'Prince Roman', which Baines describes as his 'moving tribute to the ideals of honour, service, and patriotism of a Polish aristocrat', adding that 'its vibrant sincerity ... is an indication of how very firmly Conrad had remained a Pole throughout his wanderings'.[24] And if the Western eyes of his novel are, in a profound sense, much more Conrad's own Western eyes than the English professor's, they are the eyes of a Pole whose heritage and traditions looked to the West, as they were now the eyes of a European Englishman, albeit with an imperfect command of the future tense.

It only remains to recount that when Conrad had more or less recovered from his breakdown, the family moved once again. The story of the move is best told in Jessie's own words:

It was four months before I took Conrad for his first convalescent drive. *Under Western Eyes* had been out more than a month, and had, practically, no sale whatever. It was unfortunate, yet Conrad did not seem to care, and we seemed condemned for life to that six-roomed cottage, which had grown odious to both of us. But on that day our luck changed. As we drove along a familiar lane we passed a house we had known by sight for years. It had the appearance of being unoccupied; the gate of the drive was open. I was prompted to direct the driver to turn into it; the rustic caretaker thought there was no harm in us seeing it.

Conrad was much too weak to walk about, but he sat on the low window-sill of the room that was afterwards our dining-room, while I went all over the house. It was not big, although after the cottage it seemed palatial, and John found a great delight in shouting in the empty rooms. Conrad and I felt we must have this house.

The caretaker, pocketing my half-crown, assured us that it was impossible, as the owner was going to make a weekend cottage of it for himself. Still, the caretaker gave us his name and his London address. To make a long story short, with a rapidity that seemed like enchantment but was really the magic of human kindness, the house became ours on a yearly tenancy. I sent Conrad away to the care of a friend while I directed the move (only seven miles), and put every bit of furniture in its place according to a plan which I had already in my mind's eye. Then I wired to him to come home. As I watched him come along the platform of the railway station I thought how ghostlike he still looked. Next day after breakfast he walked, still shaky, into the room which combined the functions of drawing room and study, and wrote there the first pages of 'The Smile of Fortune'.

That auspicious title ushered in a period of happy activity and comparatively good health for him.[25]

This section of the introduction to *Under Western Eyes* has been primarily an account of how the novel came into being and of that part of Conrad's biography that contributes to an understanding of its themes. I have carefully not discussed the novel itself in the belief that very many readers of this Penguin edition will not have read the novel before and would therefore find such a discussion of themes and characters virtually meaningless. But there is another reason. *Under Western Eyes* is a tense and highly dramatic story, and Conrad shaped its structure with great care so as to control the tensions, the concealments and revelations, that constitute such a large element in its psychological effect. No one can read a novel for the first time more than once, and it would be quite wrong to spoil the impact of *Under Western Eyes* for them.

So the discussion of the novel which follows should not be read at this stage except by those who have already read the novel and know its story. Readers coming to the novel for the first time should postpone reading the discussion until afterwards.

The Themes and Structure of the Novel

At the conclusion of *Under Western Eyes*, most readers probably feel depleted, as Conrad himself felt depleted to the point of nervous and physical collapse. But at the same time the reader may also feel strangely elated. For this is a novel of great moral force entwined with its moments of physical violence. Councillor Mikulin's 'soft' question, '"Where to?"' has an uncanny familiarity as well as a menacing ambiguity. It feels to be as much a question that Conrad is putting to himself as one put to Razumov, as he turns his head at the door.

Under Western Eyes has not been generally regarded as one of Conrad's most assured successes. But that may be because it leaves the reader unassured and disturbed. Conrad is, of course, a master of ironic ambiguity, of the inscrutable and the incalculable. Partly he achieves this, in some of his novels and tales, through the use of multiple narrators who serve to mask his own attitude towards the story. This is certainly the case in *Under Western Eyes*, where there are many more narrators than the English professor of languages. As a result, Conrad's novels have given rise to a great volume of commentary and interpretation, and particularly they have offered scope to critics who start with a theoretical framework which enables them to 'know' what Conrad intended and what were his underlying preoccupations. For instance, Conrad's 'last works embrace Nietzschean realism and seek to reconcile a modified altruism with Nietzschean "egoism" ... his choice of subject seems dictated by Nietzsche's criticism of English and French "sociology" for knowing only "the decadent form of society"', writes John Saveson.[26] In fact, Saveson's study contains many illuminating

22

interpretations of Conrad's novels; as do Bernard Meyer's psycho-analytic biography and Irving Howe's political analysis of *The Secret Agent* and *Under Western Eyes* in his book *Politics and the Novel,* 'those terrible surveys of desolation' – Conrad remarked, without enthusiasm, that *Under Western Eyes* 'has become already a sort of historical novel' only by 'the mere force of circumstances'.

Under Western Eyes lends itself to such specialized interpretations even more than the majority of Conrad's novels because Russia, as he presents it, is such a vast, imponderable presence; the Slav enigma baffles the English professor, and it has baffled many critics and readers. Moreover, this novel, as described earlier in this Intro-duction, presented Conrad with unusual difficulties and worries of a personal character. His subsequent collapse testifies to the strain of going back in imagination to the years of his exiled childhood in Russia; to memories of that passionate rebel, his father, and the deaths and imprisonment of his uncles; and to the misty memory of his mother's death as a result of the severity of their ordeal. Going over these memories of such disturbing resonances and trying to achieve objectivity in his recreation of Russia and the revolutionary movements; trying to re-involve himself and yet hold himself aloof was as if to deny his father's commitment.

If the task of writing *Under Western Eyes* presented Conrad with 'a black wall of helplessness', it is only to be expected that the task of reading it has presented readers and critics with difficulties and disagreements. This is not, however, the place to summarize these multiple readings or to advance yet one more theoretical interpreta-tion; but rather to help the reader unravel the novel's complexities as one retraces it along its route.

Conrad was one of the most meticulous of novelists. Shakespeare, Turgenev, Flaubert and James were among the authors he most admired, authors who attended with the greatest care to each word on every page they wrote, and who also had in a rare degree the sculptor's ability to control and shape the work as a whole. This is the distinctive art of the great story-teller, and Conrad was one of the most accomplished.

Under Western Eyes began as a short tale, but it persisted in growing and growing as it was written. If that does not sound like the sculptor's art, which is steadily to pare down the wood or stone on which he is working, it seems in Conrad's case that this continual expansion of his original idea was accompanied by an uncanny eye for the balance, the proportions of the finished work. If the central theme of the novel is Razumov's tormenting journey towards self-knowledge, its dominating preoccupation is Russia and the Russian revolutionists. Thus the novel gives the impression of beginning and ending with Razumov in Russia. It begins with him as a student in St Petersburg, 'a tall, well-proportioned young man, quite unusually dark for a Russian from the Central Provinces. His good looks would have been unquestionable if it had not been for a peculiar lack of fineness in the features ... His manner, too, was good' (p. 57). And it ends with him dying 'in the south'; in 'a little two-roomed wooden house, in the suburb of some very small town, hiding within the high plank-fence of a yard overgrown with nettles. He was crippled, ill, getting weaker every day ...' (p. 347). In one sense this is an accurate recollection: the novel does begin and end with Razumov.

Yet just as Conrad altered the name of his story from *Razumov* to *Under Western Eyes*, so he was careful to place Razumov and Russia within the Western frame provided by the English professor in Geneva. Thus in fact the novel begins in Geneva with the outside observer, the professor, addressing himself to the reader: 'To begin with I wish to disclaim the possession of those high gifts of imagination and expression ...' And it ends in Geneva also, with the professor's account of Sophia Antonovna's farewell which seems to represent, in the same breath, *his* farewell to the reader.

The story, as recounted by the English professor in four parts, begins in St Petersburg; and the whole of the magnificently tense and yet controlled Part I is located in that Russian city. Conrad endows the story as a whole with an atmosphere of eerie fatality: it seems to progress inexorably through the sequence of its four parts from Razumov's student ambitions to his hopeless near-death. But it is interesting to recollect that the actual *time* sequence of the novel begins, not in St Petersburg, but in Geneva in Part II, six months earlier, when 'I made the acquaintance of these ladies ...

By "these ladies" I mean, of course, the mother and the sister of the unfortunate Haldin' (p. 131). The West is there first, and with it the Western eyes that are to observe these Russians and Russian happenings, though Conrad was dramatically right to present his story out of sequence. Indeed, the four parts do not, except for Parts II and III, progress sequentially, but with a backwards and forwards movement that can be best seen diagrammatically:

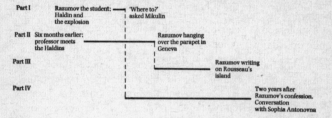

There is something aesthetically satisfying in the way Parts I and IV and Parts II and III are continuous, taking up at the point where the other ends. However, I think one should not make too much of the pattern revealed in the diagram, not least because Conrad constructed his story so adroitly, the joins and overlaps are so tidily executed, that the workmanship does not obtrude in this novel as it does, for instance, in *Chance*.

None the less, observing the shaping and sequencing of the four parts helps to explain the novel's claustrophobic intensity, for it reveals the way in which Parts II and IV encompass, embrace, earlier sequences that have already been recounted. In this way, they provide views from a different vantage-point which may have helped Conrad to achieve the objectivity he was so anxiously seeking. At the same time, by returning in Part II to the events surrounding the assassination and Haldin's arrest, Conrad is placing the reader in a privileged position, for unlike the people in Geneva the reader is already in the know; and Conrad fully exploits the ironies that this offers. On the other hand, it is not until Part IV, which returns to Councillor Mikulin's question and then recounts what ensued, that Conrad reveals to the reader the truth behind Razumov's presence in Geneva: he has come to spy on the revolutionists as a tool – or is it as an accomplice? – of Mikulin and General T—. As a result, the reader who knows about the assassination while reading Parts II and III, is simultaneously in ignorance and perplexity about Razumov's role in Geneva: and that sets up a cluster of very different and conflicting ironies.

Finally there are the subtleties which arise from the fact that the English professor reads Razumov's manuscript for the first time only towards the end of the novel, so that he is an *uninformed observer* for most of the time; above all he does not know of Razumov's betrayal of Haldin nor why he has come to Geneva. But he is, of course, an *informed story-teller*, for his story, when he eventually comes to write it, is largely based on Razumov's journal and confessions. This means that the English professor, who expresses himself puzzled by what is going on in Parts II and III, is actually being described by the professor who has read the facts in Razumov's manuscript in Part IV.

Part I: Confrontations

Writing his Author's Note some years later, Conrad described *Under Western Eyes* as 'an attempt to render not so much the political state as the psychology of Russia itself'; and he refers also to his concern to 'express imaginatively the general truth which underlies its action', which, he felt, 'could be reduced to the formula of senseless desperation provoked by senseless tyranny'. As novelist, Conrad's 'greatest anxiety was in being able to strike and sustain the note of scrupulous impartiality'. But speaking as individual, he could not restrain himself from describing the Russian situation in far more vehement terms: 'The ferocity and imbecility of an autocratic rule rejecting all legality and in fact basing itself upon complete moral anarchism provokes the no less imbecile and atrocious answer of a purely Utopian revolutionism encompassing destruction by the first means to hand ...' (Author's Note).

Conrad's triumph in this novel, and nowhere is this triumph more striking than in Part I, is to have succeeded in translating this political conflict into an imaginative drama embodying 'the aspect, the character, and the fate of the individuals' involved. It is a study of human conflict rather than of conflict between classes and vast national forces.

Yet these vast forces lie menacingly in the immediate background, and in the early pages of the novel Conrad rightly presents this background in powerful colours. The English professor speaks of 'the moral corruption of an oppressed society where the noblest aspirations of humanity ... are prostituted to the lusts of hate and fear' (p. 58), and it could be Conrad's voice we hear; just as the words of Haldin the conspirator sound as if they were uttered by Conrad's father, the poet Apollo, when he reminds Razumov of 'the sound of weeping and gnashing of teeth this man [Mr de P—] raised in the land ... Three more years of his work would have put us back fifty years into bondage' (p. 65). Not many hours later Razumov, however strongly he may wish to disassociate himself from the revolutionists, describes in his journal the 'vile den' where Ziemianitch may be found as 'an enormous slum, a hive of human vermin, a monumental abode of misery towering on the verge of starvation

27

and despair' (p. 75). These voices of protest from differing sources within the novel, and also in a ghostly fashion from without, speak in unison. But Russia itself, the vast mass of the people, seems to Razumov to be lying inert under the blanket of snow, and one's sense is of a blanket of apathy and impotence.

Then, for one sudden moment, the blanket is pierced by the two explosions with their 'terrific concentrated violence'. And simultaneously Razumov's blanket of industrious self-sufficiency is pierced by the strange figure in black who looms 'lithe and martial' in his lodging. This horribly startling confrontation with Victor Haldin is the first of the rapid sequence of confrontations that assail Razumov in the next few days, conflicting confrontations which give Part I its distinctive nightmare quality.

Conrad describes Razumov in his Author's Note as 'an ordinary young man' with 'an average conscience'. But more significantly, he is 'nobody's child' and thus 'feels rather more keenly than another would that he is a Russian – or he is nothing'. Rootless and without identity, he is intent on creating a meaning for his existence, a 'solid beginning' represented in his mind by winning the silver medal and gaining a footing in a career that would perhaps see him 'a celebrated old professor, decorated, possibly a Privy Councillor'. As befits his name ('man of reason'), his is to be an achievement of the intellect, of the mind. So it comes as a grotesque shock that, hard upon these day-dreams of intellectual success, it is precisely to his 'superior mind' that Haldin feels he can appeal: '"Men like me are necessary to make room for self-contained, thinking men like you"' (p. 68). And later he adds, with unbearable irony, '"It's you thinkers who are in everlasting revolt. I am one of the resigned."' But Razumov, as if from 'the bottom of an abyss', can only see himself, as a result of this first dislocating encounter, implicated in the assassination, deported, robbed of hope: 'He saw ... his strength give way, his mind become an abject thing ... dying unattended in some filthy hole of a room' (p. 69). One of Conrad's great triumphs in this novel is his study of what happens to the powerful mind of this 'ordinary young man' when confronted by individuals and forces which undermine his precarious self-sufficiency and deepen his isolation. As he loses, step by step, his shreds of identity, his intellectual acumen turns into a self-protective and contemptuous cynicism.

Haldin presents himself to Razumov and to the reader – and one must remember that the portrait of Haldin in Part I can only have been derived from Razumov's account of him in his journal – as a person of 'lofty daring' and idealism. He is horrified by his mission which, he feels, derives inescapably from 'The Russian soul that lives in all of us'. Why else, he asks Razumov, should he have done this, '"reckless – like a butcher – in the middle of all these innocent people – scattering death – I! I! ... I wouldn't hurt a fly!"' (p. 70). And sitting down, 'he wept for a long time'. Though Conrad wrote with some contempt of the 'purely Utopian revolutionism encompassing destruction by the first means to hand', he makes Haldin, as the novel develops, into a figure who is seen only with loving admiration in the memories of his mother and sister; a revolutionist maybe, but one compared with whom the other revolutionists gathered in Geneva appear like 'the apes of a sinister jungle' (Author's Note). And later in the novel the English professor says that Haldin 'appeared to me not as a sinister conspirator, but as a pure enthusiast'. As Razumov leaves on his mission to find Ziemianitch, Haldin calls after him, '"Go with God, thou silent soul."' And one recollects that after he had 'resigned' himself to throw his lethal 'engine', Haldin thought to himself: '"God's will be done."'

The nightmare quality of Razumov's walk through the night is marvellously evoked by Conrad. In his mounting horror at the prospect of 'sinking into the lowest social depths among the hopeless and destitute', he suddenly confronts an old beggar woman tied up in ragged shawls; but what strikes him, ironically, is 'the peace of her mind and the serenity of her fate'. In contrast, a little later, is the pretty woman, 'like a frail and beautiful savage', whose brilliant glance rests on him with a 'mocking tenderness'. In the midst of these encounters, Razumov finds Ziemianitch in his 'vile den', and suddenly he sees that between the drunkenness and apathy of the peasant and the 'dream-intoxication' of the idealist Haldin, 'he is done for'. So, in belabouring Ziemianitch with 'insatiable fury', and in deciding to give Haldin up after he has had the illusion of walking over his outstretched body in the snow, it is as f Razumov tries to destroy, obliterate, them both. Yet both are to remain riveted to his life. Well may he feel the 'touch of grace on his forehead' – if this, in Razumov's journal, is Russian mysticism, in Conrad's novel it is tinged with irony.

The nightmare is not ended. Razumov has to try to square his conscience ('"Oh, thou vile wretch!"' a brawling cab-driver yells in his ear); but above all he desperately needs to be understood, in his 'naked terror' of 'true loneliness'; 'No human being could bear a steady view of moral solitude without going mad' (p. 83). Almost every line and phrase in this section of Part I echoes forward, as it were, into the later pages of the novel. Here it leads him to Prince K—, the 'man of showy missions', and from him to General T—, one of those formidably menacing creations of Conrad's that remind one of Dickens. Razumov's encounter with these twin pillars of the autocracy fills him with a mixture of contempt and terror, for he perceives that they represent the third force, along with the peasants and the revolutionists, threatening his quest for the silver medal of respectable success and identity.

And so he returns to confront Haldin again (unlike Spontini's sculpture, the Youth has not Flown), and to justify his refusal to let '"my intelligence, my aspirations ... be robbed ... at the will of violent enthusiasts"' (p. 100). It is a despairing cry, for he will shortly travel westwards and be received by the 'violent enthusiasts' in Geneva as Haldin's accomplice, who also 'scattered a few drops of blood on the snow'. As Haldin leaves to his arrest and execution, Razumov finds that his watch has stopped.

Part I concludes with the encounter with the inscrutable Councillor Mikulin of the soft, homely physiognomy and the mild gaze, whose sentences trail off into his beard. After the hectic, see-saw turmoil of the previous days, the ominous quietness of Mikulin's 'comedy of persecution' confounds Razumov, for all that he feels the lucidity of his mind is now restored. And Mikulin confounds the reader too. What does he want with Razumov? What will Razumov, this rootless man, do with his dislocated life, 'with a bad secret police note tacked on to his record'? Will he find himself drawn, in spite of himself, into collaborating with the revolutionists, will he even become a spiritual accomplice of Haldin whom he has helped to destroy? As Conrad brings the curtain down on this compelling first act, Mikulin's unanswerable question, '"Where to?"' gathers into a tight knot all the doubts and ambiguities that have assailed Razumov, and perplexed the reader, since Haldin first appeared in his room and extolled the generosity of his sentiments and the solidity of his character. '"He does not throw his soul to the winds,"' Haldin had said of Razumov. But now, Razumov is left with 'three years of good work gone, the course of forty more perhaps jeopardized'; and Mikulin's soft, inescapable question.

Part II: Women

Part II begins six months before the assassination in Geneva, with the English professor introducing Mrs Haldin and her daughter Nathalie. Once again the reader may perhaps feel perplexed by this business of Conrad writing a story about a non-story, for the professor disclaims all the skills of the story-teller and only offers to tell the facts. Conrad admitted that the English professor 'has been much criticized', and these criticisms have continued to this day:

Conrad's use of the English teacher as narrator is a most unsatisfactory device. This is partly a technical weakness. His presence during the confession scene between Razumov and Natalia is embarrassing, as if he were a voyeur peeping in at this scene of torment. We may echo Razumov's complaint: 'How did this old man come here?' His insistence on his lack of imagination appears ridiculous, for he recounts his tale with compelling force ... He is himself a participant during important scenes, and this double role, as uncomprehending bystander and imaginative narrator, muddles his effects, particularly when he is describing his impressions of Razumov in Geneva.[27]

In his Author's Note to the novel, Conrad only remarks that the English professor was 'useful to me and therefore I think that he must be useful to the reader', for he serves as eye-witness in Geneva, and he acts as a sympathetic friend to Miss Haldin. The first is an odd explanation, for the author himself can be presumed to be an eye-witness, whether in Geneva or St Petersburg. None the less, Conrad very frequently seemed to feel the need to locate an eye-witness within the story and so to tell the story at one remove.

Marlowe is his most notable raconteur. But the English professor is no Marlowe; he is at pains to describe himself as unimaginative and unskilled; and he invariably apologizes for his interpolations. Familiar with Russia and the Russians, he offers to understand the mystique of the Russian character: which he sees as cynicism. In spite of this, as already remarked, he frequently confesses himself baffled. And this may prompt the reader to wonder whether the professor is Conrad's device for incorporating his own thoughts and feelings into the novel, but in a kind of thin disguise. For Irving Howe, 'he signifies a wish on Conrad's part to disassociate himself from his own imagination ... to be insulated from all that Russia implies ... The narrator expresses Conrad's opinions, the narrative incarnates Conrad's vision'.[28] This is well said; and yet it may be more subtle than that. If the professor expresses something of Conrad's views, it is in a crude and heavy-handed way; and thus he may at once have served to release some of the tensions Conrad felt in writing the novel, and also have helped him to maintain his distance. For John Palmer, 'this emotional withdrawal yields a narrator who is full of theory instead of feeling, and whose pompous abstractions often hide the book's subject, instead of bringing it closer'.[29] But surely, if the professor is long on abstractions, he is not short on feelings, either about Russia and revolutionists, or about Nathalie Haldin.

The Western eyes of the novel's final title are ostensibly the English professor's. But if he sees much of the story, he does not see them as the reader sees them, who also sees them through the eyes of other narrators. The professor is an important observer, but his importance lies partly in his very limitations, in his lack of imagination: in what he does not see and comprehend. In saying this, I am really insisting that the Western eyes of the title are above all Conrad's. The reader observes the professor as one of the individuals within the story who provides a vantage-point outside the Slav participants and a certain detachment and liberal idealism. But what the reader makes of the story is derived from seeing with Conrad's eyes and through his imagination, and these were Western eyes, English by adoption. It cannot be emphasized too strongly that Conrad was a Pole who looked to the West, who felt himself a cultural citizen of Western Europe, and who became as English as a Pole could then be. Not only are Conrad's eyes not the professor's; they are far more penetrating, and their moral scope and subtlety are infinitely greater. It is as if the English professor has one seeing and one partially-sighted eye. Indeed, even when in possession of the facts he sees very poorly into the depths of the Russian story he is recounting: as he says, 'I was like a traveller in a strange country.' As a result, his account of the Russian 'mystery' often reads more like his own mystification.

It has been remarked that eyes dominate this novel. To a remarkable degree Conrad focuses on his characters' eyes as a means of defining not just their mood of the moment, but their personality and even their moral worth. In Part I Haldin tells how the watchman in the woodyard suddenly started shouting, '"Take yourself and your ugly eyes away"'; and subsequently Razumov becomes morbidly obsessed with the way Haldin lay with 'the backs of his hands over his eyes'. as if to blot out the violence of his act. When he talks to Razumov about his sister, Haldin says, '"She has the most trustful eyes of any human being that ever walked this earth"' (p. 70). In the depth of his lethargy, after seeing Haldin leave to his arrest, Razumov 'caught sight of his own face in the looking-glass ... The eyes which returned his stare were the most unhappy eyes he had ever seen' (p. 106). He thinks uneasily about General T—, 'whose goggle eyes could express a mortal hatred of all rebellion' (p. 108); whereas Mikulin, that functionary of the autocracy, confronts him with a 'mild gaze', later with a 'misty gaze'. It may well be, oddly, that the only character whose eyes are not described is the English professor.

The second of Conrad's reasons for needing the presence of the professor is his friendship with Nathalie Haldin, and this has considerable substance. It does seem essential for her to be able to talk with and even confide in someone other than her mother, if her distinctive qualities are to be realized for the reader. At the opening of Part II, six months before the drama of Part I, the English professor is narrator in his own right. For all that he has 'no talent', he brings Nathalie and her mother vividly before the reader, the mother with 'the almost lifeless beauty of her face, and the living benign glance of her big dark eyes', the daughter with 'her grey eyes shaded by black eyelashes . . . Her glance was as direct and trustful as that of a young man . . . it was intrepid' (pp. 132–3). And there is their son and brother: 'a brilliant intellect, a most noble unselfish nature' – a description which the reader may well recognize.

There are critics for whom Nathalie is too idealized a figure, not sufficiently filled out as a character, to carry the great load that Conrad places on her. She is one of a small group of women who give *Under Western Eyes* a quality of compassion that distinguishes this novel so sharply from *The Secret Agent*. Conrad is rightly felt to have had difficulties with his women characters and not surprisingly this provides a major theme for Meyer in his *Psychoanalytic Biography*: He finds that there are traces in Nathalie Haldin of 'those Amazonian characters [in Conrad's work], who are endowed more with gladiatorial than with maternal qualities. Such women do not conjure up fantasies of intimacy; they are worshipped from afar, secretly, as if they partake of awe-inspiring attributes'.[30] If this corresponds somewhat with the English professor's view of her (and of his feelings towards her), she emerges, in a story of concealments and subterfuge, as a person of 'clear-eyed simplicity' and transparent honesty. When the professor tells her of the assassination of Mr de P—, she speaks with a child-like naïveté about '"concord [being] not so very far off"' and she denies that it is a class conflict in Russia: '"It is something quite different."' The professor confides to the reader that 'one must be a Russian to understand Russian simplicity, a terrible corroding simplicity in which mystic phrases clothe a naïve and hopeless cynicism' (p. 134). But he has to exempt her from this charge of cynicism and when, a week later, he has to tell her of Haldin's arrest, he speaks of 'her indefinable charm [which] was revealed to me in the conjunction of passion and stoicism' (p. 144). For her it is essential to believe that some person, some Judas, has been guilty of betraying her brother, though 'She harboured no evil thoughts against any one'. As they part, 'The grip of her strong, shapely hand had a seductive frankness, a sort of exquisite virility' (p. 145). From that

stage onwards, the English professor uses all the reticent influence
he can muster up to protect Nathalie from the malign revolutionary
forces which he associates with Peter Ivanovitch and Madame de
S— at the Château Borel, as they seek to enlist her in the insurrec-
tionary cause for which her brother gave his life.

If the English professor is the narrator of the Haldins' story, Part
II includes three other narrators, Peter Ivanovitch and Tekla, and
Nathalie herself. Peter Ivanovitch, his eyes hidden by dark glasses,
the first among the Russian revolutionists in Geneva and beyond,
is, Conrad said, 'fair game'; certainly he is treated with great gusto
and subtle contempt. Echoing Nathalie's affirmation that in Russia
there are no classes, he offers his audiences the notion that the
'greatest part of our hopes rests on women'. The story he recounts
in his book, of wandering in his chain in the forests and bogs of
Siberia, would be grotesque if Conrad did not, at the same time,
make it compellingly effective. Because his 'cult of the woman' and
'his rites of special devotion to the transcendental merits of a certain
Madame de S—' are so much charlatanry, the significance of the
women in his story is generally missed. They share many of
Nathalie's genuinely humane qualities, above all her devotion and
her compassion: first the 'quiet, pale-faced girl' who had worked her
way across Siberia to help free her lover and who gave Peter
Ivanovitch the precious file; and then the woman, faced with the
savage creature with wild head and red staring eyes, whose
'sudden, unexpected cry of profound pity, the insight of her feminine
compassion ... restored him to the ranks of humanity' (p. 150).
These two women survive the unbelievable story he tells, and they
provide a telling and exposing contrast to the absurd pretensions of
Madame de S— 'with a pair of big gleaming eyes, rolling restlessly
behind a short veil of black lace' (p. 151).

This positive feminine element in the story, which is unusual in
Conrad's novels in being treated with such unsentimentalized
strength, is then taken up by the strange, 'girlish, elderly woman'
with the cat, whom Nathalie discovers at the château and who
explains that she is the *dame de compagnie* and also secretary to Peter
Ivanovitch. She is led on to recount to Nathalie her life in Russia,
living in cellars with the proletariat and trying to make herself

'useful to the utterly hopeless', and particularly to the journeyman lithographer, a 'martyr, a simple man' for whom she alone cared in his destitution. Her story is all the more powerful for following upon Peter Ivanovitch's. The picture she presents of slave-like devotion is redeemed by its lack of sentimentality and by her mental alertness; and it underscores his self-regarding afflatus.

It is the great strength of this Part II of the novel that the struggle is presented not in familiar political terms but in the dramatic contrast between the feminine values represented by Nathalie above all (with 'her true and delicate humanity') and the bogus cult of the woman paraded by Peter Ivanovitch. The English professor describes him with his 'Egeria' driving about Geneva in their landau: 'Thus, facing each other, with no one else in the roomy carriage, their airings suggested a conscious public manifestation' (p. 151). Jacques Berthoud comments effectively:

What is most striking about this vignette is its ambiguity. Is it a public demonstration of avant-garde ideals, or is it the shameless exposure of a perverted liaison? What makes the intellectual pose – if that is what it is – so disturbing and absurd is the incongruity of the suspected alternative. It is possible that this solemn pair is attempting to match such former leaders of fashionable thought as Voltaire and Madame de Staël, both of whom 'sheltered ... on the republican territory of Geneva'. But if so, they are nothing but extravagant parodies. Even their fashionable garments look like disguises: Peter Ivanovitch's ... His feminist idealism barely masks a copious virility, and his general worship of women (as his brutal exploitation of his pathetically devoted secretary Tekla indicates) conceals a ruthlessly un-compromising will to power. Every one of his aspirations is cancelled out by a contradictory reality: the Château Borel, whence flows his stream of revolutionary utopianism, reveals itself to be an appropriately squalid rented villa; and its priestess, Madame de S—, turns out to be a vulgar occulist whom he cultivates solely for the money she supplies.[31]

It is into this world of the Château Borel that Nathalie feels herself being drawn because of her brother's status as a hero of the incipient revolution, and from which the English professor and Tekla are desperately anxious to protect her. To the former she protests, '"I believe that you hate revolution; you fancy it's not quite honest"' (p. 157). And ironically it is at the château that Nathalie

36

INTRODUCTION

then meets the not quite honest revolutionist Razumov for the first time. His appearance in Geneva seems to answer Mikulin's question '"Where to?"', though it does not answer the reader's question, 'Why has he come to Geneva?' For Nathalie, at any rate, he is the person described in her brother's letter as a man of 'unstained, lofty, and solitary existence', and so for her he is not only her brother's friend, but surely an unflinching co-conspirator. She confesses – and it is important that Nathalie herself is the narrator of this most dramatic of all the encounters in the novel – that at this unbearable moment 'her lips trembled, her eyes ran full of tears', and she is able only to gasp out her brother's name. As Razumov suddenly '"put out both his hands then to me, I may say flung them out at me, with the greatest readiness and warmth"' (p. 187), Nathalie feels that the friendship between Razumov and her brother '"must have been the very brotherhood of souls"'; and she now has the strength to escape from the château: '"I walked away quickly. There was no need to run"' (p. 188). Razumov, apparently caught up in the very revolutionary entanglements he had tried so desperately to escape, turns into the château to meet the 'Arch-Patron of revolutionary parties', as the professor calls him.

The English professor takes up the narrative for the final section of Part II. If (like the reader) he finds Razumov's behaviour abrupt and his tone sneering, he attributes it to 'a conspirator [being] everlastingly on his guard against self-betrayal in a world of secret spies' (p. 199), though of course it is Razumov himself who is the secret spy. '"I think that you people are under a curse"', the professor tells him, and wondering what ails him, he can only hope that if it were anything to do with Victor Haldin, 'he would keep it to himself for ever'. At the time neither he (nor the reader) can know that Razumov's escape from the curse now hanging over him will turn on this. Only when writing his story after having read Razumov's journal could he explain the reasons for the 'tone of cynicism . . . of moral negation, and even of moral distress' (to quote earlier words of his about the Russians) which at present lie concealed within the puzzling figure 'hanging far over the parapet of the bridge'.

Part III: Revolutionists

The water running violent and deep under the bridge could not, 'had it flowed through Razumov's breast ... have washed away the accumulated bitterness the wrecking of his life had deposited there' (p. 207).

Part III is based mainly on Razumov's journal, and the English professor imagines that Razumov must have seen it 'as a man looks at himself in a mirror, [to find] reassuring excuses for his appearance marked by the taint of some insidious hereditary disease' (p. 220). In recounting this part of the drama, the professor concentrates on Razumov's mood, on his torment of falsehood; at the time neither he nor Nathalie nor the revolutionists know the deep-seated cause of Razumov's cynicism, which provides a cloak for his anxiety. Like these characters within the novel, the reader tries to comprehend what Razumov is at, what is this mission he speaks of occasionally: but unlike them, the reader knows of Razumov's betrayal of Haldin and so can understand something of his mood of insecurity and suspicion.

He has good grounds for anxiety, for he has now to confront the revolutionists as they assemble in the Château Borel. He has only two weapons with which to counter their mixture of grudging admiration and suspicion: his intelligence, and his sense of being more genuinely Russian than these émigrés – as he says aggressively to Peter Ivanovitch, '"Russia *can't* disown me. She cannot! ... I am *it!*"'

The duel between Razumov and the revolutionists is managed with great adroitness by Conrad and, at times, with unnerving tension. At intervals the reader is reminded of the setting in which they encounter each other. Geneva certainly does not appeal to Razumov: 'the whole view ... had the uninspiring, glittering quality of a very fresh oleograph ... the very perfection of mediocrity' (p. 211), and Razumov turns his back on it with contempt. On a later occasion he walks 'along the quay, through a pretty, dull garden, where dull people sat on chairs under the trees ... he saw the green slopes framing the Petit Lac in all the marvellous banality of the picturesque' (pp. 277–8). There is no evidence that this was

Conrad's own opinion of the place; or that he shared Razumov's opinion of Geneva as '"the heart of democracy ... A fit heart for it; no bigger than a parched pea and about as much value"' (p. 213). But one can see that, for the purpose of his theme, Conrad felt the need to disassociate himself from Western democratic institutions as much as from Russian autocracy and Russian revolutionists. Moreover, he may have wanted to contrast Western superficial insipidity with Russian 'mystery', with the sense of a giant slumbering, however inertly.

Turning from the view of the lake and town, Razumov enters the grounds of the château. The château, haunted perhaps by futile middle-class ghosts, looks 'damp and gloomy and deserted'. With its 'cracked white paint' and 'tarnished gilt' it seems to resemble its tawdry owner, the 'famous – or notorious – Madame de S—'. With her 'appalling grimace of graciousness', it is 'the white gleam of the big eyeballs setting off the black, fathomless stare of the enlarged pupils' that impresses Razumov most; she seems to him 'a witch in Parisian clothes' (p. 220). As for her revolutionary zeal to 'spiritualize the discontent' and set the Balkans alight, this seems entirely motivated by her fanatical wish to punish the thieves of her private fortune and possessions. She, like Peter Ivanovitch, was clearly 'fair game' for Conrad.

The château harbours nothing but 'dust and emptiness', like the revolutionists who pass in and out of its doors. As presented to the reader by Razumov they seem, with the exception of Sophia Antonovna, a dusty and empty group. The apparent leader among them, Peter Ivanovitch, is most revealingly described by Tekla as 'an awful despot' who 'cares for no one'; and she adds, wrily, '"He is a great man. Great men are horrible"' (p. 234). Conrad invests him with a formidable intelligence to match his formidable presence. In particular it is he who defines with great if 'baffling' prescience '"a chasm [that yawns] between the past and the future. It can never be bridged by foreign liberalism. All attempts at it are either folly or cheating. Bridged it can never be! It has to be filled up"' (p. 217). Yet with his great bulk and his 'hairy and obscene' appearance (as Razumov describes him), Peter Ivanovitch is portrayed, along with the other revolutionists, in caricature. He is almost invariably given some mocking label; usually he is the 'burly' or the 'great feminist', as Madame de S— is invariably his Egeria. 'Apes of a sinister jungle', Conrad treats them 'as their grimaces deserve'. In this Conrad may, as Saveson suggests, have been influenced by a set of editorials on anarchists in *Blackwood's Magazine* with which he would have been familiar and which relied on a classification of anarchists as criminal degenerates, usually with physical deformities of some kind. Such is the portrait of the sinister Nikita, with his 'great white hairless face, double chin, prominent stomach'; and Conrad does not forget to describe, with forbidding irony, his 'thin voice piping with comic peevishness' (p. 260).

The exception among these revolutionists is Sophia Antonovna, with whom Razumov has his longest and most searching encounter. Though he judges her as being 'a distinct danger in his path', he discovers 'that he could not despise her as he despised all the others' (p. 242). It is one of Conrad's major achievements in this novel to treat her, to create her, with considerable respect and even sympathy:

> Razumov looked at her white hair; and this mark of so many uneasy years seemed nothing but a testimony to the invincible vigour of revolt. It threw out into an astonishing relief the unwrinkled face, the brilliant black glance, the upright compact figure, the simple, brisk self-possession of the mature personality - as though in her revolutionary pilgrimage she had discovered the secret, not of everlasting youth, but of everlasting endurance (p. 258).

She seems allied in quality and spirit with Haldin; like him, and in 'the true spirit of the destructive revolution', she insists that it is better 'to burn than to rot'. Compared with the 'perfect fierceness of conviction' of the active revolutionist, like his supposed accomplice Haldin, she feels that Razumov is not whole-hearted; she sees him as a moody egoist. When he is with her, or with Peter Ivanovitch, Razumov refuses to accept the revolutionary doctrine blindly: "I would scorn to be a slave even to an idea"', he says (p. 242). In response to her warning that he will go mad with his anger at everyone and his bitterness with himself, Razumov feels 'choking fumes of falsehood had taken him by the throat' (p. 263). But her news that Ziemianitch has hanged himself (and it is an astute stroke that she is made the bearer of this news) seems suddenly to save him from the traps lying around him, some of them traps of his own making: above all the 'degrading method of direct lying which at times he found it almost impossible to practise' (p. 271), and perhaps also 'the envenomed recklessness of his temper'. If he now feels safe and free, Conrad manages to conceal from the reader what or who it is he feels safe from: from Mikulin? from his conscience? or simply from the revolutionists in Geneva?

And so, prompted by the diminutive 'violent pamphleteer' Laspara to 'write something for us', Razumov finds his way to the safety and solitude of Rousseau's little isle, to write – but to write what, and to whom? It does not seem necessary to fabricate great significance out of the contrasts between Razumov and Rousseau as writers and thinkers: Conrad lets the gentle irony speak for itself. As Razumov sits in the deepening twilight, thinking to himself that '"There can be no doubt that now I am safe,"' Conrad ends Part III with the unassuming words that carry a far more significant and horrifying dramatic irony: 'His fine ear could detect the faintly accentuated murmurs of the current breaking against the point of the island, and he forgot himself in listening to them with interest. But even to his acute sense of hearing the sound was too elusive' (p. 280).

Part IV: Confessions

This part of the novel has the greatest span of all, taking the reader back to Mikulin's question and on to the end of the drama and beyond.

Though Razumov may have commented in his journal that Councillor Mikulin's question was not menacing, it checked him at the door, held him back; and it compelled him to attend further meetings with Mikulin – at an oculist's shop, of all ironic places in this novel of eyes. At long last the reader is shown the missing pieces of the puzzle, as Mikulin suddenly realizes that Razumov could make a 'perfectly fitted' tool as an informer. In the event Razumov turns out to be a flawed tool, but so does Mikulin himself. During their conversation Mikulin remarks that he believes firmly in providence, and immediately adds: '"Such a confession on the lips of an old hardened official like me may sound to you funny."' The word seems to stick in Razumov's mind, for once out in the street

the consciousness of his position presented itself to him as something so ugly, dangerous, and absurd, the difficulty of ever freeing himself from the toils of that complication so insoluble, that the idea of going back and, as he termed it to himself, *confessing* to Councillor Mikulin flashed through his mind.

Go back! What for? Confess! To what? (p. 284).

The italics are Conrad's: the need to be understood is Razumov's, and it assails him throughout his stay in Geneva until it overwhelms him.

Returning to Rousseau's island, the reader now sees Razumov as the 'fine tool', writing a report to Mikulin. But the English professor, still in the dark about Razumov's motives and actions, sees him shortly afterwards and noticing that he is deeply discomposed, he reflects that he is all that is left to Natalia and her mother of their son and brother. The re-introduction of the Haldins may well seem to many readers to be overdue. Natalia's virtual absence throughout Part III seems, in retrospect, a mistake on Conrad's part, for it might seem to weaken her presence in the rest of the novel and even render her somewhat insubstantial at a time, during the crucial meetings with Razumov in Part IV, when she has psychologically so potent a role to play.

As if to overcome any sense of her remoteness, Conrad brings her back in a flurry of activity, late at night, going out to find Razumov. Among the assembled revolutionists on the top floor of a great hotel, where she and the professor look first, Natalia seems strikingly out of place. She is able to communicate only with Sophia Antonovna. They return to her home, to find that Razumov is already there with her mother; at the moment when he believes that the news of Ziemianitch's death renders him secure, this first meeting with Victor Haldin's mother disturbs him deeply. He may, as he reminds himself, have been able to walk over Haldin's phantom 'lying powerless and passive on the pavement covered with snow', and yet he has now had to face the phantom's mother, 'her white, inclined profile suggest[ing] the contemplation of something in her lap, as

42

though a beloved head were resting there' (p. 316). It could easily be a moment of misplaced melodrama, but Conrad keeps his hand steady, as it were, and perceives that this experience fills Razumov not with renewed fear, but with anger and, what is more unbearable, with 'something like enviousness' for *he* would never 'exist in the affection of [a] mourning old woman'. Distracted by his discovery that he cannot escape Haldin's phantom presence, Razumov hears Natalia say that '"it is in you that we can find all that is left of his generous soul"'. And the professor, standing awkwardly watching, reiterates that 'of course, they had to come together, the sister and the friend of that dead man' (p. 322).

The complexities that lie beneath the surface of that naïve phrase, 'they had to come together', are revealed only obliquely, hintingly, by Conrad, but with a passionate restraint of great moral force. Natalia is revealed, perhaps for the first time, in her most compelling femininity:

> While speaking she raised her hands above her head to untie her veil, and that movement displayed for an instant the seductive grace of her youthful figure, clad in the simplest of mourning. In the transparent shadow the hat rim threw on her face her grey eyes had an enticing lustre. Her voice, with its unfeminine yet exquisite timbre, was steady . . . (pp. 322–3).

Razumov listens to her (the emphasis is now all on his *hearing*) 'with the air of a man who is listening to a strain of music' and even when Natalia has finished, 'he seemed to listen yet, motionless, as under the spell of suggestive sound'. It is as if the answer to Mikulin's question, '"Where to?"' has now been answered for Razumov: 'To Victor Haldin's sister'. It was Haldin who described her eyes as trustful, and for Razumov that means, he says, '"that there is in you no guile, no deception, no falsehood, no suspicion"'; and he is compelled to add, he who has been living a constant lie, that '"nothing in your heart . . . could give you a conception of a living, acting, speaking lie, if ever it came in your way"' (p. 324). Under the compulsion of her truthfulness, he at once confesses his love for her and his betrayal of her brother. The two confessions are inextricably linked.

The dramatic force of these confessions is in the strongest contrast to the story as Conrad originally planned it, where Razumov betrays Haldin and then marries his sister. In this final version, having struggled back to his room feeling 'washed clean', he writes his passionate confession to Natalia. In the end Razumov had found himself unable to commit the 'unpardonable sin of stealing a soul' (p. 332): '"I looked into your eyes – and that was enough ... You were appointed to undo the evil by making me betray myself back into truth and peace"' (p. 331). And at last he is able to add, to her and thus to himself, that in giving Victor Haldin up, '"it was myself ... whom I have betrayed most basely"' (p. 333). In this avowal he rediscovers a self which the reader has not previously met and which he himself may not have met either up till this moment. As on that previous night in St Petersburg, he sits with his watch in front of him, waiting for midnight, and it seems as if Victor Haldin is 'timing his conduct in the present', even helping to save him. But Razumov knows that only he can complete the process of his 'escape from the prison of lies'.

For Irving Howe the revolutionists are such a feeble and contemptible bunch that it is hard to conceive that Razumov can 'suppose them worthy to hear his *mea culpa* ... By refusing to extend his radicals the necessary credit, if only later to call it in, Conrad fails to establish the dramatic ground for his denouement'.[32] Certainly they are portrayed by Conrad as a bundle of grotesques. But in the first place Razumov's need to confess to the revolutionists is a need to redeem himself and to escape from his own inner prison. And then the revolutionists, much though Razumov despises them, are capable of providing a dramatic and moral climax to the novel. The enormous and shocking physical violence of Nikita's attack on Razumov is the culmination of all the overt and suppressed violences of the novel, from the 'terrific concentrated violence' of the initial explosions which killed Mr de P—, to the simmering explosions of Razumov's encounters with the revolutionists, and to his final outburst of confessions to Natalia. Conrad's control and restraint are wonderfully judged: even to the final twist that Nikita is himself a spy, like Razumov an agent of General T— and Councillor Mikulin. As for Razumov, who has throughout felt himself rootless and isolated, his confessions and his self-discovery have their

culmination in the isolation of deafness, an isolation all the deeper
for one with such a 'fine ear' and 'acute sense of hearing'.

The novel is brought to its close by its main and most positive
women characters. Its final momentum is back towards Russia – it
is interesting that the professor now calls Nathalie by her Russian
name Natalia. Tekla rescues Razumov and somewhere in the south
she 'tended him unweariedly with the pure joy of unselfish devotion': she has 'found work to do after her own heart'. Sophia
Antonovna, whom the English professor meets two years later, has
made a point of visiting Razumov and she alone, that 'much-trusted
revolutionary', is able to find the words to commend him: '"... how
many of them would deliver themselves up deliberately to perdition
... rather than go on living, secretly debased in their own eyes? How
many? ... There's character in such a discovery."' It is Sophia
Antonovna who has the very last words in the novel, as she says
farewell to the professor: '... in the very doorway, where I attended
her, she turned round for an instant, and declared in a firm voice
– "Peter Ivanovitch is an inspired man"' (p. 349). Inescapably the
reader remembers Razumov also turning his head at the door to
receive Councillor Mikulin's question. Were this the play of the
novel that Conrad failed to write, the visual echo would surely be
carefully emphasized upon the stage. If it makes an effectively ironic
curtain line, it may justify Conrad's comment, in his Author's Note,
that she is 'wrong-headed'.

But the main reason for Sophia Antonovna's wish to speak to the
English professor is to convey a friendly message from Natalia. She
gives a picture of her, 'sharing her compassionate labours between
the horrors of over-crowded jails, and the heart-rending misery of
bereaved homes', that allies her with the 'good Samaritan' Tekla
rather than with the good revolutionist Sophia Antonovna. If there
is any resolution in this novel it must be found, one feels, in the last
words that Natalia speaks. In her final meeting with the professor,
she reveals 'something grave and measured in her voice, in her
movements, in her manner. It was the perfection of collected
independence' (p. 342). Neither of the West nor of the revolutionists, Natalia represents Conrad's symbol of hope and integrity.
After giving the professor Razumov's journal, she says, '"My

eyes are open at last"', and she utters her paean of hope for the future:

'I must own to you that I shall never give up looking forward to the day when all discord shall be silenced. Try to imagine its dawn! The tempest of blows and of execrations is over; all is still; the new sun is rising, and the weary men united at last, taking count in their conscience of the ended contest, feel saddened by their victory, because so many ideas have perished for the triumph of one, so many beliefs have abandoned them without support. They feel alone on the earth and gather close together. Yes, there must be many bitter hours! But at last the anguish of hearts shall be extinguished in love' (p. 345).

If her words are naïve, they have, in this grim and anguished novel, the virtue of naïveté. Speaking without the irony that informs and controls so much of the rest of the novel, she seems to be speaking not only from her own heart and wisdom, but for Conrad himself.

Notes to the Introduction

1. Letter to Galsworthy, 6 May 1907.
2. *Notes by Joseph Conrad*, p. 20.
3. Letter to Pinker, 5 March 1906.
4. Zdzislaw Najder, *Joseph Conrad*, p. 324. Throughout this Introduction I am greatly indebted to Najder's definitive biography.
5. Letter to Pinker, 7 January 1908.
6. Letter to Harriet Mary Capes, 10 September 1907.
7. Letter to Galsworthy, 6 January 1908.
8. Quoted by Najder, pp. 334–5.
9. ibid., p. 335.
10. Conrad, Author's Note to *Under Western Eyes*.
11. Najder, p. 4.
12. Quoted by Najder, p. 11.
13. Korzeniowski's letter to Kascewski, 1 February 1866; quoted by Najder, p. 21.
14. Najder, p. 29.
15. ibid., p. 36.
16. Morton Dauwen Zabel, Introduction to Anchor Books edition, reprinted in Marvin Mudrick (ed.), *Conrad: A Collection of Critical Essays*, p. 120.

17. Jocelyn Baines, *Joseph Conrad: A Critical Biography*, p. 352.
18. Jessie Conrad, *Joseph Conrad As I Knew Him*, pp. 135–7.
19. Jessie Conrad, letter to David Meldrum, 6 February 1910.
20. Letter to Hugh Clifford, 19 May 1910.
21. Najder, p. 361.
22. Author's Note to *Chance*.
23. Author's Note to *'Twixt Land and Sea*.
24. Baines, pp. 373–4.
25. Jessie Conrad, pp. 58–60.
26. *Conrad: The Later Moralist*, pp. 73, 90–91.
27. C. B. Cox, *Joseph Conrad: The Modern Imagination*, p. 104.
28. *Politics and the Novel*, p. 89.
29. *Joseph Conrad's Fiction*, p. 131.
30. Bernard C. Meyer, *Joseph Conrad: A Psychoanaylitic Biography*, p. 217.
31. *Joseph Conrad: The Major Phase*, pp. 167–8.
32. Howe, p. 92.

SELECT BIBLIOGRAPHY

Biographical Studies

Jocelyn Baines, *Joseph Conrad: A Critical Biography* (Greenwood Press, 1976)

Jessie Conrad, *Joseph Conrad As I Knew Him* (Heinemann, 1926; Scholarly, Honston, 1972)

Zdzislaw Najder, *Joseph Conrad* (Cambridge University Press, 1984)

Studies of *Under Western Eyes*

Jacques Berthoud, *Joseph Conrad: The Major Phase* (Cambridge University Press, 1978)

Christopher Cooper, *Conrad and the Human Dilemma* (Chatto & Windus, 1970)

A. J. Guerard, *Conrad the Novelist* (Harvard University Press, 1958)

Irving Howe, 'Order and Anarchy' in *Politics and the Novel* (Meridian Books, Inc., 1957)

Bernard C. Meyer, *Joseph Conrad: A Psychoanalytic Biography* (Princeton University Press, 1967)

John A. Palmer, *Joseph Conrad's Fiction* (Cornell University Press, 1969)

Royal Roussel, *The Metaphysics of Darkness* (Johns Hopkins Press, 1971)

John E. Saveson, *Conrad: The Later Moralist* (Editions Rodopi, 1974)

Norman Sherry (ed.), *Conrad: The Critical Heritage* (Routledge & Kegan Paul, 1973)

Morton Dauwen Zabel, 'Introduction to *Under Western Eyes*' in Marvin Mudrick (ed.), *Conrad: A Collection of Critical Essays* (Prentice–Hall, 1966)

48

AUTHOR'S NOTE

It must be admitted that by the mere force of circumstances *Under Western Eyes* has become already a sort of historical novel dealing with the past.

This reflection bears entirely upon the events of the tale; but being as a whole an attempt to render not so much the political state as the psychology of Russia itself, I venture to hope that it has not lost all its interest. I am encouraged in this flattering belief by noticing that in many articles on Russian affairs of the present day reference is made to certain sayings and opinions uttered in the pages that follow, in a manner testifying to the clearness of my vision and the correctness of my judgement. I need not say that in writing this novel I had no other object in view than to express imaginatively the general truth which underlies its action, together with my honest convictions as to the moral complexion of certain facts more or less known to the whole world.

As to the actual creation I may say that when I began to write I had a distinct conception of the first part only, with the three figures of Haldin, Razumov, and Councillor Mikulin, defined exactly in my mind. It was only after I had finished writing the first part that the whole story revealed itself to me in its tragic character and in the march of its events as unavoidable and sufficiently ample in its outline to give free play to my creative instinct and to the dramatic possibilities of the subject.

The course of action need not be explained. It has suggested itself more as a matter of feeling than a matter of thinking. It is the result not of a special experience but of general knowledge, fortified by earnest meditation. My greatest anxiety was in being able to strike and sustain the note of scrupulous impartiality. The obligation of absolute fairness was imposed on me historically and hereditarily, by the peculiar experience of race and family, in addition to my primary conviction that truth alone is the justification of any fiction which makes the least claim to the quality of art or may hope to take its place in the culture of men and women of its time. I had never been called before to a greater effort of detachment: detachment from all passions, prejudices and even from personal memories. *Under Western Eyes* on its first appearance in England was a failure with the public, perhaps because of that very detachment. I obtained my reward some six years later when I first heard that the book had found universal recognition in Russia and had been re-published there in many editions.

The various figures playing their part in the story also owe their existence to no special experience but to the general knowledge of the condition of Russia and of the moral and emotional reactions of the Russian temperament to the pressure of tyrannical lawlessness, which, in general human terms, could be reduced to the formula of senseless desperation provoked by senseless tyranny. What I was concerned with mainly was the aspect, the character, and the fate of the individuals as they appeared to the Western Eyes of the old teacher of languages. He himself has been much criticized; but I will not at this late hour undertake to justify his existence. He was useful to me and therefore I think that he must be useful to the reader both in the way of comment and by the part he plays in the development of the story. In my desire to produce the effect of actuality it seemed to me indispensable to have an eye-witness of the transactions in Geneva. I needed also a sympathetic friend for Miss Haldin, who otherwise would have been too much alone and unsupported to be perfectly credible. She would have had no one to whom she could give a glimpse of her idealistic faith, of her great heart, and of her simple emotions.

Razumov is treated sympathetically. Why should he not be? He is an ordinary young man, with a healthy capacity for work and sane ambitions. He has an average conscience. If he is slightly abnormal it is only in his sensitiveness to his position. Being nobody's child he feels rather more keenly than another would that he is a Russian – or he is nothing. He is perfectly right in looking on all Russia as his heritage. The sanguinary futility of the crimes and the sacrifices seething in that amorphous mass envelops and crushes him. But I don't think that in his distraction he is ever monstrous. Nobody is exhibited as a monster here – neither the simple-minded Tekla nor the wrong headed Sophia Antonovna. Peter Ivanovitch and Madame de S–. are fair game. They are the apes of a sinister jungle and are treated as their grimaces deserve. As to Nikita – nicknamed Necator – he is the perfect flower of the terroristic wilderness. What troubled me most in dealing with him was not his monstrosity but his banality. He has been exhibited to the public eye for years in so-called 'disclosures' in newspaper articles, in secret histories, in sensational novels.

The most terrifying reflection (I am speaking now for myself) is that all these people are not the product of the exceptional but of the general – of the normality of their place, and time, and race. The ferocity and imbecility of an autocratic rule rejecting all legality and in fact basing itself upon complete moral anarchism provokes the no less imbecile and atrocious answer of a purely Utopian revolutionism encompassing destruction by the first means to hand, in the strange conviction that a fundamental change of hearts must follow the downfall of any given human institutions. These people are unable to see that all they can effect is merely a change of names. The oppressors and the oppressed are all Russians together; and the world is brought once more face to face with the truth of the saying that the tiger cannot change his stripes nor the leopard his spots.

1920   J.C.

UNDER
WESTERN EYES

*'I would take liberty from any hand as a
hungry man would snatch a piece of bread'*

—MISS HALDIN

To Agnes Tobin
who brought to our door
her genius for friendship
from the uttermost shore
of the west

PART FIRST

To begin with I wish to disclaim the possession of those high gifts of imagination and expression which would have enabled my pen to create for the reader the personality of the man who called himself, after the Russian custom, Cyril son of Isidor – Kirylo Sidorovitch – Razumov.[1]

If I have ever had these gifts in any sort of living form they have been smothered out of existence a long time ago under a wilderness of words. <u>Words, as is well known, are the great foes of reality</u>. I have been for many years a teacher of languages. It is an occupation which at length becomes fatal to whatever share of imagination, observation, and insight an ordinary person may be heir to. To a teacher of languages there comes a time when the world is but a place of many words and man appears a mere talking animal not much more wonderful than a parrot.

This being so, I could not have observed Mr Razumov or guessed at his reality by the force of insight, much less have imagined him as he was. Even to invent the mere bald facts of his life would have been utterly beyond my powers. But I think that without this declaration the readers of these pages will be able to detect in the story the marks of documentary evidence. And that is perfectly correct. It is based on a document; all I have brought to it is my knowledge of the Russian language, which is sufficient for what is attempted here. The document, of course, is something in the nature of a journal, a diary, yet not exactly that in its actual form. For instance, most of it was not written up from day to day, though all the entries are dated. Some of these entries cover months of time and extend over dozens of pages. All the earlier part is a retrospect, in a narrative form, relating to an event which took place about a year before.

I must mention that I have lived for a long time in Geneva. A whole quarter of that town, on account of many Russians residing there, is called La Petite Russie – Little Russia. I had a rather extensive connection in Little Russia at that time. Yet I confess that I have no comprehension of the Russian character. The illogicality of their attitude, the arbitrariness of their conclusions, the frequency of the exceptional, should present no difficulty to a student of many grammars; but there must be something else in the way, some special human trait – one of those subtle differences that are beyond the ken of mere professors. What must remain striking to a teacher of languages is the Russians' extraordinary love of words. They gather them up; they cherish them, but they don't hoard them in their breasts; on the contrary, they are always ready to pour them out by the hour or by the night with an enthusiasm, a sweeping abundance, with such an aptness of application sometimes that, as in the case of very accomplished parrots, one can't defend oneself from the suspicion that they really understand what they say. There is a generosity in their ardour of speech which removes it as far as possible from common loquacity; and it is ever too disconnected to be classed as eloquence . . . But I must apologize for this digression.

It would be idle to inquire why Mr Razumov has left this record behind him. It is inconceivable that he should have wished any human eye to see it. A mysterious impulse of human nature comes into play here. Putting aside Samuel Pepys, who has forced in this way the door of immortality, innumerable people, criminals, saints, philosophers, young girls, statesmen, and simple imbeciles, have kept self-revealing records from vanity no doubt, but also from other more inscrutable motives. There must be a wonderful soothing power in mere words since so many men have used them for self-communion. Being myself a quiet individual I take it that what all men are really after is some form or perhaps only some formula of peace. Certainly they are crying loud enough for it at the present day. What sort of peace Kirylo Sidorovitch Razumov expected to find in the writing up of his record it passeth my understanding to guess.

The fact remains that he has written it.

Mr Razumov was a tall, well-proportioned young man, quite unusually dark for a Russian from the Central Provinces. His good looks would have been unquestionable if it had not been for a peculiar lack of fineness in the features. It was as if a face modelled vigorously in wax (with some approach even to a classical correctness of type) had been held close to a fire till all sharpness of line had been lost in the softening of the material. His manner, too, was good. In discussion he was easily swayed by argument and authority. With his younger compatriots he took the attitude of an inscrutable listener, a listener of the kind that hears you out intelligently and then – just changes the subject.

This sort of trick, which may arise either from intellectual insufficiency or from an imperfect trust in one's own convictions, procured for Mr Razumov a reputation of profundity. Amongst a lot of exuberant talkers, in the habit of exhausting themselves daily by ardent discussion, a comparatively taciturn personality is naturally credited with reserve power. By his comrades at the St Petersburg[2] University, Kirylo Sidorovitch Razumov, third year's student in philosophy, was looked upon as a strong nature – an altogether trustworthy man. This, in a country where an opinion may be a legal crime visited by death or sometimes by a fate worse than mere death, meant that he was worthy of being trusted with forbidden opinions. He was liked also for his amiability and for his quiet readiness to oblige his comrades even at the cost of personal inconvenience.

Mr Razumov was supposed to be the son of an Archpriest[3] and to be protected by a distinguished nobleman – perhaps of his own distant province. But his outward appearance accorded badly with such humble origin. Such a descent was not credible. It was, indeed, suggested that Mr Razumov was the son of an Archpriest's pretty daughter – which, of course, would put a different complexion on the matter. This theory also rendered intelligible the protection of the distinguished nobleman. All this, however, had never been investigated maliciously or otherwise. No one knew or cared who the nobleman in question was. Razumov received a modest but very sufficient allowance from the hands of an obscure attorney, who seemed to act as his guardian in some measure. Now and then he appeared at some professor's informal reception. Apart from that Razumov was not known to have any social relations in the town. He attended the obligatory lectures regularly and was considered by the authorities as a very promising student. He worked at home in the manner of a man who means to get on, but did not shut himself up severely for that purpose. He was always accessible, and there was nothing secret or reserved in his life.

I

The origin of Mr Razumov's record is connected with an event characteristic of modern Russia in the actual fact: the assassination of a prominent statesman – and still more characteristic of the moral corruption of an oppressed society where the noblest aspirations of humanity, the desire of freedom, an ardent patriotism, the love of justice, the sense of pity, and even the fidelity of simple minds are prostituted to the lusts of hate and fear, the inseparable companions of an uneasy despotism.

The fact alluded to above is the successful attempt on the life of Mr de P—⁴, the President of the notorious Repressive Commission of some years ago, the Minister of State invested with extraordinary powers. The newspapers made noise enough about that fanatical, narrow-chested figure in gold-laced uniform, with a face of crumpled parchment, insipid, bespectacled eyes and the cross of the Order of St Procopius hung under the skinny throat. For a time, it may be remembered, not a month passed without his portrait appearing in some one of the illustrated papers of Europe. He served the monarchy by imprisoning, exiling, or sending to the gallows men and women, young and old, with an equable, unwearied industry. In his mystic acceptance of the principle of autocracy he was bent on extirpating from the land every vestige of anything that resembled freedom in public institutions; and in his ruthless persecution of the rising generation he seemed to aim at the destruction of the very hope of liberty itself.

It is said that this execrated personality had not enough imagination to be aware of the hate he inspired. It is hardly credible; but

58

it is a fact that he took very few precautions for his safety. In the preamble of a certain famous State paper he had declared once that 'the thought of liberty has never existed in the Act of the Creator. From the multitude of men's counsel nothing could come but revolt and disorder; and revolt and disorder in a world created for obedience and stability is sin. It was not Reason but Authority which expressed the Divine Intention. God was the Autocrat of the Universe ...' It may be that the man who made this declaration believed that heaven itself was bound to protect him in his remorseless defence of Autocracy on this earth.

No doubt the vigilance of the police saved him many times; but, as a matter of fact, when his appointed fate overtook him, the competent authorities could not have given him any warning. They had no knowledge of any conspiracy against the Minister's life, had no hint of any plot through their usual channels of information, had seen no signs, were aware of no suspicious movements or dangerous persons.

Mr de P— was being driven towards the railway station in a two-horse uncovered sleigh with footman and coachman on the box. Snow had been falling all night, making the roadway, uncleared as yet at this early hour, very heavy for the horses. It was still falling thickly. But the sleigh must have been observed and marked down. As it drew over to the left before taking a turn, the footman noticed a peasant walking slowly on the edge of the pavement with his hands in the pockets of his sheepskin coat and his shoulders hunched up to his ears under the falling snow. On being overtaken this peasant suddenly faced about and swung his arm. In an instant there was a terrible shock, a detonation muffled in the multitude of snowflakes; both horses lay dead and mangled on the ground and the coachman, with a shrill cry, had fallen off the box mortally wounded. The footman (who survived) had no time to see the face of the man in the sheepskin coat. After throwing the bomb this last got away, but it is supposed that, seeing a lot of people surging up on all sides of him in the falling snow, and all running towards the scene of the explosion, he thought it safer to turn back with them.

In an incredibly short time an excited crowd assembled round the sledge. The Minister-President, getting out unhurt into the deep snow, stood near the groaning coachman and addressed the people repeatedly in his weak, colourless voice: 'I beg of you to keep off. For the love of God, I beg of you good people to keep off.'

It was then that a tall young man who had remained standing perfectly still within a carriage gateway, two houses lower down, stepped out into the street and walking up rapidly flung another bomb over the heads of the crowd. It actually struck the Minister-President on the shoulder as he stooped over his dying servant, then falling between his feet exploded with a terrific concentrated violence, striking him dead to the ground, finishing the wounded man and practically annihilating the empty sledge in the twinkling of an eye. With a yell of horror the crowd broke up and fled in all directions, except for those who fell dead or dying where they stood nearest to the Minister-President, and one or two others who did not fall till they had run a little way.

The first explosion had brought together a crowd as if by enchant-ment, the second made as swiftly a solitude in the street for hundreds of yards in each direction. Through the falling snow people looked from afar at the small heap of dead bodies lying upon each other near the carcasses of the two horses. Nobody dared to approach till some Cossacks[5] of a street-patrol galloped up and, dismounting, began to turn over the dead. Amongst the innocent victims of the second explosion laid out on the pavement there was a body dressed in a peasant's sheepskin coat; but the face was unrecognizable, there was absolutely nothing found in the pockets of its poor cloth-ing, and it was the only one whose identity was never established.

That day Mr Razumov got up at his usual hour and spent the morning within the University buildings listening to the lectures and working for some time in the library. He heard the first vague rumour of something in the way of bomb-throwing at the table of the students' ordinary, where he was accustomed to eat his two o'clock dinner. But this rumour was made up of mere whispers, and this was Russia, where it was not always safe, for a student especi-ally, to appear too much interested in certain kinds of whispers. Razumov was one of those men who, living in a period of mental and political unrest, keep an instinctive hold on normal, practical, everyday life. He was aware of the emotional tension of his time;

he even responded to it in an indefinite way. But his main concern was with his work, his studies, and with his own future.

Officially and in fact without a family (for the daughter of the Archpriest had long been dead), no home influences had shaped his opinions or his feelings. He was as lonely in the world as a man swimming in the deep sea. The word Razumov was the mere label of a solitary individuality. There were no Razumovs belonging to him anywhere. His closest parentage was defined in the statement that he was a Russian. Whatever good he expected from life would be given to or withheld from his hopes by that connection alone. This immense parentage suffered from the throes of internal dissensions, and he shrank mentally from the fray as a good-natured man may shrink from taking definite sides in a violent family quarrel.

Razumov, going home, reflected that having prepared all the matters of the forthcoming examination, he could now devote his time to the subject of the prize essay. He hankered after the silver medal. The prize was offered by the Ministry of Education; the names of the competitors would be submitted to the Minister himself. The mere fact of trying would be considered meritorious in the higher quarters; and the possessor of the prize would have a claim to an administrative appointment of the better sort after he had taken his degree. The student Razumov in an access of elation forgot the dangers menacing the stability of the institutions which give rewards and appointments. But remembering the medallist of the year before, Razumov, the young man of no parentage, was sobered. He and some others happened to be assembled in their comrade's rooms at the very time when that last received the official advice of his success. He was a quiet, unassuming young man: 'Forgive me,' he had said with a faint apologetic smile and taking up his cap, 'I am going out to order up some wine. But I must first send a telegram to my folk at home. I say! Won't the old people make it a festive time for the neighbours for twenty miles around our place.'

Razumov thought there was nothing of that sort for him in the world. His success would matter to no one. But he felt no bitterness against the nobleman his protector, who was not a provincial magnate as was generally supposed. He was in fact nobody less than

Prince K——, once a great and splendid figure in the world and now, his day being over, a Senator and a gouty invalid, living in a still splendid but more domestic manner. He had some young children and a wife as aristocratic and proud as himself.

In all his life Razumov was allowed only once to come into personal contact with the Prince.

It had the air of a chance meeting in the little attorney's office. One day Razumov, coming in by appointment, found a stranger standing there – a tall, aristocratic-looking personage with silky, grey side-whiskers. The bald-headed, sly little lawyer-fellow called out, 'Come in – come in, Mr Razumov,' with a sort of ironic heartiness. Then turning deferentially to the stranger with the grand air, 'A ward of mine, your Excellency. One of the most promising students of his faculty in the St Petersburg University.'

To his intense surprise Razumov saw a white shapely hand extended to him. He took it in great confusion (it was soft and passive) and heard at the same time a condescending murmur in which he caught only the words 'Satisfactory' and 'Persevere'. But the most amazing thing of all was to feel suddenly a distinct pressure of the white shapely hand just before it was withdrawn: a light pressure like a secret sign. The emotion of it was terrible. Razumov's heart seemed to leap into his throat. When he raised his eyes the aristocratic personage, motioning the little lawyer aside, had opened the door and was going out.

The attorney rummaged amongst the papers on his desk for a time. 'Do you know who that was?' he asked suddenly.

Razumov, whose heart was thumping hard yet, shook his head in silence.

'That was Prince K——. You wonder what he could be doing in the hole of a poor legal rat like myself – eh? These awfully great people have their sentimental curiosities like common sinners. But if I were you, Kirylo Sidorovitch,' he continued, leering and laying a peculiar emphasis on the patronymic, 'I wouldn't boast at large of the introduction. It would not be prudent, Kirylo Sidorovitch. Oh dear no! It would be in fact dangerous for your future.'

The young man's ears burned like fire; his sight was dim. 'That man!' Razumov was saying to himself. 'He!'

Henceforth it was by this monosyllable that Mr Razumov got into the habit of referring mentally to the stranger with grey silky side-whiskers. From that time too, when walking in the more fashionable quarters, he noted with interest the magnificent horses and carriages with Prince K——'s liveries on the box. Once he saw the Princess get out – she was shopping – followed by two girls, of which one was nearly a head taller than the other. Their fair hair hung loose down their backs in the English style; they had merry eyes, their coats, muffs, and little fur caps were exactly alike, and their cheeks and noses were tinged a cheerful pink by the frost. They crossed the pavement in front of him, and Razumov went on his way smiling shyly to himself. 'His' daughters. They resembled 'Him'. The young man felt a glow of warm friendliness towards these girls who would never know of his existence. Presently they would marry Generals or Kammerherrs* and have girls and boys of their own, who perhaps would be aware of him as a celebrated old professor, decorated, possibly a Privy Councillor, one of the glories of Russia – nothing more!

But a celebrated professor was a somebody. Distinction would convert the label Razumov into an honoured name. There was nothing strange in the student Razumov's wish for distinction. A man's real life is that accorded to him in the thoughts of other men by reason of respect or natural love. Returning home on the day of the attempt on Mr de P——'s life, Razumov resolved to have a good try for the silver medal.

Climbing slowly the four flights of the dark, dirty staircase in the house where he had his lodgings, he felt confident of success. The winner's name would be published in the papers on New Year's Day. And at the thought that 'He' would most probably read it there, Razumov stopped short on the stairs for an instant, then went on smiling faintly at his own emotion. 'This is but a shadow,' he said to himself, 'but the medal is a solid beginning.'

With those ideas of industry in his head the warmth of his room was agreeable and encouraging. 'I shall put in four hours of good work,' he thought. But no sooner had he closed the door than he

* Chamberlain; gentleman-in-waiting at the court.

63

was horribly startled. All black against the usual tall stove of white tiles gleaming in the dusk, stood a strange figure, wearing a skirted, close-fitting, brown cloth coat strapped round the waist, in long boots, and with a little Astrakhan cap on its head. It loomed lithe and martial. Razumov was utterly confounded. It was only when the figure advancing two paces asked in an untroubled, grave voice if the outer door was closed that he regained his power of speech.

'Haldin! . . . Victor Victorovitch! . . . Is that you? . . . Yes. The outer door is shut all right. But this is indeed unexpected.'

Victor Haldin, a student older than most of his contemporaries at the University, was not one of the industrious set. He was hardly ever seen at lectures; the authorities had marked him as 'restless' and 'unsound' – very bad notes. But he had a great personal prestige with his comrades and influenced their thoughts. Razumov had never been intimate with him. They had met from time to time at gatherings in other students' houses. They had even had a discussion together – one of those discussions on first principles dear to the sanguine minds of youth.

Razumov wished the man had chosen some other time to come for a chat. He felt in good trim to tackle the prize essay. But as Haldin could not be slightingly dismissed Razumov adopted the tone of hospitality, asking him to sit down and smoke.

'Kirylo Sidorovitch,' said the other, flinging off his cap, 'we are not perhaps in exactly the same camp. Your judgement is more philosophical. You are a man of few words, but I haven't met anybody who dared to doubt the generosity of your sentiments. There is a solidity about your character which cannot exist without courage.'

Razumov felt flattered and began to murmur shyly something about being very glad of his good opinion, when Haldin raised his hand.

'That is what I was saying to myself,' he continued, 'as I dodged in the woodyard down by the river-side. "He has a strong character this young man," I said to myself. "He does not throw his soul to the winds." Your reserve has always fascinated me, Kirylo Sidorovitch. So I tried to remember your address. But look here – it was

64

a piece of luck. Your dvornik* was away from the gate talking to a sleigh-driver on the other side of the street. I met no one on the stairs, not a soul. As I came up to your floor I caught sight of your landlady coming out of your rooms. But she did not see me. She crossed the landing to her own side, and then I slipped in. I have been here two hours expecting you to come in every moment.'

Razumov had listened in astonishment; but before he could open his mouth Haldin added, speaking deliberately, 'It was I who removed de P—this morning.'

Razumov kept down a cry of dismay. The sentiment of his life being utterly ruined by this contact with such a crime expressed itself quaintly by a sort of half-derisive mental exclamation, 'There goes my silver medal!'

Haldin continued after waiting a while –

'You say nothing, Kirylo Sidorovitch! I understand your silence. To be sure, I cannot expect you with your frigid English manner to embrace me. But never mind your manners. You have enough heart to have heard the sound of weeping and gnashing of teeth this man raised in the land. That would be enough to get over any philosophical hopes. He was uprooting the tender plant. He had to be stopped. He was a dangerous man – a convinced man. Three more years of his work would have put us back fifty years into bondage – and look at all the lives wasted, at all the souls lost in that time.'

His curt, self-confident voice suddenly lost its ring and it was in a dull tone that he added, 'Yes, brother, I have killed him. It's weary work.'

Razumov had sunk into a chair. Every moment he expected a crowd of policemen to rush in. There must have been thousands of them out looking for that man walking up and down in his room. Haldin was talking again in a restrained, steady voice. Now and then he flourished an arm, slowly, without excitement.

He told Razumov how he had brooded for a year; how he had not slept properly for weeks. He and 'Another' had a warning of the Minister's movements from 'a certain person' late the evening

* Porter, concierge.

65

before. He and that 'Another' prepared their 'engines' and resolved to have no sleep till 'the deed' was done. They walked the streets under the falling snow with the 'engines' on them, exchanging not a word the livelong night. When they happened to meet a police patrol they took each other by the arm and pretended to be a couple of peasants on the spree. They reeled and talked in drunken hoarse voices. Except for these strange outbreaks they kept silence, moving on ceaselessly. Their plans had been previously arranged. At daybreak they made their way to the spot which they knew the sledge must pass. When it appeared in sight they exchanged a muttered good-bye and separated. The 'other' remained at the corner. Haldin took up a position a little farther up the street . . .

After throwing his 'engine' he ran off and in a moment was overtaken by the panic-struck people flying away from the spot after the second explosion. They were wild with terror. He was jostled once or twice. He slowed down for the rush to pass him and then turned to the left into a narrow street. There he was alone.

He marvelled at this immediate escape. The work was done. He could hardly believe it. He fought with an almost irresistible longing to lie down on the pavement and sleep. But this sort of faintness – a drowsy faintness – passed off quickly. He walked faster, making his way to one of the poorer parts of the town in order to look up Ziemianitch.

This Ziemianitch, Razumov understood, was a sort of town-peasant who had got on; owner of a small number of sledges and horses for hire. Haldin paused in his narrative to exclaim –

'A bright spirit! A hardy soul! The best driver in St Petersburg. He has a team of three horses there . . . Ah! He's a fellow!'

This man had declared himself willing to take out safely, at any time, one or two persons to the second or third railway station on one of the southern lines. But there had been no time to warn him the night before. His usual haunt seemed to be a low-class eating-house on the outskirts of the town. When Haldin got there the man was not to be found. He was not expected to turn up again till the evening. Haldin wandered away restlessly.

He saw the gate of a woodyard open and went in to get out of the wind which swept the bleak broad thoroughfare. The great rectangular piles of cut wood loaded with snow resembled the hut of a village. At first the watchman who discovered him crouching amongst them talked in a friendly manner. He was a dried-up old man wearing two ragged army coats one over the other; his wizened little face, tied up under the jaw and over the ears in a dirty red handkerchief, looked comical. Presently he grew sulky, and then all at once without rhyme or reason began to shout furiously.

'Aren't you ever going to clear out of this, you loafer? We know all about factory hands of your sort. A big, strong, young chap! You aren't even drunk. What do you want here? You don't frighten us. Take yourself and your ugly eyes away.'

Haldin stopped before the sitting Razumov. His supple figure, with the white forehead above which the fair hair stood straight up, had an aspect of lofty daring.

'He did not like my eyes,' he said. 'And so . . . here I am.'

Razumov made an effort to speak calmly.

'But pardon me, Victor Victorovitch. We know each other so little . . . I don't see why you . . .'

'Confidence,' said Haldin.

This word sealed Razumov's lips as if a hand had been clapped on his mouth. His brain seethed with arguments.

'And so – here you are,' he muttered through his teeth.

The other did not detect the tone of anger. Never suspected it.

'Yes. And nobody knows I am here. You are the last person that could be suspected – should I get caught. That's an advantage, you see. And then – speaking to a superior mind like yours I can well say all the truth. It occurred to me that you – you have no one belonging to you – no ties, no one to suffer for it if this came out by some means. There have been enough ruined Russian homes as it is. But I don't see how my passage through your rooms can be ever known. If I should be got hold of, I'll know how to keep silent – no matter what they may be pleased to do to me,' he added grimly.

He began to walk again while Razumov sat still, appalled.

'You thought that –' he faltered out almost sick with indignation.

'Yes, Razumov. Yes, brother. Some day you shall help to build. You suppose that I am a terrorist, now – a destructor of what is. But consider that the true destroyers are they who destroy the spirit

67

of progress and truth, not the avengers who merely kill the bodies of the persecutors of human dignity. Men like me are necessary to make room for self-contained, thinking men like you. Well, we have made the sacrifice of our lives, but all the same I want to escape if it can be done. It is not my life I want to save, but my power to do. I won't live idle. Oh no! Don't make any mistake, Razumov. Men like me are rare. And, besides, an example like this is more awful to oppressors when the perpetrator vanishes without a trace. They sit in their offices and palaces and quake. All I want you to do is to help me to vanish. No great matter that. Only to go by and by and see Ziemianitch for me at that place where I went this morning. Just tell him, "He whom you know wants a well-horsed sledge to pull up half an hour after midnight at the seventh lamp-post on the left counting from the upper end of Karabelnaya. If nobody gets in, the sledge is to run round a block or two, so as to come back past the same spot in ten minutes' time." '

Razumov wondered why he had not cut short that talk and told this man to go away long before. Was it weakness or what?

He concluded that it was a sound instinct. Haldin must have been seen. It was impossible that some people should not have noticed the face and appearance of the man who threw the second bomb. Haldin was a noticeable person. The police in their thousands must have had his description within the hour. With every moment the danger grew. Sent out to wander in the streets he could not escape being caught in the end.

The police would very soon find out all about him. They would set about discovering a conspiracy. Everybody Haldin had ever known would be in the greatest danger. Unguarded expressions, little facts in themselves innocent would be counted for crimes. Razumov remembered certain words he said, the speeches he had listened to, the harmless gatherings he had attended – it was almost impossible for a student to keep out of that sort of thing, without becoming suspect to his comrades.

Razumov saw himself shut up in a fortress, worried, badgered, perhaps ill-used. He saw himself deported by an administrative order, his life broken, ruined, and robbed of all hope. He saw himself – at best – leading a miserable existence under police supervision, in some small, far-away provincial town, without friends to assist his necessities or even take any steps to alleviate his lot – as others had. Others had fathers, mothers, brothers, relations, connections, to move heaven and earth on their behalf – he had no one. The very officials that sentenced him some morning would forget his existence before sunset.

He saw his youth pass away from him in misery and half starvation – his strength give way, his mind become an abject thing. He saw himself creeping, broken down and shabby, about the streets – dying unattended in some filthy hole of a room, or on the sordid bed of a Government hospital.

He shuddered. Then the peace of bitter calmness came over him. It was best to keep this man out of the streets till he could be got rid of with some chance of escaping. That was the best that could be done. Razumov, of course, felt the safety of his lonely existence to be permanently endangered. This evening's doings could turn up against him at any time as long as this man lived and the present institutions endured. They appeared to him rational and indestructible at that moment. They had a force of harmony – in contrast with the horrible discord of this man's presence. He hated the man. He said quietly –

'Yes, of course, I will go. You must give me precise directions, and for the rest – depend on me.'

'Ah! You are a fellow! Collected – cool as a cucumber. A regular Englishman. Where did you get your soul from? There aren't many like you. Look here, brother! Men like me leave no posterity, but their souls are not lost. No man's soul is ever lost. It works for itself – or else where would be the sense of self-sacrifice, of martyrdom, of conviction, of faith – the labours of the soul? What will become of my soul when I die in the way I must die – soon – very soon perhaps? It shall not perish. Don't make a mistake, Razumov. This is not murder – it is war, war. My spirit shall go on warring in some Russian body till all falsehood is swept out of the world. The modern civilization is false, but a new revelation shall come out of Russia. Ha! you say nothing. You are a sceptic. I respect your philosophical scepticism, Razumov, but don't touch the soul. The Russian soul that lives in all of us. It has a future. It has a mission, I tell you, or else why should I have been moved to do this – reckless – like a butcher – in the middle of all these innocent people – scattering death – I! I! . . . I wouldn't hurt a fly!'

'Not so loud,' warned Razumov harshly.

Haldin sat down abruptly, and leaning his head on his folded arms burst into tears. He wept for a long time. The dusk had deepened in the room. Razumov, motionless in sombre wonder, listened to the sobs.

The other raised his head, got up and with an effort mastered his voice.

'Yes. Men like me leave no posterity,' he repeated in a subdued tone. 'I have a sister though. She's with my old mother – I persuaded them to go abroad this year – thank God. Not a bad little girl my sister. She has the most trustful eyes of any human being that ever walked this earth. She will marry well, I hope. She may have children – sons perhaps. Look at me. My father was a Government official in the provinces. He had a little land too. A simple servant of God – a true Russian in his way. His was the soul of obedience. But I am not like him. They say I resemble my mother's eldest brother, an officer. They shot him in '28. Under Nicholas,[6] you know. Haven't I told you that this is war, war . . . But God of Justice! This is weary work.'

Razumov, in his chair, leaning his head on his hand, spoke as if from the bottom of an abyss.

'You believe in God, Haldin?'

'There you go catching at words that are wrung from one. What does it matter? What was it the Englishman said: "There is a divine soul in things . . ." Devil take him – I don't remember now. But he spoke the truth. When the day of you thinkers comes don't you forget what's divine in the Russian soul – and that's resignation. Respect that in your intellectual restlessness and don't let your arrogant wisdom spoil its message to the world. I am speaking to you now like a man with a rope round his neck. What do you imagine I am? A being in revolt? No. It's you thinkers who are in everlasting revolt. I am one of the resigned. When the necessity of this heavy work came to me and I understood that it had to be done – what did I do? Did I exult? Did I take pride in my purpose? Did I try to weigh its worth and consequences? No! I was resigned. I thought "God's will be done."'

He threw himself full length on Razumov's bed and putting the backs of his hands over his eyes remained perfectly motionless and silent. Not even the sound of his breathing could be heard. The dead stillness of the room remained undisturbed till in the darkness Razumov said gloomily –

'Haldin.'

'Yes,' answered the other readily, quite invisible now on the bed and without the slightest stir.

'Isn't it time for me to start?'

'Yes, brother.' The other was heard, lying still in the darkness as though he were talking in his sleep. 'The time has come to put fate to the test.'

He paused, then gave a few lucid directions in the quiet impersonal voice of a man in a trance. Razumov made ready without a word of answer. As he was leaving the room the voice in the bed said after him –

'Go with God, thou silent soul.'

On the landing, moving softly, Razumov locked the door and put the key in his pocket.

II

The words and events of that evening must have been graven as if with a steel tool on Mr Razumov's brain since he was able to write his relation with such fullness and precision a good many months afterwards.

The record of the thoughts which assailed him in the street is even more minute and abundant. They seem to have rushed upon him with the greater freedom because his thinking powers were no longer crushed by Haldin's presence – the appalling presence of a great crime and the stunning force of a great fanaticism. On looking through the pages of Mr Razumov's diary I own that a 'rush of thoughts' is not an adequate image.

The more adequate description would be a tumult of thoughts –

71

the faithful reflection of the state of his feelings. The thoughts in themselves were not numerous – they were like the thoughts of most human beings, few and simple – but they cannot be reproduced here in all their exclamatory repetitions which went on in an endless and weary turmoil – for the walk was long.

If to the Western reader they appear shocking, inappropriate, or even improper, it must be remembered that as to the first this may be the effect of my crude statement. For the rest I will only remark here that this is not a story of the West of Europe.

Nations it may be have fashioned their Governments, but the Governments have paid them back in the same coin. It is unthinkable that any young Englishman should find himself in Razumov's situation. This being so it would be a vain enterprise to imagine what he would think. The only safe surmise to make is that he would not think as Mr Razumov thought at this crisis of his fate. He would not have an hereditary and personal knowledge of the means by which a historical autocracy represses ideas, guards its power, and defends its existence. By an act of mental extravagance he might imagine himself arbitrarily thrown into prison, but it would never occur to him unless he were delirious (and perhaps not even then) that he could be beaten with whips as a practical measure either of investigation or of punishment.

This is but a crude and obvious example of the different conditions of Western thought. I don't know that this danger occurred specially to Mr Razumov. No doubt it entered unconsciously into the general dread and the general appallingness of this crisis. Razumov, as has been seen, was aware of more subtle ways in which an individual may be undone by the proceedings of a despotic Government. A simple expulsion from the University (the very least that could happen to him), with an impossibility to continue his studies anywhere, was enough to ruin utterly a young man depending entirely upon the development of his natural abilities for his place in the world. He was a Russian: and for him to be implicated meant simply sinking into the lowest social depths amongst the hopeless and the destitute – the night birds of the city.

The peculiar circumstances of Razumov's parentage, or rather of his lack of parentage, should be taken into the account of his thoughts. And he remembered them too. He had been lately reminded of them in a peculiarly atrocious way by this fatal Haldin. 'Because I haven't that, must everything else be taken away from me?' he thought.

He nerved himself for another effort to go on. Along the roadway sledges glided phantom-like and jingling through a fluttering whiteness on the black face of the night. 'For it is a crime,' he was saying to himself. 'A murder is a murder. Though, of course, some sort of liberal institutions . . .'

A feeling of horrible sickness came over him. 'I must be courageous,' he exhorted himself mentally. All his strength was suddenly gone as if taken out by a hand. Then by a mighty effort of will it came back because he was afraid of fainting in the street and being picked up by the police with the key of his lodgings in his pocket. They would find Haldin there, and then, indeed, he would be undone.

Strangely enough it was this fear which seems to have kept him up to the end. The passers-by were rare. They came upon him suddenly, looming up black in the snowflakes close by, then vanishing all at once – without footfalls.

It was the quarter of the very poor. Razumov noticed an elderly woman tied up in ragged shawls. Under the street lamp she seemed a beggar off duty. She walked leisurely in the blizzard as though she had no home to hurry to, she hugged under one arm a round loaf of black bread with an air of guarding a priceless booty; and Razumov averting his glance envied her the peace of her mind and the serenity of her fate.

To one reading Mr Razumov's narrative it is really a wonder how he managed to keep going as he did along one interminable street after another on pavements that were gradually becoming blocked with snow. It was the thought of Haldin locked up in his rooms and the desperate desire to get rid of his presence which drove him forward. No rational determination had any part in his exertions. Thus, when on arriving at the low eating-house he heard that the man of horses, Ziemianitch, was not there, he could only stare stupidly.

The waiter, a wild-haired youth in tarred boots and a pink shirt, exclaimed, uncovering his pale gums in a silly grin, that Ziemian-itch had got his skinful early in the afternoon and had gone away with a bottle under each arm to keep it up amongst the horses – he supposed.

The owner of the vile den, a bony short man in a dirty cloth caftan coming down to his heels, stood by, his hands tucked into his belt, and nodded confirmation.

The reek of spirits, the greasy rancid steam of food got Razumov by the throat. He struck a table with his clenched hand and shouted violently –

'You lie.'

Bleary unwashed faces were turned to his direction. A mild-eyed ragged tramp drinking tea at the next table moved farther away. A murmur of wonder arose with an undertone of uneasiness. A laugh was heard too, and an exclamation, 'There! there!' jeeringly soothing. The waiter looked all round and announced to the room –

'The gentleman won't believe that Ziemianitch is drunk.'

From a distant corner a hoarse voice belonging to a horrible, nondescript, shaggy being with a black face like the muzzle of a bear grunted angrily –

'The cursed driver of thieves. What do we want with his gentle-men here? We are all honest folk in this place.'

Razumov, biting his lip till blood came to keep himself from bursting into imprecations, followed the owner of the den, who, whispering 'Come along, little father,' led him into a tiny hole of a place behind the wooden counter, whence proceeded a sound of splashing. A wet and bedraggled creature, a sort of sexless and shivering scarecrow, washed glasses in there, bending over a wooden tub by the light of a tallow dip.

'Yes, little father,' the man in the long caftan said plaintively. He had a brown, cunning little face, a thin greyish beard. Trying to light a tin lantern he hugged it to his breast and talked garrulously the while.

He would show Ziemianitch to the gentleman to prove there were no lies told. And he would show him drunk. His woman, it seems, ran away from him last night. 'Such a hag she was! Thin! Pfui!' He spat. They were always running away from that driver of the devil – and he sixty years old too; could never get used to it. But each heart knows sorrow after its own kind and Ziemianitch was a born fool all his days. And then he would fly to the bottle. '"Who could bear life in our land without the bottle?" he says. A proper Russian man – the little pig ... Be pleased to follow me.'

Razumov crossed a quadrangle of deep snow enclosed between high walls with innumerable windows. Here and there a dim yellow light hung within the four-square mass of darkness. The house was an enormous slum, a hive of human vermin, a monumental abode of misery towering on the verge of starvation and despair.

In a corner the ground sloped sharply down, and Razumov followed the light of the lantern through a small doorway into a long cavernous place like a neglected subterranean byre. Deep within, three shaggy little horses tied up to rings hung their heads together, motionless and shadowy in the dim light of the lantern. It must have been the famous team of Haldin's escape. Razumov peered fearfully into the gloom. His guide pawed in the straw with his foot.

'Here he is. Ah! the little pigeon. A true Russian man. "No heavy hearts for me," he says. "Bring out the bottle and take your ugly mug out of my sight." Ha! ha! ha! That's the fellow he is.'

He held the lantern over a prone form of a man, apparently fully dressed for outdoors. His head was lost in a pointed cloth hood. On the other side of a heap of straw protruded a pair of feet in monstrous thick boots.

'Always ready to drive,' commented the keeper of the eating-house. 'A proper Russian driver that. Saint or devil, night or day is all one to Ziemianitch when his heart is free from sorrow. "I don't ask who you are, but where you want to go," he says. He would drive Satan himself to his own abode and come back chirruping to his horses. Many a one he has driven who is clanking his chains in the Nertchinsk mines[7] by this time.'

Razumov shuddered.

'Call him, wake him up,' he faltered out.

The other set down his light, stepped back and launched a kick at the prostrate sleeper. The man shook at the impact but did not move. At the third kick he grunted but remained inert as before.

The eating-house keeper desisted and fetched a deep sigh.

'You see for yourself how it is. We have done what we can for you.'

He picked up the lantern. The intense black spokes of shadow swung about in the circle of light. A terrible fury – the blind rage of self-preservation – possessed Razumov.

'Ah! The vile beast,' he bellowed out in an unearthly tone which made the lantern jump and tremble! 'I shall wake you! Give me . . . Give me . . .'

He looked round wildly, seized the handle of a stablefork and rushing forward struck at the prostrate body with inarticulate cries. After a time his cries ceased, and the rain of blows fell in the stillness and shadows of the cellar-like stable. Razumov belaboured Ziemianitch with an insatiable fury, in great volleys of sounding thwacks. Except for the violent movements of Razumov nothing stirred, neither the beaten man nor the spoke-like shadows on the walls. And only the sound of blows was heard. It was a weird scene.

Suddenly there was a sharp crack. The stick broke and half of it flew far away into the gloom beyond the light. At the same time Ziemianitch sat up. At this Razumov became as motionless as the man with the lantern – only his breast heaved for air as if ready to burst.

Some dull sensation of pain must have penetrated at last the consoling night of drunkenness enwrapping the 'bright Russian soul', of Haldin's enthusiastic praise. But Ziemianitch evidently saw nothing. His eyeballs blinked all white in the light once, twice – then the gleam went out. For a moment he sat in the straw with closed eyes with a strange air of weary meditation, then fell over slowly on his side without making the slightest sound. Only the straw rustled a little. Razumov stared wildly, fighting for his breath. After a second or two he heard a light snore.

He flung from him the piece of stick remaining in his grasp, and went off with great hasty strides without looking back once.

After going heedlessly for some fifty yards along the street he walked into a snowdrift and was up to his knees before he stopped.

This recalled him to himself; and glancing about he discovered he had been going in the wrong direction. He retraced his steps, but now at a more moderate pace. When passing before the house he had just left he flourished his fist at the sombre refuge of misery and crime rearing its sinister bulk on the white ground. It had an air of brooding. He let his arm fall by his side – discouraged.

Ziemianitch's passionate surrender to sorrow and consolation had baffled him. That was the people. A true Russian man! Razumov was glad he had beaten that brute – the 'bright soul' of the other. Here they were: the people and the enthusiast.

Between the two he was done for. Between the drunkenness of the peasant incapable of action and the dream-intoxication of the idealist incapable of perceiving the reason of things, and the true character of men. It was a sort of terrible childishness. But children had their masters. 'Ah! the stick, the stick, the stern hand,' thought Razumov, longing for power to hurt and destroy.

He was glad he had thrashed that brute. The physical exertion had left his body in a comfortable glow. His mental agitation too was clarified as if all the feverishness had gone out of him in a fit of outward violence. Together with the persisting sense of terrible danger he was conscious now of a tranquil, unquenchable hate.

He walked slower and slower. And indeed, considering the guest he had in his rooms, it was no wonder he lingered on the way. It was like harbouring a pestilential disease that would not perhaps take your life, but would take from you all that made life worth living – a subtle pest that would convert earth into a hell.

What was he doing now? Lying on the bed as if dead, with the back of his hands over his eyes? Razumov had a morbidly vivid vision of Haldin on his bed – the white pillow hollowed by the head, the legs in long boots, the upturned feet. And in his abhorrence he said to himself, 'I'll kill him when I get home.' But he knew very well that that was of no use. The corpse hanging round his neck would be nearly as fatal as the living man. Nothing short of complete annihilation would do. And that was impossible. What then? Must one kill oneself to escape this visitation?

Razumov's despair was too profoundly tinged with hate to accept that issue.

77

And yet it was despair – nothing less – at the thought of having to live with Haldin for an indefinite number of days in mortal alarm at every sound. But perhaps when he heard that this 'bright soul' of Ziemianitch suffered from a drunken eclipse the fellow would take his infernal resignation somewhere else. And that was not likely on the face of it.

Razumov thought: 'I am being crushed – and I can't even run away.' Other men had somewhere a corner of the earth – some little house in the provinces where they had a right to take their troubles. A material refuge. He had nothing. He had not even a moral refuge – the refuge of confidence. To whom could he go with this tale – in all this great, great land?

Razumov stamped his foot – and under the soft carpet of snow felt the hard ground of Russia, inanimate, cold, inert, like a sullen and tragic mother hiding her face under a winding-sheet – his native soil! – his very own – without a fireside, without a heart!

He cast his eyes upwards and stood amazed. The snow had ceased to fall, and now, as if by a miracle, he saw above his head the clear black sky of the northern winter, decorated with the sumptuous fires of the stars. It was a canopy fit for the resplendent purity of the snows.

Razumov received an almost physical impression of endless space and of countless millions.

He responded to it with the readiness of a Russian who is born to an inheritance of space and numbers. Under the sumptuous immensity of the sky, the snow covered the endless forests, the frozen rivers, the plains of an immense country, obliterating the landmarks, the accidents of the ground, levelling everything under its uniform whiteness, like a monstrous blank page awaiting the record of an inconceivable history. It covered the passive land with its lives of countless people like Ziemianitch and its handful of agitators like this Haldin – murdering foolishly.

It was a sort of sacred inertia. Razumov felt a respect for it. A voice seemed to cry within him, 'Don't touch it.' It was a guarantee of duration, of safety, while the travail of maturing destiny went on – a work not of revolutions with their passionate levity of action and their shifting impulses – but of peace. What it needed was not the conflicting aspirations of a people, but a will strong and one: it wanted not the babble of many voices, but a man – strong and one!

Razumov stood on the point of conversion. He was fascinated by its approach, by its overpowering logic. For a train of thought is never false. The falsehood lies deep in the necessities of existence, in secret fears and half-formed ambitions, in the secret confidence combined with a secret mistrust of ourselves in the love of hope and the dread of uncertain days.

In Russia, the land of spectral ideas and disembodied aspirations, many brave minds have turned away at last from the vain and endless conflict to the one great historical fact of the land. They turned to autocracy for the peace of their patriotic conscience as a weary unbeliever, touched by grace, turns to the faith of his fathers for the blessing of spiritual rest. Like other Russians before him, Razumov, in conflict with himself, felt the touch of grace upon his forehead.

'Haldin means disruption,' he thought to himself, beginning to walk again. 'What is he with his indignation, with his talk of bondage – with his talk of God's justice? All that means disruption. Better that thousands should suffer than that a people should become a disintegrated mass, helpless like dust in the wind. Obscurantism is better than the light of incendiary torches. The seed germinates in the night. Out of the dark soil springs the perfect plant. But a volcanic eruption is sterile, the ruin of the fertile ground. And am I, who love my country – who have nothing but that to love and put my faith in – am I to have my future, perhaps my usefulness, ruined by this sanguinary fanatic?'

The grace entered into Razumov. He believed now in the man who would come at the appointed time.

What is a throne? A few pieces of wood upholstered in velvet. But a throne is a seat of power too. The form of government is the shape of a tool – an instrument. But twenty thousand bladders inflated by the noblest sentiments and jostling against each other in the air are a miserable incumbrance of space, holding no power, possessing no will, having nothing to give.

He went on thus, heedless of the way, holding a discourse with himself with extraordinary abundance and facility. Generally his

79

phrases came to him slowly, after a conscious and painstaking wooing. Some superior power had inspired him with a flow of masterly argument as certain converted sinners become overwhelmingly loquacious.

He felt an austere exultation.

'What are the luridly smoky lucubrations of that fellow to the clear grasp of my intellect?' he thought. 'Is not this my country? Have I not got forty million brothers?' he asked himself, unanswerably victorious in the silence of his breast. And the fearful thrashing he had given the inanimate Ziemianitch seemed to him a sign of intimate union, a pathetically severe necessity of brotherly love. 'No! If I must suffer let me at least suffer for my convictions, not for a crime my reason – my cool superior reason – rejects.'

He ceased to think for a moment. The silence in his breast was complete. But he felt a suspicious uneasiness, such as we may experience when we enter an unlighted strange place – the irrational feeling that something may jump upon us in the dark – the absurd dread of the unseen.

Of course he was far from being a moss-grown reactionary. Everything was not for the best. Despotic bureaucracy ... abuses ... corruption ... and so on. Capable men were wanted. Enlightened intelligences. Devoted hearts. But absolute power should be preserved – the tool ready for the man – for the great autocrat of the future. Razumov believed in him. The logic of history made him unavoidable. The state of the people demanded him. 'What else?' he asked himself ardently, 'could move all that mass in one direction? Nothing could. Nothing but a single will.'

He was persuaded that he was sacrificing his personal longings of liberalism – rejecting the attractive error for the stern Russian truth. 'That's patriotism,' he observed mentally, and added, 'There's no stopping midway on that road,' and then remarked to himself, 'I am not a coward.'

And again there was a dead silence in Razumov's breast. He walked with lowered head, making room for no one. He walked slowly and his thoughts returning spoke within him with solemn slowness.

'What is this Haldin? And what am I? Only two grains of sand.

But a great mountain is made up of just such insignificant grains. And the death of a man or of many men is an insignificant thing. Yet we combat a contagious pestilence. Do I want his death? No! I would save him if I could – but no one can do that – he is the withered member which must be cut off. If I must perish through him, let me at least not perish with him, and associated against my will with his sombre folly that understands nothing either of men or things. Why should I leave a false memory?'

It passed through his mind that there was no one in the world who cared what sort of memory he left behind him. He exclaimed to himself instantly, 'Perish vainly for a falsehood! ... What a miserable fate!'

He was now in a more animated part of the town. He did not remark the crash of two colliding sledges close to the curb. The driver of one bellowed tearfully at his fellow –

'Oh, thou vile wretch!'

This hoarse yell, let out nearly in his ear, disturbed Razumov. He shook his head impatiently and went on looking straight before him. Suddenly on the snow, stretched on his back right across his path, he saw Haldin, solid, distinct, real, with his inverted hands over his eyes, clad in a brown close-fitting coat and long boots. He was lying out of the way a little, as though he had selected that place on purpose. The snow round him was untrodden.

This hallucination had such a solidity of aspect that the first movement of Razumov was to reach for his pocket to assure himself that the key of his rooms was there. But he checked the impulse with a disdainful curve of his lips. He understood. His thought, concentrated intensely on the figure left lying on his bed, had culminated in this extraordinary illusion of the sight. Razumov tackled the phenomenon calmly. With a stern face, without a check and gazing far beyond the vision, he walked on, experiencing nothing but a slight tightening of the chest. After passing he turned his head for a glance, and saw only the unbroken track of his footsteps over the place where the breast of the phantom had been lying.

Razumov walked on and after a little time whispered his wonder to himself.

'Exactly as if alive! Seemed to breathe! And right in my way too! I have had an extraordinary experience.'

He made a few steps and muttered through his set teeth –

'I shall give him up.'

Then for some twenty yards or more all was blank. He wrapped his cloak closer round him. He pulled his cap well forward over his eyes.

'Betray. A great word. What is betrayal? They talk of a man betraying his country, his friends, his sweetheart. There must be a moral bond first. All a man can betray is his conscience. And how is my conscience engaged here; by what bond of common faith, of common conviction, am I obliged to let that fanatical idiot drag me down with him? On the contrary – every obligation of true courage is the other way.'

Razumov looked round from under his cap.

'What can the prejudice of the world reproach me with? Have I provoked his confidence? No! Have I by a single word, look, or gesture given him reason to suppose that I accepted his trust in me? No! It is true that I consented to go and see his Ziemianitch. Well, I have been to see him. And I broke a stick on his back too – the brute.'

Something seemed to turn over in his head bringing uppermost a singularly hard, clear facet of his brain.

'It would be better, however,' he reflected with a quite different mental accent, 'to keep that circumstance altogether to myself.'

He had passed beyond the turn leading to his lodgings, and had reached a wide and fashionable street. Some shops were still open, and all the restaurants. Lights fell on the pavement where men in expensive fur coats, with here and there the elegant figure of a woman, walked with an air of leisure. Razumov looked at them with the contempt of an austere believer for the frivolous crowd. It was the world – those officers, dignitaries, men of fashion, officials, members of the Yacht Club. The event of the morning affected them all. What would they say if they knew what this student in a cloak was going to do?

'Not one of them is capable of feeling and thinking as deeply as I can. How many of them could accomplish an act of conscience?'

Razumov lingered in the well-lighted street. He was firmly decided. Indeed, it could hardly be called a decision. He had simply discovered what he had meant to do all along. And yet he felt the need of some other mind's sanction.

With something resembling anguish he said to himself –

'I want to be understood.' The universal aspiration with all its profound and melancholy meaning assailed heavily Razumov, who, amongst eighty millions of his kith and kin, had no heart to which he could open himself.

The attorney was not to be thought of. He despised the little agent of chicane too much. One could not go and lay one's conscience before the policeman at the corner. Neither was Razumov anxious to go to the chief of his district's police – a common-looking person whom he used to see sometimes in the street in a shabby uniform and with a smouldering cigarette stuck to his lower lip. 'He would begin by locking me up most probably. At any rate, he is certain to get excited and create an awful commotion,' thought Razumov practically.

An act of conscience must be done with outward dignity.

Razumov longed desperately for a word of advice, for moral support. Who knows what true loneliness is – not the conventional word, but the naked terror? To the lonely themselves it wears a mask. The most miserable outcast hugs some memory or some illusion. Now and then a fatal conjunction of events may lift the veil for an instant. For an instant only. No human being could bear a steady view of moral solitude without going mad.

Razumov had reached that point of vision. To escape from it he embraced for a whole minute the delirious purpose of rushing to his lodgings and flinging himself on his knees by the side of the bed with the dark figure stretched on it; to pour out a full confession in passionate words that would stir the whole being of that man to its innermost depths; that would end in embraces and tears; in an incredible fellowship of souls – such as the world had never seen. It was sublime!

Inwardly he wept and trembled already. But to the casual eyes that were cast upon him he was aware that he appeared as a tranquil student in a cloak, out for a leisurely stroll. He noted, too, the sidelong, brilliant glance of a pretty woman – with a delicate head, and covered in the hairy skins of wild beasts down to her feet, like a frail and beautiful savage – which rested for a moment with a sort of mocking tenderness on the deep abstraction of that good-looking young man.

Suddenly Razumov stood still. The glimpse of a passing grey whisker, caught and lost in the same instant, had evoked the complete image of Prince K—, the man who once had pressed his hand as no other man had pressed it – a faint but lingering pressure like a secret sign, like a half-unwilling caress.

And Razumov marvelled at himself. Why did he not think of him before!

'A senator, a dignitary, a great personage, the very man – He!'

A strange softening emotion came over Razumov – made his knees shake a little. He repressed it with a new-born austerity. All that sentiment was pernicious nonsense. He couldn't be quick enough; and when he got into a sledge he shouted to the driver –

'To the K— Palace. Get on – you! Fly!'

The startled moujik, bearded up to the very whites of his eyes, answered obsequiously –

'I hear, your high Nobility.'

It was lucky for Razumov that Prince K— was not a man of timid character. On the day of Mr de P—'s murder an extreme alarm and despondency prevailed in the high official spheres.

Prince K—, sitting sadly alone in his study, was told by his alarmed servants that a mysterious young man had forced his way into the hall, refused to tell his name and the nature of his business, and would not move from there till he had seen his Excellency in private. Instead of locking himself up and telephoning for the police, as nine out of ten personages would have done that evening, the Prince gave way to curiosity and came quietly to the door of his study.

In the hall, the front door standing wide open, he recognized at once Razumov, pale as death, his eyes blazing, and surrounded by perplexed lackeys.

The Prince was vexed beyond measure, and even indignant. But his humane instincts and a subtle sense of self-respect could not allow him to let this young man be thrown out into the street by base menials. He retreated unseen into his room, and after a little rang his bell. Razumov heard in the hall an ominously raised harsh voice saying somewhere far away –

'Show the gentleman in here.'

Razumov walked in without a tremor. He felt himself invulnerable – raised far above the shallowness of common judgement. Though he saw the Prince looking at him with black displeasure, the lucidity of his mind, of which he was very conscious, gave him an extraordinary assurance. He was not asked to sit down.

Half an hour later they appeared in the hall together. The lackeys stood up, and the Prince, moving with difficulty on his gouty feet, was helped into his furs. The carriage had been ordered before. When the great double door was flung open with a crash, Razumov, who had been standing silent with a lost gaze but with every faculty intensely on the alert, heard the Prince's voice –

'Your arm, young man.'

The mobile, superficial mind of the ex-Guards officer, man of showy missions, experienced in nothing but the arts of gallant intrigue and worldly success, had been equally impressed by the more obvious difficulties of such a situation and by Razumov's quiet dignity in stating them.

He had said, 'No. Upon the whole I can't condemn the step you ventured to take by coming to me with your story. It is not an affair for police understrappers. The greatest importance is attached to ... Set your mind at rest. I shall see you through this most extraordinary and difficult situation.'

Then the Prince rose to ring the bell, and Razumov, making a short bow, had said with deference –

'I have trusted my instinct. A young man having no claim upon anybody in the world has in an hour of trial involving his deepest political convictions turned to an illustrious Russian – that's all.'

The Prince had exclaimed hastily –

'You have done well.'

In the carriage – it was a small brougham on sleigh runners – Razumov broke the silence in a voice that trembled slightly.

'My gratitude surpasses the greatness of my presumption.'

85

He gasped, feeling unexpectedly in the dark a momentary pressure on his arm.

'You have done well,' repeated the Prince.

When the carriage stopped the Prince murmured to Razumov, who had never ventured a single question –

'The house of General T—.'

In the middle of the snow-covered roadway blazed a great bonfire. Some Cossacks, the bridles of their horses over the arm, were warming themselves around it. Two sentries stood at the door, several gendarmes lounged under the great carriage gateway, and on the first-floor landing two orderlies rose and stood at attention. Razumov walked at the Prince's elbow.

A surprising quantity of hot-house plants in pots cumbered the floor of the ante-room. Servants came forward. A young man in civilian clothes arrived hurriedly, was whispered to, bowed low, and exclaiming zealously, 'Certainly – this minute,' fled within somewhere. The Prince signed to Razumov.

They passed through a suite of reception-rooms all barely lit and one of them prepared for dancing. The wife of the General had put off her party. An atmosphere of consternation pervaded the place. But the General's own room, with heavy sombre hangings, two massive desks, and deep armchairs, had all the lights turned on. The footman shut the door behind them and they waited.

There was a coal fire in an English grate; Razumov had never before seen such a fire; and the silence of the room was like the silence of the grave; perfect, measureless, for even the clock on the mantelpiece made no sound. Filling a corner, on a black pedestal, stood a quarter-life-size smooth-limbed bronze of an adolescent figure, running. The Prince observed in an undertone –

'Spontini's. "Flight of Youth". Exquisite.'

'Admirable, assented Razumov faintly.

They said nothing more after this, the Prince silent with his grand air, Razumov staring at the statue. He was worried by a sensation resembling the gnawing of hunger.

He did not turn when he heard an inner door fly open, and a quick footstep, muffled on the carpet.

The Prince's voice immediately exclaimed, thick with excitement –

'We have got him – *ce misérable*. A worthy young man came to me – No! It's incredible ...'

Razumov held his breath before the bronze as if expecting a crash. Behind his back a voice he had never heard before insisted politely –

'*Asseyez-vous donc.*'*

The Prince almost shrieked, '*Mais comprenez-vous, mon cher!*† *L'assassin!* the murderer – we have got him ...'

Razumov spun round. The General's smooth big cheeks rested on the stiff collar of his uniform. He must have been already looking at Razumov, because that last saw the pale blue eyes fastened on him coldly.

The Prince from a chair waved an impressive hand.

'This is a most honourable young man whom Providence itself ... Mr Razumov.'

The General acknowledged the introduction by frowning at Razumov, who did not make the slightest movement.

Sitting down before his desk the General listened with compressed lips. It was impossible to detect any sign of emotion on his face.

Razumov watched the immobility of the fleshy profile. But it lasted only a moment, till the Prince had finished; and when the General turned to the providential young man, his florid complexion, the blue, unbelieving eyes and the bright white flash of an automatic smile had an air of jovial, careless cruelty. He expressed no wonder at the extraordinary story – no pleasure or excitement – no incredulity either. He betrayed no sentiment whatever. Only with a politeness almost deferential suggested that 'the bird might have flown while Mr – Mr Razumov was running about the streets'.

Razumov advanced to the middle of the room and said, 'The door is locked and I have the key in my pocket.'

His loathing for the man was intense. It had come upon him so unawares that he felt he had not kept it out of his voice. The General looked up at him thoughtfully, and Razumov grinned.

All this went over the head of Prince K— seated in a deep armchair, very tired and impatient.

---

* 'Please be seated.'
† 'But don't you understand, my friend?'

87

'A student called Haldin,' said the General thoughtfully.

Razumov ceased to grin.

'That is his name,' he said, unnecessarily loud. 'Victor Victoro-vitch Haldin – a student.'

The General shifted his position a little.

'How is he dressed? Would you have the goodness to tell me?'

Razumov angrily described Haldin's clothing in a few jerky words. The General stared all the time, then addressing the Prince –

'We were not without some indications,' he said in French.[8] 'A good woman who was in the street described to us somebody wearing a dress of the sort as the thrower of the second bomb. We have detained her at the Secretariat, and everyone in a Tcherkess coat[9] we could lay our hands on has been brought to her to look at. She kept on crossing herself and shaking her head at them. It was exasperating . . .'

He turned to Razumov, and in Russian, with friendly re-proach –

'Take a chair, Mr Razumov – do. Why are you standing?'

Razumov sat down carelessly and looked at the General.

'This goggle-eyed imbecile understands nothing,' he thought.

The Prince began to speak loftily.

'Mr Razumov is a young man of conspicuous abilities. I have it at heart that his future should not . . .'

'Certainly,' interrupted the General, with a movement of the hand. 'Has he any weapons on him, do you think, Mr Razumov?'

The General employed a gentle musical voice. Razumov answered with suppressed irritation –

'No. But my razors are lying about – you understand.'

The General lowered his head approvingly.

'Precisely.'

Then to the Prince, explaining courteously –

'We want that bird alive. It will be the devil if we can't make him sing a little before we are done with him.'

The grave-like silence of the room with its mute clock fell upon the polite modulations of this terrible phrase. The Prince, hidden in the chair, made no sound.

The General unexpectedly developed a thought.

'Fidelity to menaced institutions on which depend the safety of a throne and of a people is no child's play. We know that, *mon Prince*, and – *tenez* –' he went on with a sort of flattering harshness, 'Mr Razumov here begins to understand that too.'

His eyes which he turned upon Razumov seemed to be starting out of his head. This grotesqueness of aspect no longer shocked Razumov. He said with gloomy conviction –

'Haldin will never speak.'

'That remains to be seen,' muttered the General.

'I am certain,' insisted Razumov. 'A man like this never speaks ... Do you imagine that I am here from fear?' he added violently. He felt ready to stand by his opinion of Haldin to the last extremity.

'Certainly not,' protested the General, with great simplicity of tone. 'And I don't mind telling you, Mr Razumov, that if he had not come with his tale to such a staunch and loyal Russian as you, he would have disappeared like a stone in the water ... which would have had a detestable effect,' he added, with a bright, cruel smile under his stony stare. 'So you see, there can be no suspicion of any fear here.'

The Prince intervened, looking at Razumov round the back of the armchair.

'Nobody doubts the moral soundness of your action. Be at ease in that respect, pray.'

He turned to the General uneasily.

'That's why I am here. You may be surprised why I should ...'

The General hastened to interrupt.

'Not at all. Extremely natural. You saw the importance ...'

'Yes,' broke in the Prince. 'And I venture to ask insistently that mine and Mr Razumov's intervention should not become public. He is a young man of promise – of remarkable aptitudes.'

'I haven't a doubt of it,' murmured the General. 'He inspires confidence.'

'All sorts of pernicious views are so widespread nowadays – they taint such unexpected quarters – that, monstrous as it seems, he might suffer ... His studies ... His ...'

The General, with his elbows on the desk, took his head between his hands.

'Yes. Yes. I am thinking it out . . . How long is it since you left him at your rooms, Mr Razumov?'

Razumov mentioned the hour which nearly corresponded with the time of his distracted flight from the big slum house. He had made up his mind to keep Ziemianitch out of the affair completely. To mention him at all would mean imprisonment for the 'bright soul', perhaps cruel floggings, and in the end a journey to Siberia in chains. Razumov, who had beaten Ziemianitch, felt for him now a vague, remorseful tenderness.

The General, giving way for the first time to his secret sentiments, exclaimed contemptuously –

'And you say he came in to make you this confidence like this – for nothing – *à propos des bottes*.'*

Razumov felt danger in the air. The merciless suspicion of despotism had spoken openly at last. Sudden fear sealed Razumov's lips. The silence of the room resembled now the silence of a deep dungeon, where time does not count, and a suspect person is sometimes forgotten for ever. But the Prince came to the rescue.

'Providence itself has led the wretch in a moment of mental aberration to seek Mr Razumov on the strength of some old, utterly misinterpreted exchange of ideas – some sort of idle speculative conversation – months ago – I am told – and completely forgotten till now by Mr Razumov.'

'Mr Razumov,' queried the General meditatively, after a short silence, 'do you often indulge in speculative conversation?'

'No, Excellency,' answered Razumov, coolly, in a sudden access of self-confidence. 'I am a man of deep convictions. Crude opinions are in the air. They are not always worth combating. But even the silent contempt of a serious mind may be misinterpreted by head-long utopists.'

The General stared from between his hands. Prince K— murmured –

'A serious young man. *Un esprit supérieur*.'

* 'Without any reason.'

'I see that, *mon cher Prince*,' said the General. 'Mr Razumov is quite safe with me. I am interested in him. He has, it seems, the great and useful quality of inspiring confidence. What I was wondering at is why the other should mention anything at all – I mean even the bare fact alone – if his object was only to obtain temporary shelter for a few hours. For, after all, nothing was easier than to say nothing about it unless, indeed, he were trying, under a crazy misapprehension of your true sentiments, to enlist your assistance – eh, Mr Razumov?'

It seemed to Razumov that the floor was moving slightly. This grotesque man in a tight uniform was terrible. It was right that he should be terrible.

'I can see what your Excellency has in your mind. But I can only answer that I don't know why.'

'I have nothing in my mind,' murmured the General with gentle surprise.

'I am his prey – his helpless prey,' thought Razumov. The fatigues and the disgusts of that afternoon, the need to forget, the fear which he could not keep off, reawakened his hate for Haldin.

'Then I can't help your Excellency. I don't know what he meant. I only know there was a moment when I wished to kill him. There was also a moment when I wished myself dead. I said nothing. I was overcome. I provoked no confidence – I asked for no explanations –'

Razumov seemed beside himself; but his mind was lucid. It was really a calculated outburst.

'It is rather a pity,' the General said, 'that you did not. Don't you know at all what he means to do?'

Razumov calmed down and saw an opening there.

'He told me he was in hopes that a sledge would meet him about half an hour after midnight at the seventh lamp-post on the left from the upper end of Karabelnaya. At any rate, he meant to be there at that time. He did not even ask me for a change of clothes.'

'*Ah voilà!*' said the General, turning to Prince K— with an air of satisfaction. 'There is a way to keep your *protégé*, Mr Razumov, quite clear of any connection with the actual arrest. We shall be ready for that gentleman in Karabelnaya.'

91

The Prince expressed his gratitude. There was real emotion in his voice. Razumov, motionless, silent, sat staring at the carpet. The General turned to him.

'Half an hour after midnight. Till then we have to depend on you, Mr Razumov. You don't think he is likely to change his purpose?'

'How can I tell?' said Razumov. 'Those men are not of the sort that ever changes its purpose.'

'What men do you mean?'

'Fanatical lovers of liberty in general. Liberty with a capital L, Excellency. Liberty that means nothing precise. Liberty in whose name crimes are committed.'

The General murmured –

'I detest rebels of every kind. I can't help it. It's my nature!'

He clenched a fist and shook it, drawing back his arm. 'They shall be destroyed, then.'

'They have made a sacrifice of their lives beforehand,' said Razumov with malicious pleasure and looking the General straight in the face. 'If Haldin does change his purpose tonight, you may depend on it that it will not be to save his life by flight in some other way. He would have thought then of something else to attempt. But that is not likely.'

The General repeated as if to himself, 'They shall be destroyed.'

Razumov assumed an impenetrable expression.

The Prince exclaimed –

'What a terrible necessity!'

The General's arm was lowered slowly.

'One comfort there is. That brood leaves no posterity. I've always said it; one effort, pitiless, persistent, steady – and we are done with them for ever.'

Razumov thought to himself that this man entrusted with so much arbitrary power must have believed what he said or else he could not have gone on bearing the responsibility.

The General repeated again with extreme animosity –

'I detest rebels. These subversive minds! These intellectual *debauchés*! My existence has been built on fidelity. It's a feeling. To defend it I am ready to lay down my life – and even my honour – if that were needed. But pray tell me what honour can there be as against rebels – against people that deny God Himself – perfect unbelievers! Brutes. It is horrible to think of.'

During this tirade Razumov, facing the General, had nodded slightly twice. Prince K—, standing on one side with his grand air, murmured, casting up his eyes –

'*Hélas!*'

Then lowering his glance and with great decision declared –

'This young man, General, is perfectly fit to apprehend the bearing of your memorable words.'

The General's whole expression changed from dull resentment to perfect urbanity.

'I would ask now, Mr Razumov,' he said, 'to return to his home. Note that I don't ask Mr Razumov whether he has justified his absence to his guest. No doubt he did this sufficiently. But I don't ask. Mr Razumov inspires confidence. It is a great gift. I only suggest that a more prolonged absence might awaken the criminal's suspicions and induce him perhaps to change his plans.'

He rose and with a scrupulous courtesy escorted his visitors to the ante-room encumbered with flower-pots.

Razumov parted with the Prince at the corner of a street. In the carriage he had listened to speeches where natural sentiment struggled with caution. Evidently the Prince was afraid of encouraging any hopes of future intercourse. But there was a touch of tenderness in the voice uttering in the dark the guarded general phrases of goodwill. And the Prince too said –

'I have perfect confidence in you, Mr Razumov.'

'They all, it seems, have confidence in me,' thought Razumov dully. He had an indulgent contempt for the man sitting shoulder to shoulder with him in the confined space. Probably he was afraid of scenes with his wife. She was said to be proud and violent.

It seemed to him bizarre that secrecy should play such a large part in the comfort and safety of lives. But he wanted to put the Prince's mind at ease; and with a proper amount of emphasis he said that, being conscious of some small abilities and confident in his power of work, he trusted his future to his own exertions. He expressed his gratitude for the helping hand. Such dangerous situations did not occur twice in the course of one life – he added.

93

'And you have met this one with a firmness of mind and correctness of feeling which give me a high idea of your worth,' the Prince said solemnly. 'You have now only to persevere – to persevere.'

On getting out on the pavement Razumov saw an ungloved hand extended to him through the lowered window of the brougham. It detained his own in its grasp for a moment, while the light of a street lamp fell upon the Prince's long face and old-fashioned grey whiskers.

'I hope you are perfectly reassured now as to the consequences ...'

'After what your Excellency has condescended to do for me, I can only rely on my conscience.'

'*Adieu,*' said the whiskered head with feeling.

Razumov bowed. The brougham glided away with a slight swish in the snow – he was alone on the edge of the pavement.

He said to himself that there was nothing to think about, and began walking towards his home.

He walked quietly. It was a common experience to walk thus home to bed after an evening spent somewhere with his fellows or in the cheaper seats of a theatre. After he had gone a little way the familiarity of things got hold of him. Nothing was changed. There was the familiar corner; and when he turned it he saw the familiar dim light of the provision shop kept by a German woman. There were loaves of stale bread, bunches of onions and strings of sausages behind the small window-panes. They were closing it. The sickly lame fellow whom he knew so well by sight staggered out into the snow embracing a large shutter.

Nothing would change. There was the familiar gateway yawning black with feeble glimmers marking the arches of the different staircases.

The sense of life's continuity depended on trifling bodily impressions. The trivialities of daily existence were an armour for the soul. And this thought reinforced the inward quietness of Razumov as he began to climb the stairs familiar to his feet in the dark, with his hand on the familiar clammy banister. The exceptional could not prevail against the material contacts which make one day resemble another. Tomorrow would be like yesterday.

It was only on the stage that the unusual was outwardly acknowledged.

'I suppose,' thought Razumov, 'that if I had made up my mind to blow out my brains on the landing I would be going up these stairs as quietly as I am doing it now. What's a man to do? What must be must be. Extraordinary things do happen. But when they have happened they are done with. Thus, too, when the mind is made up. That question is done with. And the daily concerns, the familiarities of our thoughts swallow it up – and the life goes on as before with its mysterious and secret sides quite out of sight, as they should be. Life is a public thing.'

Razumov unlocked his door and took the key out; entered very quietly and bolted the door behind him carefully.

He thought, 'He hears me,' and after bolting the door he stood still holding his breath. There was not a sound. He crossed the bare outer room, stepping deliberately in the darkness. Entering the other, he felt all over his table for the matchbox. The silence, but for the groping of his hand, was profound. Could the fellow be sleeping so soundly?

He struck a light and looked at the bed. Haldin was lying on his back as before, only both his hands were under his head. His eyes were open. He stared at the ceiling.

Razumov held the match up. He saw the clear-cut features, the firm chin, the white forehead and the top-knot of fair hair against the white pillow. There he was, lying flat on his back. Razumov thought suddenly, 'I have walked over his chest.'

He continued to stare till the match burnt itself out; then struck another and lit the lamp in silence without looking towards the bed any more. He had turned his back on it and was hanging his coat on a peg when he heard Haldin sigh profoundly, then ask in a tired voice –

'Well! And what have you arranged?'

The emotion was so great that Razumov was glad to put his hands against the wall. A diabolical impulse to say, 'I have given you up to the police,' frightened him exceedingly. But he did not say that. He said, without turning round, in a muffled voice –

'It's done.'

Again he heard Haldin sigh. He walked to the table, sat down with the lamp before him, and only then looked towards the bed.

In the distant corner of the large room far away from the lamp, which was small and provided with a very thick china shade, Haldin appeared like a dark and elongated shape – rigid with the immobility of death. This body seemed to have less substance than its own phantom walked over by Razumov in the street white with snow. It was more alarming in its shadowy, persistent reality than the distinct but vanishing illusion.

Haldin was heard again.

'You must have had a walk – such a walk . . .' he murmured deprecatingly. 'This weather . . .'

Razumov answered with energy –

'Horrible walk . . . A nightmare of a walk.'

He shuddered audibly. Haldin sighed once more, then –

'And so you have seen Ziemianitch – brother?'

'I've seen him.'

Razumov, remembering the time he had spent with the Prince, thought it prudent to add, 'I had to wait some time.'

'A character – eh? It's extraordinary what a sense of the necessity of freedom there is in that man. And he has sayings too – simple, to the point, such as only the people can invent in their rough sagacity. A character that . . .'

'I, you understand, haven't had much opportunity . . .' Razumov muttered through his teeth.

Haldin continued to stare at the ceiling.

'You see, brother, I have been a good deal in that house of late. I used to take there books – leaflets. Not a few of the poor people who live there can read. And, you see, the guests for the feast of freedom must be sought for in byways and hedges. The truth is, I have almost lived in that house of late. I slept sometimes in the stable. There is a stable . . .'

'That's where I had my interview with Ziemianitch,' interrupted Razumov gently. A mocking spirit entered into him and he added, 'It was satisfactory in a sense. I came away from it much relieved.'

'Ah! he's a fellow,' went on Haldin, talking slowly at the ceiling. 'I came to know him in that way, you see. For some weeks now, ever since I resigned myself to do what had to be done, I tried to isolate myself. I gave up my rooms. What was the good of exposing a decent widow woman to the risk of being worried out of her mind by the police? I gave up seeing any of our comrades ...'

Razumov drew to himself a half-sheet of paper and began to trace lines on it with a pencil.

'Upon my word,' he thought angrily, 'he seems to have thought of everybody's safety but mine.'

Haldin was talking on.

'This morning – ah! this morning – that was different. How can I explain to you? Before the deed was done I wandered at night and lay hid in the day, thinking it out, and I felt restful. Sleepless but restful. What was there for me to torment myself about? But this morning – after! Then it was that I became restless. I could not have stopped in that big house full of misery. The miserable of this world can't give you peace. Then when that silly caretaker began to shout, I said to myself, "There is a young man in this town head and shoulders above common prejudices."'

'Is he laughing at me?' Razumov asked himself, going on with his aimless drawing of triangles and squares. And suddenly he thought: 'My behaviour must appear to him strange. Should he take fright at my manner and rush off somewhere I shall be undone completely. That infernal General ...'

He dropped the pencil and turned abruptly towards the bed with the shadowy figure extended full length on it – so much more indistinct than the one over whose breast he had walked without faltering. Was this, too, a phantom?

The silence had lasted a long time. 'He is no longer here,' was the thought against which Razumov struggled desperately, quite frightened at its absurdity. 'He is already gone and this ... only ...'

He could resist no longer. He sprang to his feet, saying aloud, 'I am intolerably anxious,' and in a few headlong strides stood by the side of the bed. His hand fell lightly on Haldin's shoulder, and directly he felt its reality he was beset by an insane temptation to grip that exposed throat and squeeze the breath out of that body, lest it should escape his custody, leaving only a phantom behind.

Haldin did not stir a limb, but his overshadowed eyes moving a

97

little gazed upwards at Razumov with wistful gratitude for this manifestation of feeling.

Razumov turned away and strode up and down the room. 'It would have been possibly a kindness,' he muttered to himself, and was appalled by the nature of that apology for a murderous intention his mind had found somewhere within him. And all the same he could not give it up. He became lucid about it. 'What can he expect?' he thought. 'The halter – in the end. And I . . .'

This argument was interrupted by Haldin's voice.

'Why be anxious for me? They can kill my body, but they cannot exile my soul from this world. I tell you what – I believe in this world so much that I cannot conceive eternity otherwise than as a very long life. That is perhaps the reason I am so ready to die.'

'H'm,' muttered Razumov, and biting his lower lip he continued to walk up and down and to carry on his strange argument.

Yes, to a man in such a situation – of course it would be an act of kindness. The question, however, was not how to be kind, but how to be firm. He was a slippery customer . . .

'I too, Victor Victorovitch, believe in this world of ours,' he said with force. 'I too, while I live . . . But you seem determined to haunt it. You can't seriously mean . . .'

The voice of the motionless Haldin began –

'Haunt it! Truly, the oppressors of thought which quickens the world, the destroyers of souls which aspire to perfection of human dignity, they shall be haunted. As to the destroyers of my mere body, I have forgiven them beforehand.'

Razumov had stopped apparently to listen, but at the same time he was observing his own sensations. He was vexed with himself for attaching so much importance to what Haldin said.

'The fellow's mad,' he thought firmly, but this opinion did not mollify him towards Haldin. It was a particularly impudent form of lunacy – and when it got loose in the sphere of public life of a country, it was obviously the duty of every good citizen . . .

This train of thought broke off short there and was succeeded by a paroxysm of silent hatred towards Haldin, so intense that Razumov hastened to speak at random.

'Yes. Eternity, of course. I, too, can't very well represent it to myself . . . I imagine it, however, as something quiet and dull. There would be nothing unexpected – don't you see? The element of time would be wanting.'

He pulled out his watch and gazed at it. Haldin turned over on his side and looked on intently.

Razumov got frightened at this movement. A slippery customer this fellow with a phantom. It was not midnight yet. He hastened on –

'And unfathomable mysteries! Can you conceive secret places in Eternity? Impossible. Whereas life is full of them. There are secrets of birth, for instance. One carries them on to the grave. There is something comical . . . but never mind. And there are secret motives of conduct. A man's most open actions have a secret side to them. That is interesting and so unfathomable! For instance, a man goes out of a room for a walk. Nothing more trivial in appearance. And yet it may be momentous. He comes back – he has seen perhaps a drunken brute, taken particular notice of the snow on the ground – and behold he is no longer the same man. The most unlikely things have a secret power over one's thoughts – the grey whiskers of a particular person – the goggle eyes of another.'

Razumov's forehead was moist. He took a turn or two in the room, his head low and smiling to himself viciously.

'Have you ever reflected on the power of goggle eyes and grey whiskers? Excuse me. You seem to think I must be crazy to talk in this vein at such a time. But I am not talking lightly. I have seen instances. It has happened to me once to be talking to a man whose fate was affected by physical facts of that kind. And the man did not know it. Of course, it was a case of conscience, but the material facts such as these brought about the solution . . . And you tell me, Victor Victorovitch, not to be anxious! Why! I am responsible for you,' Razumov almost shrieked.

He avoided with difficulty a burst of Mephistophelian laughter. Haldin, very pale, raised himself on his elbow.

'And the surprises of life,' went on Razumov, after glancing at the other uneasily. 'Just consider their astonishing nature. A mysterious impulse induces you to come here. I don't say you have done wrong. Indeed, from a certain point of view you could not have done better.

You might have gone to a man with affections and family ties. You have such ties yourself. As to me, you know I have been brought up in an educational institute where they did not give us enough to eat. To talk of affection in such a connection – you perceive yourself ... As to ties, the only ties I have in the world are social. I must get acknowledged in some way before I can act at all. I sit here working ... And don't you think I am working for progress too? I've got to find my own ideas of the true way ... Pardon me,' continued Razumov, after drawing breath and with a short, throaty laugh, 'but I haven't inherited a revolutionary inspiration together with a resemblance from an uncle.'

He looked again at his watch and noticed with sickening disgust that there were yet a good many minutes to midnight. He tore watch and chain off his waistcoat and laid them on the table well in the circle of bright lamplight. Haldin, reclining on his elbow, did not stir. Razumov was made uneasy by this attitude. 'What move is he meditating over so quietly?' he thought. 'He must be prevented. I must keep on talking to him.'

He raised his voice.

'You are a son, a brother, a nephew, a cousin – I don't know what – to no end of people. I am just a man. Here I stand before you. A man with a mind. Did it ever occur to you how a man who had never heard a word of warm affection or praise in his life would think on matters on which you would think first with or against your class, your domestic tradition – your fireside prejudices? ... Did you ever consider how a man like that would feel? I have no domestic tradition. I have nothing to think against. My tradition is historical. What have I to look back to but that national past from which you gentlemen want to wrench away your future? Am I to let my intelligence, my aspirations towards a better lot, be robbed of the only thing it has to go upon at the will of violent enthusiasts? You come from your province, but all this land is mine – or I have nothing. No doubt you shall be looked upon as a martyr some day – a sort of hero – a political saint. But I beg to be excused. I am content in fitting myself to be a worker. And what can you people do by scattering a few drops of blood on the snow? On this Immensity. On this unhappy Immensity! I tell you,' he cried, in a vibrating, subdued voice, and advancing one step nearer the bed, 'that what it needs is not a lot of haunting phantoms that I could walk through – but a man!'

Haldin threw his arms forward as if to keep him off in horror.

'I understand it all now,' he exclaimed, with awestruck dismay. 'I understand – at last.'

Razumov staggered back against the table. His forehead broke out in perspiration while a cold shudder ran down his spine.

'What have I been saying?' he asked himself. 'Have I let him slip through my fingers after all?'

He felt his lips go stiff like buckram, and instead of a reassuring smile only achieved an uncertain grimace.

'What will you have?' he began in a conciliating voice which got steady after the first trembling word or two. 'What will you have? Consider – a man of studious, retired habits – and suddenly like this ... I am not practised in talking delicately. But ...'

He felt anger, a wicked anger, get hold of him again.

'What were we to do together till midnight? Sit here opposite each other and think of your – your – shambles?'

Haldin had a subdued, heartbroken attitude. He bowed his head; his hands hung between his knees. His voice was low and pained but calm.

'I see now how it is, Razumov – brother. You are a magnanimous soul, but my action is abhorrent to you – alas ...'

Razumov stared. From fright he had set his teeth so hard that his whole face ached. It was impossible for him to make a sound.

'And even my person, too, is loathsome to you perhaps,' Haldin added mournfully, after a short pause, looking up for a moment, then fixing his gaze on the floor. 'For indeed, unless one ...'

He broke off, evidently waiting for a word. Razumov remained silent. Haldin nodded his head dejectedly twice.

'Of course. Of course,' he murmured ... 'Ah! – weary work!'

He remained perfectly still for a moment, then made Razumov's leaden heart strike a ponderous blow by springing up briskly.

'So be it,' he cried sadly in a low, distinct tone. 'Farewell then.'

Razumov started forward, but the sight of Haldin's raised hand checked him before he could get away from the table. He leaned on it heavily, listening to the faint sounds of some town clock tolling the hour. Haldin, already at the door, tall and straight as an arrow, with his pale face and a hand raised attentively, might have posed for the statue of a daring youth listening to an inner voice. Razumov mechanically glanced down at his watch. When he looked towards the door again Haldin had vanished. There was a faint rustling in the outer room, the feeble click of a bolt drawn back lightly. He was gone – almost as noiseless as a vision.

Razumov ran forward unsteadily, with parted, voiceless lips. The outer door stood open. Staggering out on the landing, he leaned far over the banister. Gazing down into the deep black shaft with a tiny glimmering flame at the bottom, he traced by ear the rapid spiral descent of somebody running down the stairs on tiptoe. It was a light, swift, pattering sound, which sank away from him into the depths: a fleeting shadow passed over the glimmer – a wink of the tiny flame. Then stillness.

Razumov hung over, breathing the cold raw air tainted by the evil smells of the unclean staircase. All quiet.

He went back into his room slowly, shutting the doors after him. The peaceful steady light of his reading-lamp shone on the watch. Razumov stood looking down at the little white dial. It wanted yet three minutes to midnight. He took the watch into his hand fumblingly.

'Slow,' he muttered, and a strange fit of nervelessness came over him. His knees shook, the watch and chain slipped through his fingers in an instant and fell on the floor. He was so startled that he nearly fell himself. When at last he regained enough confidence in his limbs to stoop for it he held it to his ear at once. After a while he growled –

'Stopped,' and paused for quite a long time before he muttered sourly –

'It's done ... And now to work.'

He sat down, reached haphazard for a book, opened it in the middle and began to read; but after going conscientiously over two lines he lost his hold on the print completely and did not try to regain it. He thought –

'There was to a certainty a police agent of some sort watching the house across the street.'

He imagined him lurking in a dark gateway, goggle-eyed, muffled up in a cloak to the nose and with a General's plumed, cocked hat on his head. This absurdity made him start in the chair convulsively. He literally had to shake his head violently to get rid of it. The man would be disguised perhaps as a peasant ... a beggar ... Perhaps he would be just buttoned up in a dark overcoat and carrying a loaded stick – a shifty-eyed rascal, smelling of raw onions and spirits.

This evocation brought on positive nausea. 'Why do I want to bother about this?' thought Razumov with disgust. 'Am I a gendarme? Moreover, it is done.'

He got up in great agitation. It was not done. Not yet. Not till half-past twelve. And the watch had stopped. This reduced him to despair. Impossible to know the time! The landlady and all the people across the landing were asleep. How could he go and ... God knows what they would imagine, or how much they would guess. He dared not go into the streets to find out. 'I am a suspect now. There's no use shirking that fact,' he said to himself bitterly. If Haldin from some cause or another gave them the slip and failed to turn up in the Karabelnaya the police would be invading his lodging. And if he were not in he could never clear himself. Never. Razumov looked wildly about as if for some means of seizing upon time which seemed to have escaped him altogether. He had never, as far as he could remember, heard the striking of that town clock in his rooms before this night. And he was not even sure now whether he had heard it really on this night.

He went to the window and stood there with slightly bent head on the watch for the faint sound. 'I will stay here till I hear something,' he said to himself. He stood still, his ear turned to the panes. An atrocious aching numbness with shooting pains in his back and legs tortured him. He did not budge. His mind hovered on the borders of delirium. He heard himself suddenly saying, 'I confess,' as a person might do on the rack. 'I am on the rack.' he thought. He felt ready to swoon. The faint deep boom of the distant clock seemed to explode in his head – he heard it so clearly ... One!

If Haldin had not turned up the police would have been already here ransacking the house. No sound reached him. This time it was done.

He dragged himself painfully to the table and dropped into the chair. He flung the book away and took a square sheet of paper. It was like the pile of sheets covered with his neat minute hand-writing, only blank. He took a pen brusquely and dipped it with a vague notion of going on with the writing of his essay – but his pen remained poised over the sheet. It hung there for some time before it came down and formed long scrawly letters.

Still-faced and his lips set hard, Razumov began to write. When he wrote a large hand his neat writing lost its character altogether – became unsteady. almost childish. He wrote five lines one under the other.

History not Theory.
Patriotism not Internationalism.
Evolution not Revolution.
Direction not Destruction.
Unity not Disruption.

He gazed at them dully. Then his eyes strayed to the bed and remained fixed there for a good many minutes, while his right hand groped all over the table for the penknife.

He rose at last, and walking up with measured steps stabbed the paper with the penknife to the lath and plaster wall at the head of the bed. This done he stepped back a pace and flourished his hand with a glance round the room.

After that he never looked again at the bed. He took his big cloak down from its peg and, wrapping himself up closely, went to lie down on the hard horse-hair sofa at the other side of his room. A leaden sleep closed his eyelids at once. Several times that night he woke up shivering from a dream of walking through drifts of snow in a Russia where he was as completely alone as any betrayed autocrat could be; an immense, wintry Russia which, somehow, his view could embrace in all its enormous expanse as if it were a map. But after each shuddering start his heavy eyelids fell over his glazed eyes and he slept again.

III

Approaching this part of Mr Razumov's story, my mind, the decent mind of an old teacher of languages, feels more and more the difficulty of the task.

The task is not in truth the writing in the narrative form a *précis* of a strange human document, but the rendering – I perceive it now clearly – of the moral conditions ruling over a large portion of this earth's surface; conditions not easily to be understood, much less discovered in the limits of a story, till some key-word is found; a word that could stand at the back of all the words covering the pages, a word which, if not truth itself, may perchance hold truth enough to help the moral discovery which should be the object of every tale.

I turn over for the hundredth time the leaves of Mr Razumov's record, I lay it aside, I take up the pen – and the pen being ready for its office of setting down black on white I hesitate. For the word that persists in creeping under its point is no other word than 'cynicism'.

For that is the mark of Russian autocracy and of Russian revolt. In its pride of numbers, in its strange pretensions of sanctity, and in the secret readiness to abase itself in suffering, the spirit of Russia is the spirit of cynicism. It informs the declarations of statesmen, the theories of her revolutionists, and the mystic vaticinations of prophets to the point of making freedom look like a form of debauch, and the Christian virtues themselves appear actually indecent ... But I must apologize for the digression. It proceeds from the consideration of the course taken by the story of Mr Razumov after his conservative convictions, diluted in a vague liberalism natural to the ardour of his age, had become crystallized by the shock of his contact with Haldin.

Razumov woke up for the tenth time perhaps with a heavy shiver. Seeing the light of day in his window, he resisted the inclination to lay himself down again. He did not remember anything, but he did not think it strange to find himself on the sofa in his cloak and chilled to the bone. The light coming through the window seemed strangely cheerless, containing no promise as the light of each new day should for a young man. It was the awakening of a man mortally ill, or of a man ninety years old. He looked at the lamp which had burnt itself out. It stood there, the extinguished beacon of his labours a cold object of brass and porcelain, amongst the scattered pages of his notes and small piles of books – a mere litter of blackened paper – dead matter – without significance or interest.

He got on his feet, and divesting himself of his cloak hung it on the peg, going through all the motions mechanically. An incredible dullness, a ditch-water stagnation was sensible to his perceptions as though life had withdrawn itself from all things and even from his own thoughts. There was not a sound in the house.

Turning away from the peg, he thought in that same lifeless manner that it must be very early yet; but when he looked at the watch on his table he saw both hands arrested at twelve o'clock.

'Ah! yes,' he mumbled to himself, and as if beginning to get roused a little he took a survey of his room. The paper stabbed to the wall arrested his attention. He eyed it from the distance without approval or perplexity; but when he heard the servant-girl beginning to bustle about in the outer room with the *samovar** for his morning tea, he walked up to it and took it down with an air of profound indifference.

While doing this he glanced down at the bed on which he had not slept that night. The hollow in the pillow made by the weight of Haldin's head was very noticeable.

Even his anger at this sign of the man's passage was dull. He did not try to nurse it into life. He did nothing all that day; he neglected even to brush his hair. The idea of going out never occurred to him – and if he did not start a connected train of thought it was not because he was unable to think. It was because he was not interested enough.

He yawned frequently. He drank large quantities of tea, he walked about aimlessly, and when he sat down he did not budge for a long time. He spent some time drumming on the window with his fingertips quietly. In his listless wanderings round about the table he caught sight of his own face in the looking-glass and that arrested him. The eyes which returned his stare were the most unhappy eyes

* Copper urn for boiling water and keeping tea hot.

he had ever seen. And this was the first thing which disturbed the mental stagnation of that day.

He was not affected personally. He merely thought that life without happiness is impossible. What was happiness? He yawned and went on shuffling about and about between the walls of his room. Looking forward was happiness – that's all – nothing more. To look forward to the gratification of some desire, to the gratification of some passion, love, ambition, hate – hate too indubitably. Love and hate. And to escape the dangers of existence, to live without fear, was also happiness. There was nothing else. Absence of fear – looking forward. 'Oh! the miserable lot of humanity!' he exclaimed mentally; and added at once in his thought, 'I ought to be happy enough as far as that goes.' But he was not excited by that assurance. On the contrary, he yawned again as he had been yawning all day. He was mildly surprised to discover himself being overtaken by night. The room grew dark swiftly though time had seemed to stand still. How was it that he had not noticed the passing of that day? Of course, it was the watch being stopped ...

He did not light his lamp, but went over to the bed and threw himself on it without any hesitation. Lying on his back, he put his hands under his head and stared upward. After a moment he thought, 'I am lying here like that man. I wonder if he slept while I was struggling with the blizzard in the streets. No, he did not sleep. But why should I not sleep?' and he felt the silence of the night press upon all his limbs like a weight.

In the calm of the hard frost outside, the clear-cut strokes of the town clock counting off midnight penetrated the quietness of his suspended animation.

Again he began to think. It was twenty-four hours since that man left his room. Razumov had a distinct feeling that Haldin in the fortress was sleeping that night. It was a certitude which made him angry because he did not want to think of Haldin, but he justified it to himself by physiological and psychological reasons. The fellow had hardly slept for weeks on his own confession, and now every incertitude was at an end for him. No doubt he was looking forward to the consummation of his martyrdom. A man who resigns himself to kill need not go very far for resignation to die. Haldin slept perhaps more soundly than General T—, whose task – weary work too – was not done, and over whose head hung the sword of revolutionary vengeance.

Razumov, remembering the thick-set man with his heavy jowl resting on the collar of his uniform, the champion of autocracy, who had let no sign of surprise, incredulity, or joy escape him, but whose goggle eyes could express a mortal hatred of all rebellion – Razumov moved uneasily on the bed.

'He suspected me,' he thought. 'I suppose he must suspect everybody. He would be capable of suspecting his own wife, if Haldin had gone to her boudoir with his confession.'

Razumov sat up in anguish. Was he to remain a political suspect all his days? Was he to go through life as a man not wholly to be trusted – with a bad secret police note tacked on to his record? What sort of future could he look forward to?

'I am now a suspect,' he thought again; but the habit of reflection and that desire of safety, of an ordered life, which was so strong in him came to his assistance as the night wore on. His quiet, steady, and laborious existence would vouch at length for his loyalty. There were many permitted ways to serve one's country. There was an activity that made for progress without being revolutionary. The field of influence was great and infinitely varied – once one had conquered a name.

His thought like a circling bird reverted after four-and-twenty hours to the silver medal, and as it were poised itself there.

When the day broke he had not slept, not for a moment, but he got up not very tired and quite sufficiently self-possessed for all practical purposes.

He went out and attended three lectures in the morning. But the work in the library was a mere dumb show of research. He sat with many volumes open before him trying to make notes and extracts. His new tranquillity was like a flimsy garment, and seemed to float at the mercy of a casual word. Betrayal! Why! the fellow had done all that was necessary to betray himself. Precious little had been needed to deceive him.

'I have said no word to him that was not strictly true. Not one word,' Razumov argued with himself.

Once engaged on this line of thought there could be no question of doing useful work. The same ideas went on passing through his mind, and he pronounced mentally the same words over and over again. He shut up all the books and rammed all his papers into his pocket with convulsive movements, raging inwardly against Haldin.

As he was leaving the library a long bony student in a threadbare overcoat joined him, stepping moodily by his side. Razumov answered his mumbled greeting without looking at him at all.

'What does he want with me?' he thought with a strange dread of the unexpected which he tried to shake off lest it should fasten itself upon his life for good and all. And the other, muttering cautiously with downcast eyes, supposed that his comrade had seen the news of de P—'s executioner – that was the expression he used – having been arrested the night before last . . .

'I've been ill – shut up in my rooms,' Razumov mumbled through his teeth.

The tall student, raising his shoulders, shoved his hands deep into his pockets. He had a hairless, square, tallowy chin which trembled slightly as he spoke, and his nose nipped bright red by the sharp air looked like a false nose of painted cardboard between the sallow cheeks. His whole appearance was stamped with the mark of cold and hunger. He stalked deliberately at Razumov's elbow with his eyes on the ground.

'It's an official statement,' he continued in the same cautious mutter. 'It may be a lie. But there was somebody arrested between midnight and one in the morning on Tuesday. This is certain.'

And talking rapidly under the cover of his downcast air, he told Razumov that this was known through an inferior Government clerk employed at the Central Secretariat. That man belonged to one of the revolutionary circles. 'The same, in fact, I am affiliated to,' remarked the student.

They were crossing a wide quadrangle. An infinite distress possessed Razumov, annihilated his energy, and before his eyes everything appeared confused and as if evanescent. He dared not leave the fellow there. 'He may be affiliated to the police,' was the thought that passed through his mind. 'Who could tell?' But eyeing the miserable frost-nipped, famine-struck figure of his companion he perceived the absurdity of his suspicion.

'But I – you know – I don't belong to any circle. I . . .'

He dared not say any more. Neither dared he mend his pace. The other, raising and setting down his lamentably shod feet with exact deliberation, protested in a low tone that it was not necessary for everybody to belong to an organization. The most valuable personalities remained outside. Some of the best work was done outside the organization. Then very fast, with whispering, feverish lips –

'The man arrested in the street was Haldin.'

And accepting Razumov's dismayed silence as natural enough, he assured him that there was no mistake. That Government clerk was on night duty at the Secretariat. Hearing a great noise of footsteps in the hall and aware that political prisoners were brought over sometimes at night from the fortress, he opened the door of the room in which he was working, suddenly. Before the gendarme on duty could push him back and slam the door in his face, he had seen a prisoner being partly carried, partly dragged along the hall by a lot of policemen. He was being used very brutally. And the clerk had recognized Haldin perfectly. Less than half an hour afterwards General T— arrived at the Secretariat to examine that prisoner personally.

'Aren't you astonished?' concluded the gaunt student.

'No,' said Razumov roughly – and at once regretted his answer.

'Everybody supposed Haldin was in the provinces – with his people. Didn't you?'

The student turned his big hollow eyes upon Razumov, who said unguardedly –

'His people are abroad.'

He could have bitten his tongue out with vexation. The student pronounced in a tone of profound meaning –

'So! You alone were aware . . .' and stopped.

'They have sworn my ruin,' thought Razumov. 'Have you spoken of this to anyone else?' he asked with bitter curiosity.

The other shook his head.

'No, only to you. Our circle thought that as Haldin had been often heard expressing a warm appreciation of your character . . .'

Razumov could not restrain a gesture of angry despair which the other must have misunderstood in some way, because he ceased speaking and turned away his black, lack-lustre eyes.

They moved side by side in silence. Then the gaunt student began to whisper again, with averted gaze –

'As we have at present no one affiliated inside the fortress so as to make it possible to furnish him with a packet of poison, we have considered already some sort of retaliatory action – to follow very soon ...'

Razumov trudging on interrupted –

'Were you acquainted with Haldin? Did he know where you live?'

'I had the happiness to hear him speak twice,' his companion answered in the feverish whisper contrasting with the gloomy apathy of his face and bearing. 'He did not know where I live ... I am lodging poorly ... with an artisan family ... I have just a corner in a room. It is not very practicable to see me there but if you should need me for anything I am ready ...'

Razumov trembled with rage and fear. He was beside himself, but kept his voice low.

'You are not to come near me. You are not to speak to me. Never address a single word to me. I forbid you.'

'Very well,' said the other submissively, showing no surprise whatever at this abrupt prohibition. 'You don't wish for secret reasons ... perfectly ... I understand.'

He edged away at once, not looking up even; and Razumov saw his gaunt, shabby, famine-stricken figure cross the street obliquely with lowered head and that peculiar exact motion of the feet.

He watched him as one would watch a vision out of a nightmare, then he continued on his way, trying not to think. On his landing the landlady seemed to be waiting for him. She was a short, thick, shapeless woman with a large yellow face wrapped up everlastingly in a black woollen shawl. When she saw him come up the last flight of stairs she flung both her arms up excitedly, then clasped her hands before her face.

'Kirylo Sidorovitch – little father – what have you been doing? And such a quiet young man, too! The police are just gone this moment after searching your rooms.'

Razumov gazed down at her with silent, scrutinizing attention. Her puffy yellow countenance was working with emotion. She screwed up her eyes at him entreatingly.

'Such a sensible young man! Anybody can see you are sensible. And now – like this – all at once ... What is the good of mixing yourself up with these Nihilists? Do give over, little father. They are unlucky people.'

Razumov moved his shoulders slightly.

'Or is it that some secret enemy has been calumniating you, Kirylo Sidorovitch? The world is full of black hearts and false denunciations nowadays. There is much fear about.'

'Have you heard that I have been denounced by someone?' asked Razumov, without taking his eyes off her quivering face.

But she had not heard anything. She had tried to find out by asking the police captain while his men were turning the room upside down. The police captain of the district had known her for the last eleven years and was a humane person. But he said to her on the landing looking very black and vexed –

'My good woman, do not ask questions. I don't know anything myself. The order comes from higher quarters.'

And indeed there had appeared, shortly after the arrival of the policemen of the district, a very superior gentleman in a fur coat and a shiny hat, who sat down in the room and looked through all the papers himself. He came alone and went away by himself, taking nothing with him. She had been trying to put things straight a little since they left.

Razumov turned away brusquely and entered his rooms.

All his books had been shaken and thrown on the floor. His landlady followed him, and stooping painfully began to pick them up into her apron. His papers and notes which were kept always neatly sorted (they all related to his studies) had been shuffled up and heaped together into a ragged pile in the middle of the table.

This disorder affected him profoundly, unreasonably. He sat down and stared. He had a distinct sensation of his very existence being undermined in some mysterious manner, of his moral supports falling away from him one by one. He even experienced a slight physical giddiness and made a movement as if to reach for something to steady himself with.

The old woman, rising to her feet with a low groan, shot all the books she had collected in her apron on to the sofa and left the room muttering and sighing.

It was only then that he noticed that the sheet of paper which for one night had remained stabbed to the wall above his empty bed was lying on top of the pile.

When he had taken it down the day before he had folded it in four, absent-mindedly, before dropping it on the table. And now he saw it lying uppermost, spread out, smoothed out even and covering all the confused pile of pages, the record of his intellectual life for the last three years. It had not been flung there. It had been placed there – smoothed out, too! He guessed in that an intention of profound meaning – or perhaps some inexplicable mockery.

He sat staring at the piece of paper till his eyes began to smart. He did not attempt to put his papers in order, either that evening or the next day – which he spent at home in a state of peculiar irresolution. This irresolution bore upon the question whether he should continue to live – neither more nor less. But its nature was very far removed from the hesitation of a man contemplating suicide. The idea of laying violent hands upon his body did not occur to Razumov. The unrelated organism bearing that label, walking, breathing, wearing these clothes, was of no importance to any one, unless maybe to the landlady. The true Razumov had his being in the willed, in the determined future – in that future menaced by the lawlessness of autocracy – for autocracy knows no law – and the lawlessness of revolution. The feeling that his moral personality was at the mercy of these lawless forces was so strong that he asked himself seriously if it were worth while to go on accomplishing the mental functions of that existence which seemed no longer his own.

'What is the good of exerting my intelligence, of pursuing the systematic development of my faculties and all my plans of work?' he asked himself. 'I want to guide my conduct by reasonable convictions, but what security have I against something – some destructive horror – walking in upon me as I sit here? ...'

Razumov looked apprehensively towards the door of the outer

room as if expecting some shape of evil to turn the handle and appear before him silently.

'A common thief,' he said to himself, 'finds more guarantees in the law he is breaking, and even a brute like Ziemianitch has his consolation.' Razumov envied the materialism of the thief and the passion of the incorrigible lover. The consequences of their actions were always clear and their lives remained their own.

But he slept as soundly that night as though he had been consoling himself in the manner of Ziemianitch. He dropped off suddenly, lay like a log, remembered no dream on waking. But it was as if his soul had gone out in the night to gather the flowers of wrathful wisdom. He got up in a mood of grim determination and as if with a new knowledge of his own nature. He looked mockingly on the heap of papers on his table; and left his room to attend the lectures, muttering to himself, 'We shall see.'

He was in no humour to talk to anybody or hear himself questioned as to his absence from lectures the day before. But it was difficult to repulse rudely a very good comrade with a smooth pink face and fair hair, bearing the nickname amongst his fellow-students of 'Madcap Kostia'. He was the idolized only son of a very wealthy and illiterate Government contractor, and attended the lectures only during the periodical fits of contrition following upon tearful paternal remonstrances. Noisily blundering like a retriever puppy, his elated voice and great gestures filled the bare academy corridors with the joy of thoughtless animal life, provoking indulgent smiles at a great distance. His usual discourses treated of trotting horses, wine-parties in expensive restaurants, and the merits of persons of easy virtue, with a disarming artlessness of outlook. He pounced upon Razumov about midday, somewhat less uproariously than his habit was, and led him aside.

'Just a moment, Kirylo Sidorovitch. A few words here in this quiet corner.'

He felt Razumov's reluctance, and insinuated his hand under his arm caressingly.

'No – pray do. I don't want to talk to you about any of my silly scrapes. What are my scrapes? Absolutely nothing. Mere childishness. The other night I flung a fellow out of a certain place where

114

I was having a fairly good time. A tyrannical little beast of a quill-driver from the Treasury department . . . He was bullying the people of the house. I rebuked him. "You are not behaving humanely to God's creatures that are a jolly sight more estimable than yourself," I said. I can't bear to see any tyranny, Kirylo Sidorovitch. Upon my word I can't. He didn't take it in good part at all. "Who's that impudent puppy?" he begins to shout. I was in excellent form as it happened, and he went through the closed window very suddenly. He flew quite a long way into the yard. I raged like – like a – minotaur. The women clung to me and screamed, the fiddlers got under the table . . . Such fun! My dad had to put his hand pretty deep into his pocket, I can tell you.'

He chuckled.

'My dad is a very useful man. Jolly good thing it is for me, too. I do get into unholy scrapes.'

His elation fell. That was just it. What was his life? Insignificant; no good to any one; a mere festivity. It would end some fine day in his getting his skull split with a champagne bottle in a drunken brawl. At such times, too, when men were sacrificing themselves to ideas. But he could never get any ideas into his head. His head wasn't worth anything better than to be split by a champagne bottle.

Razumov, protesting that he had no time, made an attempt to get away. The other's tone changed to confidential earnestness.

'For God's sake, Kirylo, my dear soul, let me make some sort of sacrifice. It would not be a sacrifice really. I have my rich dad behind me. There's positively no getting to the bottom of his pocket.'

And rejecting indignantly Razumov's suggestion that this was drunken raving, he offered to lend him some money to escape abroad with. He could always get money from his dad. He had only to say that he had lost it at cards or something of that sort, and at the same time promise solemnly not to miss a single lecture for three months on end. That would fetch the old man; and he, Kostia, was quite equal to the sacrifice. Though he really did not see what was the good for him to attend the lectures. It was perfectly hopeless.

'Won't you let me be of some use?' he pleaded to the silent Razumov, who with his eyes on the ground and utterly unable to penetrate the real drift of the other's intention, felt a strange reluctance to clear up the point.

'What makes you think I want to go abroad?' he asked at last very quietly.

Kostia lowered his voice.

'You had the police in your rooms yesterday. There are three or four of us who have heard of that. Never mind how we know. It is sufficient that we do. So we have been consulting together.'

'Ah! You got to know that so soon,' muttered Razumov negligently.

'Yes. We did. And it struck us that a man like you ...'

'What sort of a man do you take me to be?' Razumov interrupted him.

'A man of ideas – and a man of action too. But you are very deep, Kirylo. There's no getting to the bottom of your mind. Not for fellows like me. But we all agreed that you must be preserved for our country. Of that we have no doubt whatever – I mean all of us who have heard Haldin speak of you on certain occasions. A man doesn't get the police ransacking his rooms without there being some devilry hanging over his head ... And so if you think that it would be better for you to bolt at once ...'

Razumov tore himself away and walked down the corridor, leaving the other motionless with his mouth open. But almost at once he returned and stood before the amazed Kostia, who shut his mouth slowly. Razumov looked him straight in the eyes, before saying with marked deliberation and separating his words –

'I thank – you – very – much.'

He went away again rapidly. Kostia, recovering from his surprise at these manoeuvres, ran up behind him pressingly.

'No! Wait! Listen. I really mean it. It would be like giving your compassion to a starving fellow. Do you hear, Kirylo? And any disguise you may think of, that too I could procure from a costumier, a Jew I know. Let a fool be made serviceable according to his folly. Perhaps also a false beard or something of that kind may be needed.'

Razumov turned at bay.

116

'There are no false beards needed in this business. Kostia – you good-hearted lunatic, you. What do you know of my ideas ? My ideas may be poison to you.'

The other began to shake his head in energetic protest.

'What have you got to do with ideas? Some of them would make an end of your dad's money-bags. Leave off meddling with what you don't understand. Go back to your trotting horses and your girls, and then you'll be sure at least of doing no harm to anybody, and hardly any to yourself.'

The enthusiastic youth was overcome by this disdain.

'You're sending me back to my pig's trough, Kirylo. That settles it. I am an unlucky beast – and I shall die like a beast too. But mind – it's your contempt that has done for me.'

Razumov went off with long strides. That this simple and grossly festive soul should have fallen too under the revolutionary curse affected him as an ominous symptom of the time. He reproached himself for feeling troubled. Personally he ought to have felt re-assured. There was an obvious advantage in this conspiracy of mis-taken judgement taking him for what he was not. But was it not strange?

Again he experienced that sensation of his conduct being taken out of his hands by Haldin's revolutionary tyranny. His solitary and laborious existence had been destroyed – the only thing he could call his own on this earth. By what right? he asked himself furiously. In what name?

What infuriated him most was to feel that the 'thinkers' of the University were evidently connecting him with Haldin – as a sort of confidant in the background apparently. A mysterious con-nection! Ha! ha! ... He had been made a personage without know-ing anything about it. How that wretch Haldin must have talked about him! Yet it was very likely that Haldin had said very little. The fellow's casual utterances were caught up and treasured and pondered over by all these imbeciles. And was not all secret revolu-tionary action based upon folly, self-deception, and lies?

'Impossible to think of anything else,' muttered Razumov to himself. 'I'll become an idiot if this goes on. The scoundrels and the fools are murdering my intelligence.'

He lost all hope of saving his future, which depended on the free use of his intelligence.

He reached the doorway of his house in a state of mental discouragement which enabled him to receive with apparent indifference an official-looking envelope from the dirty hand of the dvornik.

'A gendarme brought it,' said the man. 'He asked if you were at home. I told him "No, he's not at home." So he left it. "Give it into his own hands," says he. Now you've got it – eh?'

He went back to his sweeping, and Razumov climbed his stairs, envelope in hand. Once in his room he did not hasten to open it. Of course this official missive was from the superior direction of the police. A suspect! A suspect!

He stared in dreary astonishment at the absurdity of his position. He thought with a sort of dry, unemotional melancholy; three years of good work gone, the course of forty more perhaps jeopardized – turned from hope to terror, because events started by human folly link themselves into a sequence which no sagacity can foresee and no courage can break through. Fatality enters your rooms while your landlady's back is turned; you come home and find it in possession bearing a man's name, clothed in flesh – wearing a brown cloth coat and long boots – lounging against the stove. It asks you, 'Is the outer door closed?' – and you don't know enough to take it by the throat and fling it downstairs. You don't know. You welcome the crazy fate. 'Sit down,' you say. And it is all over. You cannot shake it off any more. It will cling to you for ever. Neither halter nor bullet can give you back the freedom of your life and the sanity of your thought ... It was enough to make one dash one's head against a wall.

Razumov looked slowly all round the walls as if to select a spot to dash his head against. Then he opened the letter. It directed the student Kirylo Sidorovitch Razumov to present himself without delay at the General Secretariat.

Razumov had a vision of General T—'s goggle eyes waiting for him – the embodied power of autocracy, grotesque and terrible. He embodied the whole power of autocracy because he was its guardian. He was the incarnate suspicion, the incarnate anger, the incarnate ruthlessness of a political and social régime on its defence.

He loathed rebellion by instinct. And Razumov reflected that the man was simply unable to understand a reasonable adherence to the doctrine of absolutism.

'What can he want with me precisely – I wonder?' he asked himself.

As if that mental question had evoked the familiar phantom, Haldin stood suddenly before him in the room with the extraordinary completeness of detail. Though the short winter day had passed already into the sinister twilight of a land buried in snow, Razumov saw plainly the narrow leather strap round the Tcherkess coat. The illusion of that hateful presence was so perfect that he half expected it to ask, 'Is the outer door closed?' He looked at it with hatred and contempt. Souls do not take a shape of clothing. Moreover, Haldin could not be dead yet. Razumov stepped forward menacingly; the vision vanished – and turning short on his heel he walked out of his room with infinite disdain.

But after going down the first flight of stairs it occurred to him that perhaps the superior authorities of police meant to confront him with Haldin in the flesh. This thought struck him like a bullet, and had he not clung with both hands to the banister he would have rolled down to the next landing most likely. His legs were of no use for a considerable time ... But why? For what conceivable reason? To what end?

There could be no rational answer to these questions; but Razumov remembered the promise made by the General to Prince K —. His action was to remain unknown.

He got down to the bottom of the stairs, lowering himself as it were from step to step, by the banister. Under the gate he regained much of his firmness of thought and limb. He went out into the street without staggering visibly. Every moment he felt steadier mentally. And yet he was saying to himself that General T — was perfectly capable of shutting him up in the fortress for an indefinite time. His temperament fitted his remorseless task, and his omnipotence made him inaccessible to reasonable argument.

But when Razumov arrived at the Secretariat he discovered that he would have nothing to do with General T —. It is evident from Mr Razumov's diary that this dreaded personality was to remain in the background. A civilian of superior rank received him in a private room after a period of waiting in outer offices where a lot of scribbling went on at many tables in a heated and stuffy atmosphere.

The clerk in uniform who conducted him said in the corridor –

'You are going before Gregory Matvieitch Mikulin.'

There was nothing formidable about the man bearing that name. His mild, expectant glance was turned on the door already when Razumov entered. At once, with the penholder he was holding in his hand, he pointed to a deep sofa between two windows. He followed Razumov with his eyes while that last crossed the room and sat down. The mild gaze rested on him, not curious, not inquisitive – certainly not suspicious – almost without expression. In its passionless persistence there was something resembling sympathy.

Razumov, who had prepared his will and his intelligence to encounter General T— himself, was profoundly troubled. All the moral bracing up against the possible excesses of power and passion went for nothing before this sallow man, who wore a full unclipped beard. It was fair, thin, and very fine. The light fell in coppery gleams on the protuberances of a high, rugged forehead. And the aspect of the broad, soft physiognomy was so homely and rustic that the careful middle parting of the hair seemed a pretentious affectation.

The diary of Mr Razumov testifies to some irritation on his part. I may remark here that the diary proper consisting of the more or less daily entries seems to have been begun on that very evening after Mr Razumov had returned home.

Mr Razumov, then, was irritated. His strung-up individuality had gone to pieces within him very suddenly.

'I must be very prudent with him,' he warned himself in the silence during which they sat gazing at each other. It lasted some little time, and was characterized (for silences have their character) by a sort of sadness imparted to it perhaps by the mild and thoughtful manner of the bearded official. Razumov learned later that he was the chief of a department in the General Secretariat, with a rank in the civil service equivalent to that of a colonel in the army.

Razumov's mistrust became acute. The main point was, not to be drawn into saying too much. He had been called there for some

120

reason. What reason? To be given to understand that he was a suspect – and also no doubt to be pumped. As to what precisely? There was nothing. Or perhaps Haldin had been telling lies . . . Every alarming uncertainty beset Razumov. He could bear the silence no longer, and cursing himself for his weakness spoke first, though he had promised himself not to do so on any account.

'I haven't lost a moment's time,' he began in a hoarse, provoking tone; and then the faculty of speech seemed to leave him and enter the body of Councillor Mikulin, who chimed in approvingly –

'Very proper. Very proper. Though as a matter of fact . . .'

But the spell was broken, and Razumov interrupted him boldly, under a sudden conviction that this was the safest attitude to take. With a great flow of words he complained of being totally misunderstood. Even as he talked with a perception of his own audacity he thought that the word 'misunderstood' was better than the word 'mistrusted', and he repeated it again with insistence. Suddenly he ceased, being seized with fright before the attentive immobility of the official. 'What am I talking about?' he thought, eyeing him with a vague gaze. Mistrusted – not misunderstood – was the right symbol of these people. Misunderstood was the other kind of curse. Both had been brought on his head by that fellow Haldin. And his head ached terribly. He passed his hand over his brow – an involuntary gesture of suffering, which he was too careless to restrain.

At that moment Razumov beheld his own brain suffering on the rack – a long, pale figure drawn asunder horizontally with terrific force in the darkness of a vault, whose face he failed to see. It was as though he had dreamed for an infinitesimal fraction of time of some dark print of the Inquisition . . .

It is not to be seriously supposed that Razumov had actually dozed off and had dreamed in the presence of Councillor Mikulin, of an old print of the Inquisition. He was indeed extremely exhausted, and he records a remarkably dream-like experience of anguish at the circumstance that there was no one whatever near the pale and extended figure. The solitude of the racked victim was particularly horrible to behold. The mysterious impossibility to see the face, he also notes, inspired a sort of terror. All these characteristics of an ugly dream were present. Yet he is certain that he never lost the consciousness of himself on the sofa, leaning forward with his hands between his knees and turning his cap round and round in his fingers. But everything vanished at the voice of Councillor Mikulin. Razumov felt profoundly grateful for the even simplicity of its tone.

'Yes. I have listened with interest. I comprehend in a measure your ... But, indeed, you are mistaken in what you ...' Councillor Mikulin uttered a series of broken sentences. Instead of finishing them he glanced down his beard. It was a deliberate curtailment which somehow made the phrases more impressive. But he could talk fluently enough as became apparent when changing his tone to persuasiveness he went on: 'By listening to you as I did, I think I have proved that I do not regard our intercourse as strictly official. In fact, I don't want it to have that character at all ... Oh yes! I admit that the request for your presence here had an official form. But I put it to you whether it was a form which would have been used to secure the attendance of a ...'

'Suspect,' exclaimed Razumov, looking straight into the official's eyes. They were big with heavy eyelids, and met his boldness with a dim, steadfast gaze. 'A suspect.' The open repetition of that word which had been haunting all his waking hours gave Razumov a strange sort of satisfaction. Councillor Mikulin shook his head slightly. 'Surely you do know that I've had my rooms searched by the police?'

'I was about to say a "misunderstood person", when you interrupted me.' insinuated quietly Councillor Mikulin.

Razumov smiled without bitterness. The renewed sense of his intellectual superiority sustained him in the hour of danger. He said a little disdainfully –

'I know I am but a reed. But I beg you to allow me the superiority of the thinking reed over the unthinking forces that are about to crush him out of existence. Practical thinking in the last instance is but criticism. I may perhaps be allowed to express my wonder at this action of the police being delayed for two full days during which, of course, I could have annihilated everything compromising by burning it – let us say – and getting rid of the very ashes, for that matter.'

'You are angry,' remarked the official, with an unutterable simplicity of tone and manner. 'Is that reasonable?'

Razumov felt himself colouring with annoyance.

'I am reasonable. I am even – permit me to say – a thinker, though to be sure, this name nowadays seems to be the monopoly of hawkers of revolutionary wares, the slaves of some French or German thought – devil knows what foreign notions. But I am not an intellectual mongrel. I think like a Russian. I think faithfully – and I take the liberty to call myself a thinker. It is not a forbidden word, as far as I know.'

'No. Why should it be a forbidden word?' Councillor Mikulin turned in his seat with crossed legs and resting his elbow on the table propped his head on the knuckles of a half-closed hand. Razumov noticed a thick forefinger clasped by a massive gold band set with a blood-red stone – a signet ring that, looking as if it could weigh half a pound, was an appropriate ornament for that ponderous man with the accurate middle-parting of glossy hair above a rugged Socratic forehead.

'Could it be a wig?' Razumov detected himself wondering with an unexpected detachment. His self-confidence was much shaken. He resolved to chatter no more. Reserve! Reserve! All he had to do was to keep the Ziemianitch episode secret with absolute determination, when the questions came. Keep Ziemianitch strictly out of all the answers.

Councillor Mikulin looked at him dimly. Razumov's self-confidence abandoned him completely. It seemed impossible to keep Ziemianitch out. Every question would lead to that, because, of course, there was nothing else. He made an effort to brace himself up. It was a failure. But Councillor Mikulin was surprisingly detached too.

'Why should it be forbidden?' he repeated. 'I too consider myself a thinking man, I assure you. The principal condition is to think correctly. I admit it is difficult sometimes at first for a young man abandoned to himself – with his generous impulses undisciplined, so to speak – at the mercy of every wild wind that blows. Religious belief, of course, is a great ...'

Councillor Mikulin glanced down his beard, and Razumov,

whose tension was relaxed by that unexpected and discursive turn, murmured with gloomy discontent –

'That man, Haldin, believed in God.'

'Ah! You are aware,' breathed out Councillor Mikulin, making the point softly, as if with discretion, but making it nevertheless plainly enough, as if he too were put off his guard by Razumov's remark. The young man preserved an impassive, moody countenance, though he reproached himself bitterly for a pernicious fool, to have given thus an utterly false impression of intimacy. He kept his eyes on the floor. 'I must positively hold my tongue unless I am obliged to speak,' he admonished himself. And at once against his will the question, 'Hadn't I better tell him everything?' presented itself with such force that he had to bite his lower lip. Councillor Mikulin could not, however, have nourished any hope of confession. He went on –

'You tell me more than his judges were able to get out of him. He was judged by a commission of three. He would tell them absolutely nothing. I have the report of the interrogatories here, by me. After every question there stands "Refuses to answer – refuses to answer." It's like that page after page. You see, I have been entrusted with some further investigations around and about this affair. He has left me nothing to begin my investigations on. A hardened miscreant. And so, you say, he believed in ...'

Again Councillor Mikulin glanced down his beard with a faint grimace; but he did not pause for long. Remarking with a shade of scorn that blasphemers also had that sort of belief, he concluded by supposing that Mr Razumov had conversed frequently with Haldin on the subject.

'No,' said Razumov loudly, without looking up. 'He talked and I listened. That is not a conversation.'

'Listening is a great art,' observed Mikulin parenthetically.

'And getting people to talk is another,' mumbled Razumov.

'Well, no – that is not very difficult,' Mikulin said innocently, 'except, of course, in special cases. For instance, this Haldin. Nothing could induce him to talk. He was brought four times before the delegated judges. Four secret interrogatories – and even during the last, when your personality was put forward ...'

'My personality put forward?' repeated Razumov, raising his head brusquely. 'I don't understand.'

Councillor Mikulin turned squarely to the table, and taking up some sheets of grey foolscap dropped them one after another, retaining only the last in his hand. He held it before his eyes while speaking.

'It was – you see – judged necessary. In a case of that gravity no means of action upon the culprit should be neglected. You understand that yourself, I am certain.'

Razumov stared with enormous wide eyes at the side view of Councillor Mikulin, who now was not looking at him at all.

'So it was decided (I was consulted by General T——) that a certain question should be put to the accused. But in deference to the earnest wishes of Prince K—— your name has been kept out of the documents and even from the very knowledge of the judges themselves. Prince K—— recognized the propriety, the necessity of what we proposed to do, but he was concerned for your safety. Things do leak out – that we can't deny. One cannot always answer for the discretion of inferior officials. There was, of course, the secretary of the special tribunal – one or two gendarmes in the room. Moreover, as I have said, in deference to Prince K—— even the judges themselves were to be left in ignorance. The question ready framed was sent to them by General T—— (I wrote it out with my own hand) with instructions to put it to the prisoner the very last of all. Here it is.'

Councillor Mikulin threw back his head into proper focus and went on reading monotonously: 'Question – Has the man well known to you, in whose rooms you remained for several hours on Monday and on whose information you have been arrested – has he had any previous knowledge of your intention to commit a political murder? . . . Prisoner refuses to reply.

'Question repeated. Prisoner preserves the same stubborn silence.

'The venerable Chaplain of the Fortress being then admitted and exhorting the prisoner to repentance, entreating him also to atone for his crime by an unreserved and full confession which should help to liberate from the sin of rebellion against the Divine laws and the sacred Majesty of the Ruler, our Christ-loving land – the prisoner opens his lips for the first time during this morning's audience and in a loud, clear voice rejects the venerable Chaplain's ministrations.

'At eleven o'clock the Court pronounces in summary form the death sentence.

'The execution is fixed for four o'clock in the afternoon, subject to further instructions from superior authorities.'

Councillor Mikulin dropped the page of foolscap, glanced down his beard, and turning to Razumov, added in an easy, explanatory tone –

'We saw no object in delaying the execution. The order to carry out the sentence was sent by telegraph at noon. I wrote out the telegram myself. He was hanged at four o'clock this afternoon.'

The definite information of Haldin's death gave Razumov the feeling of general lassitude which follows a great exertion or a great excitement. He kept very still on the sofa, but a murmur escaped him –

'He had a belief in a future existence.'

Councillor Mikulin shrugged his shoulders slightly, and Razumov got up with an effort. There was nothing now to stay for in that room. Haldin had been hanged at four o'clock. There could be no doubt of that. He had, it seemed, entered upon his future existence, long boots, Astrakhan fur cap and all, down to the very leather strap round his waist. A flickering, vanishing sort of existence. It was not his soul, it was his mere phantom he had left behind on this earth – thought Razumov, smiling caustically to himself while he crossed the room, utterly forgetful of where he was and of Councillor Mikulin's existence. The official could have set a lot of bells ringing all over the building without leaving his chair. He let Razumov go quite up to the door before he spoke.

'Come, Kirylo Sidorovitch – what are you doing?'

Razumov turned his head and looked at him in silence. He was not in the least disconcerted. Councillor Mikulin's arms were stretched out on the table before him and his body leaned forward a little with an effort of his dim gaze.

'Was I actually going to clear out like this?' Razumov wondered at himself with an impassive countenance. And he was aware of this impassiveness concealing a lucid astonishment.

'Evidently I was going out if he had not spoken,' he thought. 'What would he have done then? I must end this affair one way or another. I must make him show his hand.'

For a moment longer he reflected behind the mask as it were, then let go the door-handle and came back to the middle of the room.

'I'll tell you what you think,' he said explosively, but not raising his voice. 'You think that you are dealing with a secret accomplice of that unhappy man. No, I do not know that he was unhappy. He did not tell me. He was a wretch from my point of view, because to keep alive a false idea is a greater crime than to kill a man. I suppose you will not deny that? I hated him! Visionaries work everlasting evil on earth. Their Utopias inspire in the mass of mediocre minds a disgust of reality and a contempt for the secular logic of human development.'

Razumov shrugged his shoulders and stared. 'What a tirade!' he thought. The silence and immobility of Councillor Mikulin impressed him. The bearded bureaucrat sat at his post, mysteriously self-possessed like an idol with dim, unreadable eyes. Razumov's voice changed involuntarily.

'If you were to ask me where is the necessity of my hate for such as Haldin, I would answer you – there is nothing sentimental in it. I did not hate him because he had committed the crime of murder. Abhorrence is not hate. I hated him simply because I am sane. It is in that character that he outraged me. His death . . .'

Razumov felt his voice growing thick in his throat. The dimness of Councillor Mikulin's eyes seemed to spread all over his face and made it indistinct to Razumov's sight. He tried to disregard these phenomena.

'Indeed,' he pursued, pronouncing each word carefully, 'what is his death to me? If he were lying here on the floor I could walk over his breast . . . The fellow is a mere phantom . . .'

Razumov's voice died out very much against his will. Mikulin behind the table did not allow himself the slightest movement. The silence lasted for some little time before Razumov could go on again.

'He went about talking of me . . . Those intellectual fellows sit in each other's rooms and get drunk on foreign ideas in the same way young Guards' officers treat each other with foreign wines. Merest debauchery ... Upon my word,' – Razumov, enraged by a sudden recollection of Ziemianitch, lowered his voice forcibly, – 'upon my word, we Russians are a drunken lot. Intoxication of some sort we must have: to get ourselves wild with sorrow or maudlin with resignation; to lie inert like a log or set fire to the house. What is a sober man to do, I should like to know? To cut oneself entirely from one's kind is impossible. To live in a desert one must be a saint. But if a drunken man runs out of the grog-shop, falls on your neck and kisses you on both cheeks because something about your appearance has taken his fancy, what then – kindly tell me? You may break, perhaps, a cudgel on his back and yet not succeed in beating him off ...'

Councillor Mikulin raised his hand and passed it down his face deliberately.

'That's ... of course,' he said in an undertone.

The quiet gravity of that gesture made Razumov pause. It was so unexpected, too. What did it mean? It had an alarming aloofness. Razumov remembered his intention of making him show his hand.

'I have said all this to Prince K—,' he began with assumed indifference, but lost it on seeing Councillor Mikulin's slow nod of assent. 'You know it? You've heard ... Then why should I be called here to be told of Haldin's execution? Did you want to confront me with his silence now that the man is dead? What is his silence to me? This is incomprehensible. You want in some way to shake my moral balance.'

'No. Not that,' murmured Councillor Mikulin, just audibly. 'The service you have rendered is appreciated ...'

'Is it?' interrupted Razumov ironically.

'... and your position too.' Councillor Mikulin did not raise his voice. 'But only think! You fall into Prince K—'s study as if from the sky with your startling information ... You are studying yet, Mr Razumov, but we are serving already – don't forget that ... And naturally some curiosity was bound to ...'

Councillor Mikulin looked down his beard. Razumov's lips trembled.

'An occurrence of that sort marks a man,' the homely murmur

128

went on. 'I admit I was curious to see you. General T— thought it would be useful, too ... Don't think I am incapable of understanding your sentiments. When I was young like you I studied ...'

'Yes – you wished to see me,' said Razumov in a tone of profound distaste. 'Naturally you have the right – I mean the power. It all amounts to the same thing. But it is perfectly useless, if you were to look at me and listen to me for a year. I begin to think there is something about me which people don't seem able to make out. It's unfortunate. I imagine, however, that Prince K— understands. He seemed to.'

Councillor Mikulin moved slightly and spoke.

'Prince K— is aware of everything that is being done, and I don't mind informing you that he approved my intention of becoming personally acquainted with you.'

Razumov concealed an immense disappointment under the accents of railing surprise.

'So he is curious too! ... Well – after all, Prince K— knows me very little. It is really very unfortunate for me, but – it is not exactly my fault.'

Councillor Mikulin raised a hasty deprecatory hand and inclined his head slightly over his shoulder.

'Now, Mr Razumov – is it necessary to take it in that way? Everybody I am sure can ...'

He glanced rapidly down his beard, and when he looked up again there was for a moment an interested expression in his misty gaze. Razumov discouraged it with a cold, repellent smile.

'No. That's of no importance to be sure – except that in respect of all this curiosity being aroused by a very simple matter ... What is to be done with it? It is unappeasable. I mean to say there is nothing to appease it with. I happen to have been born a Russian with patriotic instincts – whether inherited or not I am not in a position to say.'

Razumov spoke consciously with elaborate steadiness.

'Yes, patriotic instincts developed by a faculty of independent thinking – of detached thinking. In that respect I am more free than any social democratic revolution could make me. It is more than probable that I don't think exactly as you are thinking. Indeed, how

129

could it be? You would think most likely at this moment that I am elaborately lying to cover up the track of my repentance.'

Razumov stopped. His heart had grown too big for his breast. Councillor Mikulin did not flinch.

'Why so?' he said simply. 'I assisted personally at the search of your rooms. I looked through all the papers myself. I have been greatly impressed by a sort of political confession of faith. A very remarkable document. Now may I ask for what purpose ...'

'To deceive the police naturally,' said Razumov savagely ... 'What is all this mockery? Of course, you can send me straight from this room to Siberia. That would be intelligible. To what is intelligible I can submit. But I protest against this comedy of persecution. The whole affair is becoming too comical altogether for my taste. A comedy of errors, phantoms, and suspicions. It's positively indecent ...'

Councillor Mikulin turned an attentive ear.

'Did you say phantoms?' he murmured.

'I could walk over dozens of them.' Razumov, with an impatient wave of his hand, went on headlong, 'But, really, I must claim the right to be done once for all with that man. And in order to accomplish this I shall take the liberty ...'

Razumov on his side of the table bowed slightly to the seated bureaucrat.

'... To retire – simply to retire,' he finished with great resolution.

He walked to the door, thinking, 'Now he must show his hand. He must ring and have me arrested before I am out of the building, or he must let me go. And either way ...'

An unhurried voice said –

'Kirylo Sidorovitch.'

Razumov at the door turned his head.

'To retire,' he repeated.

'Where to?' asked Councillor Mikulin softly.

PART SECOND

I

In the conduct of an invented story there are, no doubt, certain proprieties to be observed for the sake of clearness and effect. A man of imagination, however inexperienced in the art of narrative, has his instinct to guide him in the choice of his words, and in the development of the action. A grain of talent excuses many mistakes. But this is not a work of imagination; I have no talent; my excuse for this undertaking lies not in its art, but in its artlessness. Aware of my limitations and strong in the sincerity of my purpose, I would not try (were I able) to invent anything. I push my scruples so far that I would not even invent a transition.

Dropping then Mr Razumov's record at the point where Councillor Mikulin's question 'Where to?' comes in with the force of an insoluble problem, I shall simply say that I made the acquaintance of these ladies about six months before that time. By 'these ladies' I mean, of course, the mother and the sister of the unfortunate Haldin.

By what arguments he had induced his mother to sell their little property and go abroad for an indefinite time, I cannot tell precisely. I have an idea that Mrs Haldin, at her son's wish, would have set fire to her house and emigrated to the moon without any sign of surprise or apprehension; and that Miss Haldin – Nathalie, caressingly Natalka – would have given her assent to the scheme.

Their proud devotion to that young man became clear to me in a very short time. Following his directions they went straight to Switzerland – to Zürich – where they remained the best part of a year. From Zürich, which they did not like, they came to Geneva. A friend of mine in Lausanne, a lecturer in history at the University (he had married a Russian lady, a distant connection of Mrs Haldin's), wrote to me suggesting I should call on these ladies. It was a very kindly meant business suggestion. Miss Haldin wished to go through a course of reading the best English authors with a competent teacher.

Mrs Haldin received me very kindly. Her bad French, of which she was smilingly conscious, did away with the formality of the first interview. She was a tall woman in a black silk dress. A wide brow, regular features, and delicately cut lips, testified to her past beauty. She sat upright in an easy chair and in a rather weak, gentle voice told me that her Natalka simply thirsted after knowledge. Her thin hands were lying on her lap, her facial immobility had in it something monachal.* 'In Russia,' she went on, 'all knowledge was tainted with falsehood. Not chemistry and all that, but education generally,' she explained. The Government corrupted the teaching for its own purposes. Both her children felt that. Her Natalka had obtained a diploma of a Superior School for Women and her son was a student at the St Petersburg University. He had a brilliant intellect, a most noble unselfish nature, and he was the oracle of his comrades. Early next year, she hoped he would join them and they would then go to Italy together. In any other country but their own she would have been certain of a great future for a man with the extraordinary abilities and the lofty character of her son – but in Russia . . .

The young lady sitting by the window turned her head and said – 'Come, mother. Even with us things change with years.'

Her voice was deep, almost harsh, and yet caressing in its harshness. She had a dark complexion, with red lips and a full figure. She gave the impression of strong vitality. The old lady sighed.

'You are both young – you two. It is easy for you to hope. But I, too, am not hopeless. Indeed, how could I be with a son like this.'

I addressed Miss Haldin, asking her what authors she wished to read. She directed upon me her grey eyes shaded by black eyelashes, and I became aware, notwithstanding my years, how attractive physically her personality could be to a man capable of appreciating

* Monastic.

132

in a woman something else than the mere grace of femininity. Her glance was as direct and trustful as that of a young man yet unspoiled by the world's wise lessons. And it was intrepid, but in this intrepidity there was nothing aggressive. A naïve yet thoughtful assurance is a better definition. She had reflected already (in Russia the young begin to think early), but she had never known deception as yet because obviously she had never yet fallen under the sway of passion. She was – to look at her was enough – very capable of being roused by an idea or simply by a person. At least, so I judged with I believe an unbiased mind; for clearly my person could not be the person – and as to my ideas! . . .

We became excellent friends in the course of our reading. It was very pleasant. Without fear of provoking a smile, I shall confess that I became very much attached to that young girl. At the end of four months I told her that now she could very well go on reading English by herself. It was time for the teacher to depart. My pupil looked unpleasantly surprised.

Mrs Haldin, with her immobility of feature and kindly expression of the eyes, uttered from her armchair in her uncertain French, *'Mais l'ami reviendra.'** And so it was settled. I returned – not four times a week as before, but pretty frequently. In the autumn we made some short excursions together in company with other Russians. My friendship with these ladies gave me a standing in the Russian colony which otherwise I could not have had.

The day I saw in the papers the news of Mr de P —'s assassination – it was a Sunday – I met the two ladies in the street and walked with them for some distance. Mrs Haldin wore a heavy grey cloak, I remember, over her black silk dress, and her fine eyes met mine with a very quiet expression.

'We have been to the late service,' she said. 'Natalka came with me. Her girl-friends, the students here, of course don't . . . With us in Russia the church is so identified with oppression, that it seems almost necessary when one wishes to be free in this life, to give up all hope of a future existence. But I cannot give up praying for my son.'

* 'But our friend will return.'

She added with a sort of stony grimness, colouring slightly, and in French, *'Ce n'est peut être qu'une habitude.'* ('It may be only habit.')

Miss Haldin was carrying the prayer-book. She did not glance at her mother.

'You and Victor are both profound believers,' she said.

I communicated to them the news from their country which I had just read in a café. For a whole minute we walked together fairly briskly in silence. Then Mrs Haldin murmured –

'There will be more trouble, more persecutions for this. They may be even closing the University. There is neither peace nor rest in Russia for one but in the grave.

'Yes. The way is hard,' came from the daughter, looking straight before her at the Chain of Jura covered with snow, like a white wall closing the end of the street. 'But concord is not so very far off.'

'That is what my children think,' observed Mrs Haldin to me.

I did not conceal my feeling that these were strange times to talk of concord. Nathalie Haldin surprised me by saying, as if she had thought very much on the subject, that the occidentals did not understand the situation. She was very calm and youthfully superior.

'You think it is a class conflict, or a conflict of interests, as social contests are with you in Europe. But it is not that at all. It is something quite different.'

'It is quite possible that I don't understand,' I admitted.

That propensity of lifting every problem from the plane of the understandable by means of some sort of mystic expression, is very Russian. I knew her well enough to have discovered her scorn for all the practical forms of political liberty known to the western world. I suppose one must be a Russian to understand Russian simplicity, a terrible corroding simplicity in which mystic phrases clothe a naïve and hopeless cynicism. I think sometimes that the psychological secret of the profound difference of that people consists in this, that they detest life, the irremediable life of the earth as it is, whereas we westerners cherish it with perhaps an equal exaggeration of its sentimental value. But this is a digression indeed . . .

I helped these ladies into the tramcar and they asked me to call in the afternoon. At least Mrs Haldin asked me as she climbed up, and her Natalka smiled down at the dense westerner indulgently from the rear platform of the moving car. The light of the clear wintry forenoon was softened in her grey eyes.

Mr Razumov's record, like the open book of fate, revives for me the memory of that day as something startlingly pitiless in its freedom from all forebodings. Victor Haldin was still with the living, but with the living whose only contact with life is the expectation of death. He must have been already referring to the last of his earthly affections, the hours of that obstinate silence, which for him was to be prolonged into eternity. That afternoon the ladies entertained a good many of their compatriots – more than was usual for them to receive at one time; and the drawing-room on the ground floor of a large house on the Boulevard des Philosophes was very much crowded.

I outstayed everybody; and when I rose Miss Haldin stood up too. I took her hand and was moved to revert to that morning's conversation in the street.

'Admitting that we occidentals do not understand the character of your people . . .' I began.

It was as if she had been prepared for me by some mysterious fore-knowledge. She checked me gently –

'Their impulses – their . . .' she sought the proper expression and found it, but in French . . . 'their *mouvements d'âme*.'*

Her voice was not much above a whisper.

'Very well,' I said. 'But still we are looking at a conflict. You say it is not a conflict of classes and not a conflict of interests. Suppose I admitted that. Are antagonistic ideas then to be reconciled more easily – can they be cemented with blood and violence into that concord which you proclaim to be so near?'

She looked at me searchingly with her clear grey eyes, without answering my reasonable question – my obvious, my unanswerable question.

'It is inconceivable,' I added, with something like annoyance.

'Everything is inconceivable,' she said. 'The whole world is

---

* Spiritual inclinations.

inconceivable to the strict logic of ideas. And yet the world exists to our senses, and we exist in it. There must be a necessity superior to our conceptions. It is a very miserable and a very false thing to belong to the majority. We Russians shall find some better form of national freedom than an artificial conflict of parties – which is wrong because it is a conflict and contemptible because it is artificial. It is left for us Russians to discover a better way.'

Mrs Haldin had been looking out of the window. She turned upon me the almost lifeless beauty of her face, and the living benign glance of her big dark eyes.

'That's what my children think,' she declared.

'I suppose,' I addressed Miss Haldin, 'that you will be shocked if I tell you that I haven't understood – I won't say a single word; I've understood all the words . . . But what can be this era of disembodied concord you are looking forward to. Life is a thing of form. It has its plastic shape and a definite intellectual aspect. The most idealistic conceptions of love and forbearance must be clothed in flesh as it were before they can be made understandable.'

I took my leave of Mrs Haldin, whose beautiful lips never stirred. She smiled with her eyes only. Nathalie Haldin went with me as far as the door, very amiable.

'Mother imagines that I am the slavish echo of my brother Victor. It is not so. He understands me better than I can understand him. When he joins us and you come to know him you will see what an exceptional soul it is.' She paused. 'He is not a strong man in the conventional sense, you know,' she added. 'But his character is without a flaw.'

'I believe that it will not be difficult for me to make friends with your brother Victor.'

'Don't expect to understand him quite,' she said, a little maliciously. 'He is not at all – at all – western at bottom.'

And on this unnecessary warning I left the room with another bow in the doorway to Mrs Haldin in her armchair by the window. The shadow of autocracy all unperceived by me had already fallen upon the Boulevard des Philosophes, in the free, independent and democratic city of Geneva, where there is a quarter called 'La Petite Russie'. Whenever two Russians come together, the shadow of autocracy is with them, tinging their thoughts, their views, their most intimate feelings, their private life, their public utterances – haunting the secret of their silences.

What struck me next in the course of a week or so was the silence of these ladies. I used to meet them walking in the public garden near the University. They greeted me with their usual friendliness, but I could not help noticing their taciturnity. By that time it was generally known that the assassin of Mr de P— had been caught, judged, and executed. So much had been declared officially to the news agencies. But for the world at large he remained anonymous. The official secrecy had withheld his name from the public. I really cannot imagine for what reason.

One day I saw Miss Haldin walking alone in the main valley of the Bastions under the naked trees.

'Mother is not very well,' she explained.

As Mrs Haldin had, it seemed, never had a day's illness in her life, this indisposition was disquieting. It was nothing definite, too.

'I think she is fretting because we have not heard from my brother for rather a long time.'

'No news – good news,' I said cheerfully, and we began to walk slowly side by side.

'Not in Russia,' she breathed out so low that I only just caught the words. I looked at her with more attention.

'You too are anxious?'

She admitted after a moment of hesitation that she was.

'It is really such a long time since we heard . . .'

And before I could offer the usual banal suggestions she confided in me.

'Oh! But it is much worse than that. I wrote to a family we know in Petersburg. They had not seen him for more than a month. They thought he was already with us. They were even offended a little that he should have left Petersburg without calling on them. The husband of the lady went at once to his lodgings. Victor had left there and they did not know his address.'

I remember her catching her breath rather pitifully. Her brother had not been seen at lectures for a very long time either. He only turned up now and then at the University gate to ask the porter for his letters. And the gentleman friend was told that the student Haldin did not come to claim the last two letters for him. But the police came to inquire if the student Haldin ever received any correspondence at the University and took them away.

'My two last letters,' she said.

We faced each other. A few snow-flakes fluttered under the naked boughs. The sky was dark.

'What do you think could have happened?' I asked.

Her shoulders moved slightly.

'One can never tell – in Russia.'

I saw then the shadow of autocracy lying upon Russian lives in their submission or their revolt. I saw it touch her handsome open face nestled in a fur collar and darken her clear eyes that shone upon me brilliantly grey in the murky light of a beclouded, inclement afternoon.

'Let us move on,' she said. 'It is cold standing today.'

She shuddered a little and stamped her little feet. We moved briskly to the end of the alley and back to the great gates of the garden.

'Have you told your mother?' I ventured to ask.

'No. Not yet. I came out to walk off the impression of this letter.'

I heard a rustle of paper somewhere. It came from her muff. She had the letter with her in there.

'What is it that you are afraid of?' I asked.

To us Europeans of the West, all ideas of political plots and conspiracies seem childish, crude inventions for the theatre or a novel. I did not like to be more definite in my inquiry.

'For us – for my mother specially, what I am afraid of is incertitude. People do disappear. Yes, they do disappear. I leave you to imagine what it is – the cruelty of the dumb weeks – months – years! This friend of ours has abandoned his inquiries when he heard of the police getting hold of the letters. I suppose he was afraid of compromising himself. He has a wife and children – and why should he, after all ... Moreover, he is without influential *connections* and not rich. What could he do? ... Yes, I am afraid of silence – for my poor mother. She won't be able to bear it. For my brother I am afraid of ...' she became almost indistinct, 'of anything.'

We were now near the gate opposite the theatre. She raised her voice.

'But lost people do turn up even in Russia. Do you know what my last hope is? Perhaps the next thing we know, we shall see him walking into our rooms.'

I raised my hat and she passed out of the gardens, graceful and strong, after a slight movement of the head to me, her hands in the muff, crumpling the cruel Petersburg letter.

On returning home I opened the newspaper I receive from London, and glancing down the correspondence from Russia – not the telegrams but the correspondence – the first thing that caught my eye was the name of Haldin. Mr de P —'s death was no longer an actuality, but the enterprising correspondent was proud of having ferreted out some unofficial information about that fact of modern history. He had got hold of Haldin's name, and had picked up the story of the midnight arrest in the street. But the sensation from a journalistic point of view was already well in the past. He did not allot to it more than twenty lines out of a full column. It was quite enough to give me a sleepless night. I perceived that it would have been a sort of treason to let Miss Haldin come without preparation upon that journalistic discovery which would infallibly be reproduced on the morrow by French and Swiss newspapers. I had a very bad time of it till the morning, wakeful with nervous worry and nightmarish with the feeling of being mixed up with something theatrical and morbidly affected. The incongruity of such a complication in those two women's lives was sensible to me all night in the form of absolute anguish. It seemed due to their refined simplicity that it should remain concealed from them for ever. Arriving at an unconscionably early hour at the door of their apartment, I felt as if I were about to commit an act of vandalism ...

The middle-aged servant woman led me into the drawing-room where there was a duster on a chair and a broom leaning against the centre table. The motes danced in the sunshine; I regretted I had not written a letter instead of coming myself, and was thankful for the brightness of the day. Miss Haldin in a plain black dress came lightly out of her mother's room with a fixed uncertain smile on her lips.

I pulled the paper out of my pocket. I did not imagine that a number of the *Standard* could have the effect of Medusa's head.[10] Her face went stony in a moment – her eyes – her limbs. The most terrible thing was that being stony she remained alive. One was conscious of her palpitating heart. I hope she forgave me the delay of my clumsy circumlocution. It was not very prolonged; she could not have kept so still from head to foot for more than a second or two; and then I heard her draw a breath. As if the shock had paralysed her moral resistance, and affected the firmness of her muscles, the contours of her face seemed to have given way. She was frightfully altered. She looked aged – ruined. But only for a moment. She said with decision –

'I am going to tell my mother at once.'

'Would that be safe in her state?' I objected.

'What can be worse than the state she has been in for the last month? We understand this in another way. The crime is not at his door. Don't imagine I am defending him before you.'

She went to the bedroom door, then came back to ask me in a low murmur not to go till she returned. For twenty interminable minutes not a sound reached me. At last Miss Haldin came out and walked across the room with her quick light step. When she reached the armchair she dropped into it heavily as if completely exhausted.

Mrs Haldin, she told me, had not shed a tear. She was sitting up in bed, and her immobility, her silence, were very alarming. At last she lay down gently and had motioned her daughter away.

'She will call me in presently,' added Miss Haldin. 'I left a bell near the bed.'

I confess that my very real sympathy had no standpoint. The Western readers for whom this story is written will understand what I mean. It was, if I may say so, the want of experience. Death is a remorseless spoliator. The anguish of irreparable loss is familiar to us all. There is no life so lonely as to be safe against that experience. But the grief I had brought to these two ladies had gruesome associations. It had the associations of bombs and gallows – a lurid, Russian colouring which made the complexion of my sympathy uncertain.

I was grateful to Miss Haldin for not embarrassing me by an

outward display of deep feeling. I admired her for that wonderful command over herself, even while I was a little frightened at it. It was the stillness of a great tension. What if it should suddenly snap? Even the door of Mrs Haldin's room, with the old mother alone in there, had a rather awful aspect.

Nathalie Haldin murmured sadly –

'I suppose you are wondering what my feelings are?'

Essentially that was true. It was that very wonder which unsettled my sympathy of a dense Occidental. I could get hold of nothing but of some commonplace phrases, those futile phrases that give the measure of our impotence before each other's trials. I mumbled something to the effect that, for the young, life held its hopes and compensations. It held duties too – but of that I was certain it was not necessary to remind her.

She had a handkerchief in her hands and pulled at it nervously.

'I am not likely to forget my mother,' she said. 'We used to be three. Now we are two – two women. She's not so very old. She may live quite a long time yet. What have we to look for in the future? For what hope and what consolation?'

'You must take a wider view,' I said resolutely, thinking that with this exceptional creature this was the right note to strike. She looked at me steadily for a moment, and then the tears she had been keeping down flowed unrestrained. She jumped up and stood in the window with her back to me.

I slipped away without attempting even to approach her. Next day I was told at the door that Mrs Haldin was better. The middle-aged servant remarked that a lot of people – Russians – had called that day, but Mrs Haldin had not seen anybody. A fortnight later, when making my daily call, I was asked in and found Mrs Haldin sitting in her usual place by the window.

At first one would have thought that nothing was changed. I saw across the room the familiar profile, a little sharper in outline and overspread by a uniform pallor as might have been expected in an invalid. But no disease could have accounted for the change in her black eyes, smiling no longer with gentle irony. She raised them as she gave me her hand. I observed the three weeks' old number of the *Standard* folded with the correspondence from Russia uppermost, lying on a little table by the side of the armchair. Mrs Haldin's voice was startlingly weak and colourless. Her first words to me framed a question.

'Has there been anything more in your newspapers?'

I released her long emaciated hand, shook my head negatively, and sat down.

'The English press is wonderful. Nothing can be kept secret from it, and all the world must hear. Only our Russian news is not always easy to understand. Not always easy . . . But English mothers do not look for news like that . . .'

She laid her hand on the newspaper and took it away again. I said –

'We too have had tragic times in our history.'

'A long time ago. A very long time ago.'

'Yes.'

'There are nations that have made their bargain with fate,' said Miss Haldin, who had approached us. 'We need not envy them.'

'Why this scorn?' I asked gently. 'It may be that our bargain was not a very lofty one. But the terms men and nations obtain from Fate are hallowed by the price.'

Mrs Haldin turned her head away and looked out of the window for a time, with that new, sombre, extinct gaze of her sunken eyes which so completely made another woman of her.

'That Englishman, this correspondent,' she addressed me suddenly, 'do you think it is possible that he knew my son?'

To this strange question I could only say that it was possible of course. She saw my surprise.

'If one knew what sort of man he was one could perhaps write to him,' she murmured.

'Mother thinks,' explained Miss Haldin, standing between us, with one hand resting on the back of my chair, 'that my poor brother perhaps did not try to save himself.'

I looked up at Miss Haldin in sympathetic consternation, but Miss Haldin was looking down calmly at her mother. The latter said –

'We do not know the address of any of his friends. Indeed, we know nothing of his Petersburg comrades. He had a multitude of young friends, only he never spoke much of them. One could guess

142

that they were his disciples and that they idolized him. But he was so modest. One would think that with so many devoted . . .'

She averted her head again and looked down the Boulevard des Philosophes, a singularly arid and dusty thoroughfare, where nothing could be seen at the moment but two dogs, a little girl in a pinafore hopping on one leg, and in the distance a workman wheeling a bicycle.

'Even amongst the Apostles of Christ there was found a Judas,' she whispered as if to herself, but with the evident intention to be heard by me.

The Russian visitors assembled in little knots, conversed amongst themselves meantime, in low murmurs, and with brief glances in our direction. It was a great contrast to the usual loud volubility of these gatherings. Miss Haldin followed me into the ante-room.

'People will come,' she said. 'We cannot shut the door in their faces.'

While I was putting on my overcoat she began to talk to me of her mother. Poor Mrs Haldin was fretting after more news. She wanted to go on hearing about her unfortunate son. She could not make up her mind to abandon him quietly to the dumb unknown. She would persist in pursuing him in there through the long days of motionless silence face to face with the empty Boulevard des Philosophes. She could not understand why he had not escaped — as so many other revolutionists and conspirators had managed to escape in other instances of that kind. It was really inconceivable that the means of secret revolutionary organizations should have failed so inexcusably to preserve her son. But in reality the inconceivable that staggered her mind was nothing but the cruel audacity of Death passing over her head to strike at that young and precious heart.

Miss Haldin mechanically, with an absorbed look, handed me my hat. I understood from her that the poor woman was possessed by the sombre and simple idea that her son must have perished because he did not want to be saved. It could not have been that he despaired of his country's future. That was impossible. Was it possible that his mother and sister had not known how to merit his confidence; and that, after having done what he was compelled to do, his spirit

143

became crushed by an intolerable doubt, his mind distracted by a sudden mistrust.

I was very much shocked by this piece of ingenuity.

'Our three lives were like that!' Miss Haldin twined the fingers of both her hands together in demonstration, then separated them slowly, looking straight into my face. 'That's what poor mother found to torment herself and me with, for all the years to come,' added the strange girl. At that moment her indefinable charm was revealed to me in the conjunction of passion and stoicism. I imagined what her life was likely to be by the side of Mrs Haldin's terrible immobility, inhabited by that fixed idea. But my concern was reduced to silence by my ignorance of her modes of feeling. Difference of nationality is a terrible obstacle for our complex Western natures. But Miss Haldin probably was too simple to suspect my embarrassment. She did not wait for me to say anything, but as if reading my thoughts on my face she went on courageously –

'At first poor mother went numb, as our peasants say; then she began to think and she will go on now thinking and thinking in that unfortunate strain. You see yourself how cruel that is . . .'

I never spoke with greater sincerity than when I agreed with her that it would be deplorable in the highest degree. She took an anxious breath.

'But all these strange details in the English paper,' she exclaimed suddenly. 'What is the meaning of them? I suppose they are true? But is it not terrible that my poor brother should be caught wandering alone, as if in despair, about the streets at night . . .'

We stood so close to each other in the dark ante-room that I could see her biting her lower lip to suppress a dry sob. After a short pause she said –

'I suggested to mother that he may have been betrayed by some false friend or simply by some cowardly creature. It may be easier for her to believe that.'

I understood now the poor woman's whispered allusion to Judas.

'It may be easier,' I admitted, admiring inwardly the directness and the subtlety of the girl's outlook. She was dealing with life as it was made for her by the political conditions of her country. She faced cruel realities, not morbid imaginings of her own making. I could not defend myself from a certain feeling of respect when she added simply –

'Time they say can soften every sort of bitterness. But I cannot believe that it has any power over remorse. It is better that mother should think some person guilty of Victor's death, than that she should connect it with a weakness of her son or a shortcoming of her own.'

'But you, yourself, don't suppose that . . .' I began.

She compressed her lips and shook her head. She harboured no evil thoughts against any one, she declared – and perhaps nothing that happened was unnecessary. On these words, pronounced low and sounding mysterious in the half obscurity of the ante-room, we parted with an expressive and warm handshake. The grip of her strong, shapely hand had a seductive frankness, a sort of exquisite virility. I do not know why she should have felt so friendly to me. It may be that she thought I understood her much better than I was able to do. The most precise of her sayings seemed always to me to have enigmatical prolongations vanishing somewhere beyond my reach. I am reduced to suppose that she appreciated my attention and my silence. The attention she could see was quite sincere, so that the silence could not be suspected of coldness. It seemed to satisfy her. And it is to be noted that if she confided in me it was clearly not with the expectation of receiving advice, for which, indeed, she never asked.

II

Our daily relations were interrupted at this period for something like a fortnight. I had to absent myself unexpectedly from Geneva. On my return I lost no time in directing my steps up the Boulevard des Philosophes.

Through the open door of the drawing-room I was annoyed to hear a visitor holding forth steadily in an unctuous deep voice.[11]

Mrs Haldin's armchair by the window stood empty. On the sofa, Nathalie Haldin raised her charming grey eyes in a glance of greeting accompanied by the merest hint of a welcoming smile. But she made no movement. With her strong white hands lying inverted in the lap of her mourning dress she faced a man who presented to me a robust back covered with black broadcloth, and well in keeping with the deep voice. He turned his head sharply over his shoulder, but only for a moment.

'Ah! your English friend. I know. I know. That's nothing.'

He wore spectacles with smoked glasses, a tall silk hat stood on the floor by the side of his chair. Flourishing slightly a big soft hand he went on with his discourse, precipitating his delivery a little more.

'I have never changed the faith I held while wandering in the forests and bogs of Siberia. It sustained me then – it sustains me now. The great Powers of Europe are bound to disappear – and the cause of their collapse will be very simple. They will exhaust themselves struggling against their proletariat. In Russia it is different. In Russia we have no classes to combat each other, one holding the power of wealth, and the other mighty with the strength of numbers. We have only an unclean bureaucracy in the face of a people as great and as incorruptible as the ocean. No, we have no classes. But we have the Russian woman. The admirable Russian woman! I receive most remarkable letters signed by women. So elevated in tone, so courageous, breathing such a noble ardour of service! The greatest part of our hopes rests on women. I behold their thirst for knowledge. It is admirable. Look how they absorb, how they are making it their own. It is miraculous. But what is knowledge? ... I understand that you have not been studying anything especially – medicine for instance. No? That's right. Had I been honoured by being asked to advise you on the use of your time when you arrived here I would have been strongly opposed to such a course. Knowledge in itself is mere dross.'

He had one of those bearded Russian faces without shape, a mere appearance of flesh and hair with not a single feature having any sort of character. His eyes being hidden by the dark glasses there was an utter absence of all expression. I knew him by sight. He was a Russian refugee of mark. All Geneva knew his burly black-coated figure. At one time all Europe was aware of the story of his life written by himself and translated into seven or more languages. In his youth he had led an idle, dissolute life. Then a society girl he was about to marry died suddenly and thereupon he abandoned the world of fashion, and began to conspire in a spirit of repentance, and, after that, his native autocracy took good care that the usual things should happen to him. He was imprisoned in fortresses, beaten within an inch of his life, and condemned to work in mines, with common criminals. The great success of his book, however, was the chain.

I do not remember now the details of the weight and length of the fetters riveted on his limbs by an 'Administrative' order, but it was in the number of pounds and the thickness of links an appalling assertion of the divine right of autocracy. Appalling and futile too, because this big man managed to carry off that simple engine of government with him into the woods. The sensational clink of these fetters is heard all through the chapters describing his escape – a subject of wonder to two continents. He had begun by concealing himself successfully from his guard in a hole on a river bank. It was the end of the day; with infinite labour he managed to free one of his legs. Meantime night fell. He was going to begin on his other leg when he was overtaken by a terrible misfortune. He dropped his file.

All this is precise yet symbolic; and the file had its pathetic history. It was given to him unexpectedly one evening, by a quiet, pale-faced girl. The poor creature had come out to the mines to join one of his fellow convicts, a delicate young man, a mechanic and a social democrat, with broad cheekbones and large staring eyes. She had worked her way across half Russia and nearly the whole of Siberia to be near him, and, as it seems, with the hope of helping him to escape. But she arrived too late. Her lover had died only a week before.

Through that obscure episode, as he says, in the history of ideas in Russia, the file came into his hands, and inspired him with an ardent resolution to regain his liberty. When it slipped through his fingers it was as if it had gone straight into the earth. He could by no manner of means put his hand on it again in the dark. He groped systematically in the loose earth, in the mud, in the water; the night was passing meantime, the precious night on which he counted to get away into the forests, his only chance of escape. For a moment he was tempted by despair to give up; but recalling the quiet, sad face of the heroic girl, he felt profoundly ashamed of his weakness. She had selected him for the gift of liberty and he must show himself worthy of the favour conferred by her feminine, indomitable soul. It appeared to be a sacred trust. To fail would have been a sort of treason against the sacredness of self-sacrifice and womanly love.

There are in his book whole pages of self-analysis whence emerges like a white figure from a dark confused sea the conviction of woman's spiritual superiority – his new faith confessed since in several volumes. His first tribute to it, the great act of his conversion, was his extraordinary existence in the endless forests of the Okhotsk Province, with the loose end of the chain wound about his waist. A strip torn off his convict shirt secured the end firmly. Other strips fastened it at intervals up his left leg to deaden the clanking and to prevent the slack links from getting hooked in the bushes. He became very fierce. He developed an unsuspected genius for the arts of a wild and hunted existence. He learned to creep into villages without betraying his presence by anything more than an occasional faint jingle. He broke into outhouses with an axe he managed to purloin in a wood-cutters' camp. In the deserted tracts of country he lived on wild berries and hunted for honey. His clothing dropped off him gradually. His naked tawny figure glimpsed vaguely through the bushes with a cloud of mosquitoes and flies hovering about the shaggy head, spread tales of terror through whole districts. His temper grew savage as the days went by, and he was glad to discover that there was so much of a brute in him. He had nothing else to put his trust in. For it was as though there had been two human beings indissolubly joined in that enterprise. The civilized man, the enthusiast of advanced humanitarian ideals thirsting for the triumph of spiritual love and political liberty; and the stealthy, primeval savage, pitilessly cunning in the preservation of his freedom from day to day, like a tracked wild beast.

The wild beast was making its way instinctively eastward to the Pacific coast, and the civilized humanitarian in fearful anxious dependence watched the proceedings with awe. Through all these weeks he could never make up his mind to appeal to human compassion. In the wary primeval savage this shyness might have been natural, but the other too, the civilized creature, the thinker, the escaping 'political' had developed an absurd form of morbid pessimism, a form of temporary insanity, originating perhaps in the physical worry and discomfort of the chain. These links, he fancied, made him odious to the rest of mankind. It was a repugnant and suggestive load. Nobody could feel any pity at the disgusting sight of a man escaping with a broken chain. His imagination became affected by his fetters in a precise, matter-of-fact manner. It seemed to him impossible that people could resist the temptation of fastening the loose end to a staple in the wall while they went for the nearest police official. Crouching in holes or hidden in thickets, he had tried to read the faces of unsuspecting free settlers working in the clearings or passing along the paths within a foot or two of his eyes. His feeling was that no man on earth could be trusted with the temptation of the chain.

One day, however, he chanced to come upon a solitary woman. It was on an open slope of rough grass outside the forest. She sat on the bank of a narrow stream; she had a red handkerchief on her head and a small basket was lying on the ground near her hand. At a little distance could be seen a cluster of log cabins, with a water-mill over a dammed pool shaded by birch trees and looking bright as glass in the twilight. He approached her silently, his hatchet stuck in his iron belt, a thick cudgel in his hand; there were leaves and bits of twig in his tangled hair, in his matted beard; bunches of rags he had wound round the links fluttered from his waist. A faint clink of his fetters made the woman turn her head. Too terrified by this savage apparition to jump up or even to scream, she was yet too stout-hearted to faint ... Expecting nothing less than to be murdered on the spot she covered her eyes with her hands to avoid the sight of the descending axe. When at last she found courage to look again, she saw the shaggy wild man sitting on the bank six feet away from her. His thin, sinewy arms hugged his naked legs; the long beard covered the knees on which he rested his chin; all these clasped, folded limbs, the bare shoulders, the wild head with red staring eyes, shook and trembled violently while the bestial creature was making efforts to speak. It was six weeks since he had heard the sound of his own voice. It seemed as though he had lost the faculty of speech. He had become a dumb and despairing brute, till the woman's sudden, unexpected cry of profound pity, the insight of her feminine compassion discovering the complex misery of the man under the terrifying aspect of the monster, restored him to the ranks of humanity. This point of view is presented in his book, with a very effective eloquence. She ended, he says, by shedding tears over him, sacred, redeeming tears, while he also wept with joy in the manner of a converted sinner. Directing him to hide in the bushes and wait patiently (a police patrol was expected in the Settlement) she went away towards the houses, promising to return at night.

As if providentially appointed to be the newly wedded wife of the village blacksmith, the woman persuaded her husband to come out with her, bringing some tools of his trade, a hammer, a chisel, a small anvil ... 'My fetters' – the book says – 'were struck off on the banks of the stream, in the starlight of a calm night by an athletic, taciturn young man of the people, kneeling at my feet, while the woman like a liberating genius stood by with clasped hands.' Obviously a symbolic couple. At the same time they furnished his regained humanity with some decent clothing, and put heart into the new man by the information that the sea-coast of the Pacific was only a very few miles away. It could be seen, in fact, from the top of the next ridge ...

The rest of his escape does not lend itself to mystic treatment and symbolic interpretation. He ended by finding his way to the West by the Suez Canal route in the usual manner. Reaching the shores of South Europe he sat down to write his autobiography – the great literary success of its year. This book was followed by other books written with the declared purpose of elevating humanity. In these works he preached generally the cult of the woman. For his own part he practised it under the rites of special devotion to the trans-cendental merits of a certain Madame de S—, a lady of advanced views, no longer very young, once upon a time the intriguing wife of a now dead and forgotten diplomat. Her loud pretensions to be one of the leaders of modern thought and of modern sentiment, she sheltered (like Voltaire and Mme de Staël) on the republican territory of Geneva. Driving through the streets in her big landau she exhibited to the indifference of the natives and the stares of the tourists a long-waisted, youthful figure of hieratic stiffness, with a pair of big gleaming eyes, rolling restlessly behind a short veil of black lace, which, coming down no further than her vividly red lips, resembled a mask. Usually the 'heroic fugitive' (this name was bestowed upon him in a review of the English edition of his book) – the 'heroic fugitive' accompanied her, sitting, portentously bearded and darkly bespectacled, not by her side, but opposite her, with his back to the horses. Thus, facing each other, with no one else in the roomy carriage, their airings suggested a conscious public manifestation. Or it may have been unconscious. Russian simplicity often marches innocently on the edge of cynicism for some lofty purpose. But it is a vain enterprise for sophisticated Europe to try and understand these doings. Considering the air of gravity extending even to the physiognomy of the coachman and the action of the showy horses, this quaint display might have possessed a mystic significance, but to the corrupt frivolity of a Western mind, like my own, it seemed hardly decent.

However, it is not becoming for an obscure teacher of languages to criticize a 'heroic fugitive' of worldwide celebrity. I was aware from hearsay that he was an industrious busy-body, hunting up his compatriots in hotels, in private lodgings, and – I was told – conferring upon them the honour of his notice in public gardens when a suitable opening presented itself. I was under the impression that after a visit or two, several months before, he had given up the ladies Haldin – no doubt reluctantly, for there could be no question of his being a determined person. It was perhaps to be expected that he should reappear again on this terrible occasion, as a Russian and a revolutionist, to say the right thing, to strike the true, perhaps a comforting, note. But I did not like to see him sitting there. I trust that an unbecoming jealousy of my privileged position had nothing to do with it. I made no claim to a special standing for my silent friendship. Removed by the difference of age and nationality as if into the sphere of another existence, I produced, even upon myself, the effect of a dumb helpless ghost, of an anxious immaterial thing that could only hover about without the power to protect or guide

151

by as much as a whisper. Since Miss Haldin with her sure instinct had refrained from introducing me to the burly celebrity, I would have retired quietly and returned later on, had I not met a peculiar expression in her eyes which I interpreted as a request to stay, with the view, perhaps, of shortening an unwelcome visit.

He picked up his hat, but only to deposit it on his knees.

'We shall meet again, Natalia Victorovna. Today I have called only to mark those feelings towards your honoured mother and yourself, the nature of which you cannot doubt. I needed no urging, but Eleanor – Madame de S— herself has in a way sent me. She extends to you the hand of feminine fellowship. There is positively in all the range of human sentiments no joy and no sorrow that woman cannot understand, elevate, and spiritualize by her interpretation. That young man newly arrived from St Petersburg, I have mentioned to you, is already under the charm.'

At this point Miss Haldin got up abruptly. I was glad. He did not evidently expect anything so decisive and, at first, throwing his head back, he tilted up his dark glasses with bland curiosity. At last, recollecting himself, he stood up hastily, seizing his hat off his knees with great adroitness.

'How is it, Natalia Victorovna, that you have kept aloof so long, from what after all is – let disparaging tongues say what they like – a unique centre of intellectual freedom and of effort to shape a high conception of our future? In the case of your honoured mother I understand in a measure. At her age new ideas – new faces are not perhaps ... But you! Was it mistrust – or indifference? You must come out of your reserve. We Russians have no right to be reserved with each other. In our circumstances it is almost a crime against humanity. The luxury of private grief is not for us. Nowadays the devil is not combated by prayers and fasting. And what is fasting after all but starvation. You must not starve yourself, Natalia Victorovna. Strength is what we want. Spiritual strength, I mean. As to the other kind, what could withstand us Russians if we only put it forth? Sin is different in our day, and the way of salvation for pure souls is different too. It is no longer to be found in monasteries but in the world, in the ...'

The deep sound seemed to rise from under the floor, and one felt steeped in it to the lips. Miss Haldin's interruption resembled the effort of a drowning person to keep above water. She struck in with an accent of impatience –

'But, Peter Ivanovitch, I don't mean to retire into a monastery. Who would look for salvation there?'

'I spoke figuratively,' he boomed.

'Well, then, I am speaking figuratively too. But sorrow is sorrow and pain is pain in the old way. They make their demands upon people. One has got to face them the best way one can. I know that the blow which has fallen upon us so unexpectedly is only an episode in the fate of a people. You may rest assured that I don't forget that. But just now I have to think of my mother. How can you expect me to leave her to herself . . . ?'

'That is putting it in a very crude way,' he protested in his great effortless voice.

Miss Haldin did not wait for the vibration to die out.

'And run about visiting amongst a lot of strange people. The idea is distasteful for me; and I do not know what else you may mean?'

He towered before her, enormous, deferential, cropped as close as a convict; and this big pinkish poll evoked for me the vision of a wild head with matted locks peering through parted bushes, glimpses of naked, tawny limbs slinking behind the masses of sodden foliage under a cloud of flies and mosquitoes. It was an involuntary tribute to the vigour of his writing. Nobody could doubt that he had wandered in Siberian forests, naked and girt with a chain. The black broadcloth coat invested his person with a character of austere decency – something recalling a missionary.

'Do you know what I want, Natalia Victorovna?' he uttered solemnly. 'I want you to be a fanatic.'

'A fanatic?'

'Yes. Faith alone won't do.'

His voice dropped to a still lower tone. He raised for a moment one thick arm; the other remained hanging down against his thigh, with the fragile silk hat at the end.

'I shall tell you now something which I entreat you to ponder over carefully. Listen, we need a force that would move heaven and earth – nothing less.'

153

The profound, subterranean note of this 'nothing less' made one shudder, almost, like the deep muttering of wind in the pipes of an organ.

'And are we to find that force in the salon of Madame de S—? Excuse me, Peter Ivanovitch, if I permit myself to doubt it. Is not that lady a woman of the great world, an aristocrat?'

'Prejudice!' he cried. 'You astonish me. And suppose she was all that! She is also a woman of flesh and blood. There is always something to weigh down the spiritual side in all of us. But to make of it a reproach is what I did not expect from you. No! I did not expect that. One would think you have listened to some malevolent scandal.'

'I have heard no gossip, I assure you. In our province how could we? But the world speaks of her. What can there be in common in a lady of that sort and an obscure country girl like me?'

'She is a perpetual manifestation of a noble and peerless spirit,' he broke in. 'Her charm – no, I shall not speak of her charm. But, of course, everybody who approaches her falls under the spell ... Contradictions vanish, trouble falls away from one ... Unless I am mistaken – but I never make a mistake in spiritual matters – you are troubled in your soul, Natalia Victorovna.'

Miss Haldin's clear eyes looked straight at his soft enormous face; I received the impression that behind these dark spectacles of his he could be as impudent as he chose.

'Only the other evening walking back to town from Château Borel with our latest interesting arrival from Petersburg, I could notice the powerful soothing influence – I may say reconciling influence ... There he was, all these kilometres along the shores of the lake, silent, like a man who has been shown the way of peace. I could feel the leaven working in his soul, you understand. For one thing he listened to me patiently. I myself was inspired that evening by the firm and exquisite genius of Eleanor – Madame de S—, you know. It was a full moon and I could observe his face. I cannot be deceived ...'

Miss Haldin, looking down, seemed to hesitate.

'Well! I will think of what you said, Peter Ivanovitch. I shall try to call as soon as I can leave mother for an hour or two safely.'

Coldly as these words were said I was amazed at the concession. He snatched her right hand with such fervour that I thought he was going to press it to his lips or his breast. But he only held it by the fingertips in his great paw and shook it a little up and down while he delivered his last volley of words.

'That's right. That's right. I haven't obtained your full confidence as yet, Natalia Victorovna, but that will come. All in good time. The sister of Victor Haldin cannot be without importance . . . It's simply impossible. And no woman can remain sitting on the steps. Flowers, tears, applause – that has had its time; it's a medieval conception. The arena, the arena itself is the place for women!'

He relinquished her hand with a flourish, as if giving it to her for a gift, and remained still, his head bowed in dignified submission before her femininity.

'The arena! . . . You must descend into the arena, Natalia.'

He made one step backwards, inclined his enormous body, and was gone swiftly. The door fell to behind him. But immediately the powerful resonance of his voice was heard addressing in the ante-room the middle-aged servant woman who was letting him out. Whether he exhorted her too to descend into the arena I cannot tell. The thing sounded like a lecture, and the slight crash of the outer door cut it short suddenly.

III

We remained looking at each other for a time.

'Do you know who he is?'

Miss Haldin, coming forward, put this question to me in English. I took her offered hand.

'Everybody knows. He is a revolutionary feminist, a great writer, if you like, and – how shall I say it – the – the familiar guest of Madame de S—'s mystic revolutionary salon.'

Miss Haldin passed her hand over her forehead.

'You know, he was with me for more than an hour before you came in. I was so glad mother was lying down. She has many nights without sleep, and then sometimes in the middle of the day she gets a rest of several hours. It is sheer exhaustion – but still, I am thankful ... If it were not for these intervals ...'

She looked at me and, with that extraordinary penetration which used to disconcert me, shook her head.

'No. She would not go mad.'

'My dear young lady,' I cried, by way of protest, the more shocked because in my heart I was far from thinking Mrs Haldin quite sane.

'You don't know what a fine, lucid intellect mother had,' continued Nathalie Haldin, with her calm, clear-eyed simplicity, which seemed to me always to have a quality of heroism.

'I am sure ...' I murmured.

'I darkened mother's room and came out here. I've wanted for so long to think quietly.'

She paused, then, without giving any sign of distress, added, 'It's so difficult,' and looked at me with a strange fixity, as if watching for a sign of dissent or surprise.

I gave neither. I was irresistibly impelled to say –

'The visit from that gentleman has not made it any easier, I fear.'

Miss Haldin stood before me with a peculiar expression in her eyes.

'I don't pretend to understand Peter Ivanovitch completely. Some guide one must have, even if one does not wholly give up the direction of one's conduct to him. I am an inexperienced girl, but I am not slavish. There has been too much of that in Russia. Why should I not listen to him? There is no harm in having one's thoughts directed. But I don't mind confessing to you that I have not been completely candid with Peter Ivanovitch. I don't quite know what prevented me at the moment ...'

She walked away suddenly from me to a distant part of the room; but it was only to open and shut a drawer in a bureau. She returned with a piece of paper in her hand. It was thin and blackened with close handwriting. It was obviously a letter.

'I wanted to read you the very words,' she said. 'This is one of my poor brother's letters. He never doubted. How could he doubt? They make only such a small handful, these miserable oppressors, before the unanimous will of our people.'

'Your brother believed in the power of a people's will to achieve anything?'

'It was his religion,' declared Miss Haldin.

I looked at her calm face and her animated eyes.

'Of course the will must be awakened, inspired, concentrated,' she went on. 'That is the true task of real agitators. One has got to give up one's life to it. The degradation of servitude, the absolutist lies must be uprooted and swept out. Reform is impossible. There is nothing to reform. There is no legality, there are no institutions. There are only arbitrary decrees. There is only a handful of cruel – perhaps blind – officials against a nation.'

The letter rustled slightly in her hand. I glanced down at the flimsy blackened pages whose very handwriting seemed cabalistic, incomprehensible to the experience of Western Europe.

'Stated like this,' I confessed, 'the problem seems simple enough. But I fear I shall not see it solved. And if you go back to Russia I know that I shall not see you again. Yet once more I say: go back! Don't suppose that I am thinking of your preservation. No! I know that you will not be returning to personal safety. But I had much rather think of you in danger there than see you exposed to what may be met here.'

'I tell you what,' said Miss Haldin, after a moment of reflection. 'I believe that you hate revolution; you fancy it's not quite honest. You belong to a people which has made a bargain with fate and wouldn't like to be rude to it. But we have made no bargain. It was never offered to us – so much liberty for so much hard cash. You shrink from the idea of revolutionary action for those you think well of as if it were something – how shall I say it – not quite decent.'

I bowed my head.

'You are quite right,' I said. 'I think very highly of you.'

'Don't suppose I do not know it,' she began hurriedly. 'Your friendship has been very valuable.'

'I have done little else but look on.'

She was a little flushed under the eyes.

'There is a way of looking on which is valuable. I have felt less lonely because of it. It's difficult to explain.'

'Really? Well, I too have felt less lonely. That's easy to explain, though. But it won't go on much longer. The last thing I want to tell you is this: in a real revolution – not a simple dynastic change or a mere reform of institutions – in a real revolution the best characters do not come to the front. A violent revolution falls into the hands of narrow-minded fanatics and of tyrannical hypocrites at first. Afterwards comes the turn of all the pretentious intellectual failures of the time. Such are the chiefs and the leaders. You will notice that I have left out the mere rogues. The scrupulous and the just, the noble, humane, and devoted natures; the unselfish and the intelligent may begin a movement – but it passes away from them. They are not the leaders of a revolution. They are its victims: the victims of disgust, of disenchantment – often of remorse. Hopes grotesquely betrayed, ideals caricatured – that is the definition of revolutionary success. There have been in every revolution hearts broken by such successes. But enough of that. My meaning is that I don't want you to be a victim.'

'If I could believe all you have said I still wouldn't think of myself,' protested Miss Haldin. 'I would take liberty from any hand as a hungry man would snatch a piece of bread. The true progress must begin after. And for that the right men shall be found. They are already amongst us. One comes upon them in their obscurity, unknown, preparing themselves . . .'

She spread out the letter she had kept in her hand all the time, and looking down at it –

'Yes! One comes upon such men!' she repeated, and then read out the words, 'Unstained, lofty, and solitary existences.'

Folding up the letter, while I looked at her interrogatively, she explained –

'These are the words which my brother applies to a young man he came to know in St Petersburg. An intimate friend, I suppose. It must be. His is the only name my brother mentions in all his correspondence with me. Absolutely the only one, and – would you believe it? – the man is here. He arrived recently in Geneva.'

'Have you seen him?' I inquired. 'But, of course, you must have seen him.'

'No! No! I haven't! I didn't know he was here. It's Peter Ivano-vitch himself who told me. You have heard him yourself mentioning a new arrival from Petersburg ... Well, that is the man of "unstained, lofty, and solitary existence". My brother's friend!'

'Compromised politically, I suppose,' I remarked.

'I don't know. Yes. It must be so. Who knows! Perhaps it was this very friendship with my brother which ... But no! It is scarcely possible. Really, I know nothing except what Peter Ivanovitch told me of him. He has brought a letter of introduction from Father Zosim – you know, the priest-democrat; you have heard of Father Zosim?'

'Oh yes. The famous Father Zosim was staying here in Geneva for some two months about a year ago,' I said. 'When he left here he seems to have disappeared from the world.'

'It appears that he is at work in Russia again. Somewhere in the centre,' Miss Haldin said, with animation. 'But please don't mention that to any one – don't let it slip from you, because if it got into the papers it would be dangerous for him.'

'You are anxious, of course, to meet that friend of your brother?' I asked.

Miss Haldin put the letter into her pocket. Her eyes looked beyond my shoulder at the door of her mother's room.

'Not here,' she murmured. 'Not for the first time, at least.'

After a moment of silence I said good-bye, but Miss Haldin followed me into the ante-room, closing the door behind us carefully.

'I suppose you guess where I mean to go tomorrow?'

'You have made up your mind to call on Madame de S—.'

'Yes. I am going to the Château Borel. I must.'

'What do you expect to hear there?' I asked, in a low voice.

I wondered if she were not deluding herself with some impossible hope. It was not that, however.

'Only think – such a friend. The only man mentioned in his letters. He would have something to give me, if nothing more than a few poor words. It may be something said and thought in those last days. Would you want me to turn my back on what is left of my poor brother – a friend?'

'Certainly not,' I said. 'I quite understand your pious curiosity.'

'– Unstained, lofty, and solitary existences,' she murmured to herself. 'There are! There are! Well, let me question one of them about the loved dead.'

'How do you know, though, that you will meet him there? Is he staying in the Château as a guest – do you suppose?'

'I can't really tell,' she confessed. 'He brought a written introduction from Father Zosim – who, it seems, is a friend of Madame de S— too. She can't be such a worthless woman after all.'

'There were all sorts of rumours afloat about Father Zosim himself,' I observed.

She shrugged her shoulders.

'Calumny is a weapon of our government too. It's well known. Oh yes! It is a fact that Father Zosim had the protection of the Governor-General of a certain province. We talked on the subject with my brother two years ago, I remember. But his work was good. And now he is proscribed. What better proof can one require. But no matter what that priest was or is. All that cannot affect my brother's friend. If I don't meet him there I shall ask these people for his address. And, of course, mother must see him too, later on. There is no guessing what he may have to tell us. It would be a mercy if mamma could be soothed. You know what she imagines. Some explanation perhaps may be found, or – or even made up, perhaps. It would be no sin.'

'Certainly,' I said, 'it would be no sin. It may be a mistake, though.'

'I want her only to recover some of her old spirit. While she is like this I cannot think of anything calmly.'

'Do you mean to invent some sort of pious fraud for your mother's sake?' I asked.

'Why fraud? Such a friend is sure to know something of my brother in these last days. He could tell us ... There is something in the facts which will not let me rest. I am certain he meant to join us abroad – that he had some plans – some great patriotic action in view; not only for himself, but for both of us. I trusted in that. I looked forward to the time! Oh! with such hope and impatience .. I could have helped. And now suddenly this appearance of recklessness – as if he had not cared ...'

She remained silent for a time, then obstinately she concluded –

'I want to know ...'

Thinking it over, later on, while I walked slowly away from the Boulevard des Philosophes, I asked myself critically, what precisely was it that she wanted to know? What I had heard of her history was enough to give me a clue. In the educational establishment for girls where Miss Haldin finished her studies she was looked upon rather unfavourably. She was suspected of holding independent views on matters settled by official teaching. Afterwards, when the two ladies returned to their country place, both mother and daughter, by speaking their minds openly on public events, had earned for themselves a reputation of liberalism. The three-horse trap of the district police-captain began to be seen frequently in their village. 'I must keep an eye on the peasants' – so he explained his visits up at the house. 'Two lonely ladies must be looked after a little.' He would inspect the walls as though he wanted to pierce them with his eyes, peer at the photographs, turn over the books in the drawing-room negligently, and after the usual refreshments, would depart. But the old priest of the village came one evening in the greatest distress and agitation, to confess that he – the priest – had been ordered to watch and ascertain in other ways too (such as using his spiritual power with the servants) all that was going on in the house, and especially in respect of the visitors these ladies received, who they were, the length of their stay, whether any of them were strangers to that part of the country, and so on. The poor, simple old man was in an agony of humiliation and terror. 'I came to warn you. Be cautious in your conduct, for the love of God. I am burning with shame, but there is no getting out from under the net. I shall have to tell them what I see, because if I did not there is my deacon. He would make the worst of things to curry favour. And then my son-in-law, the husband of my Parasha, who is a writer in the Government Domain office, they would soon kick him out – and maybe send him away somewhere.' The old man lamented the necessities of the times – 'when people do not agree somehow' and wiped his eyes. He did not wish to spend the evening of his days with a shaven head in the penitent's cell of some monastery – 'and subjected to all the severities of ecclesiastical discipline; for they would show no mercy to an old man,' he groaned. He became almost hysterical, and the two ladies, full of commiseration, soothed him the best they could before they let him go back to his cottage. But, as a matter of fact, they had very few visitors. The neighbours – some of them old friends – began to keep away; a few from timidity, others with marked disdain, being grand people that came only for the summer – Miss Haldin explained to me – aristocrats, reactionaries. It was a solitary existence for a young girl. Her relations with her mother were of the tenderest and most open kind; but Mrs Haldin had seen the experiences of her own generation, its sufferings, its deceptions, its apostasies too. Her affection for her children was expressed by the suppression of all signs of anxiety. She maintained a heroic reserve. To Nathalie Haldin, her brother with his Petersburg existence, not enigmatical in the least (there could be no doubt of what he felt or thought) but conducted a little mysteriously, was the only visible representative of a proscribed liberty. All the significance of freedom, its indefinite promises, lived in their long discussions, which breathed the loftiest hope of action and faith in success. Then, suddenly, the action, the hopes, came to an end with the details ferreted out by the English journalist. The concrete fact, the fact of his death remained! but it remained obscure in its deeper causes. She felt herself abandoned without explanation. But she did not suspect him. What she wanted was to learn almost at any cost how she could remain faithful to his departed spirit.

IV

Several days elapsed before I met Nathalie Haldin again. I was crossing the place in front of the theatre when I made out her shapely figure in the very act of turning between the gate pillars of the unattractive public promenade of the Bastions. She walked away from me, but I knew we should meet as she returned down the main alley – unless, indeed, she were going home. In that case, I don't think I should have called on her yet. My desire to keep her away from these people was as strong as ever, but I had no illusions as to my power. I was but a Westerner, and it was clear that Miss Haldin would not, could not listen to my wisdom; and as to my desire of listening to her voice, it were better, I thought, not to indulge overmuch in that pleasure. No, I should not have gone to the Boulevard des Philosophes; but when at about the middle of the principal alley I saw Miss Haldin coming towards me, I was too curious, and too honest, perhaps, to run away.

There was something of the spring harshness in the air. The blue sky was hard, but the young leaves clung like soft mist about the uninteresting range of trees; and the clear sun put little points of gold into the grey of Miss Haldin's frank eyes, turned to me with a friendly greeting.

I inquired after the health of her mother.

She gave a slight movement of the shoulders and a little sad sigh.

'But, you see, I did come out for a walk ... for exercise, as you English say.'

I smiled approvingly, and she added an unexpected remark –

'It is a glorious day.'

Her voice, slightly harsh, but fascinating with its masculine and bird-like quality, had the accent of spontaneous conviction. I was glad of it. It was as though she had become aware of her youth – for there was but little of spring-like glory in the rectangular railed space of grass and trees, framed visibly by the orderly roof-slopes of that town, comely without grace, and hospitable without sympathy. In the very air through which she moved there was but little warmth; and the sky, the sky of a land without horizons, swept and washed clean by the April showers, extended a cold cruel blue, without elevation, narrowed suddenly by the ugly, dark wall of the Jura where, here and there, lingered yet a few miserable trails and patches of snow. All the glory of the season must have been within herself – and I was glad this feeling had come into her life, if only for a little time.

'I am pleased to hear you say these words.'

She gave me a quick look. Quick, not stealthy. If there was one thing of which she was absolutely incapable, it was stealthiness. Her sincerity was expressed in the very rhythm of her walk. It was I who was looking at her covertly – if I may say so. I knew where she had been, but I did not know what she had seen and heard in that nest of aristocratic conspiracies. I use the word aristocratic, for want of a better term. The Château Borel, embowered in the trees and thickets of its neglected grounds, had its fame in our day, like the residence of that other dangerous and exiled woman, Madame de Staël, in the Napoleonic era. Only the Napoleonic despotism, the booted heir of the Revolution, which counted that intellectual woman for an enemy worthy to be watched, was something quite unlike the autocracy in mystic vestments, engendered by the slavery of a Tartar conquest. And Madame de S— was very far from resembling the gifted author of *Corinne*. She made a great noise about being persecuted. I don't know if she were regarded in certain circles as dangerous. As to being watched, I imagine that the Château Borel could be subjected only to a most distant observation. It was in its exclusiveness an ideal abode for hatching superior plots – whether serious or futile. But all this did not interest me. I wanted to know the effect its extraordinary inhabitants and its special atmosphere had produced on a girl like Miss Haldin, so true, so honest, but so dangerously inexperienced! Her unconsciously lofty ignorance of the baser instincts of mankind left her disarmed before her own impulses. And there was also that friend of her brother, the significant new arrival from Russia . . . I wondered whether she had managed to meet him.

We walked for some time, slowly and in silence.

'You know,' I attacked her suddenly, 'if you don't intend telling me anything, you must say so distinctly, and then, of course, it shall be final. But I won't play at delicacy. I ask you point-blank for all the details.'

She smiled faintly at my threatening tone.

'You are as curious as a child.'

'No. I am only an anxious old man,' I replied earnestly.

She rested her glance on me as if to ascertain the degree of my anxiety or the number of my years. My physiognomy has never been expressive, I believe, and as to my years I am not ancient enough as yet to be strikingly decrepit. I have no long beard like the good hermit of a romantic ballad; my footsteps are not tottering, my aspect not that of a slow, venerable sage. Those picturesque advantages are not mine. I am old, alas, in a brisk, commonplace way.

And it seemed to me as though there were some pity for me in Miss Haldin's prolonged glance. She stepped out a little quicker.

'You ask for all the details. Let me see. I ought to remember them. It was novel enough for a – a village girl like me.'

After a moment of silence she began by saying that the Château Borel was almost as neglected inside as outside. It was nothing to wonder at. A Hamburg banker, I believe, retired from business, had it built to cheer his remaining days by the view of that lake whose precise, orderly, and well-to-do beauty must have been attractive to the unromantic imagination of a business man. But he died soon. His wife departed too (but only to Italy), and this house of moneyed ease, presumably unsaleable, had stood empty for several years. One went to it up a gravel drive, round a large, coarse grass-plot, with plenty of time to observe the degradation of its stuccoed front. Miss Haldin said that the impression was unpleasant. It grew more depressing as one came nearer.

She observed green stains of moss on the steps of the terrace. The front door stood wide open. There was no one about. She found herself in a wide, lofty, and absolutely empty hall, with a good many doors. These doors were all shut. A broad, bare stone staircase faced her, and the effect of the whole was of an untenanted house. She stood still, disconcerted by the solitude, but after a while she became aware of a voice speaking continuously somewhere.

'You were probably being observed all the time,' I suggested. 'There must have been eyes.'

'I don't see how that could be,' she retorted. 'I haven't seen even a bird in the grounds. I don't remember hearing a single twitter in the trees. The whole place appeared utterly deserted except for the voice.'

She could not make out the language – Russian, French, or German. No one seemed to answer it. It was as though the voice had been left behind by the departed inhabitants to talk to the bare walls. It went on volubly, with a pause now and then. It was lonely and sad. The time seemed very long to Miss Haldin. An invincible repugnance prevented her from opening one of the doors in the hall. It was so hopeless. No one would come, the voice would never stop.

She confessed to me that she had to resist an impulse to turn round and go away unseen, as she had come.

'Really? You had that impulse?' I cried, full of regret. 'What a pity you did not obey it.'

She shook her head.

'What a strange memory it would have been for one. Those deserted grounds, that empty hall, that impersonal, voluble voice, and – nobody, nothing, not a soul.'

The memory would have been unique and harmless. But she was not a girl to run away from an intimidating impression of solitude and mystery. 'No, I did not run away,' she said. 'I stayed where I was – and I did see a soul. Such a strange soul.'

As she was gazing up the broad staircase, and had concluded that the voice came from somewhere above, a rustle of dress attracted her attention. She looked down and saw a woman crossing the hall, having issued apparently through one of the many doors. Her face was averted, so that at first she was not aware of Miss Haldin.

On turning her head and seeing a stranger, she appeared very much startled. From her slender figure Miss Haldin had taken her for a young girl; but if her face was almost childishly round, it was also sallow and wrinkled, with dark rings under the eyes. A thick crop of dusty brown hair was parted boyishly on the side with a lateral wave above the dry, furrowed forehead. After a moment of dumb blinking, she suddenly squatted down on the floor.

'What do you mean by squatted down?' I asked, astonished. 'This is a very strange detail.'

Miss Haldin explained the reason. This person when first seen was carrying a small bowl in her hand. She had squatted down to put it on the floor for the benefit of a large cat, which appeared then from behind her skirts, and hid its head into the bowl greedily. She got up, and approaching Miss Haldin asked with nervous bluntness –

'What do you want? Who are you?'

Miss Haldin mentioned her name and also the name of Peter Ivanovitch. The girlish, elderly woman nodded and puckered her face into a momentary expression of sympathy. Her black silk blouse was old and even frayed in places; the black serge skirt was short and shabby. She continued to blink at close quarters, and her eyelashes and eyebrows seemed shabby too. Miss Haldin, speaking gently to her, as if to an unhappy and sensitive person, explained how it was that her visit could not be an altogether unexpected event to Madame de S——.

'Ah! Peter Ivanovitch brought you an invitation. How was I to know? A *dame de compagnie** is not consulted, as you may imagine.'

The shabby woman laughed a little. Her teeth, splendidly white and admirably even, looked absurdly out of place, like a string of pearls on the neck of a ragged tramp. 'Peter Ivanovitch is the greatest genius of the century perhaps, but he is the most inconsiderate man living. So if you have an appointment with him you must not be surprised to hear that he is not here.'

Miss Haldin explained that she had no appointment with Peter Ivanovitch. She became interested at once in that bizarre person.

'Why should he put himself out for you or any one else? Oh! these geniuses. If you only knew! Yes! And their books – I mean, of course, the books that the world admires, the inspired books. But you have not been behind the scenes. Wait till you have to sit at a table for a half a day with a pen in your hand. He can walk up and down his rooms for hours and hours. I used to get so stiff and numb that I was afraid I would lose my balance and fall off the chair all at once.'

She kept her hands folded in front of her, and her eyes, fixed on Miss Haldin's face, betrayed no animation whatever. Miss Haldin, gathering that the lady who called herself a *dame de compagnie* was proud of having acted as secretary to Peter Ivanovitch, made an amiable remark.

'You could not imagine a more trying experience,' declared the lady. 'There is an Anglo-American journalist interviewing Madame de S—— now, or I would take you up,' she continued in a changed tone and glancing towards the staircase. 'I act as master of ceremonies.'

It appeared that Madame de S—— could not bear Swiss servants about her person; and, indeed, servants would not stay for very long in the Château Borel. There were always difficulties. Miss Haldin

*Female companion.

167

had already noticed that the hall was like a dusty barn of marble and stucco with cobwebs in the corners and faint tracks of mud on the black and white tessellated floor.

'I look also after this animal,' continued the *dame de compagnie*, keeping her hands folded quietly in front of her; and she bent her worn gaze upon the cat. 'I don't mind a bit. Animals have their right; though, strictly speaking, I see no reason why they should not suffer as well as human beings. Do you? But of course they never suffer so much. That is impossible. Only, in their case it is more pitiful because they cannot make a revolution. I used to be a Republican. I suppose you are a Republican?'

Miss Haldin confessed to me that she did not know what to say. But she nodded slightly, and asked in her turn –

'And are you no longer a Republican?'

'After taking down Peter Ivanovitch from dictation for two years, it is difficult for me to be anything. First of all, you have to sit perfectly motionless. The slightest movement you make puts to flight the ideas of Peter Ivanovitch. You hardly dare to breathe. And as to coughing – God forbid. Peter Ivanovitch changed the position of the table to the wall because at first I could not help raising my eyes to look out of the window, while waiting for him to go on with his dictation. That was not allowed. He said I stared so stupidly. I was likewise not permitted to look at him over my shoulder. Instantly Peter Ivanovitch stamped his foot, and would roar, "Look down on the paper!" It seems my expression, my face, put him off. Well, I know that I am not beautiful, and that my expression is not hopeful either. He said that my air of unintelligent expectation irritated him. These are his own words.'

Miss Haldin was shocked, but admitted to me that she was not altogether surprised.

'Is it possible that Peter Ivanovitch could treat any woman so rudely?' she cried.

The *dame de compagnie* nodded several times with an air of discretion, then assured Miss Haldin that she did not mind in the least. The trying part of it was to have the secret of the composition laid bare before her; to see the great author of the revolutionary gospels grope for words as if he were in the dark as to what he meant to say.

'I am quite willing to be the blind instrument of higher ends. To give one's life for the cause is nothing. But to have one's illusions destroyed – that is really almost more than one can bear. I really don't exaggerate,' she insisted. 'It seemed to freeze my very beliefs in me – the more so that when we worked in winter Peter Ivanovitch, walking up and down the room, required no artificial heat to keep himself warm. Even when we move to the South of France there are bitterly cold days, especially when you have to sit still for six hours at a stretch. The walls of these villas on the Riviera are so flimsy. Peter Ivanovitch did not seem to be aware of anything. It is true that I kept down my shivers from fear of putting him out. I used to set my teeth till my jaws felt absolutely locked. In the moments when Peter Ivanovitch interrupted his dictation, and sometimes these intervals were very long – often twenty minutes, no less, while he walked to and fro behind my back muttering to himself – I felt I was dying by inches, I assure you. Perhaps if I had let my teeth rattle Peter Ivanovitch might have noticed my distress, but I don't think it would have had any practical effect. He's very miserly in such matters.'

The *dame de compagnie* glanced up the staircase. The big cat had finished the milk and was rubbing its whiskered cheek sinuously against her skirt. She dived to snatch it up from the floor.

'Miserliness is rather a quality than otherwise, you know,' she continued, holding the cat in her folded arms. 'With us it is misers who can spare money for worthy objects – not the so-called generous natures. But pray don't think I am a sybarite. My father was a clerk in the Ministry of Finances with no position at all. You may guess by this that our home was far from luxurious, though of course we did not actually suffer from cold. I ran away from my parents, you know, directly I began to think by myself. It is not very easy, such thinking. One has got to be put in the way of it, awakened to the truth. I am indebted for my salvation to an old apple-woman, who had her stall under the gateway of the house we lived in. She had a kind wrinkled face, and the most friendly voice imaginable. One day, casually, we began to talk about a child, a ragged little girl we had seen begging from men in the streets at dusk; and from one thing to another my eyes began to open gradually to the horrors from which innocent people are made to suffer in this world, only in order that governments might exist. After I once understood the crime of the upper classes, I could not go on living with my parents. Not a single charitable word was to be heard in our home from year's end to year's end; there was nothing but the talk of vile office intrigues, and of promotion and of salaries, and of courting the favour of the chiefs. The mere idea of marrying one day such another man as my father made me shudder. I don't mean that there was any one wanting to marry me. There was not the slightest prospect of anything of the kind. But was it not sin enough to live on a Government salary while half Russia was dying of hunger? The Ministry of Finances! What a grotesque horror it is! What does the starving, ignorant people want with a Ministry of Finances? I kissed my old folks on both cheeks, and went away from them to live in cellars, with the proletariat. I tried to make myself useful to the utterly hopeless. I suppose you understand what I mean? I mean the people who have nowhere to go and nothing to look forward to in this life. Do you understand how frightful that is – nothing to look forward to! Sometimes I think that it is only in Russia that there are such people and such a depth of misery can be reached. Well, I plunged into it, and – do you know – there isn't much that one can do in there. No, indeed – at least as long as there are Ministries of Finances and such like grotesque horrors to stand in the way. I suppose I would have gone mad there just trying to fight the vermin, if it had not been for a man. It was my old friend and teacher, the poor saintly apple-woman, who discovered him for me, quite accidentally. She came to fetch me late one evening in her quiet way. I followed her where she would lead; that part of my life was in her hand altogether, and without her my spirit would have perished miserably. The man was a young workman, a lithographer by trade, and he had got into trouble in connection with that affair of temperance tracts – you remember. There was a lot of people put in prison for that. The Ministry of Finances again! What would become of it if the poor folk ceased making beasts of themselves with drink? Upon my word, I would think that finances and all the rest of it are an invention of the devil; only that a belief in a supernatural source of evil is not necessary; men alone are quite capable of every wickedness. Finances indeed!'

Hatred and contempt hissed in her utterance of the word 'finances', but at the very moment she gently stroked the cat reposing in her arms. She even raised them slightly, and inclining her head rubbed her cheek against the fur of the animal, which received this caress with the complete detachment so characteristic of its kind. Then looking at Miss Haldin she excused herself once more for not taking her upstairs to Madame de S—. The interview could not be interrupted. Presently the journalist would be seen coming down the stairs. The best thing was to remain in the hall; and besides, all these rooms (she glanced all round at the many doors), all these rooms on the ground floor were unfurnished.

'Positively there is no chair down here to offer you,' she continued. 'But if you prefer your own thoughts to my chatter, I will sit down on the bottom step here and keep silent.'

Miss Haldin hastened to assure her that, on the contrary, she was very much interested in the story of the journeyman lithographer. He was a revolutionist, of course.

'A martyr, a simple man,' said the *dame de compagnie* with a faint sigh, and gazing through the open front door dreamily. She turned her misty brown eyes on Miss Haldin.

'I lived with him for four months. It was like a nightmare.'

As Miss Haldin looked at her inquisitively she began to describe the emaciated face of the man, his fleshless limbs, his destitution. The room into which the apple-woman had led her was a tiny garret, a miserable den under the roof of a sordid house. The plaster fallen off the walls covered the floor, and when the door was opened a horrible tapestry of black cobwebs waved in the draught. He had been liberated a few days before – flung out of prison into the streets. And Miss Haldin seemed to see for the first time, a name and a face upon the body of that suffering people whose hard fate had been the subject of so many conversations, between her and her brother, in the garden of their country house.

He had been arrested with scores and scores of other people in that affair of the lithographed temperance tracts. Unluckily, having got hold of a great many suspected persons, the police thought they could extract from some of them other information relating to the revolutionist propaganda.

'They beat him so cruelly in the course of investigation,' went on the *dame de compagnie*, 'that they injured him internally. When they had done with him he was doomed. He could do nothing for himself. I beheld him lying on a wooden bedstead without any bedding, with his head on a bundle of dirty rags, lent to him out of charity by an old rag-picker, who happened to live in the basement of the house. There he was, uncovered, burning with fever, and there was not even a jug in the room for the water to quench his thirst with. There was nothing whatever – just that bedstead and the bare floor.'

'Was there no one in all that great town amongst the liberals and revolutionaries, to extend a helping hand to a brother?' asked Miss Haldin indignantly.

'Yes. But you do not know the most terrible part of that man's misery. Listen. It seems that they ill-used him so atrociously that, at last, his firmness gave way, and he did let out some information. Poor soul, the flesh is weak, you know. What it was he did not tell me. There was a crushed spirit in that mangled body. Nothing I found to say could make him whole. When they let him out, he crept into that hole, and bore his remorse stoically. He would not go near any one he knew. I would have sought assistance for him, but, indeed, where could I have gone looking for it? Where was I to look for any one who had anything to spare or any power to help? The people living round us were all starving and drunken. They were the victims of the Ministry of Finances. Don't ask me how we lived. I couldn't tell you. It was like a miracle of wretchedness. I had nothing to sell, and I assure you my clothes were in such a state that it was impossible for me to go out in the daytime. I was indecent. I had to wait till it was dark before I ventured into the streets to beg for a crust of bread, or whatever I could get, to keep him and me alive. Often I got nothing, and then I would crawl back and lie on the floor by the side of his couch. Oh yes, I can sleep quite soundly on bare boards. That is nothing, and I am only mentioning it to you so that you should not think I am a sybarite. It was infinitely less killing than the task of sitting for hours at a table in a cold study to take the books of Peter Ivanovitch from dictation. But you shall see yourself what that is like, so I needn't say any more about it.'

'It is by no means certain that I will ever take Peter Ivanovitch from dictation,' said Miss Haldin.

'No!' cried the other incredulously. 'Not certain? You mean to say that you have not made up your mind?'

When Miss Haldin assured her that there never had been any question of that between her and Peter Ivanovitch, the woman with the cat compressed her lips tightly for a moment.

'Oh, you will find yourself settled at the table before you know that you have made up your mind. Don't make a mistake, it is disenchanting to hear Peter Ivanovitch dictate, but at the same time there is a fascination about it. He is a man of genius. Your face is certain not to irritate him; you may perhaps even help his inspiration, make it easier for him to deliver his message. As I look at you, I feel certain that you are the kind of woman who is not likely to check the flow of his inspiration.'

Miss Haldin thought it useless to protest against all these assumptions.

'But this man – this workman – did he die under your care?' she said, after a short silence.

The *dame de compagnie*, listening up the stairs where now two voices were alternating with some animation, made no answer for a time. When the loud sounds of the discussion had sunk into an almost inaudible murmur, she turned to Miss Haldin.

'Yes, he died, but not, literally speaking, in my arms, as you might suppose. As a matter of fact, I was asleep when he breathed his last. So even now I cannot say I have seen anybody die. A few days before the end, some young men found us out in our extremity. They were revolutionists, as you might guess. He ought to have trusted in his political friends when he came out of prison. He had been liked and respected before, and nobody would have dreamed of reproaching him with his indiscretion before the police. Everybody knows how they go to work, and the strongest man has his moments of weakness before pain. Why even hunger alone is enough to give one queer ideas as to what may be done. A doctor came, our lot was

173

alleviated as far as physical comforts go, but otherwise he could not be consoled – poor man. I assure you, Miss Haldin, that he was very lovable, but I had not the strength to weep. I was nearly dead myself. But there were kind hearts to take care of me. A dress was found to clothe my nakedness. I tell you, I was not decent – and after a time the revolutionists placed me with a Jewish family going abroad, as governess. Of course I could teach the children, I finished the sixth class of the Lyceum; but the real object was, that I should carry some important papers across the frontier. I was entrusted with a packet which I carried next my heart. The gendarmes at the station did not suspect the governess of a Jewish family, busy looking after three children. I don't suppose those Hebrews knew what I had on me, for I had been introduced to them in a very roundabout way by persons who did not belong to the revolutionary movement, and naturally I had been instructed to accept a very small salary. When we reached Germany I left that family and delivered my papers to a revolutionist in Stuttgart; after this I was employed in various ways. But you do not want to hear all that. I have never felt that I was very useful, but I live in hopes of seeing all the Ministries destroyed, finances and all. The greatest joy of my life has been to hear what your brother has done.'

She directed her round eyes again to the sunshine outside, while the cat reposed within her folded arms in lordly beatitude and sphinx-like meditation.

'Yes! I rejoiced,' she began again. 'For me there is a heroic ring about the very name of Haldin. They must have been trembling with fear in their Ministries – all those men with fiendish hearts. Here I stand talking to you, and when I think of all the cruelties, oppressions, and injustices that are going on at this very moment, my head begins to swim. I have looked closely at what would seem inconceivable if one's own eyes had not to be trusted. I have looked at things that made me hate myself for my helplessness. I hated my hands that had no power, my voice that could not be heard, my very mind that would not become unhinged. Ah! I have seen things. And you?'

Miss Haldin was moved. She shook her head slightly.

'No, I have seen nothing for myself as yet,' she murmured. 'We have always lived in the country. It was my brother's wish.'

'It is a curious meeting – this – between you and me,' continued the other. 'Do you believe in chance, Miss Haldin? How could I have expected to see you, his sister, with my own eyes? Do you know that when the news came the revolutionaries here were as much surprised as pleased, every bit? No one seemed to know anything about your brother. Peter Ivanovitch himself had not foreseen that such a blow was going to be struck. I suppose your brother was simply inspired. I myself think that such deeds should be done by inspiration. It is a great privilege to have the inspiration and the opportunity. Did he resemble you at all? Don't you rejoice, Miss Haldin?'

'You must not expect too much from me,' said Miss Haldin, repressing an inclination to cry which came over her suddenly. She succeeded, then added calmly, 'I am not a heroic person!'

'You think you couldn't have done such a thing yourself, perhaps?'

'I don't know. I must not even ask myself till I have lived a little longer, seen more . . .'

The other moved her head appreciatively. The purring of the cat had a loud complacency in the empty hall. No sound of voices came from upstairs. Miss Haldin broke the silence.

'What is it precisely that you heard people say about my brother? You said that they were surprised. Yes, I supposed they were. Did it not seem strange to them that my brother should have failed to save himself after the most difficult part – that is, getting away from the spot – was over? Conspirators should understand these things well. There are reasons why I am very anxious to know how it is he failed to escape.'

The *dame de compagnie* had advanced to the open hall-door. She glanced rapidly over her shoulder at Miss Haldin, who remained within the hall.

'Failed to escape,' she repeated absently. 'Didn't he make the sacrifice of his life? Wasn't he just simply inspired? Wasn't it an act of abnegation? Aren't you certain?'

'What I am certain of,' said Miss Haldin, 'is that it was not an act of despair. Have you not heard some opinion expressed here upon his miserable capture?'

The *dame de compagnie* mused for a while in the doorway.

'Did I hear? Of course, everything is discussed here. Has not all the world been speaking about your brother? For my part, the mere mention of his achievement plunges me into an envious ecstasy. Why should a man certain of immortality think of his life at all?'

She kept her back turned to Miss Haldin. Upstairs from behind a great dingy white and gold door, visible behind the balustrade of the first floor landing, a deep voice began to drone formally, as if reading over notes or something of the sort. It paused frequently, and then ceased altogether.

'I don't think I can stay any longer now,' said Miss Haldin. 'I may return another day.'

She waited for the *dame de compagnie* to make room for her exit; but the woman appeared lost in the contemplation of sunshine and shadows, sharing between themselves the stillness of the deserted grounds. She concealed the view of the drive from Miss Haldin. Suddenly she said –

'It will not be necessary; here is Peter Ivanovitch himself coming up. But he is not alone. He is seldom alone now.'

Hearing that Peter Ivanovitch was approaching, Miss Haldin was not so pleased as she might have been expected to be. Somehow she had lost the desire to see either the heroic captive or Madame de S—, and the reason of that shrinking which came upon her at the very last minute is accounted for by the feeling that those two people had not been treating the woman with the cat kindly.

'Would you please let me pass?' said Miss Haldin at last, touching lightly the shoulder of the *dame de compagnie*.

But the other, pressing the cat to her breast, did not budge.

'I know who is with him,' she said, without even looking back.

More unaccountably than ever Miss Haldin felt a strong impulse to leave the house.

'Madame de S— may be engaged for some time yet, and what I have got to say to Peter Ivanovitch is just a simple question which I might put to him when I meet him in the grounds on my way down. I really think I must go. I have been some time here, and I am anxious to get back to my mother. Will you let me pass, please?'

The *dame de compagnie* turned her head at last.

'I never supposed that you really wanted to see Madame de S——,' she said, with unexpected insight. 'Not for a moment.' There was something confidential and mysterious in her tone. She passed through the door, with Miss Haldin following her, on to the terrace, and they descended side by side the moss-grown stone steps. There was no one to be seen on the part of the drive visible from the front of the house.

'They are hidden by the trees over there,' explained Miss Haldin's new acquaintance, 'but you shall see them directly. I don't know who that young man is to whom Peter Ivanovitch has taken such a fancy. He must be one of us, or he would not be admitted here when the others come. You know what I mean by the others. But I must say that he is not at all mystically inclined. I don't know that I have made him out yet. Naturally I am never for very long in the drawing-room. There is always something to do for me, though the establishment here is not so extensive as the villa on the Riviera. But still there are plenty of opportunities for me to make myself useful.'

To the left, passing by the ivy-grown end of the stables, appeared Peter Ivanovitch and his companion. They walked very slowly conversing with some animation. They stopped for a moment, and Peter Ivanovitch was seen to gesticulate, while the young man listened motionless, with his arms hanging down and his head bowed a little. He was dressed in a dark brown suit and a black hat. The round eyes of the *dame de compagnie* remained fixed on the two figures, which had resumed their leisurely approach.

'An extremely polite young man,' she said. 'You shall see what a bow he will make; and it won't altogether be so exceptional either. He bows in the same way when he meets me alone in the hall.'

She moved on a few steps, with Miss Haldin by her side, and things happened just as she had foretold. The young man took off his hat, bowed and fell back, while Peter Ivanovitch advanced quicker, his black, thick arms extended heartily, and seized hold of

177

both Miss Haldin's hands, shook them, and peered at her through his dark glasses.

'That's right. that's right!' he exclaimed twice, approvingly. 'And so you have been looked after by . . .' He frowned slightly at the *dame de compagnie*, who was still nursing the cat. 'I conclude Eleanor – Madame de S— is engaged. I know she expected somebody today. So the newspaper man did turn up, eh? She is engaged?'

For all answer the *dame de compagnie* turned away her head.

'It is very unfortunate – very unfortunate indeed. I very much regret that you should have been . . .' He lowered suddenly his voice. 'But what is it – surely you are not departing, Natalia Victorovna? You got bored waiting, didn't you?'

'Not in the least,' Miss Haldin protested. 'Only I have been here some time, and I am anxious to get back to my mother.'

'The time seemed long, eh? I am afraid our worthy friend here' (Peter Ivanovitch suddenly jerked his head sideways towards his right shoulder and jerked it up again), – 'our worthy friend here has not the art of shortening the moments of waiting. No, distinctly she has not the art; and in that respect good intentions alone count for nothing.'

The *dame de compagnie* dropped her arms, and the cat found itself suddenly on the ground. It remained quite still after alighting, one hind leg stretched backwards. Miss Haldin was extremely indignant on behalf of the lady companion.

'Believe me, Peter Ivanovitch, that the moments I have passed in the hall of this house have been not a little interesting, and very instructive too. They are memorable. I do not regret the waiting, but I see that the object of my call here can be attained without taking up Madame de S—'s time.'

At this point I interrupted Miss Haldin. The above relation is founded on her narrative, which I have not so much dramatized as might be supposed. She had rendered, with extraordinary feeling and animation, the very accent almost of the disciple of the old apple-woman, the irreconcilable hater of Ministries, the voluntary servant of the poor. Miss Haldin's true and delicate humanity had been extremely shocked by the uncongenial fate of her new acquaintance, that lady companion, secretary, whatever she was.

For my own part, I was pleased to discover in it one more obstacle to intimacy with Madame de S—. I had a positive abhorrence for the painted, bedizened, dead-faced, glassy-eyed Egeria[12] of Peter Ivanovitch. I do not know what was her attitude to the unseen, but I know that in the affairs of this world she was avaricious, greedy, and unscrupulous. It was within my knowledge that she had been worsted in a sordid and desperate quarrel about money matters with the family of her late husband, the diplomatist. Some very august personages indeed (whom in her fury she had insisted upon scandalously involving in her affairs) had incurred her animosity. I find it perfectly easy to believe that she had come to within an ace of being spirited away, for reasons of state, into some discreet *maison de santé* – a madhouse of sorts, to be plain. It appears, however, that certain high-placed personages opposed it for reasons which . . .

But it's no use to go into details.

Wonder may be expressed at a man in the position of a teacher of languages knowing all this with such definiteness. A novelist says this and that of his personages, and if only he knows how to say it earnestly enough he may not be questioned upon the inventions of his brain in which his own belief is made sufficiently manifest by a telling phrase, a poetic image, the accent of emotion. Art is great! But I have no art, and not having invented Madame de S—, I feel bound to explain how I came to know so much about her.

My informant was the Russian wife of a friend of mine already mentioned, the professor of Lausanne University. It was from her that I learned the last fact of Madame de S—'s history, with which I intend to trouble my readers. She told me, speaking positively, as a person who trusts her sources, of the cause of Madame de S—'s flight from Russia, some years before. It was neither more nor less than this: that she became suspect to the police in connection with the assassination of the Emperor Alexander.[13] The ground of this suspicion was either some unguarded expressions that escaped her in public, or some talk overheard in her *salon*. Overheard, we must believe, by some guest, perhaps a friend, who hastened to play the informer, I suppose. At any rate, the overheard matter seemed to imply her foreknowledge of that event, and I think she was wise in not waiting for the investigation of such a charge. Some of my readers may remember a little book from her pen, published in Paris, a mystically bad-tempered, declamatory, and frightfully disconnected piece of writing, in which she all but admits the foreknowledge, more than hints at its supernatural origin, and plainly suggests in venomous innuendoes that the guilt of the act was not with the terrorists, but with a palace intrigue. When I observed to my friend, the professor's wife, that the life of Madame de S——, with its unofficial diplomacy, its intrigues, lawsuits, favours, disgrace, expulsions, its atmosphere of scandal, occultism, and charlatanism, was more fit for the eighteenth century than for the conditions of our own time, she assented with a smile, but a moment after went on in a reflective tone: 'Charlatanism? – yes, in a certain measure. Still, times are changed. There are forces now which were nonexistent in the eighteenth century. I should not be surprised if she were more dangerous than an Englishman would be willing to believe. And what's more, she is looked upon as really dangerous by certain people – *chez nous.*'*

Chez nous in this connection meant Russia in general, and the Russian political police in particular. The object of my digression from the straight course of Miss Haldin's relation (in my own words) of her visit to the Château Borel, was to bring forward that statement of my friend, the professor's wife. I wanted to bring it forward simply to make what I have to say presently of Mr Razumov's presence in Geneva, a little more credible – for this is a Russian story for Western ears, which, as I have observed already, are not attuned to certain tones of cynicism and cruelty, of moral negation, and even of moral distress already silenced at our end of Europe. And this I state as my excuse for having left Miss Haldin standing, one of the little group of two women and two men who had come together below the terrace of the Château Borel.

The knowledge which I have just stated was in my mind when, as I have said, I interrupted Miss Haldin. I interrupted her with the cry of profound satisfaction –

'So you never saw Madame de S——, after all?'

Miss Haldin shook her head. It was very satisfactory to me. She

* 'At home.'

180

had not seen Madame de S—! That was excellent, excellent! I welcomed the conviction that she would never know Madame de S— now. I could not explain the reason of the conviction but by the knowledge that Miss Haldin was standing face to face with her brother's wonderful friend. I preferred him to Madame de S— as the companion and guide of that young girl abandoned to her inexperience by the miserable end of her brother. But, at any rate, that life now ended had been sincere, and perhaps its thoughts might have been lofty, its moral sufferings profound, its last act a true sacrifice. It is not for us, the staid lovers calmed by the possession of a conquered liberty, to condemn without appeal the fierceness of thwarted desire.

I am not ashamed of the warmth of my regard for Miss Haldin. It was, it must be admitted, an unselfish sentiment, being its own reward. The late Victor Haldin – in the light of that sentiment – appeared to me not as a sinister conspirator, but as a pure enthusiast. I did not wish indeed to judge him, but the very fact that he did not escape, that fact which brought so much trouble to both his mother and his sister, spoke to me in his favour. Meantime, in my fear of seeing the girl surrender to the influence of the Château Borel revolutionary feminism, I was more than willing to put my trust in that friend of the late Victor Haldin. He was nothing but a name, you will say. Exactly! A name! And what's more, the only name; the only name to be found in the correspondence between brother and sister. The young man had turned up; they had come face to face, and, fortunately, without the direct interference of Madame de S—. What will come of it? what will she tell me presently? I was asking myself.

It was only natural that my thought should turn to the young man, the bearer of the only name uttered in all the dream-talk of a future to be brought about by a revolution. And my thought took the shape of asking myself why this young man had not called upon these ladies. He had been in Geneva for some days before Miss Haldin heard of him first in my presence from Peter Ivanovitch. I regretted that last's presence at their meeting. I would rather have had it happen somewhere out of his spectacled sight. But I supposed that, having both these young people there, he introduced them to each other.

181

I broke the silence by beginning a question on that point –

'I suppose Peter Ivanovitch ...'

Miss Haldin gave vent to her indignation. Peter Ivanovitch directly he had got his answer from her had turned upon the *dame de compagnie* in a shameful manner.

'Turned upon her?' I wondered. 'What about? For what reason?'

'It was unheard of; it was shameful,' Miss Haldin pursued, with angry eyes. '*Il lui a fait une scène** – like this, before strangers. And for what? You would never guess. For some eggs ... Oh!'

I was astonished. 'Eggs, did you say?'

'For Madame de S—. That lady observes a special diet, or something of the sort. It seems she complained the day before to Peter Ivanovitch that the eggs were not rightly prepared. Peter Ivanovitch suddenly remembered this against the poor woman, and flew out at her. It was most astonishing. I stood as if rooted.'

'Do you mean to say that the great feminist allowed himself to be abusive to a woman?' I asked.

'Oh, not that! It was something you have no conception of. It was an odious performance. Imagine, he raised his hat to begin with. He made his voice soft and deprecatory. "Ah! you are not kind to us – you will not deign to remember ..." This sort of phrase, that sort of tone. The poor creature was terribly upset. Her eyes ran full of tears. She did not know where to look. I shouldn't wonder if she would have preferred abuse, or even a blow.'

I did not remark that very possibly she was familiar with both on occasions when no one was by. Miss Haldin walked by my side, her head up in scornful and angry silence.

'Great men have their surprising peculiarities,' I observed inanely. 'Exactly like men who are not great. But that sort of thing cannot be kept up for ever. How did the great feminist wind up this very characteristic episode?'

Miss Haldin, without turning her face my way, told me that the end was brought about by the appearance of the interviewer, who had been closeted with Madame de S—.

He came up rapidly, unnoticed, lifted his hat slightly, and paused

* 'He made a scene with her.'

to say in French: 'The Baroness has asked me, in case I met a lady on my way out, to desire her to come in at once.'

After delivering this message, he hurried down the drive. The *dame de compagnie* flew towards the house, and Peter Ivanovitch followed her hastily, looking uneasy. In a moment Miss Haldin found herself alone with the young man, who undoubtedly must have been the new arrival from Russia. She wondered whether her brother's friend had not already guessed who she was.

I am in a position to say that, as a matter of fact, he had guessed. It is clear to me that Peter Ivanovitch, for some reason or other, had refrained from alluding to these ladies' presence in Geneva. But Razumov had guessed. The trustful girl! Every word uttered by Haldin lived in Razumov's memory. They were like haunting shapes; they could not be exorcized. The most vivid amongst them was the mention of the sister. The girl had existed for him ever since. But he did not recognize her at once. Coming up with Peter Ivanovitch, he did observe her; their eyes had met, even. He had responded, as no one could help responding, to the harmonious charm of her whole person, its strength, its grace, its tranquil frankness – and then he had turned his gaze away. He said to himself that all this was not for him; the beauty of women and the friendship of men were not for him. He accepted that feeling with a purposeful sternness, and tried to pass on. It was only her outstretched hand which brought about the recognition. It stands recorded in the pages of his self-confession, that it nearly suffocated him physically with an emotional reaction of hate and dismay, as though her appearance had been a piece of accomplished treachery.

He faced about. The considerable elevation of the terrace concealed them from any one lingering in the doorway of the house; and even from the upstairs windows they could not have been seen. Through the thickets run wild, and the trees of the gently sloping grounds, he had cold, placid glimpses of the lake. A moment of perfect privacy had been vouchsafed to them at this juncture. I wondered to myself what use they had made of that fortunate circumstance.

'Did you have time for more than a few words?' I asked.

That animation with which she had related to me the incidents of her visit to the Château Borel had left her completely. Strolling by my side, she looked straight before her; but I noticed a little colour on her cheek. She did not answer me.

After some little time I observed that they could not have hoped to remain forgotten for very long, unless the other two had discovered Madame de S— swooning with fatigue, perhaps, or in a state of morbid exaltation after the long interview. Either would require their devoted ministrations. I could depict to myself Peter Ivanovitch rushing busily out of the house again, bareheaded, perhaps, and on across the terrace with his swinging gait, the black skirts of the frock-coat floating clear of his stout light grey legs. I confess to having looked upon these young people as the quarry of the 'heroic fugitive'. I had the notion that they would not be allowed to escape capture. But of that I said nothing to Miss Haldin, only as she still remained uncommunicative, I pressed her a little.

'Well – but you can tell me at least your impression.'

She turned her head to look at me, and turned away again.

'Impression?' she repeated slowly, almost dreamily; then in a quicker tone –

'He seems to be a man who has suffered more from his thoughts than from evil fortune.'

'From his thoughts, you say?'

'And that is natural enough in a Russian,' she took me up. 'In a young Russian; so many of them are unfit for action, and yet unable to rest.'

'And you think he is that sort of man?'

'No, I do not judge him. How could I, so suddenly? You asked for my impression – I explain my impression. I – I – don't know the world, nor yet the people in it; I have been too solitary – I am too young to trust my own opinions.'

'Trust your instinct,' I advised her. 'Most women trust to that, and make no worse mistakes than men. In this case you have your brother's letter to help you.'

She drew a deep breath like a light sigh.

'Unstained, lofty, and solitary existences,' she quoted as if to herself. But I caught the wistful murmur distinctly.

'High praise,' I whispered to her.

'The highest possible.'

'So high that, like the award of happiness, it is more fit to come only at the end of a life. But still no common or altogether unworthy personality could have suggested such a confident exaggeration of praise and ...'

'Ah!' She interrupted me ardently. 'And if you had only known the heart from which that judgement has come!'

She ceased on that note, and for a space I reflected on the character of the words which I perceived very well must tip the scale of the girl's feeling in that young man's favour. They had not the sound of a casual utterance. Vague they were to my Western mind and to my Western sentiment, but I could not forget that, standing by Miss Haldin's side, I was like a traveller in a strange country. It had also become clear to me that Miss Haldin was unwilling to enter into the details of the only material part of their visit to the Château Borel. But I was not hurt. Somehow I didn't feel it to be a want of confidence. It was some other difficulty – a difficulty I could not resent. And it was without the slightest resentment that I said –

'Very well. But on that high ground, which I will not dispute, you, like any one else in such circumstances, you must have made for yourself a representation of that exceptional friend, a mental image of him, and – please tell me – you were not disappointed?'

'What do you mean? His personal appearance?'

'I don't mean precisely his good looks, or otherwise.'

We turned at the end of the alley and made a few steps without looking at each other.

'His appearance is not ordinary,' said Miss Haldin at last.

'No, I should have thought not – from the little you've said of your first impression. After all, one has to fall back on that word. Impression! What I mean is that something indescribable which is likely to mark a "not ordinary" person.'

I perceived that she was not listening. There was no mistaking her expression; and once more I had the sense of being out of it – not because of my age, which at any rate could draw inferences – but altogether out of it, on another plane whence I could only watch her from afar. And so ceasing to speak I watched her stepping out by my side.

'No,' she exclaimed suddenly, 'I could not have been disappointed with a man of such strong feeling.'

'Aha! Strong feeling,' I muttered, thinking to myself censoriously: like this, at once, all in a moment!

'What did you say?' inquired Miss Haldin innocently.

'Oh, nothing. I beg your pardon. Strong feeling. I am not surprised.'

'And you don't know how abruptly I behaved to him!' she cried remorsefully.

I suppose I must have appeared surprised, for, looking at me with a still more heightened colour, she said she was ashamed to admit that she had not been sufficiently collected; she had failed to control her words and actions as the situation demanded. She lost the fortitude worthy of both the men, the dead and the living; the fortitude which should have been the note of the meeting of Victor Haldin's sister with Victor Haldin's only known friend. He was looking at her keenly, but said nothing, and she was – she confessed – painfully affected by his want of comprehension. All she could say was: 'You are Mr Razumov.' A slight frown passed over his forehead. After a short, watchful pause, he made a little bow of assent, and waited.

At the thought that she had before her the man so highly regarded by her brother, the man who had known his value, spoken to him, understood him, had listened to his confidences, perhaps had encouraged him – her lips trembled, her eyes ran full of tears; she put out her hand, made a step towards him impulsively, saying with an effort to restrain her emotion, 'Can't you guess who I am?' He did not take the proffered hand. He even recoiled a pace, and Miss Haldin imagined that he was unpleasantly affected. Miss Haldin excused him, directing her displeasure at herself. She had behaved unworthily, like an emotional French girl. A manifestation of that kind could not be welcomed by a man of stern, self-contained character.

He must have been stern indeed, or perhaps very timid with women, not to respond in a more human way to the advances of a girl like Nathalie Haldin – I thought to myself. Those lofty and

186

solitary existences (I remembered the words suddenly) make a young man shy and an old man savage – often.

'Well,' I encouraged Miss Haldin to proceed.

She was still very dissatisfied with herself.

'I went from bad to worse,' she said, with an air of discouragement very foreign to her. 'I did everything foolish except actually bursting into tears. I am thankful to say I did not do that. But I was unable to speak for quite a long time.'

She had stood before him speechless, swallowing her sobs, and when she managed at last to utter something, it was only her brother's name – 'Victor – Victor Haldin!' she gasped out, and again her voice failed her.

'Of course,' she commented to me, 'this distressed him. He was quite overcome. I have told you my opinion that he is a man of deep feeling – it is impossible to doubt it. You should have seen his face. He positively reeled. He leaned against the wall of the terrace. Their friendship must have been the very brotherhood of souls! I was grateful to him for that emotion, which made me feel less ashamed of my own lack of self-control. Of course I had regained the power of speech at once, almost. All this lasted not more than a few seconds. "I am his sister," I said. "Maybe you have heard of me."'

'And had he?' I interrupted.

'I don't know. How could it have been otherwise? And yet . . . But what does that matter? I stood there before him, near enough to be touched and surely not looking like an impostor. All I know is, that he put out both his hands then to me, I may say flung them out at me, with the greatest readiness and warmth, and that I seized and pressed them, feeling that I was finding again a little of what I thought was lost to me for ever, with the loss of my brother – some of that hope, inspiration, and support which I used to get from my dear dead . . .'

I understood quite well what she meant. We strolled on slowly. I refrained from looking at her. And it was as if answering my own thoughts that I murmured –

'No doubt it was a great friendship – as you say. And that young man ended by welcoming your name, so to speak, with both hands.

187

After that, of course, you would understand each other. Yes, you would understand each other quickly.'

It was a moment before I heard her voice.

'Mr Razumov seems to be a man of few words. A reserved man – even when he is strongly moved.'

Unable to forget – or even to forgive – the bass-toned expansiveness of Peter Ivanovitch, the Arch-Patron of revolutionary parties, I said that I took this for a favourable trait of character. It was associated with sincerity – in my mind.

'And, besides, we had not much time,' she added.

'No, you would not have, of course.' My suspicion and even dread of the feminist and his Egeria was so ineradicable that I could not help asking with real anxiety, which I made smiling –

'But you escaped all right?'

She understood me, and smiled too, at my uneasiness.

'Oh yes! I escaped, if you like to call it that. I walked away quickly. There was no need to run. I am neither frightened nor yet fascinated, like that poor woman who received me so strangely.'

'And Mr – Mr Razumov . . .'

'He remained there, of course. I suppose he went into the house after I left him. You remember that he came here strongly recommended to Peter Ivanovitch – possibly entrusted with important messages for him.'

'Ah yes! From that priest who . . .'

'Father Zosim – yes. Or from others, perhaps.'

'You left him, then. But have you seen him since, may I ask?'

For some time Miss Haldin made no answer to this very direct question, then –

'I have been expecting to see him here today,' she said quietly.

'You have! Do you meet, then, in this garden? In that case I had better leave you at once.'

'No, why leave me? And we don't meet in this garden. I have not seen Mr Razumov since that first time. Not once. But I have been expecting him . . .'

She paused. I wondered to myself why that young revolutionist should show so little alacrity.

'Before we parted I told Mr Razumov that I walked here for an hour every day at this time. I could not explain to him then why I did not ask him to come and see us at once. Mother must be prepared for such a visit. And then, you see, I do not know myself what Mr Razumov has to tell us. He, too, must be told first how it is with poor mother. All these thoughts flashed through my mind at once. So I told him hurriedly that there was a reason why I could not ask him to see us at home, but that I was in the habit of walking here ... This is a public place, but there are never many people about at this hour. I thought it would do very well. And it is so near our apartments. I don't like to be very far away from mother. Our servant knows where I am in case I should be wanted suddenly.'

'Yes. It is very convenient from that point of view,' I agreed.

In fact, I thought the Bastions a very convenient place, since the girl did not think it prudent as yet to introduce that young man to her mother. It was here, then, I thought, looking round at that plot of ground of deplorable banality, that their acquaintance will begin and go on in the exchange of generous indignations and of extreme sentiments, too poignant, perhaps, for a non-Russian mind to conceive. I saw these two, escaped out of four score of millions of human beings ground between the upper and nether millstone, walking under these trees, their young heads close together. Yes, an excellent place to stroll and talk in. It even occurred to me, while we turned once more away from the wide iron gates, that when tired they would have plenty of accommodation to rest themselves. There was a quantity of tables and chairs displayed between the restaurant chalet and the bandstand, a whole raft of painted deals spread out under the trees. In the very middle of it I observed a solitary Swiss couple, whose fate was made secure from the cradle to the grave by the perfected mechanism of democratic institutions in a republic that could almost be held in the palm of one's hand. The man, colourlessly uncouth, was drinking beer out of a glittering glass; the woman, rustic and placid, leaning back in the rough chair, gazed idly around.

There is little logic to be expected on this earth, not only in the matter of thought, but also of sentiment. I was surprised to discover myself displeased with that unknown young man. A week had gone by since they met. Was he callous, or shy, or very stupid? I could not make it out.

'Do you think,' I asked Miss Haldin, after we had gone some distance up the great alley, 'that Mr Razumov understood your intention?'

'Understood what I meant?' she wondered. 'He was greatly moved. That I know! In my own agitation I could see it. But I spoke distinctly. He heard me; he seemed, indeed, to hang on my words ...'

Unconsciously she had hastened her pace. Her utterance, too, became quicker.

I waited a little before I observed thoughtfully –

'And yet he allowed all these days to pass.'

'How can we tell what work he may have to do here? He is not an idler travelling for his pleasure. His time may not be his own – nor yet his thoughts, perhaps.'

She slowed her pace suddenly, and in a lowered voice added –

'Or his very life' – then paused and stood still. 'For all I know, he may have had to leave Geneva the very day he saw me.'

'Without telling you!' I exclaimed incredulously.

'I did not give him time. I left him quite abruptly. I behaved emotionally to the end. I am sorry for it. Even if I had given him the opportunity he would have been justified in taking me for a person not to be trusted. An emotional, tearful girl is not a person to confide in. But even if he has left Geneva for a time, I am confident that we shall meet again.'

'Ah! you are confident ... I dare say. But on what ground?'

'Because I've told him that I was in great need of someone, a fellow-countryman, a fellow-believer, to whom I could give my confidence in a certain matter.'

'I see. I don't ask you what answer he made. I confess that this is good ground for your belief in Mr Razumov's appearance before long. But he has not turned up today?'

'No,' she said quietly, 'not today'; and we stood for a time in silence, like people that have nothing more to say to each other and let their thoughts run widely asunder before their bodies go off their different ways. Miss Haldin glanced at the watch on her wrist and made a brusque movement. She had already overstayed her time, it seemed.

'I don't like to be away from mother,' she murmured, shaking her head. 'It is not that she is very ill now. But somehow when I am not with her I am more uneasy than ever.'

Mrs Haldin had not made the slightest allusion to her son for the last week or more. She sat, as usual, in the armchair by the window, looking out silently on that hopeless stretch of the Boulevard des Philosophes. When she spoke, a few lifeless words, it was of indifferent, trivial things.

'For any one who knows what the poor soul is thinking of, that sort of talk is more painful than her silence. But that is bad too; I can hardly endure it, and I dare not break it.'

Miss Haldin sighed, refastening a button of her glove which had come undone. I knew well enough what a hard time of it she must be having. The stress, its causes, its nature, would have undermined the health of an Occidental girl; but Russian natures have a singular power of resistance against the unfair strains of life. Straight and supple, with a short jacket open on her black dress, which made her figure appear more slender and her fresh but colourless face more pale, she compelled my wonder and admiration.

'I can't stay a moment longer. You ought to come soon to see mother. You know she calls you "*L'ami*". It is an excellent name, and she really means it. And now *au revoir*, I must run.'

She glanced vaguely down the broad walk – the hand she put out to me eluded my grasp by an unexpected upward movement, and rested upon my shoulder. Her red lips were slightly parted, not in a smile, however, but expressing a sort of startled pleasure. She gazed towards the gates and said quickly, with a gasp –

'There! I knew it. Here he comes!'

I understood that she must mean Mr Razumov. A young man was walking up the alley, without haste. His clothes were some dull shade of brown, and he carried a stick. When my eyes first fell on him, his head was hanging on his breast as if in deep thought. While I was looking at him he raised it sharply, and at once stopped. I am certain he did, but that pause was nothing more perceptible than a faltering check in his gait, instantaneously overcome. Then he continued his approach, looking at us steadily. Miss Haldin signed to me to remain, and advanced a step or two to meet him.

I turned my head away from that meeting, and did not look at them again till I heard Miss Haldin's voice uttering his name in the way of introduction. Mr Razumov was informed, in a warm, low tone, that, besides being a wonderful teacher, I was a great support 'in our sorrow and distress'.

Of course I was described also as an Englishman. Miss Haldin spoke rapidly, faster than I have ever heard her speak, and that by contrast made the quietness of her eyes more expressive.

'I have given him my confidence,' she added, looking all the time at Mr Razumov. That young man did, indeed, rest his gaze on Miss Haldin, but certainly did not look into her eyes which were so ready for him. Afterwards he glanced backwards and forwards at us both, while the faint commencement of a forced smile, followed by the suspicion of a frown, vanished one after another; I detected them, though neither could have been noticed by a person less intensely bent upon divining him than myself. I don't know what Nathalie Haldin had observed, but my attention seized the very shades of these movements. The attempted smile was given up, the incipient frown was checked, and smoothed so that there should be no sign; but I imagined him exclaiming inwardly –

'Her confidence! To this elderly person – this foreigner!'

I imagined this because he looked foreign enough to me. I was upon the whole favourably impressed. He had an air of intelligence and even some distinction quite above the average of the students and other inhabitants of the *Petite Russie*. His features were more decided than in the generality of Russian faces; he had a line of the jaw, a clean-shaven, sallow cheek; his nose was a ridge, and not a mere protuberance. He wore the hat well down over his eyes, his dark hair curled low on the nape of his neck; in the ill-fitting brown clothes there were sturdy limbs; a slight stoop brought out a satis-factory breadth of shoulders. Upon the whole I was not disap-pointed. Studious – robust – shy . . .

Before Miss Haldin had ceased speaking I felt the grip of his hand on mine, a muscular, firm grip, but unexpectedly hot and dry. Not a word or even a mutter assisted this short and arid handshake.

I intended to leave them to themselves, but Miss Haldin touched me lightly on the forearm with a significant contact, conveying a distinct wish. Let him smile who likes, but I was only too ready to stay near Nathalie Haldin, and I am not ashamed to say that it was no smiling matter to me. I stayed, not as a youth would have stayed, uplifted, as it were poised in the air, but soberly, with my feet on the ground and my mind trying to penetrate her intention. She had turned to Razumov.

'Well. This is the place. Yes, it is here that I meant you to come. I have been walking every day ... Don't excuse yourself – I understand. I am grateful to you for coming today, but all the same I cannot stay now. It is impossible. I must hurry off home. Yes, even with you standing before me, I must run off. I have been too long away ... You know how it is?'

These last words were addressed to me. I noticed that Mr Razumov passed the tip of his tongue over his lips just as a parched, feverish man might do. He took her hand in its black glove, which closed on his, and held it – detained it quite visibly to me against a drawing-back movement.

'Thank you once more for – for understanding me,' she went on warmly. He interrupted her with a certain effect of roughness. I didn't like him speaking to this frank creature so much from under the brim of his hat, as it were. And he produced a faint, rasping voice quite like a man with a parched throat.

'What is there to thank me for? Understand you? ... How did I understand you? ... You had better know that I understand nothing. I was aware that you wanted to see me in this garden. I could not come before. I was hindered. And even today, you see ... late.'

She still held his hand.

'I can, at any rate, thank you for not dismissing me from your mind as a weak, emotional girl. No doubt I want sustaining. I am very ignorant. But I can be trusted. Indeed I can!'

'You are ignorant,' he repeated thoughtfully. He had raised his head, and was looking straight into her face now, while she held his hand. They stood like this for a long moment. She released his hand.

'Yes. You did come late. It was good of you to come on the chance of me having loitered beyond my time. I was talking with this good

193

friend here. I was talking of you. Yes, Kirylo Sidorovitch, of you. He was with me when I first heard of your being here in Geneva. He can tell you what comfort it was to my bewildered spirit to hear that news. He knew I meant to seek you out. It was the only object of my accepting the invitation of Peter Ivanovitch ...'

'Peter Ivanovitch talked to you of me,' he interrupted, in that wavering, hoarse voice which suggested a horribly dry throat.

'Very little. Just told me your name, and that you had arrived here. Why should I have asked for more? What could he have told me that I did not know already from my brother's letter? Three lines! And how much they meant to me! I will show them to you one day, Kirylo Sidorovitch. But now I must go. The first talk between us cannot be a matter of five minutes, so we had better not begin ...'

I had been standing a little aside, seeing them both in profile. At that moment it occurred to me that Mr Razumov's face was older than his age.

'If mother' – the girl had turned suddenly to me – 'were to wake up in my absence (so much longer than usual) she would perhaps question me. She seems to miss me more, you know, of late. She would want to know what delayed me – and, you see, it would be painful for me to dissemble before her.'

I understood the point very well. For the same reason she checked what seemed to be on Mr Razumov's part a movement to accompany her.

'No! No! I go alone, but meet me here as soon as possible.' Then to me in a lower, significant tone –

'Mother may be sitting at the window at this moment, looking down the street. She must not know anything of Mr Razumov's presence here till – till something is arranged.' She paused before she added a little louder, but still speaking to me, 'Mr Razumov does not quite understand my difficulty, but you know what it is.'

V

With a quick inclination of the head for us both, and an earnest, friendly glance at the young man, Miss Haldin left us covering our heads and looking after her straight, supple figure receding rapidly. Her walk was not that hybrid and uncertain gliding affected by some women, but a frank, strong, healthy movement forward. Rapidly she increased the distance – disappeared with suddenness at last. I discovered only then that Mr Razumov, after ramming his hat well over his brow, was looking me over from head to foot. I dare say I was a very unexpected fact for that young Russian to stumble upon. I caught in his physiognomy, in his whole bearing, an expression compounded of curiosity and scorn, tempered by alarm – as though he had been holding his breath while I was not looking. But his eyes met mine with a gaze direct enough. I saw then for the first time that they were of a clear brown colour and fringed with thick black eyelashes. They were the youngest feature of his face. Not at all unpleasant eyes. He swayed slightly, leaning on his stick and generally hung in the wind. It flashed upon me that in leaving us together Miss Haldin had an intention – that something was entrusted to me, since, by a mere accident I had been found at hand. On this assumed ground I put all possible friendliness into my manner. I cast about for some right thing to say, and suddenly in Miss Haldin's last words I perceived the clue to the nature of my mission.

'No,' I said gravely, if with a smile, 'you cannot be expected to understand.'

His clean-shaven lip quivered ever so little before he said, as if wickedly amused –

'But haven't you heard just now? I was thanked by that young lady for understanding so well.'

I looked at him rather hard. Was there a hidden and inexplicable sneer in this retort? No. It was not that. It might have been resentment. Yes. But what had he to resent? He looked as though he had not slept very well of late. I could almost feel on me the weight of his unrefreshed, motionless stare, the stare of a man who lies unwinking in the dark, angrily passive in the toils of disastrous thoughts. Now, when I know how true it was, I can honestly affirm that this *was* the effect produced on me. It was painful in a curiously indefinite way – for, of course, the definition comes to me now while I sit writing in the fullness of my knowledge. But this is what the effect was at that time of absolute ignorance. This new sort of uneasiness which he seemed to be forcing upon me I attempted to put down by assuming a conversational, easy familiarity.

'That extremely charming and essentially admirable young girl (I am – as you see – old enough to be frank in my expressions) was referring to her own feelings. Surely you must have understood that much?'

He made such a brusque movement that he even tottered a little.

'Must understand this! Not expected to understand that! I may have other things to do. And the girl is charming and admirable. Well – and if she is! I suppose I can see that for myself.'

This sally would have been insulting if his voice had not been practically extinct, dried up in his throat; and the rustling effort of his speech too painful to give real offence.

I remained silent, checked between the obvious fact and the subtle impression. It was open to me to leave him there and then; but the sense of having been entrusted with a mission, the suggestion of Miss Haldin's last glance, was strong upon me. After a moment of reflection I said –

'Shall we walk together a little?'

He shrugged his shoulders so violently that he tottered again. I saw it out of the corner of my eye as I moved on, with him at my elbow. He had fallen back a little and was practically out of my sight, unless I turned my head to look at him. I did not wish to indispose him still further by an appearance of marked curiosity. It might have been distasteful to such a young and secret refugee from under the pestilential shadow hiding the true, kindly face of his land. And the shadow, the attendant of his countrymen, stretching across the middle of Europe, was lying on him too, darkening his figure to my mental vision. 'Without doubt,' I said to myself, 'he seems a sombre, even a desperate revolutionist; but he is young, he may be unselfish and humane, capable of compassion, of . . .'

I heard him clear gratingly his parched throat, and became all attention.

'This is beyond everything,' were his first words. 'It is beyond everything! I find you here, for no reason that I can understand, in possession of something I cannot be expected to understand! A confidant! A foreigner! Talking about an admirable Russian girl. Is the admirable girl a fool, I begin to wonder? What are you at? What is your object?'

He was barely audible, as if his throat had no more resonance than a dry rag, a piece of tinder. It was so pitiful that I found it extremely easy to control my indignation.

'When you have lived a little longer, Mr Razumov, you will discover that no woman is an absolute fool. I am not a feminist, like that illustrious author, Peter Ivanovitch, who, to say the truth, is not a little suspect to me ...'

He interrupted me, in a surprising note of whispering astonishment.

'Suspect to you! Peter Ivanovitch suspect to you! To you! ...'

'Yes, in a certain aspect he is,' I said, dismissing my remark lightly. 'As I was saying, Mr Razumov, when you have lived long enough, you will learn to discriminate between the noble trustfulness of a nature foreign to every meanness and the flattered credulity of some women; though even the credulous, silly as they may be, unhappy as they are sure to be, are never absolute fools. It is my belief that no woman is ever completely deceived. Those that are lost leap into the abyss with their eyes open, if all the truth were known.'

'Upon my word,' he cried at my elbow, 'what is it to me whether women are fools or lunatics? I really don't care what you think of them. I – I am not interested in them. I let them be. I am not a young man in a novel. How do you know that I want to learn anything about women? ... What is the meaning of all this?'

'The object, you mean, of this conversation, which I admit I have forced upon you in a measure.'

'Forced! Object!' he repeated, still keeping half a pace or so behind me. 'You wanted to talk about women, apparently. That's a subject. But I don't care for it. I have never ... In fact, I have had other subjects to think about.'

'I am concerned here with one woman only – a young girl – the sister of your dead friend – Miss Haldin. Surely you can think a little of her. What I meant from the first was that there is a situation which you cannot be expected to understand.'

I listened to his unsteady footfalls by my side for the space of several strides.

'I think that it may prepare the ground for your next interview with Miss Haldin if I tell you of it. I imagine that she might have had something of the kind in her mind when she left us together. I believe myself authorized to speak. The peculiar situation I have alluded to has arisen in the first grief and distress of Victor Haldin's execution. There was something peculiar in the circumstances of his arrest. You no doubt know the whole truth . . .'

I felt my arm seized above the elbow, and next instant found myself swung so as to face Mr Razumov.

'You spring up from the ground before me with this talk. Who the devil are you? This is not to be borne! Why! What for? What do you know what is or is not peculiar? What have you to do with any confounded circumstances, or with anything that happens in Russia, anyway?'

He leaned on his stick with his other hand, heavily; and when he let go my arm, I was certain in my mind that he was hardly able to keep on his feet.

'Let us sit down at one of these vacant tables,' I proposed, disregarding this display of unexpectedly profound emotion. It was not without its effect on me, I confess. I was sorry for him.

'What tables? What are you talking about? Oh – the empty tables? The tables there. Certainly. I will sit at one of the empty tables.'

I led him away from the path to the very centre of the raft of deals before the *chalet*. The Swiss couple were gone by that time. We were alone on the raft, so to speak. Mr Razumov dropped into a chair, let fall his stick, and propped on his elbows, his head between his hands, stared at me persistently, openly, and continuously, while I signalled the waiter and ordered some beer. I could not quarrel with this silent inspection very well, because, truth to tell, I felt somewhat guilty of having been sprung on him with some abruptness – of having 'sprung from the ground', as he expressed it.

While waiting to be served I mentioned that, born from parents settled in St Petersburg, I had acquired the language as a child. The town I did not remember, having left it for good as a boy of nine, but in later years I had renewed my acquaintance with the language. He listened, without as much as moving his eyes the least little bit. He had to change his position when the beer came, and the instant draining of his glass revived him. He leaned back in his chair and, folding his arms across his chest, continued to stare at me squarely. It occurred to me that his clean-shaven, almost swarthy face was really of the very mobile sort, and that the absolute stillness of it was the acquired habit of a revolutionist, of a conspirator everlastingly on his guard against self-betrayal in a world of secret spies.

'But you are an Englishman – a teacher of English literature,' he murmured, in a voice that was no longer issuing from a parched throat. 'I have heard of you. People told me you have lived here for years.'

'Quite true. More than twenty years. And I have been assisting Miss Haldin with her English studies.'

'You have been reading English poetry with her,' he said, immovable now, like another man altogether, a complete stranger to the man of the heavy and uncertain footfalls a little while ago – at my elbow.

'Yes, English poetry,' I said. 'But the trouble of which I speak was caused by an English newspaper.'

He continued to stare at me. I don't think he was aware that the story of the midnight arrest had been ferreted out by an English journalist and given to the world. When I explained this to him he muttered contemptuously, 'It may have been altogether a lie.'

'I should think you are the best judge of that,' I retorted, a little disconcerted. 'I must confess that to me it looks to be true in the main.'

'How can you tell truth from lies?' he queried in his new, immovable manner.

'I don't know how you do it in Russia,' I began, rather nettled by his attitude. He interrupted me.

'In Russia, and in general everywhere – in a newspaper, for instance. The colour of the ink and the shapes of the letters are the same.'

'Well, there are other trifles one can go by. The character of the publication, the general verisimilitude of the news, the consideration of the motive, and so on. I don't trust blindly the accuracy of special correspondents – but why should this one have gone to the trouble of concocting a circumstantial falsehood on a matter of no importance to the world?'

'That's what it is,' he grumbled. 'What's going on with us is of no importance – a mere sensational story to amuse the readers of the papers – the superior contemptuous Europe. It is hateful to think of. But let them wait a bit!'

He broke off on this sort of threat addressed to the Western world. Disregarding the anger in his stare, I pointed out that whether the journalist was well- or ill-informed, the concern of the friends of these ladies was with the effect the few lines of print in question had produced – the effect alone. And surely he must be counted as one of the friends – if only for the sake of his late comrade and intimate fellow-revolutionist. At that point I thought he was going to speak vehemently; but he only astounded me by the convulsive start of his whole body. He restrained himself, folded his loosened arms tighter across his chest, and sat back with a smile in which there was a twitch of scorn and malice.

'Yes, a comrade and an intimate ... Very well,' he said.

'I ventured to speak to you on that assumption. And I cannot be mistaken. I was present when Peter Ivanovitch announced your arrival here to Miss Haldin, and I saw her relief and thankfulness when your name was mentioned. Afterwards she showed me her brother's letter, and read out the few words in which he alludes to you. What else but a friend could you have been?'

'Obviously. That's perfectly well known. A friend. Quite correct ... Go on. You were talking of some effect.'

I said to myself: 'He puts on the callousness of a stern revolu-tionist, the insensibility to common emotions of a man devoted to a destructive idea. He is young, and his sincerity assumes a pose before a stranger, a foreigner, an old man. Youth must assert itself...' As concisely as possible I exposed to him the state of mind poor Mrs Haldin had been thrown into by the news of her son's untimely end.

He listened – I felt it – with profound attention. His level stare deflected gradually downwards, left my face, and rested at last on the ground at his feet.

'You can enter into the sister's feelings. As you said, I have only read a little English poetry with her, and I won't make myself ridiculous in your eyes by trying to speak of her. But you have seen her. She is one of these rare human beings that do not want explaining. At least I think so. They had only that son, that brother, for a link with the wider world, with the future. The very groundwork of active existence for Nathalie Haldin is gone with him. Can you wonder then that she turns with eagerness to the only man her brother mentions in his letters. Your name is a sort of legacy.'

'What could he have written of me?' he cried, in a low, exasperated tone.

'Only a few words. It is not for me to repeat them to you, Mr Razumov; but you may believe my assertion that these words are forcible enough to make both his mother and his sister believe implicitly in the worth of your judgement and in the truth of anything you may have to say to them. It's impossible for you now to pass them by like strangers.'

I paused, and for a moment sat listening to the footsteps of the few people passing up and down the broad central walk. While I was speaking his head had sunk upon his breast above his folded arms. He raised it sharply.

'Must I go then and lie to that old woman!'

It was not anger; it was something else, something more poignant, and not so simple. I was aware of it sympathetically, while I was profoundly concerned at the nature of that exclamation.

'Dear me! Won't the truth do, then? I hoped you could have told them something consoling. I am thinking of the poor mother now. Your Russia *is* a cruel country.'

He moved a little in his chair.

'Yes,' I repeated. 'I thought you would have had something authentic to tell.'

The twitching of his lips before he spoke was curious.

'What if it is not worth telling?'

'Not worth – from what point of view? I don't understand.'

'From every point of view.'

I spoke with some asperity.

'I should think that anything which could explain the circumstances of that midnight arrest ...'

'Reported by a journalist for the amusement of the civilized Europe,' he broke in scornfully.

'Yes, reported ... But aren't they true? I can't make out your attitude in this. Either the man is a hero to you, or ...'

He approached his face with fiercely distended nostrils close to mine so suddenly that I had the greatest difficulty in not starting back.

'You ask me! I suppose it amuses you, all this. Look here! I am a worker. I studied. Yes, I studied very hard. There is intelligence here.' (He tapped his forehead with his finger-tips.) 'Don't you think a Russian may have sane ambitions? Yes – I had even prospects. Certainly! I had. And now you see me here, abroad, everything gone, lost, sacrificed. You see me here – and you ask! You see me, don't you? – sitting before you.'

He threw himself back violently. I kept outwardly calm.

'Yes, I see you here; and I assume you are here on account of the Haldin affair?'

His manner changed.

'You call it the Haldin affair – do you?' he observed indifferently.

'I have no right to ask you anything,' I said. 'I wouldn't presume. But in that case the mother and the sister of him who must be a hero in your eyes cannot be indifferent to you. The girl is a frank and generous creature, having the noblest – well – illusions. You will tell her nothing – or you will tell her everything. But speaking now of the object with which I've approached you: first, we have to deal with the morbid state of the mother. Perhaps something could be invented under your authority as a cure for a distracted and suffering soul filled with maternal affection.'

His air of weary indifference was accentuated, I could not help thinking, wilfully.

'Oh yes. Something might,' he mumbled carelessly.

He put his hand over his mouth to conceal a yawn. When he uncovered his lips they were smiling faintly.

'Pardon me. This has been a long conversation, and I have not had much sleep the last two nights.'

This unexpected, somewhat insolent sort of apology had the merit of being perfectly true. He had had no nightly rest to speak of since that day when, in the grounds of the Château Borel, the sister of Victor Haldin had appeared before him. The perplexities and the complex terrors – I may say – of this sleeplessness are recorded in the document I was to see later – the document which is the main source of this narrative. At the moment he looked to me convincingly tired, gone slack all over, like a man who has passed through some sort of crisis.

'I have had a lot of urgent writing to do,' he added.

I rose from my chair at once, and he followed my example, without haste, a little heavily.

'I must apologize for detaining you so long,' I said.

'Why apologize? One can't very well go to bed before night. And you did not detain me. I could have left you at any time.'

I had not stayed with him to be offended.

'I am glad you have been sufficiently interested,' I said calmly. 'No merit of mine, though – the commonest sort of regard for the mother of your friend was enough . . . As to Miss Haldin herself, she at one time was disposed to think that her brother had been betrayed to the police in some way.'

To my great surprise Mr Razumov sat down again suddenly. I stared at him, and I must say that he returned my stare without winking for quite a considerable time.

'In some way,' he mumbled, as if he had not understood or could not believe his ears.

'Some unforeseen event, a sheer accident might have done that,' I went on. 'Or, as she characteristically put it to me, the folly or weakness of some unhappy fellow-revolutionist.'

'Folly or weakness,' he repeated bitterly.

'She is a very generous creature,' I observed after a time. The man admired by Victor Haldin fixed his eyes on the ground. I turned away and moved off, apparently unnoticed by him. I nourished no resentment of the moody brusqueness with which he had treated me. The sentiment I was carrying away from that conversation was that of hopelessness. Before I had got fairly clear of the raft of chairs and tables he had rejoined me.

'H'm, yes!' I heard him at my elbow again. 'But what do you think?'

I did not look round even.

'I think that you people are under a curse.'

He made no sound. It was only on the pavement outside the gate that I heard him again.

'I should like to walk with you a little.'

After all, I preferred this enigmatical young man to his celebrated compatriot, the great Peter Ivanovitch. But I saw no reason for being particularly gracious.

'I am going now to the railway station, by the shortest way from here, to meet a friend from England,' I said, for all answer to his unexpected proposal. I hoped that something informing could come of it. As we stood on the curbstone waiting for a tramcar to pass, he remarked gloomily –

'I like what you said just now.'

'Do you?'

We stepped off the pavement together.

'The great problem,' he went on, 'is to understand thoroughly the nature of the curse.'

'That's not very difficult, I think.'

'I think so too,' he agreed with me, and his readiness, strangely enough, did not make him less enigmatical in the least.

'A curse is an evil spell,' I tried him again. 'And the important, the great problem, is to find the means to break it.'

'Yes. To find the means.'

That was also an assent, but he seemed to be thinking of something else. We had crossed diagonally the open space before the theatre, and began to descend a broad, sparsely frequented street in the direction of one of the smaller bridges. He kept on by my side without speaking for a long time.

'You are not thinking of leaving Geneva soon?' I asked.

He was silent for so long that I began to think I had been indiscreet, and should get no answer at all. Yet on looking at him I almost believed that my question had caused him something in the nature of positive anguish. I detected it mainly in the clasping of his hands, in which he put a great force stealthily. Once, however, he had overcome that sort of agonizing hesitation sufficiently to tell me that he had no such intention, he became rather communicative – at least relatively to the former off-hand curtness of his speeches. The tone, too, was more amiable. He informed me that he intended to study and also to write. He went even so far as to tell me he had been to Stuttgart. Stuttgart, I was aware, was one of the revolutionary centres. The directing committee of one of the Russian parties (I can't tell now which) was located in that town. It was there that he got into touch with the active work of the revolutionists outside Russia.

'I have never been abroad before,' he explained, in a rather inanimate voice now. Then, after a slight hesitation, altogether different from the agonizing irresolution my first simple question 'whether he meant to stay in Geneva' had aroused, he made me an unexpected confidence –

'The fact is, I have received a sort of mission from them.'

'Which will keep you here in Geneva?'

'Yes. Here. In this odious ...'

I was satisfied with my faculty for putting two and two together when I drew the inference that the mission had something to do with the person of the great Peter Ivanovitch. But I kept that surmise to myself naturally, and Mr Razumov said nothing more for some considerable time. It was only when we were nearly on the bridge we had been making for that he opened his lips again, abruptly –

'Could I see that precious article anywhere?'

I had to think for a moment before I saw what he was referring to.

'It has been reproduced in parts by the Press here. There are files to be seen in various places. My copy of the English newspaper I have left with Miss Haldin, I remember, on the day after it reached me. I was sufficiently worried by seeing it lying on a table by the side of the poor mother's chair for weeks. Then it disappeared. It was a relief, I assure you.'

He had stopped short.

'I trust,' I continued, 'that you will find time to see these ladies fairly often – that you will make time.'

He stared at me so queerly that I hardly know how to define his aspect. I could not understand it in this connection at all. What ailed him? I asked myself. What strange thought had come into his head? What vision of all the horrors that can be seen in his hopeless country had come suddenly to haunt his brain? If it were anything connected with the fate of Victor Haldin, then I hoped earnestly he would keep it to himself for ever. I was, to speak plainly, so shocked that I tried to conceal my impression by – Heaven forgive me – a smile and the assumption of a light manner.

'Surely,' I exclaimed, 'that needn't cost you a great effort.'

He turned away from me and leaned over the parapet of the bridge. For a moment I waited, looking at his back. And yet, I assure you, I was not anxious just then to look at his face again. He did not move at all. He did not mean to move. I walked on slowly on my way towards the station, and at the end of the bridge I glanced over my shoulder. No, he had not moved. He hung well over the parapet, as if captivated by the smooth rush of the blue water under the arch. The current there is swift, extremely swift; it makes some people dizzy; I myself can never look at it for any length of time without experiencing a dread of being suddenly snatched away by its destructive force. Some brains cannot resist the suggestion of irresistible power and of headlong motion.

It apparently had a charm for Mr Razumov. I left him hanging far over the parapet of the bridge. The way he had behaved to me could not be put down to mere boorishness. There was something else under his scorn and impatience. Perhaps, I thought, with sudden approach to hidden truth, it was the same thing which had kept him over a week, nearly ten days indeed, from coming near Miss Haldin. But what it was I could not tell.

PART THIRD

I

The water under the bridge ran violent and deep. Its slightly undulating rush seemed capable of scouring out a channel for itself through solid granite while you looked. But had it flowed through Razumov's breast, it could not have washed away the accumulated bitterness the wrecking of his life had deposited there.

'What is the meaning of all this?' he thought, staring downwards at the headlong flow so smooth and clean that only the passage of a faint air-bubble, or a thin vanishing streak of foam like a white hair, disclosed its vertiginous rapidity, its terrible force. 'Why has that meddlesome old Englishman blundered against me? And what is this silly tale of a crazy old woman?'

He was trying to think brutally on purpose, but he avoided any mental reference to the young girl. 'A crazy old woman,' he repeated to himself. 'It is a fatality! Or ought I to despise all this as absurd? But no! I am wrong! I can't afford to despise anything. An absurdity may be the starting-point of the most dangerous complications. How is one to guard against it? It puts to rout one's intelligence. The more intelligent one is the less one suspects an absurdity.'

A wave of wrath choked his thoughts for a moment. It even made his body leaning over the parapet quiver; then he resumed his silent thinking, like a secret dialogue with himself. And even in that privacy, his thought had some reservations of which he was vaguely conscious.

'After all, this is not absurd. It is insignificant. It is absolutely insignificant – absolutely. The craze of an old woman – the fussy officiousness of a blundering elderly Englishman. What devil put him in the way? Haven't I treated him cavalierly enough? Haven't I just? That's the way to treat these meddlesome persons. Is it possible that he still stands behind my back, waiting?'

Razumov felt a faint chill run down his spine. It was not fear. He was certain that it was not fear – not fear for himself – but it was, all the same, a sort of apprehension as if for another, for someone he knew without being able to put a name to the personality. But the recollection that the officious Englishman had a train to meet tranquillized him for a time. It was too stupid to suppose that he should be wasting his time in waiting. It was unnecessary to look round and make sure.

But what did the man mean by his extraordinary rigmarole about the newspaper, and that crazy old woman? he thought suddenly. It was a damnable presumption, anyhow, something that only an Englishman could be capable of. All this was a sort of sport for him – the sport of revolution – a game to look at from the height of his superiority. And what on earth did he mean by his exclamation, 'Won't the truth do?'

Razumov pressed his folded arms to the stone coping over which he was leaning with force. 'Won't the truth do? The truth for the crazy old mother of the –'

The young man shuddered again. Yes. The truth would do! Apparently it would do. Exactly. And receive thanks, he thought, formulating the unspoken words cynically. 'Fall on my neck in gratitude, no doubt,' he jeered mentally. But this mood abandoned him at once. He felt sad, as if his heart had become empty suddenly. 'Well, I must be cautious,' he concluded, coming to himself as though his brain had been awakened from a trance. 'There is nothing, no one, too insignificant, too absurd to be disregarded,' he thought wearily. 'I must be cautious.'

Razumov pushed himself with his hand away from the balustrade and, retracing his steps along the bridge, walked straight to his lodgings, where, for a few days, he led a solitary and retired existence. He neglected Peter Ivanovitch, to whom he was accredited by the Stuttgart group; he never went near the refugee revolutionists, to whom he had been introduced on his arrival. He kept out of that world altogether. And he felt that such conduct, causing surprise and arousing suspicion, contained an element of danger for himself.

This is not to say that during these few days he never went out. I met him several times in the streets, but he gave me no recognition. Once, going home after an evening call on the ladies Haldin, I saw him crossing the dark roadway of the Boulevard des Philosophes. He had a broad-brimmed soft hat, and the collar of his coat turned up. I watched him make straight for the house, but, instead of going in, he stopped opposite the still lighted windows, and after a time went away down a side-street.

I knew that he had not been to see Mrs Haldin yet. Miss Haldin told me he was reluctant; moreover, the mental condition of Mrs Haldin had changed. She seemed to think now that her son was living, and she perhaps awaited his arrival. Her immobility in the great armchair in front of the window had an air of expectancy, even when the blind was down and the lamps lighted.

For my part, I was convinced that she had received her death-stroke; Miss Haldin, to whom, of course, I said nothing of my forebodings, thought that no good would come from introducing Mr Razumov just then, an opinion which I shared fully. I knew that she met the young man on the Bastions. Once or twice I saw them strolling slowly up the main alley. They met every day for weeks. I avoided passing that way during the hour when Miss Haldin took her exercise there. One day, however, in a fit of absent-mindedness, I entered the gates and came upon her walking alone. I stopped to exchange a few words. Mr Razumov failed to turn up, and we began to talk about him – naturally.

'Did he tell you anything definite about your brother's activities – his end?' I ventured to ask.

'No,' admitted Miss Haldin, with some hesitation. 'Nothing definite.'

I understood well enough that all their conversations must have been referred mentally to that dead man who had brought them together. That was unavoidable. But it was in the living man that she was interested. That was unavoidable too, I suppose. And as I pushed my inquiries I discovered that he had disclosed himself to her as a by no means conventional revolutionist, contemptuous of

209

catchwords, of theories of men too. I was rather pleased at that –
but I was a little puzzled.

'His mind goes forward, far ahead of the struggle,' Miss Haldin
explained. 'Of course, he is an actual worker too,' she added.

'And do you understand him?' I inquired point-blank.

She hesitated again. 'Not altogether,' she murmured.

I perceived that he had fascinated her by an assumption of
mysterious reserve.

'Do you know what I think?' she went on, breaking through her
reserved, almost reluctant attitude: 'I think that he is observing,
studying me, to discover whether I am worthy of his trust ...'

'And that pleases you?'

She kept mysteriously silent for a moment. Then with energy, but
in a confidential tone –

'I am convinced,' she declared, 'that this extraordinary man is
meditating some vast plan, some great undertaking; he is possessed
by it – he suffers from it – and from being alone in the world.'

'And so he's looking for helpers?' I commented, turning away my
head.

Again there was a silence.

'Why not?' she said at last.

The dead brother, the dying mother, the foreign friend, had fallen
into a distant background. But, at the same time, Peter Ivanovitch
was absolutely nowhere now. And this thought consoled me. Yet
I saw the gigantic shadow of Russian life deepening around her like
the darkness of an advancing night. It would devour her presently.
I inquired after Mrs Haldin – that other victim of the deadly
shade.

A remorseful uneasiness appeared in her frank eyes. Mother
seemed no worse, but if I only knew what strange fancies she had
sometimes! Then Miss Haldin, glancing at her watch, declared that
she could not stay a moment longer, and with a hasty hand-shake
ran off lightly.

Decidedly, Mr Razumov was not to turn up that day. Incomprehensible youth!

But less than an hour afterwards, while crossing the Place
Mollard, I caught sight of him boarding a South Shore tramcar.

'He's going to the Château Borel,' I thought.

After depositing Razumov at the gates of the Château Borel, some half a mile or so from the town, the car continued its journey between two straight lines of shady trees. Across the roadway in the sunshine a short wooden pier jutted into the shallow pale water, which farther out had an intense blue tint contrasting unpleasantly with the green orderly slopes on the opposite shore. The whole view, with the harbour jetties of white stone underlining lividly the dark front of the town to the left, and the expanding space of water to the right with jutting promontories of no particular character, had the uninspiring, glittering quality of a very fresh oleograph. Razumov turned his back on it with contempt. He thought it odious – oppressively odious – in its unsuggestive finish: the very perfection of mediocrity attained at last after centuries of toil and culture. And turning his back on it, he faced the entrance to the grounds of the Château Borel.

The bars of the central way and the wrought-iron arch between the dark weather-stained stone piers were very rusty; and, though fresh tracks of wheels ran under it, the gate looked as if it had not been opened for a very long time. But close against the lodge, built of the same grey stone as the piers (its windows were all boarded up), there was a small side entrance. The bars of that were rusty too; it stood ajar and looked as though it had not been closed for a long time. In fact, Razumov, trying to push it open a little wider, discovered it was immovable.

'Democratic virtue. There are no thieves here, apparently,' he muttered to himself, with displeasure. Before advancing into the grounds he looked back sourly at an idle working man lounging on a bench in the clean, broad avenue. The fellow had thrown his feet up; one of his arms hung over the low back of the public seat; he was taking a day off in lordly repose, as if everything in sight belonged to him.

'Elector! Eligible! Enlightened!' Razumov muttered to himself. 'A brute, all the same.'

Razumov entered the grounds and walked fast up the wide sweep of the drive, trying to think of nothing – to rest his head, to rest his emotions too. But arriving at the foot of the terrace before the house he faltered, affected physically by some invisible interference. The mysteriousness of his quickened heart-beats startled him. He stopped short and looked at the brick wall of the terrace, faced with shallow arches, meagerly clothed by a few unthriving creepers, with an ill-kept narrow flower-bed along its foot.

'It is here!' he thought, with a sort of awe. 'It is here – on this very spot ...'

He was tempted to flight at the mere recollection of his first meeting with Nathalie Haldin. He confessed it to himself; but he did not move, and that not because he wished to resist an unworthy weakness, but because he knew that he had no place to fly to. Moreover, he could not leave Geneva. He recognized, even without thinking, that it was impossible. It would have been a fatal admission, an act of moral suicide. It would have been also physically dangerous. Slowly he ascended the stairs of the terrace, flanked by two stained greenish stone urns of funereal aspect.

Across the broad platform, where a few blades of grass sprouted on the discoloured gravel, the door of the house, with its ground-floor windows shuttered, faced him, wide open. He believed that his approach had been noted, because, framed in the doorway, without his tall hat, Peter Ivanovitch seemed to be waiting for his approach.

The ceremonious black frock-coat and the bared head of Europe's greatest feminist accentuated the dubiousness of his status in the house rented by Madame de S —, his Egeria. His aspect combined the formality of the caller with the freedom of the proprietor. Florid and bearded and masked by the dark blue glasses, he met the visitor, and at once took him familiarly under the arm.

Razumov suppressed every sign of repugnance by an effort which the constant necessity of prudence had rendered almost mechanical. And this necessity had settled his expression in a cast of austere, almost fanatical, aloofness. The 'heroic fugitive', impressed afresh by the severe detachment of this new arrival from revolutionary Russia, took a conciliatory, even a confidential tone. Madame de S — was resting after a bad night. She often had bad nights. He had left his hat upstairs on the landing and had come down to suggest to his young friend a stroll and a good open-hearted talk in one of the shady alleys behind the house. After voicing this proposal, the great man glanced at the unmoved face by his side, and could not restrain himself from exclaiming –

'On my word, young man, you are an extraordinary person.'

'I fancy you are mistaken, Peter Ivanovitch. If I were really an extraordinary person, I would not be here, walking with you in a garden in Switzerland, Canton of Geneva, Commune of – what's the name of the Commune this place belongs to? ... Never mind – the heart of democracy, anyhow. A fit heart for it; no bigger than a parched pea and about as much value. I am no more extraordinary than the rest of us Russians, wandering abroad.'

But Peter Ivanovitch dissented emphatically –

'No! No! You are not ordinary. I have some experience of Russians who are – well – living abroad. You appear to me, and to others too, a marked personality.'

'What does he mean by this?' Razumov asked himself, turning his eyes fully on his companion. The face of Peter Ivanovitch expressed a meditative seriousness.

'You don't suppose, Kirylo Sidorovitch, that I have not heard of you from various points where you made yourself known on your way here? I have had letters.'

'Oh, we are great in talking about each other,' interjected Razumov, who had listened with great attention. 'Gossip, tales, suspicions, and all that sort of thing, we know how to deal in to perfection. Calumny, even.'

In indulging in this sally, Razumov managed very well to conceal the feeling of anxiety which had come over him. At the same time he was saying to himself that there could be no earthly reason for anxiety. He was relieved by the evident sincerity of the protesting voice.

'Heavens!' cried Peter Ivanovitch. 'What are you talking about? What reason can *you* have to ... ?'

The great exile flung up his arms as if words had failed him in sober truth. Razumov was satisfied. Yet he was moved to continue in the same vein.

'I am talking of the poisonous plants which flourish in the world of conspirators, like evil mushrooms in a dark cellar.'

are casting aspersions,' remonstrated Peter Ivanovitch, ...as far as you are concerned –'

'No!' Razumov interrupted without heat. 'Indeed, I don't want to cast aspersions, but it's just as well to have no illusions.'

Peter Ivanovitch gave him an inscrutable glance of his dark spectacles, accompanied by a faint smile.

'The man who says that he has no illusions has at least that one,' he said, in a very friendly tone. 'But I see how it is, Kirylo Sidorovitch. You aim at stoicism.'

'Stoicism! That's a pose of the Greeks and the Romans. Let's leave it to them. We are Russians, that is – children; that is – sincere; that is – cynical, if you like. But that's not a pose.'

A long silence ensued. They strolled slowly under the lime-trees. Peter Ivanovitch had put his hands behind his back. Razumov felt the ungravelled ground of the deeply shaded walk damp and as if slippery under his feet. He asked himself, with uneasiness, if he were saying the right things. The direction of the conversation ought to have been more under his control, he reflected. The great man appeared to be reflecting on his side too. He cleared his throat slightly, and Razumov felt at once a painful reawakening of scorn and fear.

'I am astonished,' began Peter Ivanovitch gently. 'Supposing you are right in your indictment, how can you raise any question of calumny or gossip, in your case? It is unreasonable. The fact is, Kirylo Sidorovitch, there is not enough known of you to give hold to gossip or even calumny. Just now you are a man associated with a great deed, which had been hoped for, and tried for too, without success. People have perished for attempting that which you and Haldin have done at last. You come to us out of Russia, with that prestige. But you cannot deny that you have not been communicative, Kirylo Sidorovitch. People you have met imparted their impressions to me; one wrote this, another that, but I form my own opinions. I waited to see you first. You are a man out of the common. That's positively so. You are close, very close. This taciturnity, this severe brow, this something inflexible and secret in you, inspires hopes and a little wonder as to what you may mean. There is something of a Brutus ...'[14]

214

'Pray spare me those classical allusions!' burst out Razumov nervously. 'What comes Junius Brutus to do here? It is ridiculous! Do you mean to say,' he added sarcastically, but lowering his voice, 'that the Russian revolutionists are all patricians and that I am an aristocrat?'

Peter Ivanovitch, who had been helping himself with a few gestures, clasped his hands again behind his back, and made a few steps, pondering.

'Not *all* patricians,' he muttered at last. 'But you, at any rate, are one of *us*.'

Razumov smiled bitterly.

'To be sure my name is not Gugenheimer,' he said in a sneering tone. 'I am not a democratic Jew. How can I help it? Not everybody has such luck. I have no name, I have no ...'

The European celebrity showed a great concern. He stepped back a pace and his arms flew in front of his person, extended, deprecatory, almost entreating. His deep bass voice was full of pain.

'But, my dear young friend!' he cried. 'My dear Kirylo Sidorovitch ...'

Razumov shook his head.

'The very patronymic you are so civil as to use when addressing me I have no legal right to – but what of that? I don't wish to claim it. I have no father. So much the better. But I will tell you what: my mother's grandfather was a peasant – a serf. See how much I am one of *you*. I don't want any one to claim me. But Russia *can't* disown me. She cannot!'

Razumov struck his breast with his fist.

'I am *it*!'

Peter Ivanovitch walked on slowly, his head lowered. Razumov followed, vexed with himself. That was not the right sort of talk. All sincerity was an imprudence. Yet one could not renounce truth altogether, he thought, with despair. Peter Ivanovitch, meditating behind his dark glasses, became to him suddenly so odious that if he had had a knife, he fancied he could have stabbed him not only without compunction, but with a horrible triumphant satisfaction. His imagination dwelt on that atrocity in spite of himself. It was as if he were becoming light-headed. 'It is not what is expected of me,'

215

he repeated to himself. 'It is not what is – I could get away by breaking the fastening on the little gate I see there in the back wall. It is a flimsy lock. Nobody in the house seems to know he is here with me. Oh yes. The hat! These women would discover presently the hat he has left on the landing. They would come upon him, lying dead in this damp, gloomy shade – but I would be gone and no one could ever . . . Lord! Am I going mad?' he asked himself in a fright.

The great man was heard – musing in an undertone.

'H'm, yes! That – no doubt – in a certain sense . . .' He raised his voice. 'There is a deal of pride about you . . .'

The intonation of Peter Ivanovitch took on a homely, familiar ring, acknowledging, in a way, Razumov's claim to peasant descent.

'A great deal of pride, brother Kirylo. And I don't say that you have no justification for it. I have admitted you had. I have ventured to allude to the facts of your birth simply because I attach no mean importance to it. You are one of us – *un des nôtres*. I reflect on that with satisfaction.'

'I attach some importance to it also,' said Razumov quietly. 'I won't even deny that it may have some importance for you too,' he continued, after a slight pause and with a touch of grimness of which he was himself aware, with some annoyance. He hoped it had escaped the perception of Peter Ivanovitch. 'But suppose we talk no more about it?'

'Well, we shall not – not after this one time, Kirylo Sidorovitch,' persisted the noble arch-priest of Revolution. 'This shall be the last occasion. You cannot believe for a moment that I had the slightest idea of wounding your feelings. You are clearly a superior nature – that's how I read you. Quite above the common – h'm – suscepti-bilities. But the fact is, Kirylo Sidorovitch, I don't know your susceptibilities. Nobody, out of Russia, knows much of you – as yet!'

'You have been watching me?' suggested Razumov.

'Yes.'

The great man had spoken in a tone of perfect frankness, but as they turned their faces to each other Razumov felt baffled by the dark spectacles. Under their cover, Peter Ivanovitch hinted that he had felt for some time the need of meeting a man of energy and character, in view of a certain project. He said nothing more precise, however; and after some critical remarks upon the personalities of the various members of the committee of revolutionary action in Stuttgart, he let the conversation lapse for quite a long while. They paced the alley from end to end. Razumov, silent too, raised his eyes from time to time to cast a glance at the back of the house. It offered no sign of being inhabited. With its grimy, weather-stained walls and all the windows shuttered from top to bottom, it looked damp and gloomy and deserted. It might very well have been haunted in traditional style by some doleful, groaning, futile ghost of a middle-class order. The shades evoked, as worldly rumour had it, by Madame de S — to meet statesmen, diplomatists, deputies of various European Parliaments, must have been of another sort. Razumov had never seen Madame de S — but in the carriage.

Peter Ivanovitch came out of his abstraction.

'Two things I may say to you at once. I believe, first, that neither a leader nor any decisive action can come out of the dregs of a people. Now if you ask me what are the dregs of a people – h'm – it would take too long to tell. You would be surprised at the variety of ingredients that for me go to the making up of these dregs – of that which ought, *must* remain at the bottom. Moreover, such a statement might be subject to discussion. But I can tell you what is *not* the dregs. On that it is impossible for us to disagree. The peasantry of a people is not the dregs; neither is its highest class – well – the nobility. Reflect on that, Kirylo Sidorovitch! I believe you are well fitted for reflection. Everything in a people that is not genuine, not its own by origin or development, is – well – dirt! Intelligence in the wrong place is that. Foreign-bred doctrines are that. Dirt! Dregs! The second thing I would offer to your meditation is this: that for us at this moment there yawns a chasm between the past and the future. It can never be bridged by foreign liberalism. All attempts at it are either folly or cheating. Bridged it can never be! It has to be filled up.'

A sort of sinister jocularity had crept into the tones of the burly feminist. He seized Razumov's arm above the elbow, and gave it a slight shake.

'Do you understand, enigmatical young man? It has got to be just filled up.'

Razumov kept an unmoved countenance.

'Don't you think that I have already gone beyond meditation on that subject?' he said, freeing his arm by a quiet movement which increased the distance a little between himself and Peter Ivanovitch, as they went on strolling abreast. And he added that surely whole cartloads of words and theories could never fill that chasm. No meditation was necessary. A sacrifice of many lives could alone – He fell silent without finishing the phrase.

Peter Ivanovitch inclined his big hairy head slowly. After a moment he proposed that they should go and see if Madame de S— was now visible.

'We shall get some tea,' he said, turning out of the shaded gloomy walk with a brisker step.

The lady companion had been on the look out. Her dark skirt whisked into the doorway as the two men came in sight round the corner. She ran off somewhere altogether, and had disappeared when they entered the hall. In the crude light falling from the dusty glass skylight upon the black and white tessellated floor, covered with muddy tracks, their footsteps echoed faintly. The great feminist led the way up the stairs. On the balustrade of the first-floor landing a shiny tall hat reposed, rim upwards, opposite the double door of the drawing-room, haunted, it was said, by evoked ghosts, and frequented, it was to be supposed, by fugitive revolutionists. The cracked white paint of the panels, the tarnished gilt of the mouldings, permitted one to imagine nothing but dust and emptiness within. Before turning the massive brass handle, Peter Ivanovitch gave his young companion a sharp, partly critical, partly preparatory glance.

'No one is perfect,' he murmured discreetly. Thus, the possessor of a rare jewel might, before opening the casket, warn the profane that no gem perhaps is flawless.

He remained with his hand on the door-handle so long that Razumov assented by a moody 'No.'

'Perfection itself would not produce that effect,' pursued Peter

218

Ivanovitch, 'in a world not meant for it. But you shall find there a mind – no! – the quintessence of feminine intuition which will understand any perplexity you may be suffering from by the irresistible, enlightening force of sympathy. Nothing can remain obscure before that – that – inspired, yes, inspired penetration, this true light of femininity.'

The gaze of the dark spectacles in its glossy steadfastness gave his face an air of absolute conviction. Razumov felt a momentary shrinking before that closed door.

'Penetration? Light,' he stammered out. 'Do you mean some sort of thought-reading?'

Peter Ivanovitch seemed shocked.

'I mean something utterly different,' he retorted, with a faint, pitying smile.

Razumov began to feel angry, very much against his wish.

'This is very mysterious,' he muttered through his teeth.

'You don't object to being understood, to being guided?' queried the great feminist.

Razumov exploded in a fierce whisper.

'In what sense? Be pleased to understand that I am a serious person. Who do you take me for?'

They looked at each other very closely. Razumov's temper was cooled by the impenetrable earnestness of the blue glasses meeting his stare. Peter Ivanovitch turned the handle at last.

'You shall know directly,' he said, pushing the door open.

A low-pitched grating voice was heard within the room.

'Enfin. Vous voilà.'*

In the doorway, his black-coated bulk blocking the view, Peter Ivanovitch boomed in a hearty tone with something boastful in it:

'Yes. Here I am!'

He glanced over his shoulder at Razumov, who waited for him to move on.

'And I am bringing you a proved conspirator – a real one this time. *Un vrai celui là.*'

---

* 'At last. Here you are.'

219

This pause in the doorway gave the 'proved conspirator' time to make sure that his face did not betray his angry curiosity and his mental disgust.

These sentiments stand confessed in Mr Razumov's memorandum of his first interview with Madame de S—. The very words I use in my narrative are written where their sincerity cannot be suspected. The record, which could not have been meant for any one's eyes but his own, was not, I think, the outcome of that strange impulse of indiscretion common to men who lead secret lives, and accounting for the invariable existence of 'compromising documents' in all the plots and conspiracies of history. Mr Razumov looked at it, I suppose, as a man looks at himself in a mirror, with wonder, perhaps with anguish, with anger or despair. Yes, as a threatened man may look fearfully at his own face in the glass, formulating to himself reassuring excuses for his appearance marked by the taint of some insidious hereditary disease.

II

The Egeria of the 'Russian Mazzini'[15] produced, at first view, a strong effect by the death-like immobility of an obviously painted face. The eyes appeared extraordinarily brilliant. The figure, in a close-fitting dress, admirably made, but by no means fresh, had an elegant stiffness. The rasping voice inviting him to sit down; the rigidity of the upright attitude with one arm extended along the back of the sofa, the white gleam of the big eyeballs setting off the black, fathomless stare of the enlarged pupils, impressed Razumov more than anything he had seen since his hasty and secret departure from St Petersburg. A witch in Parisian clothes, he thought. A portent! He actually hesitated in his advance, and did not even comprehend, at first, what the rasping voice was saying.

'Sit down. Draw your chair nearer me. There –'

He sat down. At close quarters the rouged cheekbones, the wrinkles, the fine lines on each side of the vivid lips, astounded him. He was being received graciously, with a smile which made him think of a grinning skull.

'We have been hearing about you for some time.'

He did not know what to say, and murmured some disconnected words. The grinning skull effect vanished.

'And do you know that the general complaint is that you have shown yourself very reserved everywhere?'

Razumov remained silent for a time, thinking of his answer.

'I, don't you see, am a man of action,' he said huskily, glancing upwards.

Peter Ivanovitch stood in portentous expectant silence by the side of his chair. A slight feeling of nausea came over Razumov. What could be the relations of these two people to each other? She like a galvanized corpse out of some Hoffman's Tale[16] – he the preacher of feminist gospel for all the world, and a super-revolutionist besides! This ancient, painted mummy with unfathomable eyes, and this burly, bull-necked, deferential . . . what was it? Witchcraft, fascination . . . 'It's for her money,' he thought. 'She has millions!'

The walls, the floor of the room were bare like a barn. The few pieces of furniture had been discovered in the garrets and dragged down into service without having been properly dusted, even. It was the refuse the banker's widow had left behind her. The windows without curtains had an indigent, sleepless look. In two of them the dirty yellowy-white blinds had been pulled down. All this spoke, not of poverty, but of sordid penuriousness.

The hoarse voice on the sofa uttered angrily –

'You are looking round, Kirylo Sidorovitch. I have been shamefully robbed, positively ruined.'

A rattling laugh, which seemed beyond her control, interrupted her for a moment.

'A slavish nature would find consolation in the fact that the principal robber was an exalted and almost a sacrosanct person – a Grand Duke, in fact. Do you understand, Mr Razumov? A Grand Duke – No! You have no idea what thieves those people are! Downright thieves!'

Her bosom heaved, but her left arm remained rigidly extended along the back of the couch.

'You will only upset yourself,' breathed out a deep voice, which, to Razumov's startled glance, seemed to proceed from under the

221

steady spectacles of Peter Ivanovitch, rather than from his lips, which had hardly moved.

'What of that? I say thieves! *Voleurs! Voleurs!*'

Razumov was quite confounded by this unexpected clamour, which had in it something of wailing and croaking, and more than a suspicion of hysteria.

'*Voleurs! Voleurs! Vol . . .*'

'No power on earth can rob you of your genius,' shouted Peter Ivanovitch in an overpowering bass, but without stirring, without a gesture of any kind. A profound silence fell.

Razumov remained outwardly impassive. 'What is the meaning of this performance?' he was asking himself. But with a preliminary sound of bumping outside some door behind him, the lady companion, in a threadbare black skirt and frayed blouse, came in rapidly, walking on her heels, and carrying in both hands a big Russian samovar, obviously too heavy for her. Razumov made an instinctive movement to help which startled her so much that she nearly dropped her hissing burden. She managed, however, to land it on the table, and looked so frightened that Razumov hastened to sit down. She produced then, from an adjacent room, four glass tumblers, a teapot, and a sugar-basin, on a black iron tray.

The rasping voice asked from the sofa abruptly –

'*Les gâteaux?* Have you remembered to bring the cakes?'

Peter Ivanovitch, without a word, marched out on to the landing, and returned instantly with a parcel wrapped up in white glazed paper, which he must have extracted from the interior of his hat. With imperturbable gravity he undid the string and smoothed the paper open on a part of the table within reach of Madame de S—'s hand. The lady companion poured out the tea, then retired into a distant corner out of everybody's sight. From time to time Madame de S— extended a claw-like hand, glittering with costly rings, towards the paper of cakes, took up one and devoured it, displaying her big false teeth ghoulishly. Meantime she talked in a hoarse tone of the political situation in the Balkans. She built great hopes on some complication in the peninsula for arousing a great movement of national indignation in Russia against 'these thieves – thieves – thieves'.

'You will only upset yourself,' Peter Ivanovitch interposed, raising his glassy gaze. He smoked cigarettes and drank tea in silence, continuously. When he had finished a glass, he flourished his hand above his shoulder. At that signal the lady companion, ensconced in her corner, with round eyes like a watchful animal, would dart out to the table and pour him out another tumblerful.

Razumov looked at her once or twice. She was anxious, tremulous, though neither Madame de S— nor Peter Ivanovitch paid the slightest attention to her. 'What have they done between them to that forlorn creature?' Razumov asked himself. 'Have they terrified her out of her sense with ghosts, or simply have they only been beating her?' When she gave him his second glass of tea, he noticed that her lips trembled in the manner of a scared person about to burst into speech. But of course she said nothing, and retired into her corner, as if hugging to herself the smile of thanks he gave her.

'She may be worth cultivating,' thought Razumov suddenly.

He was calming down, getting hold of the actuality into which he had been thrown – for the first time perhaps since Victor Haldin had entered his room . . . and had gone out again. He was distinctly aware of being the object of the famous – or notorious – Madame de S—'s ghastly graciousness.

Madame de S— was pleased to discover that this young man was different from the other types of revolutionist members of committees, secret emissaries, vulgar and unmannerly fugitive professors, rough students, ex-cobblers with apostolic faces, consumptive and ragged enthusiasts, Hebrew youths, common fellows of all sorts that used to come and go around Peter Ivanovitch – fanatics, pedants, proletarians all. It was pleasant to talk to this young man of notably good appearance – for Madame de S— was not always in a mystical state of mind. Razumov's taciturnity only excited her to a quicker, more voluble utterance. It still dealt with the Balkans. She knew all the statesmen of that region, Turks, Bulgarians, Montenegrins, Roumanians, Greeks, Armenians, and nondescripts young and old, the living and the dead. With some money an intrigue could be started which would set the Peninsula in a blaze and outrage the sentiment of the Russian people. A cry of abandoned brothers could be raised, and then, with the nation seething with indignation, a couple of regiments or so would be enough to begin a military revolution in St Petersburg and make an end of these thieves . . .

'Apparently I've got only to sit still and listen,' the silent Razumov thought to himself. 'As to that hairy and obscene brute' (in such terms did Mr Razumov refer mentally to the popular expounder of a feministic conception of social state), 'as to him, for all his cunning he too shall speak out some day.'

Razumov ceased to think for a moment. Then a sombre-toned reflection formulated itself in his mind, ironical and bitter. 'I have the gift of inspiring confidence.' He heard himself laughing aloud. It was like a goad to the painted, shiny-eyed harridan on the sofa.

'You may well laugh!' she cried hoarsely. 'What else can one do! Perfect swindlers – and what base swindlers at that! Cheap Germans – Holstein-Gottorps! Though, indeed, it's hardly safe to say who and what they are. A family that counts a creature like Catherine the Great[17] in its ancestry – you understand!'

'You are only upsetting yourself,' said Peter Ivanovitch, patiently but in a firm tone. This admonition had its usual effect on the Egeria. She dropped her thick, discoloured eyelids and changed her position on the sofa. All her angular and lifeless movements seemed completely automatic now that her eyes were closed. Presently she opened them very full. Peter Ivanovitch drank tea steadily, without haste.

'Well, I declare!' She addressed Razumov directly. 'The people who have seen you on your way here are right. You are very reserved. You haven't said twenty words altogether since you came in. You let nothing of your thoughts be seen in your face either.'

'I have been listening, Madame,' said Razumov, using French for the first time, hesitatingly, not being certain of his accent. But it seemed to produce an excellent impression. Madame de S — looked meaningly into Peter Ivanovitch's spectacles, as if to convey her conviction of this young man's merit. She even nodded the least bit in his direction, and Razumov heard her murmur under her breath the words 'Later on in the diplomatic service,' which could not but refer to the favourable impression he had made. The fantastic absurdity of it revolted him because it seemed to outrage his ruined

224

hopes with the vision of a mock-career. Peter Ivanovitch, impassive as though he were deaf, drank some more tea. Razumov felt that he must say something.

'Yes,' he began deliberately, as if uttering a meditated opinion. 'Clearly. Even in planning a purely military revolution the temper of the people should be taken into account.'

'You have understood me perfectly. The discontent should be spiritualized. That is what the ordinary heads of revolutionary committees will not understand. They aren't capable of it. For instance, Mordatiev was in Geneva last month. Peter Ivanovitch brought him here. You know Mordatiev? Well, yes – you have heard of him. They call him an eagle – a hero! He has never done half as much as you have. Never attempted – not half . . .'

Madame de S — agitated herself angularly on the sofa.

'We, of course, talked to him. And do you know what he said to me? "What have we to do with Balkan intrigues? We must simply extirpate the scoundrels." Extirpate is all very well – but what then? The imbecile! I screamed at him, "But you must spiritualize – don't you understand? – spiritualize the discontent." . . .'

She felt nervously in her pocket for a handkerchief; she pressed it to her lips.

'Spiritualize?' said Razumov interrogatively, watching her heaving breast. The long ends of an old black lace scarf she wore over her head slipped off her shoulders and hung down on each side of her ghastly rosy cheeks.

'An odious creature,' she burst out again. 'Imagine a man who takes five lumps of sugar in his tea . . . Yes, I said spiritualize! How else can you make discontent effective and universal?'

'Listen to this, young man.' Peter Ivanovitch made himself heard solemnly. 'Effective and universal.'

Razumov looked at him suspiciously.

'Some say hunger will do that,' he remarked.

'Yes. I know. Our people are starving in heaps. But you can't make famine universal. And it is not despair that we want to create. There is no moral support to be got out of that. It is indignation . . .'

Madame de S — let her thin, extended arm sink on her knees.

'I am not a Mordatiev,' began Razumov.

225

'*Bien sûr!*'* murmured Madame de S—.

'Though I too am ready to say extirpate, extirpate! But in my ignorance of political work, permit me to ask: A Balkan – well – intrigue, wouldn't that take a very long time?'

Peter Ivanovitch got up and moved off quietly, to stand with his face to the window. Razumov heard a door close; he turned his head and perceived that the lady companion had scuttled out of the room.

'In matters of politics I am a supernaturalist.' Madame de S— broke the silence harshly.

Peter Ivanovitch moved away from the window and struck Razumov lightly on the shoulder. This was a signal for leaving, but at the same time he addressed Madame de S— in a peculiar reminding tone –

'Eleanor!'

Whatever it meant, she did not seem to hear him. She leaned back in the corner of the sofa like a wooden figure. The immovable peevishness of the face, framed in the limp, rusty lace, had a character of cruelty.

'As to extirpating,' she croaked at the attentive Razumov, 'there is only one class in Russia which must be extirpated. Only one. And that class consists of only one family. You understand me? That one family must be extirpated.'

Her rigidity was frightful, like the rigour of a corpse galvanized into harsh speech and glittering stare by the force of murderous hate. The sight fascinated Razumov – yet he felt more self-possessed than at any other time since he had entered this weirdly bare room. He was interested. But the great feminist by his side again uttered his appeal –

'Eleanor!'

She disregarded it. Her carmine lips vaticinated with an extraordinary rapidity. The liberating spirit would use arms before which rivers would part like Jordan, and ramparts fall down like the walls of Jericho. The deliverance from bondage would be effected by plagues and by signs, by wonders and by war. The women ...

'Eleanor!'

* 'To be sure!'

She ceased; she had heard him at last. She pressed her hand to her forehead.

'What is it? Ah yes! That girl – the sister of . . .'

It was Miss Haldin that she meant. That young girl and her mother had been leading a very retired life. They were provincial ladies – were they not? The mother had been very beautiful – traces were left yet. Peter Ivanovitch, when he called there for the first time, was greatly struck . . . But the cold way they received him was really surprising.

'He is one of our national glories,' Madame de S— cried out, with sudden vehemence. 'All the world listens to him.'

'I don't know these ladies,' said Razumov loudly, rising from his chair.

'What are you saying, Kirylo Sidorovitch? I understand that she was talking to you here, in the garden, the other day.'

'Yes, in the garden,' said Razumov gloomily. Then, with an effort, 'She made herself known to me.'

'And then ran away from us all,' Madame de S— continued, with ghastly vivacity. 'After coming to the very door! What a peculiar proceeding! Well, I have been a shy little provincial girl at one time. Yes, Razumov' (she fell into this familiarity intentionally, with an appalling grimace of graciousness. Razumov gave a perceptible start), 'yes, that's my origin. A simple provincial family.'

'You are a marvel,' Peter Ivanovitch uttered in his deepest voice.

But it was to Razumov that she gave her death's-head smile. Her tone was quite imperious.

'You must bring the wild young thing here. She is wanted. I reckon upon your success – mind!'

'She is not a wild young thing,' muttered Razumov, in a surly voice.

'Well, then – that's all the same. She may be one of these young conceited democrats. Do you know what I think? I think she is very much like you in character. There is a smouldering fire of scorn in you. You are darkly self-sufficient, but I can see your very soul.'

Her shiny eyes had a dry, intense stare, which, missing Razumov, gave him an absurd notion that she was looking at something

227

which was visible to her behind him. He cursed himself for an impressionable fool, and asked with forced calmness –

'What is it you see? Anything resembling me?'

She moved her rigidly set face from left to right, negatively.

'Some sort of phantom in my image?' pursued Razumov slowly. 'For, I suppose, a soul when it is seen is just that. A vain thing. There are phantoms of the living as well as of the dead.'

The tenseness of Madame de S—'s stare had relaxed, and now she looked at Razumov in a silence that became disconcerting.

'I myself have had an experience,' he stammered out, as if compelled. 'I've seen a phantom once.'

The unnaturally red lips moved to frame a question harshly.

'Of a dead person?'

'No. Living.'

'A friend?'

'No.'

'An enemy?'

'I hated him.'

'Ah! It was not a woman, then?'

'A woman!' repeated Razumov, his eyes looking straight into the eyes of Madame de S—. 'Why should it have been a woman? And why this conclusion? Why should I not have been able to hate a woman?'

As a matter of fact, the idea of hating a woman was new to him. At that moment he hated Madame de S—. But it was not exactly hate. It was more like the abhorrence that may be caused by a wooden or plaster figure of a repulsive kind. She moved no more than if she were such a figure; even her eyes, whose unwinking stare plunged into his own, though shining, were lifeless, as though they were as artificial as her teeth. For the first time Razumov became aware of a faint perfume, but faint as it was it nauseated him exceedingly. Again Peter Ivanovitch tapped him slightly on the shoulder. Thereupon he bowed, and was about to turn away when he received the unexpected favour of a bony, inanimate hand extended to him, with the two words in hoarse French –

'*Au revoir!*'

He bowed over the skeleton hand and left the room, escorted by the great man, who made him go out first. The voice from the sofa cried after them –

'You remain here, *Pierre*.'

'Certainly, *ma chère amie*.'*

But he left the room with Razumov, shutting the door behind him. The landing was prolonged into a bare corridor, right and left, desolate perspectives of white and gold decoration without a strip of carpet. The very light, pouring through a large window at the end, seemed dusty; and a solitary speck reposing on the balustrade of white marble – the silk top-hat of the great feminist – asserted itself extremely, black and glossy in all that crude whiteness.

Peter Ivanovitch escorted the visitor without opening his lips. Even when they had reached the head of the stairs Peter Ivanovitch did not break the silence. Razumov's impulse to continue down the flight and out of the house without as much as a nod abandoned him suddenly. He stopped on the first step and leaned his back against the wall. Below him the great hall with its chequered floor of black and white seemed absurdly large and like some public place where a great power of resonance awaits the provocation of footfalls and voices. As if afraid of awakening the loud echoes of that empty house, Razumov adopted a low tone.

'I really have no mind to turn into a dilettante spiritualist.'

Peter Ivanovitch shook his head slightly, very serious.

'Or spend my time in spiritual ecstasies or sublime meditations upon the gospel of feminism,' continued Razumov. 'I made my way here for my share of action – action, most respected Peter Ivanovitch! It was not the great European writer who attracted me, here, to this odious town of liberty. It was somebody much greater. It was the idea of the chief which attracted me. There are starving young men in Russia who believe in you so much that it seems the only thing that keeps them alive in their misery. Think of that, Peter Ivanovitch! No! But only think of that!'

The great man, thus entreated, perfectly motionless and silent, was the very image of patient, placid respectability.

'Of course I don't speak of the people. They are brutes,' added

* 'My dear friend.'

Razumov, in the same subdued but forcible tone. At this, a protesting murmur issued from the 'heroic fugitive's' beard. A murmur of
authority.

'Say – children.'

'No! Brutes!' Razumov insisted bluntly.

'But they are sound, they are innocent,' the great man pleaded
in a whisper.

'As far as that goes, a brute is sound enough,' Razumov raised
his voice at last. 'And you can't deny the natural innocence of a
brute. But what's the use of disputing about names? You just try
to give these children the power and stature of men and see what
they will be like. You just give it to them and see . . . But never mind.
I tell you, Peter Ivanovitch, that half a dozen young men do not
come together nowadays in a shabby student's room without your
name being whispered, not as a leader of thought, but as a centre
of revolutionary energies – the centre of action. What else has
drawn me near you, do you think? It is not what all the world knows
of you surely. It's precisely what the world at large does not know.
I was irresistibly drawn – let us say impelled, yes, impelled; or,
rather, compelled, driven – driven,' repeated Razumov loudly, and
ceased, as if startled by the hollow reverberation of the word 'driven'
along two bare corridors and in the great empty hall.

Peter Ivanovitch did not seem startled in the least. The young
man could not control a dry, uneasy laugh. The great revolutionist
remained unmoved with an effect of commonplace, homely
superiority.

'Curse him,' said Razumov to himself, 'he is waiting behind his
spectacles for me to give myself away.' Then aloud, with a satanic
enjoyment of the scorn prompting him to play with the greatness
of the great man –

'Ah, Peter Ivanovitch, if you only knew the force which drew –
no, which *drove* me towards you! The irresistible force.'

He did not feel any desire to laugh now. This time Peter Ivano-
vitch moved his head sideways, knowingly, as much as to say,
'Don't I?' This expressive movement was almost imperceptible.
Razumov went on in secret derision –

'All these days you have been trying to read me, Peter Ivanovitch.

That is natural. I have perceived it and I have been frank. Perhaps you may think I have not been very expansive? But with a man like you it was not needed; it would have looked like an impertinence, perhaps. And besides, we Russians are prone to talk too much as a rule. I have always felt that. And yet, as a nation, we are dumb. I assure you that I am not likely to talk to you so much again – ha! ha! –'

Razumov, still keeping on the lower step, came a little nearer to the great man.

'You have been condescending enough. I quite understood it was to lead me on. You must render me the justice that I have not tried to please. I have been impelled, compelled, or rather sent – let us say sent – towards you for a work that no one but myself can do. You would call it a harmless delusion: a ridiculous delusion at which you don't even smile. It is absurd of me to talk like this, yet some day you will remember these words, I hope. Enough of this. Here I stand before you – confessed! But one thing more I must add to complete it: a mere blind tool I can never consent to be.'

Whatever acknowledgement Razumov was prepared for, he was not prepared to have both his hands seized in the great man's grasp. The swiftness of the movement was aggressive enough to startle. The burly feminist could not have been quicker had his purpose been to jerk Razumov treacherously up on the landing and bundle him behind one of the numerous closed doors near by. This idea actually occurred to Razumov; his hands being released after a darkly eloquent squeeze, he smiled, with a beating heart, straight at the beard and the spectacles hiding that impenetrable man.

He thought to himself (it stands confessed in his handwriting), 'I won't move from here till he either speaks or turns away. This is a duel.' Many seconds passed without a sign or sound.

'Yes, yes,' the great man said hurriedly, in subdued tones, as if the whole thing had been a stolen, breathless interview. 'Exactly. Come to see us here in a few days. This must be gone into deeply – deeply, between you and me. Quite to the bottom. To the ... And, by the by, you must bring along Natalia Victorovna – you know, the Haldin girl ...'

'Am I to take this as my first instruction from you?' inquired Razumov stiffly.

Peter Ivanovitch seemed perplexed by this new attitude.

'Ah! h'm! You are naturally the proper person – *la personne indiquée*.* Everyone shall be wanted presently. Everyone.'

He bent down from the landing over Razumov, who had lowered his eyes.

'The moment of action approaches,' he murmured.

Razumov did not look up. He did not move till he heard the door of the drawing-room close behind the greatest of feminists returning to his painted Egeria. Then he walked down slowly into the hall. The door stood open, and the shadow of the house was lying aslant over the greatest part of the terrace. While crossing it slowly, he lifted his hat and wiped his damp forehead, expelling his breath with force to get rid of the last vestiges of the air he had been breathing inside. He looked at the palms of his hands, and rubbed them gently against his thighs.

He felt, bizarre as it may seem, as though another self, an independent sharer of his mind, had been able to view his whole person very distinctly indeed. 'This is curious,' he thought. After a while he formulated his opinion of it in the mental ejaculation: 'Beastly!' This disgust vanished before a marked uneasiness. 'This is an effect of nervous exhaustion,' he reflected with weary sagacity. 'How am I to go on day after day if I have no more power of resistance – moral resistance?'

He followed the path at the foot of the terrace. 'Moral resistance, moral resistance'; he kept on repeating these words mentally. Moral endurance. Yes, that was the necessity of the situation. An immense longing to make his way out of these grounds and to the other end of the town, of throwing himself on his bed and going to sleep for hours, swept everything clean out of his mind for a moment. 'Is it possible that I am but a weak creature after all?' he asked himself in sudden alarm. 'Eh! What's that?'

He gave a start as if awakened from a dream. He even swayed a little before recovering himself.

* 'The appointed person.'

232

'Ah! You stole away from us quietly to walk about here,' he said.

The lady companion stood before him, but how she came there he had not the slightest idea. Her folded arms were closely cherishing the cat.

'I have been unconscious as I walked, it's a positive fact,' said Razumov to himself in wonder. He raised his hat with marked civility.

The sallow woman blushed duskily. She had her invariably scared expression, as if somebody had just disclosed to her some terrible news. But she held her ground, Razumov noticed, without timidity. 'She is incredibly shabby,' he thought. In the sunlight her black costume looked greenish, with here and there threadbare patches where the stuff seemed decomposed by age into a velvety, black, furry state. Her very hair and eyebrows looked shabby. Razumov wondered whether she were sixty years old. Her figure, though, was young enough. He observed that she did not appear starved, but rather as if she had been fed on unwholesome scraps and leavings of plates.

Razumov smiled amiably and moved out of her way. She turned her head to keep her scared eyes on him.

'I know what you have been told in there,' she affirmed, without preliminaries. Her tone, in contrast with her manner, had an unexpectedly assured character which put Razumov at his ease.

'Do you? You must have heard all sorts of talk on many occasions in there.'

She varied her phrase, with the same incongruous effect of positiveness.

'I know to a certainty what you have been told to do.'

'Really?' Razumov shrugged his shoulders a little. He was about to pass on with a bow, when a sudden thought struck him. 'Yes. To be sure! In your confidential position you are aware of many things,' he murmured, looking at the cat.

That animal got a momentary convulsive hug from the lady companion.

'Everything was disclosed to me a long time ago,' she said.

'Everything,' Razumov repeated absently.

'Peter Ivanovitch is an awful despot,' she jerked out.

Razumov went on studying the stripes on the grey fur of the cat.

'An iron will is an integral part of such a temperament. How else could he be a leader? And I think that you are mistaken in –'

'There!' she cried. 'You tell me that I am mistaken. But I tell you all the same that he cares for no one.' She jerked her head up. 'Don't you bring that girl here. That's what you have been told to do – to bring that girl here. Listen to me; you had better tie a stone round her neck and throw her into the lake.'

Razumov had a sensation of chill and gloom, as if a heavy cloud had passed over the sun.

'The girl?' he said. 'What have I to do with her?'

'But you have been told to bring Nathalie Haldin here. Am I not right? Of course I am right. I was not in the room, but I know. I know Peter Ivanovitch sufficiently well. He is a great man. Great men are horrible. Well, that's it. Have nothing to do with her. That's the best you can do, unless you want her to become like me – disillusioned! Disillusioned!'

'Like you,' repeated Razumov, glaring at her face, as devoid of all comeliness of feature and complexion as the most miserable beggar is of money. He smiled, still feeling chilly: a peculiar sensation which annoyed him. 'Disillusioned as to Peter Ivanovitch! Is that all you have lost?'

She declared, looking frightened, but with immense conviction, 'Peter Ivanovitch stands for everything.' Then she added, in another tone, 'Keep the girl away from this house.'

'And are you absolutely inciting me to disobey Peter Ivanovitch just because – because you are disillusioned?'

She began to blink.

'Directly I saw you for the first time I was comforted. You took your hat off to me. You looked as if one could trust you. Oh!'

She shrank before Razumov's savage snarl of, 'I have heard something like this before.'

She was so confounded that she could do nothing but blink for a long time.

'It was your human manner,' she explained plaintively. 'I have been starving for, I won't say kindness, but just for a little civility, for I don't know how long. And now you are angry ...'

234

'But no, on the contrary,' he protested. 'I am very glad you trust me. It's possible that later on I may ...'

'Yes, if you were to get ill,' she interrupted eagerly, 'or meet some bitter trouble, you would find I am not a useless fool. You have only to let me know. I will come to you. I will indeed. And I will stick to you. Misery and I are old acquaintances – but this life here is worse than starving.'

She paused anxiously, then in a voice for the first time sounding really timid, she added –

'Or if you were engaged in some dangerous work. Sometimes a humble companion – I would not want to know anything. I would follow you with joy. I could carry out orders. I have the courage.'

Razumov looked attentively at the scared round eyes, at the withered, sallow, round cheeks. They were quivering about the corners of the mouth.

'She wants to escape from here,' he thought.

'Suppose I were to tell you that I am engaged in dangerous work?' he uttered slowly.

She pressed the cat to her threadbare bosom with a breathless exclamation. 'Ah!' Then not much above a whisper: 'Under Peter Ivanovitch?'

'No, not under Peter Ivanovitch.'

He read admiration in her eyes, and made an effort to smile.

'Then – alone?'

He held up his closed hand with the index raised.

'Like this finger,' he said.

She was trembling slightly. But it occurred to Razumov that they might have been observed from the house, and he became anxious to be gone. She blinked, raising up to him her puckered face, and seemed to beg mutely to be told something more, to be given a word of encouragement for her starving, grotesque, and pathetic devotion.

'Can we be seen from the house?' asked Razumov confidentially.

She answered, without showing the slightest surprise at the question –

'No, we can't, on account of this end of the stables.' And she added, with an acuteness which surprised Razumov, 'But anybody

235

looking out of an upstairs window would know that you have not passed through the gates yet.'

'Who's likely to spy out of the window?' queried Razumov. 'Peter Ivanovitch?'

She nodded.

'Why should he trouble his head?'

'He expects somebody this afternoon.'

'You know the person?'

'There's more than one.'

She had lowered her eyelids. Razumov looked at her curiously.

'Of course. You hear everything they say.'

She murmured without any animosity –

'So do the tables and chairs.'

He understood that the bitterness accumulated in the heart of that helpless creature had got into her veins and, like some subtle poison, had decomposed her fidelity to that hateful pair. It was a great piece of luck for him, he reflected; because women are seldom venal after the manner of men, who can be bought for material considerations. She would be a good ally, though it was not likely that she was allowed to hear as much as the tables and chairs of the Château Borel. That could not be expected. But still ... And, at any rate, she could be made to talk.

When she looked up her eyes met the fixed stare of Razumov, who began to speak at once.

'Well, well, dear ... but upon my word, I haven't the pleasure of knowing your name yet. Isn't it strange?'

For the first time she made a movement of the shoulders.

'Is it strange? No one is told my name. No one cares. No one talks to me, no one writes to me. My parents don't even know if I'm alive. I have no use for a name, and I have almost forgotten it myself.'

Razumov murmured gravely, 'Yes, but still ...'

She went on much slower, with indifference –

'You may call me Tekla, then. My poor Andrei called me so. I was devoted to him. He lived in wretchedness and suffering, and died in misery. That is the lot of all us Russians, nameless Russians. There is nothing else for us, and no hope anywhere, unless ...'

'Unless what?'

'Unless all these people with names are done away with,' she finished, blinking and pursing up her lips.

'It will be easier to call you Tekla, as you direct me,' said Razumov, 'if you consent to call me Kirylo, when we are talking like this – quietly – only you and me.'

And he said to himself, 'Here's a being who must be terribly afraid of the world, else she would have run away from this situation before.' Then he reflected that the mere fact of leaving the great man abruptly would make her a suspect. She could expect no support or countenance from any one. This revolutionist was not fit for an independent existence.

She moved with him a few steps, blinking and nursing the cat with a small balancing movement of her arms.

'Yes – only you and I. That's how I was with my poor Andrei, only he was dying, killed by these official brutes – while you! You are strong. You kill the monsters. You have done a great deed. Peter Ivanovitch himself must consider you. Well – don't forget me – especially if you are going back to work in Russia. I could follow you, carrying anything that was wanted – at a distance, you know. Or I could watch for hours at the corner of a street if necessary – in wet or snow – yes, I could – all day long. Or I could write for you dangerous documents, lists of names or instructions, so that in case of mischance the handwriting could not compromise you. And you need not be afraid if they were to catch me. I would know how to keep dumb. We women are not so easily daunted by pain. I heard Peter Ivanovitch say it is our blunt nerves or something. We can stand it better. And it's true; I would just as soon bite my tongue out and throw it at them as not. What's the good of speech to me? Who would ever want to hear what I could say? Ever since I closed the eyes of my poor Andrei I haven't met a man who seemed to care for the sound of my voice. I should never have spoken to you if the very first time you appeared here you had not taken notice of me so nicely. I could not help speaking of you to that charming dear girl. Oh, the sweet creature! And strong! One can see that at once. If you have a heart don't let her set her foot in here. Goodbye!'

Razumov caught her by the arm. Her emotion at being thus

seized manifested itself by a short struggle, after which she stood still, not looking at him.

'But you can tell me.' he spoke in her ear, 'why they – these people in that house there – are so anxious to get hold of her?'

She freed herself to turn upon him, as if made angry by the question.

'Don't you understand that Peter Ivanovitch must direct, inspire, influence? It is the breath of his life. There can never be too many disciples. He can't bear thinking of any one escaping him. And a woman, too! There is nothing to be done without women, he says. He has written it. He –'

The young man was staring at her passion when she broke off suddenly and ran away behind the stable.

III

Razumov, thus left to himself, took the direction of the gate. But on this day of many conversations, he discovered that very probably he could not leave the grounds without having to hold another one.

Stepping in view from beyond the lodge appeared the expected visitors of Peter Ivanovitch: a small party composed of two men and a woman. They noticed him too, immediately, and stopped short as if to consult. But in a moment the woman, moving aside, motioned with her arm to the two men, who, leaving the drive at once, struck across the large neglected lawn, or rather grass-plot, and made directly for the house. The woman remained on the path waiting for Razumov's approach. She had recognized him. He, too, had recognized her at the first glance. He had been made known to her at Zürich, where he had broken his journey while on his way from Dresden. They had been much together for the two days of his stay.

She was wearing the very same costume in which he had seen her first. A blouse of crimson silk made her noticeable at a distance. With that she wore a short brown skirt and a leather belt. Her complexion was the colour of coffee and milk, but very clear; her

238

eyes black and glittering, her figure erect. A lot of thick hair, nearly white, was done up loosely under a dusty Tyrolese hat of dark cloth, which seemed to have lost some of its trimmings.

The expression of her face was grave, intent; so grave that Razumov, after approaching her close, felt obliged to smile. She greeted him with a manly handgrasp.

'What! Are you going away?' she exclaimed. 'How is that, Razumov?'

'I am going away because I haven't been asked to stay,' Razumov answered, returning the pressure of her hand with much less force than she had put into it.

She jerked her head sideways like one who understands. Meantime Razumov's eyes had strayed after the two men. They were crossing the grass-plot obliquely, without haste. The shorter of the two was buttoned up in a narrow overcoat of some thin grey material, which came nearly to his heels. His companion, much taller and broader, wore a short, close-fitting jacket and tight trousers tucked into shabby top-boots.

The woman, who had sent them out of Razumov's way apparently, spoke in a businesslike voice.

'I had to come rushing from Zürich on purpose to meet the train and take these two along here to see Peter Ivanovitch. I've just managed it.'

'Ah! indeed,' Razumov said perfunctorily, and very vexed at her staying behind to talk to him. 'From Zürich – yes, of course. And these two, they come from ...'

She interrupted, without emphasis –

'From quite another direction. From a distance, too. A considerable distance.'

Razumov shrugged his shoulders. The two men from a distance, after having reached the wall of the terrace, disappeared suddenly at its foot as if the earth had opened to swallow them up.

'Oh, well, they have just come from America.' The woman in the crimson blouse shrugged her shoulders too a little before making that statement. 'The time is drawing near,' she interjected, as if

239

speaking to herself. 'I did not tell them who you were. Yakovlitch would have wanted to embrace you.'

'Is that he with the wisp of hair hanging from his chin, in the long coat?'

'You've guessed aright. That's Yakovlitch.'

'And they could not find their way here from the station without you coming on purpose from Zürich to show it to them? Verily, without women we can do nothing. So it stands written, and apparently so it is.'

He was conscious of an immense lassitude under his effort to be sarcastic. And he could see that she had detected it with those steady, brilliant black eyes.

'What is the matter with you?'

'I don't know. Nothing. I've had a devil of a day.'

She waited, with her black eyes fixed on his face. Then –

'What of that? You men are so impressionable and self-conscious. One day is like another, hard, hard – and there's an end of it, till the great day comes. I came over for a very good reason. They wrote to warn Peter Ivanovitch of their arrival. But where from? Only from Cherbourg on a bit of ship's notepaper. Anybody could have done that. Yakovlitch has lived for years and years in America. I am the only one at hand who had known him well in the old days. I knew him very well indeed. So Peter Ivanovitch telegraphed, asking me to come. It's natural enough, is it not?'

'You came to vouch for his identity?' inquired Razumov.

'Yes. Something of the kind. Fifteen years of a life like his make changes in a man. Lonely, like a crow in a strange country. When I think of Yakovlitch before he went to America –'

The softness of the low tone caused Razumov to glance at her sideways. She sighed; her black eyes were looking away; she had plunged the fingers of her right hand deep into the mass of nearly white hair, and stirred them there absently. When she withdrew her hand the little hat perched on the top of her head remained slightly tilted, with a queer inquisitive effect, contrasting strongly with the reminiscent murmur that escaped her.

'We were not in our first youth even then. But a man is a child always.'

Razumov thought suddenly, 'They have been living together.'
Then aloud –

'Why didn't you follow him to America?' he asked point-blank.

She looked up at him with a perturbed air.

'Don't you remember what was going on fifteen years ago? It was
a time of activity. The Revolution has its history by this time. You
are in it and yet you don't seem to know it. Yakovlitch went away
then on a mission; I went back to Russia. It had to be so. Afterwards
there was nothing for him to come back to.'

'Ah! indeed,' muttered Razumov, with affected surprise. 'Nothing!'

'What are you trying to insinuate?' she exclaimed quickly. 'Well,
and what then if he did get discouraged a little . . .'

'He looks like a Yankee, with that goatee hanging from his chin.
A regular Uncle Sam,' growled Razumov. 'Well, and you? You who
went to Russia? You did not get discouraged.'

'Never mind. Yakovlitch is a man who cannot be doubted. He,
at any rate, is the right sort.'

Her black, penetrating gaze remained fixed upon Razumov while
she spoke, and for a moment afterwards.

'Pardon me,' Razumov inquired coldly, 'but does it mean that
you, for instance, think that I am not the right sort?'

She made no protest, gave no sign of having heard the question;
she continued looking at him in a manner which he judged not to
be absolutely unfriendly. In Zürich when he passed through she had
taken him under her charge, in a way, and was with him from
morning till night during his stay of two days. She took him round
to see several people. At first she talked to him a great deal and
rather unreservedly, but always avoided all reference to herself:
towards the middle of the second day she fell silent, attending him
zealously as before, and even seeing him off at the railway station,
where she pressed his hand firmly through the lowered carriage
window, and, stepping back without a word, waited till the train
moved. He had noticed that she was treated with quiet regard. He
knew nothing of her parentage, nothing of her private history or
political record; he judged her from his own private point of view,
as being a distinct danger in his path. 'Judged' is not perhaps the

right word. It was more of a feeling, the summing up of slight impressions aided by the discovery that he could not despise her as he despised all the others. He had not expected to see her again so soon.

No, decidedly; her expression was not unfriendly. Yet he perceived an acceleration in the beat of his heart. The conversation could not be abandoned at that point. He went on in accents of scrupulous inquiry –

'Is it perhaps because I don't seem to accept blindly every development of the general doctrine – such for instance as the feminism of our great Peter Ivanovitch? If that is what makes me suspect, then I can only say I would scorn to be a slave even to an idea.'

She had been looking at him all the time, not as a listener looks at one, but as if the words he chose to say were only of secondary interest. When he finished she slipped her hand, by a sudden and decided movement, under his arm and impelled him gently towards the gate of the grounds. He felt her firmness and obeyed the impulsion at once, just as the other two men had, a moment before, obeyed unquestioningly the wave of her hand.

They made a few steps like this.

'No, Razumov, your ideas are probably all right,' she said. 'You may be valuable – very valuable. What's the matter with you is that you don't like us.'

She released him. He met her with a frosty smile.

'Am I expected then to have love as well as convictions?'

She shrugged her shoulders.

'You know very well what I mean. People have been thinking you not quite whole-hearted. I have heard that opinion from one side and another. But I have understood you at the end of the first day . . .'

Razumov interrupted her, speaking steadily.

'I assure you that your perspicacity is at fault here.'

'What phrases he uses!' she exclaimed parenthetically. 'Ah! Kirylo Sidorovitch, you like other men are fastidious, full of self-love and afraid of trifles. Moreover, you had no training. What you want is to be taken in hand by some woman. I am sorry I am not staying here a few days. I am going back to Zürich tomorrow, and shall take Yakovlitch with me most likely.'

This information relieved Razumov.

'I am sorry too,' he said. 'But, all the same, I don't think you understand me.'

He breathed more freely; she did not protest, but asked, 'And how did you get on with Peter Ivanovitch? You have seen a good deal of each other. How is it between you two?'

Not knowing what answer to make, the young man inclined his head slowly.

Her lips had been parted in expectation. She pressed them together, and seemed to reflect.

'That's all right.'

This had a sound of finality, but she did not leave him. It was impossible to guess what she had in her mind. Razumov muttered –

'It is not of me that you should have asked that question. In a moment you shall see Peter Ivanovitch himself, and the subject will come up naturally. He will be curious to know what has delayed you so long in this garden.'

'No doubt Peter Ivanovitch will have something to say to me. Several things. He may even speak of you – question me. Peter Ivanovitch is inclined to trust me generally.'

'Question you? That's very likely.'

She smiled, half serious.

'Well – and what shall I say to him?'

'I don't know. You may tell him of your discovery.'

'What's that?'

'Why – my lack of love for . . .'

'Oh! That's between ourselves,' she interrupted, it was hard to say whether in jest or earnest.

'I see that you want to tell Peter Ivanovitch something in my favour,' said Razumov, with grim playfulness. 'Well, then, you can tell him that I am very much in earnest about my mission. I mean to succeed.'

'You have been given a mission!' she exclaimed quickly.

'It amounts to that. I have been told to bring about a certain event.'

She looked at him searchingly.

'A mission,' she repeated, very grave and interested all at once. 'What sort of mission?'

'Something in the nature of propaganda work.'

'Ah! Far away from here?'

'No. Not very far,' said Razumov, restraining a sudden desire to laugh, though he did not feel joyous in the least.

'So!' she said thoughtfully. 'Well, I am not asking questions. It's sufficient that Peter Ivanovitch should know what each of us is doing. Everything is bound to come right in the end.'

'You think so?'

'I don't think, young man. I just simply believe it.'

'And is it to Peter Ivanovitch that you owe that faith?'

She did not answer the question, and they stood idle, silent, as if reluctant to part with each other.

'That's just like a man,' she murmured at last. 'As if it were possible to tell how a belief comes to one.' Her thin Mephistophelian eyebrows moved a little. 'Truly there are millions of people in Russia who would envy the life of dogs in this country. It is a horror and a shame to confess this even between ourselves. One must believe for very pity. This can't go on. No! It can't go on. For twenty years I have been coming and going, looking neither to the left nor to the right ... What are you smiling to yourself for? You are only at the beginning. You have begun well, but you just wait till you have trodden every particle of yourself under your feet in your comings and goings. For that is what it comes to. You've got to trample down every particle of your own feelings; for stop you cannot, you must not. I have been young, too – but perhaps you think that I am complaining – eh?'

'I don't think anything of the sort,' protested Razumov indifferently.

'I dare say you don't, you dear superior creature. You don't care.'

She plunged her fingers into the bunch of hair on the left side, and that brusque movement had the effect of setting the Tyrolese hat straight on her head. She frowned under it without animosity, in the manner of an investigator. Razumov averted his face carelessly.

'You men are all alike. You mistake luck for merit. You do it in good faith too! I would not be too hard on you. It's masculine nature. You men are ridiculously pitiful in your aptitude to cherish childish illusions down to the very grave. There are a lot of us who have been at work for fifteen years – I mean constantly – trying one way after another, underground and above ground, looking neither to the right nor to the left! I can talk about it. I have been one of these that never rested . . . There! What's the use of talking . . . Look at my grey hairs! And here two babies come along – I mean you and Haldin – you come along and manage to strike a blow at the very first try.'

At the name of Haldin falling from the rapid and energetic lips of the woman revolutionist, Razumov had the usual brusque consciousness of the irrevocable. But in all the months which had passed over his head he had become hardened to the experience. The consciousness was no longer accompanied by the blank dismay and the blind anger of the early days. He had argued himself into new beliefs; and he had made for himself a mental atmosphere of gloomy and sardonic reverie, a sort of murky medium through which the event appeared like a featureless shadow having vaguely the shape of a man; a shape extremely familiar, yet utterly inexpressive, except for its air of discreet waiting in the dusk. It was not alarming.

'What was *he* like?' the woman revolutionist asked unexpectedly.

'What was he like?' echoed Razumov, making a painful effort not to turn upon her savagely. But he relieved himself by laughing a little while he stole a glance at her out of the corners of his eyes. This reception of her inquiry disturbed her.

'How like a woman,' he went on. 'What is the good of concerning yourself with his appearance? Whatever it was, he is removed beyond all feminine influences now.'

A frown, making three folds at the root of her nose, accentuated the Mephistophelian slant of her eyebrows.

'You suffer, Razumov,' she suggested, in her low, confident voice.

'What nonsense!' Razumov faced the woman fairly. 'But now I think of it, I am not sure that he is beyond the influence of one woman at least; the one over there – Madame de S——, you know.

Formerly the dead were allowed to rest, but now it seems they are at the beck and call of a crazy old harridan. We revolutionists make wonderful discoveries. It is true that they are not exactly our own. We have nothing of our own. But couldn't the friend of Peter Ivanovitch satisfy your feminine curiosity? Couldn't she conjure him up for you?' – he jested like a man in pain.

Her concentrated frowning expression relaxed, and she said, a little wearily, 'Let us hope she will make an effort and conjure up some tea for us. But that is by no means certain. I am tired, Razumov.'

'You tired! What a confession! Well, there has been tea up there. I had some. If you hurry on after Yakovlitch, instead of wasting your time with such an unsatisfactory sceptical person as myself, you may find the ghost of it – the cold ghost of it – still lingering in the temple. But as to you being tired I can hardly believe it. We are not supposed to be. We mustn't. We can't. The other day I read in some paper or other an alarmist article on the tireless activity of the revolutionary parties. It impresses the world. It's our prestige.'

'He flings out continually these flouts and sneers'; the woman in the crimson blouse spoke as if appealing quietly to a third person, but her black eyes never left Razumov's face. 'And what for, pray? Simply because some of his conventional notions are shocked, some of his petty masculine standards. You might think he was one of these nervous sensitives that come to a bad end. And yet,' she went on, after a short, reflective pause and changing the mode of her address, 'and yet I have just learned something which makes me think that you are a man of character, Kirylo Sidorovitch. Yes! indeed – you are.'

The mysterious positiveness of this assertion startled Razumov. Their eyes met. He looked away and, through the bars of the rusty gate, stared at the clean, wide road shaded by the leafy trees. An electric tramcar, quite empty, ran along the avenue with a metallic rustle. It seemed to him he would have given anything to be sitting inside all alone. He was inexpressibly weary, weary in every fibre of his body, but he had a reason for not being the first to break off the conversation. At any instant, in the visionary and criminal babble of revolutionists, some momentous words might fall on his ear; from her lips, from anybody's lips. As long as he managed to preserve a clear mind and to keep down his irritability there was nothing to fear. The only condition of success and safety was indomitable will-power, he reminded himself.

He longed to be on the other side of the bars, as though he were actually a prisoner within the grounds of this centre of revolutionary plots, of this house of folly, of blindness, of villainy and crime. Silently he indulged his wounded spirit in a feeling of immense moral and mental remoteness. He did not even smile when he heard her repeat the words –

'Yes! A strong character.'

He continued to gaze through the bars like a moody prisoner, not thinking of escape, but merely pondering upon the faded memories of freedom.

'If you don't look out,' he mumbled, still looking away, 'you will certainly miss seeing as much as the mere ghost of that tea.'

She was not to be shaken off in such a way. As a matter of fact he had not expected to succeed.

'Never mind, it will be no great loss. I mean the missing of her tea and only the ghost of it at that. As to the lady, you must understand that she has her positive uses. See *that*, Razumov.'

He turned his head at this imperative appeal and saw the woman revolutionist making the motions of counting money into the palm of her hand.

'That's what it is. You see?'

Razumov uttered a slow 'I see,' and returned to his prisoner-like gazing upon the neat and shady road.

'Material means must be obtained in some way, and this is easier than breaking into banks. More certain too. There! I am joking . . . What is he muttering to himself now?' she cried under her breath.

'My admiration of Peter Ivanovitch's devoted self-sacrifice, that's all. It's enough to make one sick.'

'Oh, you squeamish, masculine creature. Sick! Makes him sick! And what do you know of the truth of it? There's no looking into the secrets of the heart. Peter Ivanovitch knew her years ago, in his worldly days, when he was a young officer in the Guards. It is not for us to judge an inspired person. That's where you men have an

247

advantage. You are inspired sometimes both in thought and action. I have always admitted that when you *are* inspired, when you manage to throw off your masculine cowardice and prudishness you are not to be equalled by us. Only, how seldom . . . Whereas the silliest woman can always be made of use. And why? Because we have passion, unappeasable passion . . . I should like to know what he is smiling at?'

'I am not smiling,' protested Razumov gloomily.

'Well! How is one to call it? You made some sort of face. Yes, I know! You men can love here and hate there and desire something or other – and you make a great to-do about it, and you call it passion! Yes! While it lasts. But we women are in love with love, and with hate, with these very things I tell you, and with desire itself. That's why we can't be bribed off so easily as you men. In life, you see, there is not much choice. You have either to rot or to burn. And there is not one of us, painted or unpainted, that would not rather burn than rot.'

She spoke with energy, but in a matter-of-fact tone. Razumov's attention had wandered away on a track of its own – outside the bars of the gate – but not out of earshot. He stuck his hands into the pockets of his coat.

'Rot or burn! Powerfully stated. Painted or unpainted. Very vigorous. Painted or . . . Do tell me – she would be infernally jealous of him, wouldn't she?'

'Who? What? The Baroness? Eleanor Maximovna? Jealous of Peter Ivanovitch? Heavens! Are these the questions the man's mind is running on? Such a thing is not to be thought of.'

'Why? Can't a wealthy old woman be jealous? Or, are they all pure spirits together?'

'But what put it into your head to ask such a question?' she wondered.

'Nothing. I just asked. Masculine frivolity, if you like.'

'I don't like,' she retorted at once. 'It is not the time to be frivolous. What are you flinging your very heart against? Or, perhaps, you are only playing a part.'

Razumov had felt that woman's observation of him like a physical contact, like a hand resting lightly on his shoulder. At that moment he received the mysterious impression of her having made up her mind for a closer grip. He stiffened himself inwardly to bear it without betraying himself.

'Playing a part,' he repeated, presenting to her an unmoved profile. 'It must be done very badly since you see through the assumption.'

She watched him, her forehead drawn into perpendicular folds, the thin black eyebrows diverging upwards like the antennae of an insect. He added hardly audibly –

'You are mistaken. I am doing it no more than the rest of us.'

'Who is doing it?' she snapped out.

'Who? Everybody,' he said impatiently. 'You are a materialist, aren't you?'

'Eh! My dear soul, I have outlived all that nonsense.'

'But you must remember the definition of Cabanis: "Man is a digestive tube." I imagine now . . .'

'I spit on him.'

'What? On Cabanis? All right. But you can't ignore the importance of a good digestion. The joy of life – you know the joy of life? – depends on a sound stomach, whereas a bad digestion inclines one to scepticism, breeds black fancies and thoughts of death. These are facts ascertained by physiologists. Well, I assure you that ever since I came over from Russia I have been stuffed with indigestible foreign concoctions of the most nauseating kind – pah!'

'You are joking,' she murmured incredulously. He assented in a detached way.

'Yes. It is all a joke. It's hardly worth while talking to a man like me. Yet for that very reason men have been known to take their own life.'

'On the contrary, I think it *is* worth while talking to you.'

He kept her in the corner of his eye. She seemed to be thinking out some scathing retort, but ended by only shrugging her shoulders slightly.

'Shallow talk! I suppose one must pardon this weakness in you,' she said, putting a special accent on the last word. There was something anxious in her indulgent conclusion.

Razumov noted the slightest shades in this conversation, which

249

he had not expected, for which he was not prepared. That was it. 'I was not prepared,' he said to himself. 'It has taken me unawares.' It seemed to him that if he only could allow himself to pant openly like a dog for a time this oppression would pass away. 'I shall never be found prepared,' he thought, with despair. He laughed a little, saying as lightly as he could –

'Thanks. I don't ask for mercy.' Then affecting a playful uneasiness, 'But aren't you afraid Peter Ivanovitch might suspect us of plotting something unauthorized together by the gate here?'

'No, I am not afraid. You are quite safe from suspicions while you are with me, my dear young man.' The humorous gleam in her black eyes went out. 'Peter Ivanovitch trusts me,' she went on, quite austerely. 'He takes my advice. I am his right hand, as it were, in certain most important things ... That amuses you – what? Do you think I am boasting?'

'God forbid. I was just only saying to myself that Peter Ivanovitch seems to have solved the woman question pretty completely.'

Even as he spoke he reproached himself for his words, for his tone. All day long he had been saying the wrong things. It was folly, worse than folly. It was weakness: it was this disease of perversity overcoming his will. Was this the way to meet speeches which certainly contained the promise of future confidences from that woman who apparently had a great store of secret knowledge and so much influence? Why give her this puzzling impression? But she did not seem inimical. There was no anger in her voice. It was strangely speculative.

'One does not know what to think, Razumov. You must have bitten something bitter in your cradle.'

Razumov gave her a sidelong glance.

'H'm! Something bitter? That's an explanation,' he muttered. 'Only it was much later. And don't you think, Sophia Antonovna, that you and I come from the same cradle?'

The woman, whose name he had forced himself at last to pronounce (he had experienced a strong repugnance in letting it pass his lips), the woman revolutionist murmured, after a pause –

'You mean – Russia?'

He disdained even to nod. She seemed softened, her black eyes very still, as though she were pursuing the simile in her thoughts to all its tender association. But suddenly she knitted her brows in a Mephistophelian frown.

'Yes. Perhaps no wonder, then. Yes. One lies there lapped up in evils, watched over by beings that are worse than ogres, ghouls, and vampires. They must be driven away, destroyed utterly. In regard of that task nothing else matters if men and women are determined and faithful. That's how I came to feel in the end. The great thing is not to quarrel amongst ourselves about all sorts of conventional trifles. Remember that, Razumov.'

Razumov was not listening. He had even lost the sense of being watched in a sort of heavy tranquillity. His uneasiness, his exasperation, his scorn were blunted at last by all these trying hours. It seemed to him that now they were blunted for ever. 'I am a match for them all,' he thought, with a conviction too firm to be exulting. The woman revolutionist had ceased speaking; he was not looking at her; there was no one passing along the road. He almost forgot that he was not alone. He heard her voice again, curt, businesslike, and yet betraying the hesitation which had been the real reason of her prolonged silence.

'I say, Razumov!'

Razumov, whose face was turned away from her, made a grimace like a man who hears a false note.

'Tell me: is it true that on the very morning of the deed you actually attended the lectures at the University?'

An appreciable fraction of a second elapsed before the real import of the question reached him, like a bullet which strikes some time after the flash of the fired shot. Luckily his disengaged hand was ready to grip a bar of the gate. He held it with a terrible force, but his presence of mind was gone. He could make only a sort of gurgling, grumpy sound.

'Come, Kirylo Sidorovitch!' she urged him. 'I know you are not a boastful man. *That* one must say for you. You are a silent man. Too silent, perhaps. You are feeding on some bitterness of your own. You are not an enthusiast. You are, perhaps, all the stronger for that. But you might tell me. One would like to understand you a little more. I was so immensely struck . . . Have you really done it?'

He got his voice back. The shot had missed him. It had been fired at random, altogether, more like a signal for coming to close quarters. It was to be a plain struggle for self-preservation. And she was a dangerous adversary too. But he was ready for battle; he was so ready that when he turned towards her not a muscle of his face moved.

'Certainly,' he said, without animation, secretly strung up but perfectly sure of himself. 'Lectures – certainly. But what makes you ask?'

It was she who was animated.

'I had it in a letter, written by a young man in Petersburg; one of us, of course. You were seen – you were observed with your notebook, impassible, taking notes ...'

He enveloped her with his fixed stare.

'What of that?'

'I call such coolness superb – that's all. It is a proof of uncommon strength of character. The young man writes that nobody could have guessed from your face and manner the part you had played only some two hours before – the great, momentous, glorious part ...'

'Oh no. Nobody could have guessed,' assented Razumov gravely, 'because, don't you see, nobody at that time ...'

'Yes, yes. But all the same you are a man of exceptional fortitude, it seems. You looked exactly as usual. It was remembered afterwards with wonder ...'

'It cost me no effort,' Razumov declared, with the same staring gravity.

'Then it's almost more wonderful still!' she exclaimed, and fell silent while Razumov asked himself whether he had not said there something utterly unnecessary – or even worse.

She raised her head eagerly.

'Your intention was to stay in Russia? You had planned ...'

'No,' interrupted Razumov without haste. 'I had made no plans of any sort.'

'You just simply walked away?' she struck in.

He bowed his head in slow assent. 'Simply – yes.' He had gradually released his hold on the bar of the gate, as though he had acquired the conviction that no random shot could knock him over now. And suddenly he was inspired to add, 'The snow was coming down very thick, you know.'

She had a slight appreciative movement of the head, like an expert in such enterprises, very interested, capable of taking every point professionally. Razumov remembered something he had heard.

'I turned into a narrow side street, you understand,' he went on negligently, and paused as if it were not worth talking about. Then he remembered another detail and dropped it before her, like a disdainful dole to her curiosity.

'I felt inclined to lie down and go to sleep there.'

She clicked her tongue at that symptom, very struck indeed. Then –

'But the notebook! The amazing notebook, man. You don't mean to say you had put it in your pocket beforehand!' she cried.

Razumov gave a start. It might have been a sign of impatience.

'I went home. Straight home to my rooms,' he said distinctly.

'The coolness of the man! You dared?'

'Why not? I assure you I was perfectly calm. Ha! Calmer than I am now perhaps.'

'I like you much better as you are now than when you indulge that bitter vein of yours, Razumov. And nobody in the house saw you return – eh? That might have appeared queer.'

'No one,' Razumov said firmly. 'Dvornik, landlady, girl, all out of the way. I went up like a shadow. It was a murky morning. The stairs were dark. I glided up like a phantom. Fate? Luck? What do you think?'

'I just see it!' The eyes of the woman revolutionist snapped darkly. 'Well – and then you considered . . .'

Razumov had it all ready in his head.

'No. I looked at my watch, since you want to know. There was just time. I took that notebook, and ran down the stairs on tiptoe. Have you ever listened to the pit-pat of a man running round and round the shaft of a deep staircase? They have a gaslight at the bottom burning night and day. I suppose it's gleaming down there now . . . The sound dies out – the flame winks . . .'

He noticed the vacillation of surprise passing over the steady curiosity of the black eyes fastened on his face as if the woman revolutionist received the sound of his voice into her pupils instead of her ears. He checked himself, passed his hand over his forehead, confused, like a man who has been dreaming aloud.

'Where could a student be running if not to his lectures in the morning? At night it's another matter. I did not care if all the house had been there to look at me. But I don't suppose there was any one. It's best not to be seen or heard. Aha! the people that are neither seen nor heard are the lucky ones – in Russia. Don't you admire my luck?'

'Astonishing,' she said. 'If you have luck as well as determination, then indeed you are likely to turn out an invaluable acquisition for the work in hand.'

Her tone was earnest; and it seemed to Razumov that it was speculative, even as though she were already apportioning him, in her mind, his share of the work. Her eyes were cast down. He waited, not very alert now, but with the grip of the ever-present danger giving him an air of attentive gravity. Who could have written about him in that letter from Petersburg? A fellow-student, surely – some imbecile victim of revolutionary propaganda, some foolish slave of foreign, subversive ideals. A long, famine-stricken red-nosed figure presented itself to his mental search. That must have been the fellow!

He smiled inwardly at the absolute wrong-headedness of the whole thing, the self-deception of a criminal idealist shattering his existence like a thunder-clap out of a clear sky, and re-echoing amongst the wreckage in the false assumptions of those other fools. Fancy that hungry and piteous imbecile furnishing to the curiosity of the revolutionist refugees this utterly fantastic detail! He appreciated it as by no means constituting a danger. On the contrary. As things stood it was for his advantage rather, a piece of sinister luck which had only to be accepted with proper caution.

'And yet, Razumov,' he heard the musing voice of the woman, 'you have not the face of a lucky man.' She raised her eyes with renewed interest. 'And so that was the way of it. After doing your work you simply walked off and made for your rooms. That sort of thing succeeds sometimes. I suppose it was agreed beforehand that, once the business over, each of you would go his own way?'

Razumov preserved the seriousness of his expression and the deliberate, if cautious, manner of speaking.

'Was not that the best thing to do?' he asked, in a dispassionate tone. 'And anyway,' he added, after waiting a moment, 'we did not give much thought to what would come after. We never discussed formally any line of conduct. It was understood, I think.'

She approved his statement with slight nods.

'You, of course, wished to remain in Russia?'

'In St Petersburg itself,' emphasized Razumov. 'It was the only safe course for me. And, moreover, I had nowhere else to go.'

'Yes! Yes! I know. Clearly. And the other – this wonderful Haldin appearing only to be regretted – you don't know what he intended?'

Razumov had foreseen that such a question would certainly come to meet him sooner or later. He raised his hands a little and let them fall helplessly by his side – nothing more.

It was the white-haired woman conspirator who was the first to break the silence.

'Very curious,' she pronounced slowly. 'And you did not think, Kirylo Sidorovitch, that he might perhaps wish to get in touch with you again?'

Razumov discovered that he could not suppress the trembling of his lips. But he thought that he owed it to himself to speak. A negative sign would not do again. Speak he must, if only to get at the bottom of what that St Petersburg letter might have contained.

'I stayed at home next day,' he said, bending down a little and plunging his glance into the black eyes of the woman so that she should not observe the trembling of his lips. 'Yes, I stayed at home. As my actions are remembered and written about, then perhaps you are aware that I was *not* seen at the lectures next day. Eh? You didn't know? Well, I stopped at home – the live-long day.'

As if moved by his agitated tone, she murmured a sympathetic 'I see! It must have been trying enough.'

'You seem to understand one's feelings,' said Razumov steadily. 'It was trying. It was horrible; it was an atrocious day. It was not the last.'

'Yes, I understand. Afterwards, when you heard they had got him. Don't I know how one feels after losing a comrade in the good fight? One's ashamed of being left. And I can remember so many. Never mind. They shall be avenged before long. And what is death? At any rate, it is not a shameful thing like some kinds of life.'

Razumov felt something stir in his breast, a sort of feeble and unpleasant tremor.

'Some kinds of life?' he repeated, looking at her searchingly.

'The subservient, submissive life. Life? No! Vegetation on the filthy heap of iniquity which the world is. Life, Razumov, not to be vile must be a revolt – a pitiless protest – all the time.'

She calmed down, the gleam of suffused tears in her eyes dried out instantly by the heat of her passion, and it was in her capable, businesslike manner that she went on –

'You understand me, Razumov. You are not an enthusiast, but there is an immense force of revolt in you. I felt it from the first, directly I set my eyes on you – you remember – in Zürich. Oh! You are full of bitter revolt. That is good. Indignation flags sometimes, revenge itself may become a weariness, but that uncompromising sense of necessity and justice which armed your and Haldin's hands to strike down that fanatical brute ... for it was that – nothing but that! I have been thinking it out. It could have been nothing else but that.'

Razumov made a slight bow, the irony of which was concealed by an almost sinister immobility of feature.

'I can't speak for the dead. As for myself, I can assure you that my conduct was dictated by necessity and by the sense of – well – retributive justice.'

'Good, that,' he said to himself, while her eyes rested upon him, black and impenetrable like the mental caverns where revolutionary thought should sit plotting the violent way of its dream of changes. As if anything could be changed! In this world of men nothing can be changed – neither happiness nor misery. They can only be displaced at the cost of corrupted consciences and broken lives – a futile game for arrogant philosophers and sanguinary triflers. Those thoughts darted through Razumov's head while he stood facing the old revolutionary hand, the respected, trusted, and influential Sophia Antonovna, whose word had such a weight in the 'active' section of every party. She was much more representative than the great Peter Ivanovitch. Stripped of rhetoric, mysticism, and theories, she was the true spirit of destructive revolution. And she was the personal adversary he had to meet. It gave him a feeling of triumphant pleasure to deceive her out of her own mouth. The epigrammatic saying that speech has been given to us for the purpose of concealing our thoughts came into his mind. Of that cynical theory this was a very subtle and a very scornful application, flouting in its own words the very spirit of ruthless revolution, embodied in that woman with her white hair and black eyebrows, like slightly sinuous lines of Indian ink, drawn together by the perpendicular folds of a thoughtful frown.

'That's it. Retributive. No pity!' was the conclusion of her silence. And this once broken, she went on impulsively in short, vibrating sentences –

'Listen to my story, Razumov! ...' Her father was a clever but unlucky artisan. No joy had lighted up his laborious days. He died at fifty; all the years of his life he had panted under the thumb of masters whose rapacity exacted from him the price of the water, of the salt, of the very air he breathed; taxed the sweat of his brow and claimed the blood of his sons. No protection, no guidance! What had society to say to him? Be submissive and be honest. If you rebel I shall kill you. If you steal I shall imprison you. But if you suffer I have nothing for you – nothing except perhaps a beggarly dole of bread – but no consolation for your trouble, no respect for your manhood, no pity for the sorrows of your miserable life.

And so he laboured, he suffered, and he died. He died in the hospital. Standing by the common grave she thought of his tormented existence – she saw it whole. She reckoned the simple joys of life, the birthright of the humblest, of which his gentle heart had been robbed by the crime of a society which nothing can absolve.

'Yes, Razumov,' she continued, in an impressive, lowered voice, 'it was like a lurid light in which I stood, still almost a child, and cursed not the toil, not the misery which had been his lot, but the great social iniquity of the system resting on unrequited toil and unpitied sufferings. From that moment I was a revolutionist.'

Razumov, trying to raise himself above the dangerous weaknesses of contempt or compassion, had preserved an impassive countenance. She, with an unaffected touch of mere bitterness, the first he could notice since he had come in contact with the woman, went on –

'As I could not go to the Church where the priests of the system exhorted such unconsidered vermin as I to resignation, I went to the secret societies as soon as I knew how to find my way. I was sixteen years old – no more, Razumov! And – look at my white hair.'

In these last words there was neither pride nor sadness. The bitterness too was gone.

'There is a lot of it. I had always magnificent hair, even as a chit of a girl. Only at that time we were cutting it short and thinking that there was the first step towards crushing the social infamy. Crush the Infamy! A fine watchword! I would placard it on the walls of prisons and palaces, carve it on hard rocks, hang it out in letters of fire on that empty sky for a sign of hope and terror – a portent of the end ...'

'You are eloquent, Sophia Antonovna,' Razumov interrupted suddenly. 'Only, so far you seem to have been writing it in water ...'

She was checked but not offended. 'Who knows? Very soon it may become a fact written all over that great land of ours,' she hinted meaningly. 'And then one would have lived long enough. White hair won't matter.'

Razumov looked at her white hair: and this mark of so many uneasy years seemed nothing but a testimony to the invincible vigour of revolt. It threw out into an astonishing relief the unwrinkled face, the brilliant black glance, the upright compact figure, the simple, brisk self-possession of the mature personality – as though in her revolutionary pilgrimage she had discovered the secret, not of everlasting youth, but of everlasting endurance.

How un-Russian she looked, thought Razumov. Her mother might have been a Jewess or an Armenian or – devil knew what. He reflected that a revolutionist is seldom true to the settled type. All revolt is the expression of strong individualism – ran his thought

vaguely. One can tell them a mile off in any society, in any sur-
roundings. It was astonishing that the police ...

'We shall not meet again very soon, I think,' she was saying. 'I
am leaving tomorrow.'

'For Zürich?' Razumov asked casually, but feeling relieved, not
from any distinct apprehension, but from a feeling of stress as if after
a wrestling match.

'Yes, Zürich – and farther on, perhaps, much farther. Another
journey. When I think of all my journeys! The last must come some
day. Never mind, Razumov. We had to have a good long talk. I
would have certainly tried to see you if we had not met. Peter
Ivanovitch knows where you live? Yes. I meant to have asked him
– but it's better like this. You see, we expect two more men; and I
had much rather wait here talking with you than up there at the
house with ...'

Having cast a glance beyond the gate, she interrupted herself.
'Here they are,' she said rapidly. 'Well, Kirylo Sidorovitch, we shall
have to say good-bye, presently.'

IV

In his incertitude of the ground on which he stood Razumov felt
perturbed. Turning his head quickly, he saw two men on the
opposite side of the road. Seeing themselves noticed by Sophia
Antonovna, they crossed over at once, and passed one after another
through the little gate by the side of the empty lodge. They looked
hard at the stranger, but without mistrust, the crimson blouse being
a flaring safety signal. The first, great white hairless face, double
chin, prominent stomach, which he seemed to carry forward consciously within a strongly distended overcoat, only nodded and
averted his eyes peevishly; his companion – lean, flushed cheek-
bones, a military red moustache below a sharp, salient nose –
approached at once Sophia Antonovna, greeting her warmly. His
voice was very strong but inarticulate. It sounded like a deep
buzzing. The woman revolutionist was quietly cordial ...

'This is Razumov,' she announced in a clear voice.

The lean new-comer made an eager half-turn. 'He will want to embrace me,' thought our young man with a deep recoil of all his being, while his limbs seemed too heavy to move. But it was a groundless alarm. He had to do now with a generation of conspirators who did not kiss each other on both cheeks; and raising an arm that felt like lead he dropped his hand into a largely outstretched palm, fleshless and hot as if dried up by fever, giving a bony pressure, expressive, seeming to say, 'Between us there's no need of words.'

The man had big, wide-open eyes. Razumov fancied he could see a smile behind their sadness.

'This is Razumov,' Sophia Antonovna repeated loudly for the benefit of the fat man, who at some distance displayed the profile of his stomach.

No one moved. Everything, sounds, attitudes, movements, and immobility seemed to be part of an experiment, the result of which was a thin voice piping with comic peevishness –

'Oh yes! Razumov. We have been hearing of nothing but Mr Razumov for months. For my part, I confess I would rather have seen Haldin on this spot instead of Mr Razumov.'

The squeaky stress put on the name 'Razumov – Mr Razumov' pierced the ear ridiculously, like the falsetto of a circus clown beginning an elaborate joke. Astonishment was Razumov's first response, followed by sudden indignation.

'What's the meaning of this?' he asked in a stern tone.

'Tut! Silliness. He's always like that.' Sophia Antonovna was obviously vexed. But she dropped the information, 'Necator,' from her lips just loud enough to be heard by Razumov. The abrupt squeaks of the fat man seemed to proceed from that thing like a balloon he carried under his overcoat. The stolidity of his attitude, the big feet, the lifeless, hanging hands, the enormous bloodless cheek, the thin wisps of hair straggling down the fat nape of the neck, fascinated Razumov into a stare on the verge of horror and laughter.

Nikita, nicknamed Necator, with a sinister aptness of alliteration! Razumov had heard of him. He had heard so much since crossing the frontier of these celebrities of the militant revolution; the legends, the stories, the authentic chronicle, which now and then peeps out before a half-incredulous world. Razumov had heard of him. He was supposed to have killed more gendarmes and police agents than any revolutionist living. He had been entrusted with executions.

The paper with the letters N.N., the very pseudonym of murder, found pinned on the stabbed breast of a certain notorious spy (this picturesque detail of a sensational murder case had got into the newspapers), was the mark of his handiwork. 'By order of the Committee. – N.N.' A corner of the curtain lifted to strike the imagination of the gaping world. He was said to have been innumerable times in and out of Russia, the Necator of bureaucrats, of provincial governors, of obscure informers. He lived between whiles, Razumov had heard, on the shores of the Lake of Como, with a charming wife, devoted to the cause, and two young children. But how could that creature, so grotesque as to set town dogs barking at its mere sight, go about on those deadly errands and slip through the meshes of the police?

'What now? what now?' the voice squeaked. 'I am only sincere. It's not denied that the other was the leading spirit. Well, it would have been better if he had been the one spared to us. More useful. I am not a sentimentalist. Say what I think ... only natural.'

Squeak, squeak, squeak, without a gesture, without a stir – the horrible squeaky burlesque of professional jealousy – this man of a sinister alliterative nickname, this executioner of revolutionary verdicts, the terrifying N.N. exasperated like a fashionable tenor by the attention attracted to the performance of an obscure amateur. Sophia Antonovna shrugged her shoulders. The comrade with the martial red moustache hurried towards Razumov full of conciliatory intentions in his strong buzzing voice.

'Devil take it! And in this place, too, in the public street, so to speak. But you can see yourself how it is. One of his fantastic sallies. Absolutely of no consequence.'

'Pray don't concern yourself,' cried Razumov, going off into a long fit of laughter. 'Don't mention it.'

The other, his hectic flush like a pair of burns on his cheek-bones, stared for a moment and burst out laughing too. Razumov, whose hilarity died out all at once, made a step forward.

'Enough of this,' he began in a clear, incisive voice, though he could hardly control the trembling of his legs. 'I will have no more of it. I shall not permit any one ... I can see very well what you are at with those allusions ... Inquire, investigate! I defy you but I will not be played with.'

He had spoken such words before. He had been driven to cry them out in the face of other suspicions. It was an infernal cycle bringing round that protest like a fatal necessity of his existence. But it was no use. He would be always played with. Luckily life does not last for ever.

'I won't have it!' he shouted, striking his fist into the palm of his other hand.

'Kirylo Sidorovitch – what has come to you?' The woman revolutionist interfered with authority. They were all looking at Razumov now; the slayer of spies and gendarmes had turned about, presenting his enormous stomach in full, like a shield.

'Don't shout. There are people passing.' Sophia Antonovna was apprehensive of another outburst. A steam-launch from Monrepos had come to the landing-stage opposite the gate, its hoarse whistle and the churning noise alongside all unnoticed, had landed a small bunch of local passengers who were dispersing their several ways. Only a specimen of early tourist in knickerbockers, conspicuous by a brand-new yellow leather glass-case, hung about for a moment, scenting something unusual about these four people within the rusty iron gates of what looked like the grounds run wild of an unoccupied private house. Ah! If he had only known what the chance of commonplace travelling had suddenly put in his way! But he was a well-bred person; he averted his gaze and moved off with short steps along the avenue, on the watch for a tramcar.

A gesture from Sophia Antonovna, 'Leave him to me,' had sent the two men away – the buzzing of the inarticulate voice growing fainter and fainter, and the thin pipe of 'What now? what's the matter?' reduced to the proportions of a squeaking toy by the distance. They had left him to her. So many things could be left safely to the experience of Sophia Antonovna. And at once, her black eyes turned to Razumov, her mind tried to get at the heart of that outburst. It had some meaning. No one is born an active revolutionist. The change comes disturbingly, with the force of a sudden vocation, bringing in its train agonizing doubts, assertive violences, an unstable state of the soul, till the final appeasement of the convert in the perfect fierceness of conviction. She had seen – often had only divined – scores of these young men and young women going through an emotional crisis. This young man looked like a moody egotist. And besides, it was a special – a unique case. She had never met an individuality which interested and puzzled her so much.

'Take care, Razumov, my good friend. If you carry on like this you will go mad. You are angry with everybody and bitter with yourself, and on the look out for something to torment yourself with.'

'It's intolerable!' Razumov could only speak in gasps. 'You must admit that I can have no illusions on the attitude which ... it isn't clear ... or rather ... only too clear.'

He made a gesture of despair. It was not his courage that failed him. The choking fumes of falsehood had taken him by the throat – the thought of being condemned to struggle on and on in that tainted atmosphere without the hope of ever renewing his strength by a breath of fresh air.

'A glass of cold water is what you want.' Sophia Antonovna glanced up the grounds at the house and shook her head, then out of the gate at the brimful placidity of the lake. With a half-comical shrug of the shoulders, she gave the remedy up in the face of that abundance.

'It is you, my dear soul, who are flinging yourself at something which does not exist. What is it? Self-reproach, or what? It's absurd. You couldn't have gone and given yourself up because your comrade was taken.'

She remonstrated with him reasonably, at some length too. He had nothing to complain of in his reception. Every new-comer was discussed more or less. Everybody had to be thoroughly understood before being accepted. No one that she could remember had been shown from the first so much confidence. Soon, very soon, perhaps sooner than he expected, he would be given an opportunity of showing his devotion to the sacred task of crushing the Infamy.

Razumov, listening quietly, thought: 'It may be that she is trying

263

to lull my suspicions to sleep. On the other hand, it is obvious that most of them are fools.' He moved aside a couple of paces and, folding his arms on his breast, leaned back against the stone pillar of the gate.

'As to what remains obscure in the fate of that poor Haldin,' Sophia Antonovna dropped into a slowness of utterance which was to Razumov like the falling of molten lead drop by drop; 'as to that – though no one ever hinted that either from fear or neglect your conduct has not been what it should have been – well, I have a bit of intelligence ...'

Razumov could not prevent himself from raising his head, and Sophia Antonovna nodded slightly.

'I have. You remember that letter from St Petersburg I mentioned to you a moment ago?'

'The letter? Perfectly. Some busybody has been reporting my conduct on a certain day. It's rather sickening. I suppose our police are greatly edified when they open these interesting and – and – superfluous letters.'

'Oh dear no! The police do not get hold of our letters as easily as you imagine. The letter in question did not leave St Petersburg till the ice broke up. It went by the first English steamer which left the Neva this spring. They have a fireman on board – one of us, in fact. It has reached me from Hull ...'

She paused as if she were surprised at the sullen fixity of Razumov's gaze, but went on at once, and much faster.

'We have some of our people there who ... but never mind. The writer of the letter relates an incident which he thinks may possibly be connected with Haldin's arrest. I was just going to tell you when those two men came along.'

'That also was an incident,' muttered Razumov, 'of a very charming kind – for me.'

'Leave off that!' cried Sophia Antonovna. 'Nobody cares for Nikita's barking. There's no malice in him. Listen to what I have to say. You may be able to throw a light. There was in St Petersburg a sort of town peasant – a man who owned horses. He came to town years ago to work for some relation as a driver and ended by owning a cab or two.'

She might well have spared herself the slight effort of the gesture: 'Wait!' Razumov did not mean to speak; he could not have interrupted her now, not to save his life. The contraction of his facial muscles had been involuntary, a mere surface stir, leaving him sullenly attentive as before.

'He was not a quite ordinary man of his class – it seems,' she went on. 'The people of the house – my informant talked with many of them – you know, one of those enormous houses of shame and misery ...'

Sophia Antonovna need not have enlarged on the character of the house. Razumov saw clearly, towering at her back, a dark mass of masonry veiled in snowflakes, with the long row of windows of the eating-shop shining greasily very near the ground. The ghost of that night pursued him. He stood up to it with rage and with weariness.

'Did the late Haldin ever by chance speak to you of that house?' Sophia Antonovna was anxious to know.

'Yes.' Razumov, making that answer, wondered whether he were falling into a trap. It was so humiliating to lie to these people that he probably could not have said no. 'He mentioned to me once,' he added, as if making an effort of memory, 'a house of that sort. He used to visit some workmen there.'

'Exactly.'

Sophia Antonovna triumphed. Her correspondent had discovered that fact quite accidentally from the talk of the people of the house, having made friends with a workman who occupied a room there. They described Haldin's appearance perfectly. He brought comforting words of hope into their misery. He came irregularly, but he came very often, and – her correspondent wrote – sometimes he spent a night in the house, sleeping, they thought, in a stable which opened upon the inner yard.

'Note that, Razumov! In a stable.'

Razumov had listened with a sort of ferocious but amused acquiescence.

'Yes. In the straw. It was probably the cleanest spot in the whole house.'

'No doubt,' assented the woman with that deep frown which

seemed to draw closer together her black eyes in a sinister fashion. No four-footed beast could stand the filth and wretchedness so many human beings were condemned to suffer from in Russia. The point of this discovery was that it proved Haldin to have been familiar with that horse-owning peasant – a reckless, independent, free-living fellow not much liked by the other inhabitants of the house. He was believed to have been the associate of a band of housebreakers. Some of these got captured. Not while he was driving them, however; but still there was a suspicion against the fellow of having given a hint to the police and ...

The woman revolutionist checked herself suddenly.

'And you? Have you ever heard your friend refer to a certain Ziemianitch?'

Razumov was ready for the name. He had been looking out for the question. 'When it comes I shall own up,' he had said to himself. But he took his time.

'To be sure!' he began slowly. 'Ziemianitch, a peasant owning a team of horses. Yes. On one occasion. Ziemianitch! Certainly! Ziemianitch of the horses ... How could it have slipped my memory like this? One of the last conversations we had together.'

'That means,' – Sophia Antonovna looked very grave, – 'that means, Razumov, it was very shortly before – eh?'

'Before what?' shouted Razumov, advancing at the woman, who looked astonished but stood her ground. 'Before ... Oh! Of course, it was before! How could it have been after? Only a few hours before.'

'And he spoke of him favourably?'

'With enthusiasm! The horses of Ziemianitch! The free soul of Ziemianitch!'

Razumov took a savage delight in the loud utterance of that name, which had never before crossed his lips audibly. He fixed his blazing eyes on the woman till at last her fascinated expression recalled him to himself.

'The late Haldin,' he said, holding himself in, with downcast eyes, 'was inclined to take sudden fancies to people, on – on – what shall I say – insufficient grounds.'

'There!' Sophia Antonovna clapped her hands. 'That, to my mind, settles it. The suspicions of my correspondent were aroused ...'

'Aha! Your correspondent,' Razumov said in an almost openly mocking tone. 'What suspicions? How aroused? By this Ziemianitch? Probably some drunken, gabbling, plausible ...'

'You talk as if you had known him.'

Razumov looked up.

'No. But I knew Haldin.'

Sophia Antonovna nodded gravely.

'I see. Every word you say confirms to my mind the suspicion communicated to me in that very interesting letter. This Ziemianitch was found one morning hanging from a hook in the stable – dead.'

Razumov felt a profound trouble. It was visible, because Sophia Antonovna was moved to observe vivaciously –

'Aha! You begin to see.'

He saw it clearly enough – in the light of a lantern casting spokes of shadow in a cellar-like stable, the body in a sheepskin coat and long boots hanging against the wall. A pointed hood, with the ends wound about up to the eyes, hid the face. 'But that does not concern me,' he reflected. 'It does not affect my position at all. He never knew who had thrashed him. He could not have known.' Razumov felt sorry for the old lover of the bottle and women.

'Yes. Some of them end like that,' he muttered. 'What is your idea, Sophia Antonovna?'

It was really the idea of her correspondent, but Sophia Antonovna had adopted it fully. She stated it in one word – 'Remorse.' Razumov opened his eyes very wide at that. Sophia Antonovna's informant, by listening to the talk of the house, by putting this and that together, had managed to come very near to the truth of Haldin's relation to Ziemianitch.

'It is I who can tell you what you were not certain of – that your friend had some plan for saving himself afterwards, for getting out of St Petersburg, at any rate. Perhaps that and no more, trusting to luck for the rest. And that fellow's horses were part of the plan.'

'They have actually got at the truth,' Razumov marvelled to himself, while he nodded judicially. 'Yes, that's possible, very possible.' But the woman revolutionist was very positive that it was so. First of all, a conversation about horses between Haldin and

267

Ziemianitch had been partly overheard. Then there were the suspicions of the people in the house when their 'young gentleman' (they did not know Haldin by his name) ceased to call at the house. Some of them used to charge Ziemianitch with knowing something of this absence. He denied it with exasperation; but the fact was that ever since Haldin's disappearance he was not himself, growing moody and thin. Finally, during a quarrel with some woman (to whom he was making up), in which most of the inmates of the house took part apparently, he was openly abused by his chief enemy, an athletic pedlar, for an informer, and for having driven 'our young gentleman to Siberia, the same as you did those young fellows who broke into houses.' In consequence of this there was a fight, and Ziemianitch got flung down a flight of stairs. Thereupon he drank and moped for a week, and then hanged himself.

Sophia Antonovna drew her conclusions from the tale. She charged Ziemianitch either with drunken indiscretion as to a driving job on a certain date, overheard by some spy in some low grog-shop – perhaps in the very eating-shop on the ground floor of the house – or, maybe, a downright denunciation, followed by remorse. A man like that would be capable of anything. People said he was a flighty old chap. And if he had been once before mixed up with the police – as seemed certain, though he always denied it – in connection with these thieves, he would be sure to be acquainted with some police underlings, always on the look out for something to report. Possibly at first his tale was not made anything of till the day that scoundrel de P— got his deserts. Ah! But then every bit and scrap of hint and information would be acted on, and fatally they were bound to get Haldin.

Sophia Antonovna spread out her hands – 'Fatally.'

Fatality – chance! Razumov meditated in silent astonishment upon the queer verisimilitude of these inferences. They were obviously to his advantage.

'It is right now to make this conclusive evidence known generally.' Sophia Antonovna was very calm and deliberate again. She had received the letter three days ago, but did not write at once to Peter Ivanovitch. She knew then that she would have the opportunity presently of meeting several men of action assembled for an important purpose.

'I thought it would be more effective if I could show the letter itself at large. I have it in my pocket now. You understand how pleased I was to come upon you.'

Razumov was saying to himself, 'She won't offer to show the letter to me. Not likely. Has she told me everything that correspondent of hers has found out?' He longed to see the letter, but he felt he must not ask.

'Tell me, please, was this an investigation ordered, as it were?'

'No, no,' she protested. 'There you are again with your sensitiveness. It makes you stupid. Don't you see, there was no starting-point for an investigation even if any one had thought of it. A perfect blank! That's exactly what some people were pointing out as the reason for receiving you cautiously. It was all perfectly accidental, arising from my informant striking an acquaintance with an intelligent skindresser lodging in that particular slum-house. A wonderful coincidence!'

'A pious person,' suggested Razumov, with a pale smile, 'would say that the hand of God has done it all.'

'My poor father would have said that.' Sophia Antonovna did not smile. She dropped her eyes. 'Not that his God ever helped him. It's a long time since God has done anything for the people. Anyway, it's done.'

'All this would be quite final,' said Razumov, with every appearance of reflective impartiality, 'if there was any certitude that the "our young gentleman" of these people was Victor Haldin. Have we got that?'

'Yes. There's no mistake. My correspondent was as familiar with Haldin's personal appearance as with your own,' the woman affirmed decisively.

'It's the red-nosed fellow beyond a doubt,' Razumov said to himself, with reawakened uneasiness. Had his own visit to that accursed house passed unnoticed? It was barely possible. Yet it was hardly probable. It was just the right sort of food for the popular gossip that gaunt busybody had been picking up. But the letter did not seem to contain any allusion to that. Unless she had suppressed it. And, if so, why? If it had really escaped the prying of that hunger-stricken democrat with a confounded genius for recognizing people from description, it could only be for a time. He would come upon it presently and hasten to write another letter – and then!

For all the envenomed recklessness of his temper, fed on hate and disdain, Razumov shuddered inwardly. It guarded him from common fear, but it could not defend him from disgust at being dealt with in any way by these people. It was a sort of superstitious dread. Now, since his position had been made more secure by their own folly at the cost of Ziemianitch, he felt the need of perfect safety, with its freedom from direct lying, with its power of moving amongst them silent, unquestioning, listening, impenetrable, like the very fate of their crimes and their folly. Was this advantage his already? Or not yet? Or never would be?

'Well, Sophia Antonovna,' his air of reluctant concession was genuine in so far that he was really loath to part with her without testing her sincerity by a question it was impossible to bring about in any way; 'well, Sophia Antonovna, if that is so, then –'

'The creature has done justice to himself,' the woman observed, as if thinking aloud.

'What? Ah yes! Remorse,' Razumov muttered with equivocal contempt.

'Don't be harsh, Kirylo Sidorovitch, if you have lost a friend.' There was no hint of softness in her tone, only the black glitter of her eyes seemed detached for an instant from vengeful visions. 'He was a man of the people. The simple Russian soul is never wholly impenitent. It's something to know that.'

'Consoling?' insinuated Razumov, in a tone of inquiry.

'Leave off railing,' she checked him explosively. 'Remember, Razumov, that women, children, and revolutionists hate irony, which is the negation of all saving instincts, of all faith, of all devotion, of all action. Don't rail! Leave off ... I don't know how it is, but there are moments when you are abhorrent to me ...'

She averted her face. A languid silence, as if all the electricity of the situation had been discharged in this flash of passion, lasted for some time. Razumov had not flinched. Suddenly she laid the tips of her fingers on his sleeve.

'Don't mind.'

'I don't mind,' he said very quietly.

He was proud to feel that she could read nothing on his face. He was really mollified, relieved, if only for a moment, from an obscure oppression. And suddenly he asked himself, 'Why the devil did I go to that house? It was an imbecile thing to do.'

A profound disgust came over him. Sophia Antonovna lingered, talking in a friendly manner with an evident conciliatory intention. And it was still about the famous letter, referring to various minute details given by her informant, who had never seen Ziemianitch. The 'victim of remorse' had been buried several weeks before her correspondent began frequenting the house. It – the house – contained very good revolutionary material. The spirit of the heroic Haldin had passed through these dens of black wretchedness with a promise of universal redemption from all the miseries that oppress mankind. Razumov listened without hearing, gnawed by the newborn desire of safety with its independence from that degrading method of direct lying which at times he found it almost impossible to practise.

No. The point he wanted to hear about could never come into this conversation. There was no way of bringing it forward. He regretted not having composed a perfect story for use abroad, in which his fatal connection with the house might have been owned up to. But when he left Russia he did not know that Ziemianitch had hanged himself. And, anyway, who could have foreseen this woman's 'informant' stumbling upon that particular slum of all the slums awaiting destruction in the purifying flame of social revolution? Who could have foreseen? Nobody! 'It's a perfect, diabolic surprise,' thought Razumov, calm-faced in his attitude of inscrutable superiority, nodding assent to Sophia Antonovna's remarks upon the psychology of 'the people'. 'Oh yes – certainly,' rather coldly, but with a nervous longing in his fingers to tear some sort of confession out of her throat.

Then, at the very last, on the point of separating, the feeling of relaxed tension already upon him he heard Sophia Antonovna allude to the subject of his uneasiness. How it came about he could only guess, his mind being absent at the moment, but it must have

271

sprung from Sophia Antonovna's complaints of the illogical absurdity of the people. For instance – that Ziemianitch was notoriously irreligious, and yet, in the last weeks of his life, he suffered from the notion that he had been beaten by the devil.

'The devil,' repeated Razumov, as though he had not heard aright.

'The actual devil. The devil in person. You may well look astonished, Kirylo Sidorovitch. Early on the very night poor Haldin was taken, a complete stranger turned up and gave Ziemianitch a most fearful thrashing while he was lying dead-drunk in the stable. The wretched creature's body was one mass of bruises. He showed them to the people in the house.'

'But you, Sophia Antonovna, you don't believe in the actual devil?'

'Do you?' retorted the woman curtly. 'Not but that there are plenty of men worse than devils to make a hell of this earth,' she muttered to herself.

Razumov watched her, vigorous and white-haired, with the deep fold between her thin eyebrows, and her black glance turned idly away. It was obvious that she did not make much of the story – unless, indeed, this was the perfection of duplicity. 'A dark young man,' she explained further. 'Never seen there before, never seen afterwards. Why are you smiling, Razumov?'

'At the devil being still young after all these ages,' he answered composedly. 'But who was able to describe him, since the victim, you say, was dead-drunk at the time?'

'Oh! The eating-house keeper has described him. An overbearing, swarthy young man in a student's cloak, who came rushing in, demanded Ziemianitch, beat him furiously, and rushed away without a word, leaving the eating-house keeper paralysed with astonishment.'

'Does he, too, believe it was the devil?'

'That I can't say. I am told he's very reserved on the matter. Those sellers of spirits are great scoundrels generally. I should think he knows more of it than anybody.'

'Well, and you, Sophia Antonovna, what's your theory?' asked

Razumov in a tone of great interest. 'Yours and your informant's, who is on the spot.'

'I agree with him. Some police-hound in disguise. Who else could beat a helpless man so unmercifully? As for the rest, if they were out that day on every trail, old and new, it is probable enough that they might have thought it just as well to have Ziemianitch at hand for more information, or for identification, or what not. Some scoundrelly detective was sent to fetch him along, and being vexed at finding him so drunk broke a stable fork over his ribs. Later on, after they had the big game safe in the net, they troubled their heads no more about that peasant.'

Such were the last words of the woman revolutionist in this conversation, keeping so close to the truth, departing from it so far in the verisimilitude of thoughts and conclusions as to give one the notion of the invincible nature of human error, a glimpse into the utmost depths of self-deception. Razumov, after shaking hands with Sophia Antonovna, left the grounds, crossed the road, and walking out on the little steamboat pier leaned over the rail.

His mind was at ease; ease such as he had not known for many days, ever since that night . . . the night. The conversation with the woman revolutionist had given him the view of his danger at the very moment this danger vanished, characteristically enough. 'I ought to have foreseen the doubts that would arise in those people's minds,' he thought. Then his attention being attracted by a stone of peculiar shape, which he could see clearly lying at the bottom, he began to speculate as to the depth of water in that spot. But very soon, with a start of wonder at this extraordinary instance of ill-timed detachment, he returned to his train of thought. 'I ought to have told very circumstantial lies from the first,' he said to himself, with a mortal distaste of the mere idea which silenced his mental utterance for quite a perceptible interval. 'Luckily, that's all right now,' he reflected, and after a time spoke to himself, half aloud, 'Thanks to the devil,' and laughed a little.

The end of Ziemianitch then arrested his wandering thoughts. He was not exactly amused at the interpretation, but he could not help detecting in it a certain piquancy. He owned to himself that, had he known of that suicide before leaving Russia, he would have been incapable of making such excellent use of it for his own purposes. He ought to be infinitely obliged to the fellow with the red nose for his patience and ingenuity, 'A wonderful psychologist apparently,' he said to himself sarcastically. Remorse, indeed! It was a striking example of your true conspirator's blindness, of the stupid subtlety of people with one idea. This was a drama of love, not of conscience, Razumov continued to himself mockingly. A woman the old fellow was making up to! A robust pedlar, clearly a rival, throwing him down a flight of stairs ... And at sixty, for a lifelong lover, it was not an easy matter to get over. That was a feminist of a different stamp from Peter Ivanovitch. Even the comfort of the bottle might conceivably fail him in this supreme crisis. At such an age nothing but a halter could cure the pangs of an unquenchable passion. And, besides, there was the wild exasperation aroused by the unjust aspersions and the contumely of the house, with the maddening impossibility to account for that mysterious thrashing, added to these simple and bitter sorrows. 'Devil, eh?' Razumov exclaimed, with mental excitement, as if he had made an interesting discovery. 'Ziemianitch ended by falling into mysticism. So many of our true Russian souls end in that way! Very characteristic.' He felt pity for Ziemianitch, a large neutral pity, such as one may feel for an unconscious multitude, a great people seen from above – like a community of crawling ants working out its destiny. It was as if this Ziemianitch could not possibly have done anything else. And Sophia Antonovna's cocksure and contemptuous 'some police-hound' was characteristically Russian in another way. But there was no tragedy there. This was a comedy of errors. It was as if the devil himself were playing a game with all of them in turn. First with him, then with Ziemianitch, then with those revolutionists. The devil's own game this ... He interrupted his earnest mental soliloquy with a jocular thought at his own expense. 'Hallo! I am falling into mysticism too.'

His mind was more at ease than ever. Turning about he put his back against the rail comfortably. 'All this fits with marvellous aptness,' he continued to think. 'The brilliance of my reputed exploit is no longer darkened by the fate of my supposed colleague. The mystic Ziemianitch accounts for that. An incredible chance has served me. No more need of lies. I shall have only to listen and to keep my scorn from getting the upper hand of my caution.'

He sighed, folded his arms, his chin dropped on his breast, and it was a long time before he started forward from that pose, with the recollection that he had made up his mind to do something important that day. What it was he could not immediately recall, yet he made no effort of memory, for he was uneasily certain that he would remember presently.

He had not gone more than a hundred yards towards the town when he slowed down, almost faltered in his walk, at the sight of a figure walking in the contrary direction, draped in a cloak, under a soft, broad-brimmed hat, picturesque but diminutive, as if seen through the big end of an opera-glass. It was impossible to avoid that tiny man, for there was no issue for retreat.

'Another one going to that mysterious meeting,' thought Razumov. He was right in his surmise, only *this* one, unlike the others who came from a distance, was known to him personally. Still, he hoped to pass on with a mere bow, but it was impossible to ignore the little thin hand with hairy wrist and knuckles protruded in a friendly wave from under the folds of the cloak, worn Spanish-wise, in disregard of a fairly warm day, a corner flung over the shoulder.

'And how is Herr Razumov?' sounded the greeting in German, by that alone made more odious to the object of the affable recognition. At closer quarters the diminutive personage looked like a reduction of an ordinary-sized man, with a lofty brow bared for a moment by the raising of the hat, the great pepper-and-salt full beard spread over the proportionally broad chest. A fine bold nose jutted over a thin mouth hidden in the mass of fine hair. All this, accented features, strong limbs in their relative smallness, appeared delicate without the slightest sign of debility. The eyes alone, almond-shaped and brown, were too big, with the whites slightly bloodshot by much pen labour under a lamp. The obscure celebrity of the tiny man was well known to Razumov. Polyglot, of unknown parentage, of indefinite nationality, anarchist, with a pedantic and ferocious temperament, and an amazingly inflammatory capacity for invective, he was a power in the background, this violent pamphle-teer clamouring for revolutionary justice, this Julius Laspara, editor of the *Living Word*, confidant of conspirators, inditer of sanguinary menaces and manifestos, suspected of being in the secret of every plot. Laspara lived in the old town in a sombre, narrow house presented to him by a naïve middle-class admirer of his humani-tarian eloquence. With him lived his two daughters, who over-topped him head and shoulders, and a pasty-faced, lean boy of six, languishing in the dark rooms in blue cotton overalls, and clumsy boots, who might have belonged to either one of them or to neither. No stranger could tell. Julius Laspara no doubt knew which of his girls it was who, after casually vanishing for a few years, had as casually returned to him possessed of that child; but, with admirable pedantry, he had refrained from asking her for details – no, not so much as the name of the father, because maternity should be an anarchist function. Razumov had been admitted twice to that suite of several small dark rooms on the top floor: dusty windowpanes, litter of all sorts of sweepings all over the place, half-full glasses of tea forgotten on every table, the two Laspara daughters prowling about enigmatically silent, sleepy-eyed, corsetless, and generally, in their want of shape and the disorder of their rumpled attire, resem-bling old dolls; the great but obscure Julius, his feet twisted round his three-legged stool, always ready to receive the visitors, the pen instantly dropped, the body screwed round with a striking display of the lofty brow and of the great austere beard. When he got down from his stool it was as though he had descended from the heights of Olympus. He was dwarfed by his daughters, by the furniture, by any caller of ordinary stature. But he very seldom left it, and still more rarely was seen walking in broad daylight.

It must have been some matter of serious importance which had driven him out in that direction that afternoon. Evidently he wished to be amiable to that young man whose arrival had made some sensation in the world of political refugees. In Russian now, which he spoke, as he spoke and wrote four or five other European languages, without distinction and without force (other than that of invective), he inquired if Razumov had taken his inscriptions at the University as yet. And the young man, shaking his head negatively –

'There's plenty of time for that. But, meantime, are you not going to write something for us?'

He could not understand how any one could refrain from writing on anything, social, economic, historical – anything. Any subject could be treated in the right spirit, and for the ends of social revolution. And, as it happened, a friend of his in London had got in touch with a review of advanced ideas. 'We must educate, educate everybody – develop the great thought of absolute liberty and of revolutionary justice.'

Razumov muttered rather surlily that he did not even know English.

'Write in Russian. We'll have it translated. There can be no difficulty. Why, without seeking further, there is Miss Haldin. My daughters go to see her sometimes.' He nodded significantly. 'She does nothing, has never done anything in her life. She would be quite competent, with a little assistance. Only write. You know you must. And so good-bye for the present.'

He raised his arm and went on. Razumov backed against the low wall, looked after him, spat violently, and went on his way with an angry mutter –

'Cursed Jew!'

He did not know anything about it. Julius Laspara might have been a Transylvanian, a Turk, an Andalusian, or a citizen of one of the Hanse towns for anything he could tell to the contrary. But this is not a story of the West, and this exclamation must be recorded, accompanied by the comment that it was merely an expression of hate and contempt, best adapted to the nature of the feelings Razumov suffered from at the time. He was boiling with rage, as though he had been grossly insulted. He walked as if blind, following instinctively the shore of the diminutive harbour along the quay, through a pretty, dull garden, where dull people sat on chairs under the trees, till, his fury abandoning him, he discovered himself in the middle of a long, broad bridge. He slowed down at once. To his right, beyond the toy-like jetties, he saw the green slopes framing the Petit Lac in all the marvellous banality of the picturesque made of painted cardboard, with the more distant stretch of water inanimate and shining like a piece of tin.

He turned his head away from that view for the tourists, and walked on slowly, his eyes fixed on the ground. One or two persons had to get out of his way, and then turned round to give a surprised stare to his profound absorption. The insistence of the celebrated subversive journalist rankled in his mind strangely. Write. Must write! He! Write! A sudden light flashed upon him. To write was the very thing he had made up his mind to do that day. He had made up his mind irrevocably to that step and then had forgotten all about it. That incorrigible tendency to escape from the grip of the situation was fraught with serious danger. He was ready to despise himself for it. What was it? Levity, or deep-seated weakness? Or an unconscious dread?

'Is it that I am shrinking? It can't be! It's impossible. To shrink now would be worse than moral suicide; it would be nothing less than moral damnation,' he thought. 'Is it possible that I have a conventional conscience?'

He rejected that hypothesis with scorn, and, checked on the edge of the pavement, made ready to cross the road and proceed up the wide street facing the head of the bridge; and that for no other reason except that it was there before him. But at the moment a couple of carriages and a slow-moving cart interposed, and suddenly he turned sharp to the left, following the quay again, but now away from the lake.

'It may be just my health,' he thought, allowing himself a very unusual doubt of his soundness; for, with the exception of a childish ailment or two, he had never been ill in his life. But that was a danger, too. Only, it seemed as though he were being looked after in a specially remarkable way. 'If I believed in an active Providence,' Razumov said to himself, amused grimly, 'I would see here the working of an ironical finger. To have a Julius Laspara put in my way as if expressly to remind me of my purpose is – Write, he had said. I must write – I must, indeed! I shall write – never fear. Certainly. That's why I am here. And for the future I shall have something to write about.'

He was exciting himself by this mental soliloquy. But the idea of writing evoked the thought of a place to write in, of shelter, of privacy, and naturally of his lodgings, mingled with a distaste for the necessary exertion of getting there, with a mistrust as of some hostile influence awaiting him within those odious four walls.

'Suppose one of these revolutionists,' he asked himself, 'were to take a fancy to call on me while I am writing?' The mere prospect of such an interruption made him shudder. One could lock one's door, or ask the tobacconist downstairs (some sort of a refugee himself) to tell inquirers that one was not in. Not very good precautions those. The manner of his life, he felt, must be kept clear of every cause for suspicion or even occasion for wonder, down to such trifling occurrences as a delay in opening a locked door. 'I wish I were in the middle of some field miles away from everywhere,' he thought.

He had unconsciously turned to the left once more and now was aware of being on a bridge again. This one was much narrower than the other, and instead of being straight, made a sort of elbow or angle. At the point of that angle a short arm joined it to a hexagonal islet with a soil of gravel and its shores faced with dressed stone, a perfection of puerile neatness. A couple of tall poplars and a few other trees stood grouped on the clean, dark gravel, and under them a few garden benches and a bronze effigy of Jean Jacques Rousseau[18] seated on its pedestal.

On setting his foot on it Razumov became aware that, except for the woman in charge of the refreshment chalet, he would be alone on the island. There was something of naïve, odious, and inane simplicity about that unfrequented tiny crumb of earth named after Jean Jacques Rousseau. Something pretentious and shabby, too. He asked for a glass of milk, which he drank standing, at one draught (nothing but tea had passed his lips since the morning), and was going away with a weary, lagging step when a thought stopped him short. He had found precisely what he needed. If solitude could ever be secured in the open air in the middle of a town, he would have it there on this absurd island, together with the faculty of watching the only approach.

He went back heavily to a garden seat, dropped into it. This was the place for making a beginning of that writing which had to be

279

done. The materials he had on him. 'I shall always come here,' he said to himself, and afterwards sat for quite a long time motionless, without thought and sight and hearing, almost without life. He sat long enough for the declining sun to dip behind the roofs of the town at his back, and throw the shadow of the houses on the lake front over the islet, before he pulled out of his pocket a fountain pen, opened a small notebook on his knee, and began to write quickly, raising his eyes now and then at the connecting arm of the bridge. These glances were needless; the people crossing over in the distance seemed unwilling even to look at the islet where the exiled effigy of the author of the *Social Contract* sat enthroned above the bowed head of Razumov in the sombre immobility of bronze. After finishing his scribbling, Razumov, with a sort of feverish haste, put away the pen, then rammed the notebook into his pocket, first tearing out the written pages with an almost convulsive brusqueness. But the folding of the flimsy batch on his knee was executed with thoughtful nicety. That done, he leaned back in his seat and remained motionless holding the papers in his left hand. The twilight had deepened. He got up and began to pace to and fro slowly under the trees.

'There can be no doubt that now I am safe,' he thought. His fine ear could detect the faintly accentuated murmurs of the current breaking against the point of the island, and he forgot himself in listening to them with interest. But even to his acute sense of hearing the sound was too elusive.

'Extraordinary occupation I am giving myself up to,' he murmured. And it occurred to him that this was about the only sound he could listen to innocently, and for his own pleasure, as it were. Yes, the sound of water, the voice of the wind – completely foreign to human passions. All the other sounds of this earth brought contamination to the solitude of a soul.

This was Mr Razumov's feeling, the soul, of course, being his own, and the word being used not in the theological sense, but standing, as far as I can understand it, for that part of Mr Razumov which was not his body, and more specially in danger from the fires of this earth. And it must be admitted that in Mr Razumov's case the bitterness of solitude from which he suffered was not an altogether morbid phenomenon.

PART FOURTH

I

That I should, at the beginning of this retrospect, mention again
that Mr Razumov's youth had no one in the world, as literally no
one as it can be honestly affirmed of any human being, is but a
statement of fact from a man who believes in the psychological
value of facts. There is also, perhaps, a desire of punctilious fairness.
Unidentified with any one in this narrative where the aspects of
honour and shame are remote from the ideas of the Western world,
and taking my stand on the ground of common humanity, it is for
that very reason that I feel a strange reluctance to state baldly here
what every reader has most likely already discovered himself. Such
reluctance may appear absurd if it were not for the thought that
because of the imperfection of language there is always something
ungracious (and even disgraceful) in the exhibition of naked truth.
But the time has come when Councillor of State Mikulin can no
longer be ignored. His simple question 'Where to?' on which we left
Mr Razumov in St Petersburg, throws a light on the general meaning of this individual case.

'Where to?' was the answer in the form of a gentle question to
what we may call Mr Razumov's declaration of independence. The
question was not menacing in the least and, indeed, had the ring
of innocent inquiry. Had it been taken in a merely topographical
sense, the only answer to it would have appeared sufficiently appalling to Mr Razumov. Where to? Back to his rooms, where the
Revolution had sought him out to put to a sudden test his dormant
instincts, his half-conscious thoughts and almost wholly unconscious ambitions, by the touch as of some furious and dogmatic
religion, with its call to frantic sacrifices, its tender resignations, its

dreams and hopes uplifting the soul by the side of the most sombre moods of despair. And Mr Razumov had let go the door-handle and had come back to the middle of the room, asking Councillor Mikulin angrily, 'What do you mean by it?'

As far as I can tell, Councillor Mikulin did not answer that question. He drew Mr Razumov into familiar conversation. It is the peculiarity of Russian natures, that, however strongly engaged in the drama of action, they are still turning their ear to the murmur of abstract ideas. This conversation (and others later on) need not be recorded. Suffice it to say that it brought Mr Razumov as we know him to the test of another faith. There was nothing official in its expression, and Mr Razumov was led to defend his attitude of detachment. But Councillor Mikulin would have none of his arguments. 'For a man like you,' were his last weighty words in the discussion, 'such a position is impossible. Don't forget that I have seen that interesting piece of paper. I understand your liberalism. I have an intellect of that kind myself. Reform for me is mainly a question of method. But the principle of revolt is a physical intoxication, a sort of hysteria which must be kept away from the masses. You agree to this without reserve, don't you? Because, you see, Kirylo Sidorovitch, abstention, reserve, in certain situations, come very near to political crime. The ancient Greeks understood that very well.'

Mr Razumov, listening with a faint smile, asked Councillor Mikulin point-blank if this meant that he was going to have him watched.

The high official took no offence at the cynical inquiry.

'No, Kirylo Sidorovitch,' he answered gravely. 'I don't mean to have you watched.'

Razumov, suspecting a lie, affected yet the greatest liberty of mind during the short remainder of that interview. The older man expressed himself throughout in familiar terms, and with a sort of shrewd simplicity. Razumov concluded that to get to the bottom of that mind was an impossible feat. A great disquiet made his heart beat quicker. The high official, issuing from behind the desk, was actually offering to shake hands with him.

'Good-bye, Mr Razumov. An understanding between intelligent

men is always a satisfactory occurrence. Is it not? And, of course, these rebel gentlemen have not the monopoly of intelligence.'

'I presume that I shall not be wanted any more?' Razumov brought out that question while his hand was still being grasped. Councillor Mikulin released it slowly.

'That, Mr Razumov,' he said with great earnestness, 'is as it may be. God alone knows the future. But you may rest assured that I never thought of having you watched. You are a young man of great independence. Yes. You are going away free as air, but you shall end by coming back to us.'

'I! I!' Razumov exclaimed in an appalled murmur of protest. 'What for?' he added feebly.

'Yes! You yourself, Kirylo Sidorovitch,' the high police functionary insisted in a low, severe tone of conviction. 'You shall be coming back to us. Some of our greatest minds had to do that in the end.'

'Our greatest minds,' repeated Razumov in a dazed voice.

'Yes, indeed! Our greatest minds . . . Good-bye.'

Razumov, shown out of the room, walked away from the door. But before he got to the end of the passage he heard heavy footsteps, and a voice calling upon him to stop. He turned his head and was startled to see Councillor Mikulin pursuing him in person. The high functionary hurried up, very simply, slightly out of breath.

'One minute. As to what we were talking about just now, it shall be as God wills it. But I may have occasion to require you again. You look surprised, Kirylo Sidorovitch. Yes, again . . . to clear up any further point that may turn up.'

'But I don't know anything,' stammered out Razumov. 'I couldn't possibly know anything.'

'Who can tell? Things are ordered in a wonderful manner. Who can tell what *may* become disclosed to you before this day is out? You have been already the instrument of Providence. You smile, Kirylo Sidorovitch; you are an *esprit fort.*'* (Razumov was not conscious of having smiled.) 'But I believe firmly in Providence. Such a confession on the lips of an old hardened official like me may

---

* 'Strong spirit.'

sound to you funny. But you yourself yet some day shall recognize
... Or else what happened to you cannot be accounted for at all. Yes,
decidedly I shall have occasion to see you again, but not here. This
wouldn't be quite – h'm ... Some convenient place shall be made
known to you. And even the written communications between us
in *that* respect or in any other had better pass through the inter-
mediacy of our – if I may express myself so – common friend, Prince
K—. Now I beg you, Kirylo Sidorovitch – don't! I am certain he'll
consent. You must give me the credit of being aware of what I am
saying. You have no better friend than Prince K—, and as to myself
it is a long time now since I've been honoured by his ...'

He glanced down his beard.

'I won't detain you any longer. We live in difficult times, in times
of monstrous chimeras and evil dreams and criminal follies. We
shall certainly meet once more. It may be some little time, though,
before we do. Till then may Heaven send you fruitful reflections!'

Once in the street, Razumov started off rapidly, without caring for
the direction. At first he thought of nothing; but in a little while the
consciousness of his position presented itself to him as something
so ugly, dangerous, and absurd, the difficulty of ever freeing himself
from the toils of that complication so insoluble, that the idea of going
back and, as he termed it to himself, *confessing* to Councillor Mikulin
flashed through his mind.

Go back! What for? Confess! To what? 'I have been speaking to
him with the greatest openness,' he said to himself with perfect
truth. 'What else could I tell him? That I have undertaken to carry
a message to that brute Ziemianitch? Establish a false complicity and
destroy what chance of safety I have won for nothing – what folly!'

Yet he could not defend himself from fancying that Councillor
Mikulin was, perhaps, the only man in the world able to understand
his conduct. To be understood appeared extremely fascinating.

On the way home he had to stop several times; all his strength
seemed to run out of his limbs; and in the movement of the busy
streets, isolated as if in a desert, he remained suddenly motionless
for a minute or so before he could proceed on his way. He reached
his rooms at last.

Then came an illness, something in the nature of a low fever,

284

which all at once removed him to a great distance from the perplexing actualities, from his very room, even. He never lost consciousness; he only seemed to himself to be existing languidly somewhere very far away from everything that had ever happened to him. He came out of this state slowly, with an effect, that is to say, of extreme slowness, though the actual number of days was not very great. And when he had got back into the middle of things they were all changed, subtly and provokingly in their nature: inanimate objects, human faces, the landlady, the rustic servant-girl, the staircase, the streets, the very air. He tackled these changed conditions in a spirit of severity. He walked to and fro to the University, ascended stairs, paced the passages, listened to lectures, took notes, crossed courtyards in angry aloofness, his teeth set hard till his jaws ached.

He was perfectly aware of madcap Kostia gazing like a young retriever from a distance, of the famished student with the red drooping nose, keeping scrupulously away as desired; of twenty others, perhaps, he knew well enough to speak to. And they all had an air of curiosity and concern as if they expected something to happen. 'This can't last much longer,' thought Razumov more than once. On certain days he was afraid that any one addressing him suddenly in a certain way would make him scream out insanely a lot of filthy abuse. Often, after returning home, he would drop into a chair in his cap and cloak and remain still for hours holding some book he had got from the library in his hand; or he would pick up the little penknife and sit there scraping his nails endlessly and feeling furious all the time – simply furious. 'This is impossible,' he would mutter suddenly to the empty room.

Fact to be noted: this room might conceivably have become physically repugnant to him, emotionally intolerable, morally uninhabitable. But no. Nothing of the sort (and he had himself dreaded it at first), nothing of the sort happened. On the contrary, he liked his lodgings better than any other shelter he, who had never known a home, had ever hired before. He liked his lodgings so well that often, on that very account, he found a certain difficulty in making up his mind to go out. It resembled a physical seduction such as, for instance, makes a man reluctant to leave the neighbourhood of a fire on a cold day.

For as, at that time, he seldom stirred except to go to the University (what else was there to do?) it followed that whenever he went abroad he felt himself at once closely involved in the moral consequences of his act. It was there that the dark prestige of the Haldin mystery fell on him, clung to him like a poisoned robe it was impossible to fling off. He suffered from it exceedingly, as well as from the conversational, commonplace, unavoidable intercourse with the other kind of students. 'They must be wondering at the change in me,' he reflected anxiously. He had an uneasy recollection of having savagely told one or two innocent, nice enough fellows to go to the devil. Once a married professor he used to call upon formerly addressed him in passing: 'How is it we never see you at our Wednesdays now, Kirylo Sidorovitch?' Razumov was conscious of meeting this advance with odious, muttering boorishness. The professor was obviously too astonished to be offended. All this was bad. And all this was Haldin, always Haldin – nothing but Haldin – everywhere Haldin: a moral spectre infinitely more effective than any visible apparition of the dead. It was only the room through which that man had blundered on his way from crime to death that his spectre did not seem to be able to haunt. Not, to be exact, that he was ever completely absent from it, but that there he had no sort of power. There it was Razumov who had the upper hand, in a composed sense of his own superiority. A vanquished phantom – nothing more. Often in the evening, his repaired watch faintly ticking on the table by the side of the lighted lamp, Razumov would look up from his writing and stare at the bed with an expectant, dispassionate attention. Nothing was to be seen there. He never really supposed that anything ever could be seen there. After a while he would shrug his shoulders slightly and bend again over his work. For he had gone to work and, at first, with some success. His unwillingness to leave that place where he was safe from Haldin grew so strong that at last he ceased to go out at all. From early morning till far into the night he wrote, he wrote for nearly a week; never looking at the time, and only throwing himself on the bed when he could keep his eyes open no longer. Then, one afternoon, quite casually, he happened to glance at his watch. He laid down his pen slowly.

'At this very hour,' was his thought, 'the fellow stole unseen into this room while I was out. And there he sat quiet as a mouse – perhaps in this very chair.'

Razumov got up and began to pace the floor steadily, glancing at the watch now and then. 'This is the time when I returned and found him standing against the stove,' he observed to himself. When it grew dark he lit his lamp. Later on he interrupted his tramping once more, only to wave away angrily the girl who attempted to enter the room with tea and something to eat on a tray. And presently he noted the watch pointing at the hour of his own going forth into the falling snow on that terrible errand.

'Complicity,' he muttered faintly, and resumed his pacing, keeping his eye on the hands as they crept on slowly to the time of his return.

'And, after all,' he thought suddenly, 'I might have been the chosen instrument of Providence. This is a manner of speaking, but there may be truth in every manner of speaking. What if that absurd saying were true in its essence?'

He meditated for a while, then sat down, his legs stretched out, with stony eyes, and with his arms hanging down on each side of the chair like a man totally abandoned by Providence – desolate.

He noted the time of Haldin's departure and continued to sit still for another half-hour; then muttering, 'And now to work,' drew up to the table, seized the pen and instantly dropped it under the influence of a profoundly disquieting reflection: 'There's three weeks gone by and no word from Mikulin.'

What did it mean? Was he forgotten? Possibly. Then why not remain forgotten – creep in somewhere? Hide. But where? How? With whom? In what hole? And was it to be for ever, or what?

But a retreat was big with shadowy dangers. The eye of the social revolution was on him, and Razumov for a moment felt an unnamed and despairing dread, mingled with an odious sense of humiliation. Was it possible that he no longer belonged to himself? This was damnable. But why not simply keep on as before? Study. Advance. Work hard as if nothing had happened (and first of all win the Silver Medal), acquire distinction, become a great reforming servant of the greatest of States. Servant, too, of the mightiest homogeneous mass of mankind with a capability for logical, guided development in a brotherly solidarity of force and aim such as the world had never dreamt of ... the Russian nation! ...

Calm, resolved, steady in his great purpose, he was stretching his hand towards the pen when he happened to glance towards the bed. He rushed at it, enraged, with a mental scream: 'It's you, crazy fanatic, who stands in the way!' He flung the pillow on the floor violently, tore the blankets aside ... Nothing there. And, turning away, he caught for an instant in the air, like a vivid detail in a dissolving view of two heads, the eyes of General T— and of Privy-Councillor Mikulin side by side fixed upon him, quite different in character, but with the same unflinching and weary and yet purposeful expression ... servants of the nation!

Razumov tottered to the washstand very alarmed about himself, drank some water and bathed his forehead. 'This will pass and leave no trace,' he thought confidently. 'I am all right.' But as to supposing that he had been forgotten it was perfect nonsense. He was a marked man on that side. And that was nothing. It was what that miserable phantom stood for which had to be got out of the way ... 'If one only could go and spit it all out at some of them – and take the consequences.'

He imagined himself accosting the red-nosed student and suddenly shaking his fist in his face. 'From that one, though,' he reflected, 'there's nothing to be got, because he has no mind of his own. He's living in a red democratic trance. Ah! you want to smash your way into universal happiness, my boy. I will give you universal happiness, you silly, hypnotized ghoul, you! And what about my own happiness, eh? Haven't I got any right to it, just because I can think for myself? ...'

And again, but with a different mental accent, Razumov said to himself, 'I am young. Everything can be lived down.' At that moment he was crossing the room slowly, intending to sit down on the sofa and try to compose his thoughts. But before he had got so far everything abandoned him – hope, courage, belief in himself, trust in men. His heart had, as it were, suddenly emptied itself. It was no use struggling on. Rest, work, solitude, and the frankness of intercourse with his kind were alike forbidden to him. Everything was gone. His existence was a great cold blank, something like the enormous plain of the whole of Russia levelled with snow and fading gradually on all sides into shadows and mists.

He sat down, with swimming head, closed his eyes, and remained like that, sitting bolt upright on the sofa and perfectly awake for the rest of the night; till the girl bustling into the outer room with the samovar thumped with her fist on the door, calling out 'Kirylo Sidorovitch, please! It is time for you to get up!'

Then, pale like a corpse obeying the dread summons of judgement, Razumov opened his eyes and got up.

Nobody will be surprised to hear, I suppose, that when the summons came he went to see Councillor Mikulin. It came that very morning, while, looking white and shaky, like an invalid just out of bed, he was trying to shave himself. The envelope was addressed in the little attorney's handwriting. That envelope contained another, superscribed to Razumov, in Prince K—'s hand, with the request 'Please forward under cover at once' in a corner. The note inside was an autograph of Councillor Mikulin. The writer stated candidly that nothing had arisen which needed clearing up, but nevertheless appointed a meeting with Mr Razumov at a certain address in town which seemed to be that of an oculist.

Razumov read it, finished shaving, dressed, looked at the note again, and muttered gloomily, 'Oculist.' He pondered over it for a time, lit a match, and burned the two envelopes and the enclosure carefully. Afterwards he waited, sitting perfectly idle and not even looking at anything in particular till the appointed hour drew near – and then went out.

Whether, looking at the unofficial character of the summons, he might have refrained from attending to it is hard to say. Probably not. At any rate, he went; but, what's more, he went with a certain eagerness, which may appear incredible till it is remembered that Councillor Mikulin was the only person on earth with whom Razumov could talk, taking the Haldin adventure for granted. And Haldin, when once taken for granted, was no longer a haunting, falsehood-breeding spectre. Whatever troubling power he exercised in all the other places of the earth, Razumov knew very well that at this oculist's address he would be merely the hanged murderer of M de P— and nothing more. For the dead can live only with the exact intensity and quality of the life imparted to them by the living. So Mr Razumov, certain of relief, went to meet Councillor Mikulin with the eagerness of a pursued person welcoming any sort of shelter.

This much said, there is no need to tell anything more of that first interview and of the several others. To the morality of a Western reader an account of these meetings would wear perhaps the sinister character of old legendary tales where the Enemy of Mankind is represented holding subtly mendacious dialogues with some tempted soul. It is not my part to protest. Let me but remark that the Evil One, with his single passion of satanic pride for the only motive, is yet, on a larger, modern view, allowed to be not quite so black as he used to be painted. With what greater latitude, then, should we appraise the exact shade of mere mortal man, with his many passions and his miserable ingenuity in error, always dazzled by the base glitter of mixed motives, everlastingly betrayed by a short-sighted wisdom.

Councillor Mikulin was one of those powerful officials who, in a position not obscure, not occult, but simply inconspicuous, exercise a great influence over the methods rather than over the conduct of affairs. A devotion to Church and Throne is not in itself a criminal sentiment; to prefer the will of one to the will of many does not argue the possession of a black heart or prove congenital idiocy. Councillor Mikulin was not only a clever but also a faithful official. Privately he was a bachelor with a love of comfort, living alone in an apartment of five rooms luxuriously furnished; and was known by his intimates to be an enlightened patron of the art of female dancing. Later on the larger world first heard of him in the very hour of his downfall, during one of those State trials which astonish and puzzle the average plain man who reads the newspapers, by a glimpse of unsuspected intrigues. And in the stir of vaguely seen monstrosities, in that momentary, mysterious disturbance of muddy waters, Councillor Mikulin went under, dignified, with only a calm, emphatic protest of his innocence – nothing more. No disclosures damaging to a harassed autocracy, complete fidelity to the secrets of the miserable *arcana imperii** deposited in his patriotic breast, a display of bureaucratic stoicism in a Russian official's ineradicable, almost sublime contempt for truth; stoicism of silence understood only by the very few of the initiated, and not without a certain cynical grandeur of self-sacrifice on the part of a sybarite. For the terribly heavy sentence turned Councillor Mikulin civilly into a corpse, and actually into something very much like a common convict.

It seems that the savage autocracy, no more than the divine democracy, does not limit its diet exclusively to the bodies of its enemies. It devours its friends and servants as well. The downfall of His Excellency Gregory Gregorievitch Mikulin (which did not occur till some years later) completes all that is known of the man. But at the time of M de P—'s murder (or execution) Councillor Mikulin, under the modest style of Head of Department at the General Secretariat, exercised a wide influence as the confidant and right-hand man of his former schoolfellow and lifelong friend, General T—. One can imagine them talking over the case of Mr Razumov, with the full sense of their unbounded power over all the lives in Russia, with cursory disdain, like two Olympians glancing at a worm. The relationship with Prince K— was enough to save Razumov from some carelessly arbitrary proceeding, and it is also very probable that after the interview at the Secretariat he would have been left alone. Councillor Mikulin would not have forgotten him (he forgot no one who ever fell under his observation), but would have simply dropped him for ever. Councillor Mikulin was a good-natured man and wished no harm to any one. Besides (with his own reforming tendencies) he was favourably impressed by that young student, the son of Prince K—, and apparently no fool.

But as fate would have it, while Mr Razumov was finding that no way of life was possible to him, Councillor Mikulin's discreet abilities were rewarded by a very responsible post – nothing less than the direction of the general police supervision over Europe. And it was then, and then only, when taking in hand the perfecting of the service which watches the revolutionist activities abroad, that

---

* Secrets of the empire or security of the state.

291

he thought again of Mr Razumov. He saw great possibilities of special usefulness in that uncommon young man on whom he had a hold already, with his peculiar temperament, his unsettled mind and shaken conscience, a struggling in the toils of a false position ... It was as if the revolutionists themselves had put into his hand that tool so much finer than the common base instruments, so perfectly fitted, if only vested with sufficient credit, to penetrate into places inaccessible to common informers. Providential! Providential! And Prince K—, taken into the secret, was ready enough to adopt that mystical view too. 'It will be necessary, though, to make a career for him afterwards,' he had stipulated anxiously. 'Oh! absolutely. We shall make that our affair,' Mikulin had agreed. Prince K—'s mysticism was of an artless kind; but Councillor Mikulin was astute enough for two.

Things and men have always a certain sense, a certain side by which they must be got hold of if one wants to obtain a solid grasp and a perfect command. The power of Councillor Mikulin consisted in the ability to seize upon that sense, that side in the men he used. It did not matter to him what it was – vanity, despair, love, hate, greed, intelligent pride or stupid conceit, it was all one to him as long as the man could be made to serve. The obscure, unrelated young student Razumov, in the moment of great moral loneliness, was allowed to feel that he was an object of interest to a small group of people of high position. Prince K— was persuaded to intervene personally, and on a certain occasion gave way to a manly emotion which, all unexpected as it was, quite upset Mr Razumov. The sudden embrace of that man, agitated by his loyalty to a throne and by suppressed paternal affection, was a revelation to Mr Razumov of something within his own breast.

'So that was it!' he exclaimed to himself. A sort of contemptuous tenderness softened the young man's grim view of his position as he reflected upon that agitated interview with Prince K—. This simpleminded, worldly ex-Guardsman and senator whose soft grey official whiskers had brushed against his cheek, his aristocratic and convinced father, was he a whit less estimable or more absurd than that famine-stricken, fanatical revolutionist, the red-nosed student?

And there was some pressure, too, besides the persuasiveness.

Mr Razumov was always being made to feel that he had committed himself. There was no getting away from that feeling, from that soft, unanswerable, 'Where to?' of Councillor Mikulin. But no suscepti-bilities were ever hurt. It was to be a dangerous mission to Geneva for obtaining, at a critical moment, absolutely reliable information from a very inaccessible quarter of the inner revolutionary circle. There were indications that a very serious plot was being matured ... The repose indispensable to a great country was at stake ... A great scheme of orderly reforms would be endangered ... The highest personages in the land were patriotically uneasy, and so on. In short, Councillor Mikulin knew what to say. This skill is to be inferred clearly from the mental and psychological self-confession, self-analysis of Mr Razumov's written journal – the pitiful resource of a young man who had near him no trusted intimacy, no natural affection to turn to.

How all this preliminary work was concealed from observation need not be recorded. The expedient of the oculist gives a sufficient instance. Councillor Mikulin was resourceful, and the task not very difficult. Any fellow-student, even the red-nosed one, was perfectly welcome to see Mr Razumov entering a private house to consult an oculist. Ultimate success depended solely on the revolutionary self-delusion which credited Razumov with a mysterious complicity in the Haldin affair. To be compromised in it was credit enough – and it was their own doing. It was precisely *that* which stamped Mr Razumov as a providential man, wide as poles apart from the usual type of agent for 'European supervision'.

And it was *that* which the Secretariat set itself the task to foster by a course of calculated and false indiscretions.

It came at last to this, that one evening, Mr Razumov was unexpectedly called upon by one of the 'thinking' students whom formerly, before the Haldin affair, he used to meet at various private gatherings; a big fellow with a quiet, unassuming manner and a pleasant voice.

Recognizing his voice raised in the ante-room, 'May one come in?' Razumov, lounging idly on his couch, jumped up. 'Suppose he were coming to stab me?' he thought sardonically, and, assuming a green shade over his left eye, said in a severe tone, 'Come in.'

The other was embarrassed; hoped he was not intruding.

'You haven't been seen for several days, and I've wondered.' He coughed a little. 'Eye better?'

'Nearly well now.'

'Good. I won't stop a minute; but you see I, that is, we – anyway, I have undertaken the duty to warn you, Kirylo Sidorovitch, that you are living in false security maybe.'

Razumov sat still with his head leaning on his hand, which nearly concealed the unshaded eye.

'I have that idea, too.'

'That's all right, then. Everything seems quiet now, but those people are preparing some move of general repression. That's of course. But it isn't that I came to tell you.' He hitched his chair closer, dropped his voice. 'You will be arrested before long – we fear.'

An obscure scribe in the Secretariat had overheard a few words of a certain conversation, and had caught a glimpse of a certain report. This intelligence was not to be neglected.

Razumov laughed a little, and his visitor became very anxious.

'Ah! Kirylo Sidorovitch, this is no laughing matter. They have left you alone for a while, but ...! Indeed, you had better try to leave the country, Kirylo Sidorovitch, while there's yet time.'

Razumov jumped up and began to thank him for the advice with mocking effusiveness, so that the other, colouring up, took himself off with the notion that this mysterious Razumov was not a person to be warned or advised by inferior mortals.

Councillor Mikulin, informed the next day of the incident, expressed his satisfaction. 'H'm. Ha! Exactly what was wanted to ...' and glanced down his beard.

'I conclude,' said Razumov, 'that the moment has come for me to start on my mission.'

'The psychological moment,' Councillor Mikulin insisted softly – very gravely – as if awed.

All the arrangements to give verisimilitude to the appearance of a difficult escape were made. Councillor Mikulin did not expect to see Mr Razumov again before his departure. These meetings were a risk, and there was nothing more to settle.

'We have said everything to each other by now, Kirylo Sidorovitch,' said the high official feelingly, pressing Razumov's hand with that unreserved heartiness a Russian can convey in his manner. 'There is nothing obscure between us. And I will tell you what! I consider myself fortunate in having – h'm – your . . .'

He glanced down his beard, and, after a moment of thoughtful silence, handed to Razumov a half-sheet of notepaper – an abbreviated note of matters already discussed, certain points of inquiry, the line of conduct agreed on, a few hints as to personalities, and so on. It was the only compromising document in the case, but, as Councillor Mikulin observed, it could be easily destroyed. Mr Razumov had better not see any one now – till on the other side of the frontier, when, of course, it will be just that . . . See and hear and . . .

He glanced down his beard; but when Razumov declared his intention to see one person at least before leaving St Petersburg, Councillor Mikulin failed to conceal a sudden uneasiness. The young man's studious, solitary, and austere existence was well known to him. It was the greatest guarantee of fitness. He became deprecatory. Had his dear Kirylo Sidorovitch considered whether, in view of such a momentous enterprise, it wasn't really advisable to sacrifice every sentiment . . .

Razumov interrupted the remonstrance scornfully. It was not a young woman, it was a young fool he wished to see for a certain purpose. Councillor Mikulin was relieved, but surprised.

'Ah! And what for – precisely?'

'For the sake of improving the aspect of verisimilitude,' said Razumov curtly, in a desire to affirm his independence. 'I must be trusted in what I do.'

Councillor Mikulin gave way tactfully, murmuring, 'Oh, certainly, certainly. Your judgement . . .'

And with another handshake they parted.

The fool of whom Mr Razumov had thought was the rich and festive student known as madcap Kostia. Feather-headed, loquacious, excitable, one could make certain of his utter and complete indiscretion. But that riotous youth, when reminded by Razumov of his offers of service some time ago, passed from his usual elation into boundless dismay.

'Oh, Kirylo Sidorovitch, my dearest friend – my saviour – what shall I do? I've blown last night every rouble I had from my dad the other day. Can't you give me till Thursday? I shall rush round to all the usurers I know ... No, of course, you can't! Don't look at me like that. What shall I do? No use asking the old man. I tell you he's given me a fistful of big notes three days ago. Miserable wretch that I am.'

He wrung his hands in despair. Impossible to confide in the old man. 'They' had given him a decoration, a cross on the neck only last year, and he had been cursing the modern tendencies ever since. Just then he would see all the intellectuals in Russia hanged in a row rather than part with a single rouble.

'Kirylo Sidorovitch, wait a moment. Don't despise me. I have it. I'll, yes – I'll do it – I'll break into his desk. There's no help for it. I know the drawer where he keeps his plunder, and I can buy a chisel on my way home. He will be terribly upset, but, you know, the dear old duffer really loves me. He'll have to get over it – and I, too. Kirylo, my dear soul, if you can only wait for a few hours – till this evening – I shall steal all the blessed lot I can lay my hands on! You doubt me! Why? You've only to say the word.'

'Steal, by all means,' said Razumov, fixing him stonily.

'To the devil with the ten commandments!' cried the other, with the greatest animation. 'It's the new future now.'

But when he entered Razumov's room late in the evening it was with an unaccustomed soberness of manner, almost solemnly.

'It's done,' he said.

Razumov sitting bowed, his clasped hands hanging between his knees, shuddered at the familiar sound of these words. Kostia deposited slowly in the circle of lamplight a small brown-paper parcel tied with a piece of string.

'As I've said – all I could lay my hands on. The old boy'll think the end of the world has come.'

Razumov nodded from the couch, and contemplated the hare-brained fellow's gravity with a feeling of malicious pleasure.

'I've made my little sacrifice,' sighed mad Kostia. 'And I've to thank you, Kirylo Sidorovitch, for the opportunity.'

'It has cost you something?'

'Yes, it has. You see, the dear old duffer really loves me. He'll be hurt.'

'And you believe all they tell you of the new future and the sacred will of the people?'

'Implicitly. I would give my life ... Only, you see I am like a pig at a trough. I am no good. It's my nature.'

Razumov, lost in thought, had forgotten his existence till the youth's voice, entreating him to fly without loss of time, roused him unpleasantly.

'All right. Well – good-bye.'

'I am not going to leave you till I've seen you out of St Petersburg,' declared Kostia unexpectedly, with calm determination. 'You can't refuse me that now. For God's sake, Kirylo, my soul, the police may be here any moment, and when they get you they'll immure you somewhere for ages – till your hair turns grey. I have down there the best trotter of dad's stables and a light sledge. We shall do thirty miles before the moon sets, and find some roadside station ...'

Razumov looked up amazed. The journey was decided – unavoidable. He had fixed the next day for his departure on the mission. And now he discovered suddenly that he had not believed in it. He had gone about listening, speaking, thinking, planning his simulated flight, with the growing conviction that all this was preposterous. As if anybody ever did such things! It was like a game of make-believe. And now he was amazed! Here was somebody who believed in it with desperate earnestness. 'If I don't go now, at once,' thought Razumov, with a start of fear, 'I shall never go.' He rose without a word, and the anxious Kostia thrust his cap on him, helped him into his cloak, or else he would have left the room bareheaded as he stood. He was walking out silently when a sharp cry arrested him.

'Kirylo!'

'What?' He turned reluctantly in the doorway. Upright, with a stiffly extended arm, Kostia, his face set and white, was pointing an eloquent forefinger at the brown little packet lying forgotten in the circle of bright light on the table. Razumov hesitated, came back for it under the severe eyes of his companion, at whom he tried to smile. But the boyish, mad youth was frowning. 'It's a dream,' thought

Razumov, putting the little parcel into his pocket and descending the stairs; 'nobody does such things.' The other held him under the arm, whispering of dangers ahead, and of what he meant to do in certain contingencies. 'Preposterous,' murmured Razumov, as he was being tucked up in the sledge. He gave himself up to watching the development of the dream with extreme attention. It continued on foreseen lines, inexorably logical – the long drive, the wait at the small station sitting by a stove. They did not exchange half a dozen words altogether. Kostia, gloomy himself, did not care to break the silence. At parting they embraced twice – it had to be done; and then Kostia vanished out of the dream.

When dawn broke, Razumov, very still in a hot, stuffy railway-car full of bedding and of sleeping people in all its dimly lighted length, rose quietly, lowered the glass a few inches, and flung out on the great plain of snow a small brown-paper parcel. Then he sat down again muffled up and motionless. 'For the people,' he thought, staring out of the window. The great white desert of frozen, hard earth glided past his eyes without a sign of human habitation.

That had been a waking act; and then the dream had him again: Prussia, Saxony, Würtemberg, faces, sights, words – all a dream, observed with an angry, compelled attention. Zürich, Geneva – still a dream, minutely followed, wearing one into harsh laughter, to fury, to death – with the fear of awakening at the end ...

II

'Perhaps life is just that,' reflected Razumov, pacing to and fro under the trees of the little island, all alone with the bronze statue of Rousseau. 'A dream and a fear.' The dusk deepened. The pages written over and torn out of his notebook were the first-fruit of his 'mission'. No dream that. They contained the assurance that he was on the eve of real discoveries. 'I think there is no longer anything in the way of my being completely accepted.'

He had resumed his impressions in those pages, some of the conversations. He even went so far as to write: 'By the by, I have discovered the personality of that terrible N. N. A horrible, paunchy brute. If I hear anything of his future movements I shall send a warning.'

The futility of all this overcame him like a curse. Even then he could not believe in the reality of his mission. He looked round despairingly, as if for some way to redeem his existence from that unconquerable feeling. He crushed angrily in his hand the pages of the notebook. 'This must be posted,' he thought.

He gained the bridge and returned to the north shore, where he remembered having seen in one of the narrower streets a little obscure shop stocked with cheap wood carvings, its walls lined with extremely dirty cardboard-bound volumes of a small circulating library. They sold stationery there, too. A morose, shabby old man dozed behind the counter. A thin woman in black, with a sickly face, produced the envelope he had asked for without even looking at him. Razumov thought that these people were safe to deal with because they no longer cared for anything in the world. He addressed the envelope on the counter with the German name of a certain person living in Vienna. But Razumov knew that this, his first communication for Councillor Mikulin, would find its way to the Embassy there, be copied in cypher by somebody trustworthy, and sent on to its destination, all safe, along with the diplomatic correspondence. That was the arrangement contrived to cover up the track of the information from all unfaithful eyes, from all indiscretions, from all mishaps and treacheries. It was to make him safe – absolutely safe.

He wandered out of the wretched shop and made for the post office. It was then that I saw him for the second time that day. He was crossing the Rue Mont Blanc with every appearance of an aimless stroller. He did not recognize me, but I made him out at some distance. He was very good-looking, I thought, this remarkable friend of Miss Haldin's brother. I watched him go up to the letter-box and then retrace his steps. Again he passed me very close, but I am certain he did not see me that time, either. He carried his head well up, but he had the expression of a somnambulist struggling with the very dream which drives him forth to wander in dangerous places. My thoughts reverted to Natalia Haldin, to her mother. He was all that was left to them of their son and brother.

The Westerner in me was discomposed. There was something shocking in the expression of that face. Had I been myself a conspirator, a Russian political refugee, I could have perhaps been able to draw some practical conclusion from this chance glimpse. As it was, it only discomposed me strongly, even to the extent of awakening an indefinite apprehension in regard to Natalia Haldin. All this is rather inexplicable, but such was the origin of the purpose I formed there and then to call on these ladies in the evening, after my solitary dinner. It was true that I had met Miss Haldin only a few hours before, but Mrs Haldin herself I had not seen for some considerable time. The truth is, I had shirked calling of late.

Poor Mrs Haldin! I confess she frightened me a little. She was one of those natures, rare enough, luckily, in which one cannot help being interested, because they provoke both terror and pity. One dreads their contact for oneself, and still more for those one cares for, so clear it is that they are born to suffer and to make others suffer, too. It is strange to think that, I won't say liberty, but the mere liberalism of outlook which for us is a matter of words, of ambitions, of votes (and if of feeling at all, then of the sort of feeling which leaves our deepest affections untouched) may be for other beings very much like ourselves and living under the same sky, a heavy trial of fortitude, a matter of tears and anguish and blood. Mrs Haldin had felt the pangs of her own generation. There was that enthusiast brother of hers – the officer they shot under Nicholas. A faintly ironic resignation is no armour for a vulnerable heart. Mrs Haldin, struck at through her children, was bound to suffer afresh from the past, and to feel the anguish of the future. She was of those who do not know how to heal themselves, of those who are too much aware of their heart, who, neither cowardly nor selfish, look passionately at its wounds – and count the cost.

Such thoughts as these seasoned my modest, lonely bachelor's meal. If anybody wishes to remark that this was a roundabout way of thinking of Natalia Haldin, I can only retort that she was well worth some concern. She had all her life before her. Let it be admitted, then, that I was thinking of Natalia Haldin's life in terms of her mother's character, a manner of thinking about a girl permissible for an old man, not too old yet to have become a stranger to pity. There was almost all her youth before her; a youth robbed arbitrarily of its natural lightness and joy, overshadowed by an un-European despotism; a terribly sombre youth given over to the hazards of a furious strife between equally ferocious antagonisms.

I lingered over my thoughts more than I should have done. One felt so helpless, and even worse – so unrelated, in a way. At the last moment I hesitated as to going there at all. What was the good?

The evening was already advanced when, turning into the Boulevard des Philosophes, I saw the light in the window at the corner. The blind was down, but I could imagine behind it Mrs Haldin seated in the chair, in her usual attitude, looking out for someone, which had lately acquired the poignant quality of mad expectation.

I thought that I was sufficiently authorized by the light to knock at the door. The ladies had not retired as yet. I only hoped they would not have any visitors of their own nationality. A broken-down, retired Russian official was to be found there sometimes in the evening. He was infinitely forlorn and wearisome by his mere dismal presence. I think these ladies tolerated his frequent visits because of an ancient friendship with Mr Haldin, the father, or something of that sort. I made up my mind that if I found him prosing away there in his feeble voice I should remain but a very few minutes.

The door surprised me by swinging open before I could ring the bell. I was confronted by Miss Haldin, in hat and jacket, obviously on the point of going out. At that hour! For the doctor, perhaps?

Her exclamation of welcome reassured me. It sounded as if I had been the very man she wanted to see. My curiosity was awakened. She drew me in, and the faithful Anna, the elderly German maid, closed the door, but did not go away afterwards. She remained near it as if in readiness to let me out presently. It appeared that Miss Haldin had been on the point of going out to find me.

She spoke in a hurried manner very unusual with her. She would have gone straight and rung at Mrs Ziegler's door, late as it was, for Mrs Ziegler's habits ...

Mrs Ziegler, the widow of a distinguished professor who was an intimate friend of mine, lets me have three rooms out of her very large and fine apartment, which she didn't give up after her husband's death; but I have my own entrance opening on the same landing. It was an arrangement of at least ten years' standing. I said that I was very glad that I had the idea to . . .

Miss Haldin made no motion to take off her outdoor things. I observed her heightened colour, something pronouncedly resolute in her tone. Did I know where Mr Razumov lived?

Where Mr Razumov lived? Mr Razumov? At this hour – so urgently? I threw my arms up in sign of utter ignorance. I had not the slightest idea where he lived. If I could have foreseen her question only three hours ago, I might have ventured to ask him on the pavement before the new post office building, and possibly he would have told me, but very possibly, too he would have dismissed me rudely to mind my own business. And possibly, I thought, remembering that extraordinary hallucined, anguished, and absent expression, he might have fallen down in a fit from the shock of being spoken to. I said nothing of all this to Miss Haldin, not even mentioning that I had a glimpse of the young man so recently. The impression had been so extremely unpleasant that I would have been glad to forget it myself.

'I don't see where I could make inquiries,' I murmured helplessly. I would have been glad to be of use in any way, and would have set off to fetch any man, young or old, for I had the greatest confidence in her common sense. 'What made you think of coming to me for that information?' I asked.

'It wasn't exactly for that,' she said, in a low voice. She had the air of someone confronted by an unpleasant task.

'Am I to understand that you must communicate with Mr Razumov this evening?'

Natalia Haldin moved her head affirmatively then after a glance at the door of the drawing-room, said in French –

'C'est maman,' and remained perplexed for a moment. Always serious, not a girl to be put out by any imaginary difficulties, my curiosity was suspended on her lips, which remained closed for a moment. What was Mr Razumov's connection with this mention of her mother? Mrs Haldin had not been informed of her son's friend's arrival in Geneva.

302

'May I hope to see your mother this evening?' I inquired.

Miss Haldin extended her hand as if to bar the way.

'She is in a terrible state of agitation. Oh, you would not be able to detect ... It's inward, but I who know mother, I am appalled. I haven't the courage to face it any longer. It's all my fault; I suppose I cannot play a part; I've never before hidden anything from mother. There has never been an occasion for anything of that sort between us. But you know yourself the reason why I refrained from telling her at once of Mr Razumov's arrival here. You understand, don't you? Owing to her unhappy state. And – there – I am no actress. My own feelings being strongly engaged, I somehow ... I don't know. She noticed something in my manner. She thought I was concealing something from her. She noticed my longer absences, and, in fact, as I have been meeting Mr Razumov daily, I used to stay away longer than usual when I went out. Goodness knows what suspicions arose in her mind. You know that she has not been herself ever since ... So this evening she – who has been so awfully silent for weeks – began to talk all at once. She said that she did not want to reproach me; that I had my character as she had her own; that she did not want to pry into my affairs or even into my thoughts; for her part, she had never had anything to conceal from her children ... cruel things to listen to. And all this in her quiet voice, with that poor, wasted face as calm as a stone. It was unbearable.'

Miss Haldin talked in an undertone and more rapidly than I had ever heard her speak before. That in itself was disturbing. The ante-room being strongly lighted, I could see under the veil the heightened colour of her face. She stood erect, her left hand was resting lightly on a small table. The other hung by her side without stirring. Now and then she caught her breath slightly.

'It was too startling. Just fancy! She thought that I was making preparations to leave her without saying anything. I knelt by the side of her chair and entreated her to think of what she was saying! She put her hand on my head, but she persists in her delusion all the same. She had always thought that she was worthy of her children's confidence, but apparently it was not so. Her son could not trust her love nor yet her understanding – and now I was

303

planning to abandon her in the same cruel and unjust manner, and so on, and so on. Nothing I could say ... It is morbid obstinacy ... She said that she felt there was something, some change in me ... If my convictions were calling me away, why this secrecy, as though she had been a coward or a weakling not safe to trust? "As if my heart could play traitor to my children," she said ... It was hardly to be borne. And she was smoothing my head all the time ... It was perfectly useless to protest. She is ill. Her very soul is ...'

I did not venture to break the silence which fell between us. I looked into her eyes, glistening through the veil.

'I! Changed!' she exclaimed in the same low tone. 'My convictions calling me away! It was cruel to hear this, because my trouble is that I am weak and cannot see what I ought to do. You know that. And to end it all I did a selfish thing. To remove her suspicions of myself I told her of Mr Razumov. It was selfish of me. You know we were completely right in agreeing to keep the knowledge away from her. Perfectly right. Directly I told her of our poor Victor's friend being here I saw how right we have been. She ought to have been prepared; but in my distress I just blurted it out. Mother got terribly excited at once. How long has he been here? What did he know, and why did he not come to see us at once, this friend of her Victor? What did that mean? Was she not to be trusted even with such memories as there were left of her son? ... Just think how I felt seeing her, white as a sheet, perfectly motionless, with her thin hands gripping the arms of the chair. I told her it was all my fault.'

I could imagine the motionless dumb figure of the mother in her chair, there, behind the door, near which the daughter was talking to me. The silence in there seemed to call aloud for vengeance against an historical fact and the modern instances of its working. That view flashed through my mind, but I could not doubt that Miss Haldin had had an atrocious time of it. I quite understood when she said that she could not face the night upon the impression of that scene. Mrs Haldin had given way to most awful imaginings, to most fantastic and cruel suspicions. All this had to be lulled at all costs and without loss of time. It was no shock to me to learn that Miss Haldin had said to her, 'I will go and bring him here at once.' There was nothing absurd in that cry. no exaggeration of sentiment. I was not even doubtful in my 'Very well, but how?'

It was perfectly right that she should think of me, but what could I do in my ignorance of Mr Razumov's quarters.

'And to think he may be living near by, within a stone's-throw, perhaps!' she exclaimed.

I doubted it; but I would have gone off cheerfully to fetch him from the other end of Geneva. I suppose she was certain of my readiness, since her first thought was to come to me. But the service she meant to ask of me really was to accompany her to the Château Borel.

I had an unpleasant mental vision of the dark road, of the sombre grounds, and the desolately suspicious aspect of that home of necromancy and intrigue and feminist adoration. I objected that Madame de S— most likely would know nothing of what we wanted to find out. Neither did I think it likely that the young man would be found there. I remembered my glimpse of his face, and somehow gained the conviction that a man who looked worse than if he had seen the dead would want to shut himself up somewhere where he could be alone. I felt a strange certitude that Mr Razumov was going home when I saw him.

'It is really of Peter Ivanovitch that I was thinking,' said Miss Haldin quietly.

Ah! He, of course, would know. I looked at my watch. It was twenty minutes past nine only ... Still.

'I would try his hotel, then,' I advised. 'He has rooms at the Cosmopolitan, somewhere on the top floor.'

I did not offer to go by myself, simply from mistrust of the reception I should meet with. But I suggested the faithful Anna, with a note asking for the information.

Anna was still waiting by the door at the other end of the room, and we two discussed the matter in whispers. Miss Haldin thought she must go herself. Anna was timid and slow. Time would be lost in bringing back the answer, and from that point of view it was getting late, for it was by no means certain that Mr Razumov lived near by.

'If I go myself,' Miss Haldin argued, 'I can go straight to him from the hotel. And in any case I should have to go out, because I must explain to Mr Razumov personally – prepare him in a way. You have no idea of mother's state of mind.'

Her colour came and went. She even thought that both for her mother's sake and for her own it was better that they should not be together for a little time. Anna, whom her mother liked, would be at hand.

'She could take her sewing into the room.' Miss Haldin continued, leading the way to the door. Then, addressing in German the maid who opened it before us. 'You may tell my mother that this gentleman called and is gone with me to find Mr Razumov. She must not be uneasy if I am away for some length of time.'

We passed out quickly into the street, and she took deep breaths of the cool night air. 'I did not even ask you,' she murmured.

'I should think not,' I said, with a laugh. The manner of my reception by the great feminist could not be considered now. That he would be annoyed to see me, and probably treat me to some solemn insolence, I had no doubt, but I supposed that he would not absolutely dare to throw me out. And that was all I cared for. 'Won't you take my arm?' I asked.

She did so in silence, and neither of us said anything worth recording till I let her go first into the great hall of the hotel. It was brilliantly lighted, and with a good many people lounging about.

'I could very well go up there without you,' I suggested.

'I don't like to be left waiting in this place,' she said in a low voice. 'I will come too.'

I led her straight to the lift then. At the top floor the attendant directed us to the right: 'End of the corridor.'

The walls were white, the carpet red, electric lights blazed in profusion, and the emptiness, the silence, the closed doors all alike and numbered, made me think of the perfect order of some severely luxurious model penitentiary on the solitary confinement principle. Up there under the roof of that enormous pile for housing travellers no sound of any kind reached us, the thick crimson felt muffled our footsteps completely. We hastened on, not looking at each other till we found ourselves before the very last door of that long passage. Then our eyes met, and we stood thus for a moment lending ear to a faint murmur of voices inside.

'I suppose this is it,' I whispered unnecessarily. I saw Miss Haldin's lips move without a sound, and after my sharp knock the murmur of voices inside ceased. A profound stillness lasted for a few seconds, and then the door was brusquely opened by a short, black-eyed woman in a red blouse, with a great lot of nearly white hair, done up negligently in an untidy and unpicturesque manner. Her thin, jetty eyebrows were drawn together. I learned afterwards with interest that she was the famous – or the notorious – Sophia Antonovna, but I was struck then by the quaint Mephistophelian character of her inquiring glance, because it was so curiously evil-less, so – I may say – un-devilish. It got softened still more as she looked up at Miss Haldin, who stated, in her rich, even voice, her wish to see Peter Ivanovitch for a moment.

'I am Miss Haldin,' she added.

At this, with her brow completely smoothed out now, but without a word in answer, the woman in the red blouse walked away to a sofa and sat down, leaving the door wide open.

And from the sofa, her hands lying on her lap, she watched us enter, with her black glittering eyes.

Miss Haldin advanced into the middle of the room; I, faithful to my part of mere attendant, remained by the door after closing it behind me. The room, quite a large one, but with a low ceiling, was scantily furnished, and an electric bulb with a porcelain shade pulled low down over a big table (with a very large map spread on it) left its distant parts in a dim, artificial twilight. Peter Ivanovitch was not to be seen, neither was Mr Razumov present. But, on the sofa, near Sophia Antonovna, a bony-faced man with a goatee beard leaned forward with his hands on his knees, staring hard with a kindly expression. In a remote corner a broad, pale face and a bulky shape could be made out, uncouth, and as if insecure on the low seat on which it rested. The only person known to me was little Julius Laspara, who seemed to have been poring over the map, his feet twined tightly round the chair-legs. He got down briskly and bowed to Miss Haldin, looking absurdly like a hook-nosed boy with a beautiful false pepper-and-salt beard. He advanced, offering his seat, which Miss Haldin declined. She had only come in for a moment to say a few words to Peter Ivanovitch.

307

His high-pitched voice became painfully audible in the room.

'Strangely enough, I was thinking of you this very afternoon, Natalia Victorovna. I met Mr Razumov. I asked him to write me an article on anything he liked. You could translate it into English – with such a teacher.'

He nodded complimentarily in my direction. At the name of Razumov an indescribable sound, a sort of feeble squeak, as of some angry small animal, was heard in the corner occupied by the man who seemed much too large for the chair on which he sat. I did not hear what Miss Haldin said. Laspara spoke again.

'It's time to do something, Natalia Victorovna. But I suppose you have your own ideas. Why not write something yourself? Suppose you came to see us soon? We could talk it over. Any advice ...'

Again I did not catch Miss Haldin's words. It was Laspara's voice once more.

'Peter Ivanovitch? He's retired for a moment into the other room. We are all waiting for him.'

The great man, entering at that moment, looked bigger, taller, quite imposing in a long dressing-gown of some dark stuff. It descended in straight lines down to his feet. He suggested a monk or a prophet, a robust figure of some desert-dweller – something Asiatic; and the dark glasses in conjunction with this costume made him more mysterious than ever in the subdued light.

Little Laspara went back to his chair to look at the map, the only brilliantly lit object in the room. Even from my distant position by the door I could make out, by the shape of the blue part representing the water, that it was a map of the Baltic provinces. Peter Ivanovitch exclaimed slightly, advancing towards Miss Haldin, checked himself on perceiving me, very vaguely no doubt, and peered with his dark, bespectacled stare. He must have recognized me by my grey hair, because, with a marked shrug of his broad shoulders, he turned to Miss Haldin in benevolent indulgence. He seized her hand in his thick cushioned palm, and put his other big paw over it like a lid.

While those two standing in the middle of the floor were exchanging a few inaudible phrases no one else moved in the room: Laspara, with his back to us, kneeling on the chair, his elbows propped on the big-scale map, the shadowy enormity in the corner, the frankly staring man with the goatee on the sofa, the woman in the red blouse by his side – not one of them stirred. I suppose that really they had no time, for Miss Haldin withdrew her hand immediately from Peter Ivanovitch and before I was ready for her was moving to the door. A disregarded Westerner, I threw it open hurriedly and followed her out, my last glance leaving them all motionless in their varied poses: Peter Ivanovitch alone standing up, with his dark glasses like an enormous blind teacher, and behind him the vivid patch of light on the coloured map, pored over by the diminutive Laspara.

Later on, much later on, at the time of the newspaper rumours (they were vague and soon died out) of an abortive military conspiracy in Russia, I remembered the glimpse I had of that motionless group with its central figure. No details ever came out, but it was known that the revolutionary parties abroad had given their assistance, had sent emissaries in advance, that even money was found to dispatch a steamer with a cargo of arms and conspirators to invade the Baltic provinces. And while my eyes scanned the imperfect disclosures (in which the world was not much interested) I thought that the old, settled Europe had been given in my person attending that Russian girl something like a glimpse behind the scenes. A short, strange glimpse on the top floor of a great hotel of all places in the world: the great man himself; the motionless great bulk in the corner of the slayer of spies and gendarmes; Yakovlitch the veteran of ancient terrorist campaigns; the woman with her hair as white as mine and the lively black eyes, all in a mysterious half-light, with the strongly lighted map of Russia on the table. The woman I had the opportunity to see again. As we were waiting for the lift she came hurrying along the corridor, with her eyes fastened on Miss Haldin's face, and drew her aside as if for a confidential communication. It was not long. A few words only.

Going down in the lift, Natalia Haldin did not break the silence. It was only when out of the hotel and as we moved along the quay in the fresh darkness spangled by the quay lights, reflected in the black water of the little port on our left hand, and with lofty piles of hotels on our right, that she spoke.

'That was Sophia Antonovna – you know the woman? . . .'

'Yes, I know – the famous . . .'

'The same. It appears that after we went out Peter Ivanovitch told them why I had come. That was the reason she ran out after us. She named herself to me, and then she said, "You are the sister of a brave man who shall be remembered. You may see better times." I told her I hoped to see the time when all this would be forgotten, even if the name of my brother were to be forgotten too. Something moved me to say that, but you understand?'

'Yes,' I said. 'You think of the era of concord and justice.'

'Yes. There is too much hate and revenge in that work. It must be done. It is a sacrifice – and so let it be all the greater. Destruction is the work of anger. Let the tyrants and the slayers be forgotten together, and only the reconstructors be remembered.'

'And did Sophia Antonovna agree with you?' I asked sceptically.

'She did not say anything except, "It is good for you to believe in love." I should think she understood me. Then she asked me if I hoped to see Mr Razumov presently. I said I trusted I could manage to bring him to see my mother this evening, as my mother had learned of his being here and was morbidly impatient to learn if he could tell us something of Victor. He was the only friend of my brother we knew of, and a great intimate. She said, "Oh! Your brother – yes. Please tell Mr Razumov that I have made public the story which came to me from St Petersburg. It concerns your brother's arrest," she added. "He was betrayed by a man of the people who has since hanged himself. Mr Razumov will explain it all to you. I gave him the full information this afternoon. And please tell Mr Razumov that Sophia Antonovna sends him her greetings. I am going away early in the morning – far away."'

And Miss Haldin added, after a moment of silence –

'I was so moved by what I heard so unexpectedly that I simply could not speak to you before . . . A man of the people! Oh, our poor people!'

She walked slowly, as if tired out suddenly. Her head drooped; from the windows of a building with terraces and balconies came the banal sound of hotel music; before the low mean portals of the Casino two red posters blazed under the electric lamps, with a cheap provincial effect – and the emptiness of the quays, the desert aspect of the streets, had an air of hypocritical respectability and of inexpressible dreariness.

I had taken for granted she had obtained the address, and let myself be guided by her. On the Mont Blanc bridge, where a few dark figures seemed lost in the wide and long perspective defined by the lights, she said –

'It isn't very far from our house. I somehow thought it couldn't be. The address is Rue de Carouge. I think it must be one of those big new houses for artisans.'

She took my arm confidingly, familiarly, and accelerated her pace. There was something primitive in our proceedings. We did not think of the resources of civilization. A late tramcar overtook us; a row of *fiacres* stood by the railing of the gardens. It never entered our heads to make use of these conveyances. She was too hurried, perhaps, and as to myself – well, she had taken my arm confidingly. As we were ascending the easy incline of the Corraterie, all the shops shuttered and no light in any of the windows (as if all the mercenary population had fled at the end of the day), she said tentatively –

'I could run in for a moment to have a look at mother. It would not be much out of the way.'

I dissuaded her. If Mrs Haldin really expected to see Razumov that night it would have been unwise to show herself without him. The sooner we got hold of the young man and brought him along to calm her mother's agitation the better. She assented to my reasoning, and we crossed diagonally the Place de Théâtre, bluish grey with its floor of slabs of stone, under the electric light, and the lonely equestrian statue all black in the middle. In the Rue de Carouge we were in the poorer quarters and approaching the outskirts of the town. Vacant building plots alternated with high, new houses. At the corner of a side street the crude light of a whitewashed shop fell into the night, fan-like, through a wide doorway. One could see from a distance the inner wall with its scantily furnished shelves, and the deal counter painted brown. That was the house. Approaching it along the dark stretch of a fence of tarred planks, we saw the narrow pallid face of the cut angle, five single windows high, without a gleam in them, and crowned by the heavy shadow of a jutting roof slope.

311

'We must inquire in the shop,' Miss Haldin directed me.

A sallow, thinly whiskered man, wearing a dingy white collar and a frayed tie, laid down a newspaper, and, leaning familiarly on both elbows far over the bare counter, answered that the person I was inquiring for was indeed his *locataire* on the third floor, but that for the moment he was out.

'For the moment,' I repeated, after a glance at Miss Haldin. 'Does this mean that you expect him back at once?'

He was very gentle, with ingratiating eyes and soft lips. He smiled faintly as though he knew all about everything. Mr Razumov, after being absent all day, had returned early in the evening. He was very surprised about half an hour or a little more ago to see him come down again. Mr Razumov left his key, and in the course of some words which passed between them had remarked that he was going out because he needed air.

From behind the bare counter he went on smiling at us, his head held between his hands. Air. Air. But whether that meant a long or a short absence it was difficult to say. The night was very close, certainly.

After a pause, his ingratiating eyes turned to the door, he added –

'The storm will drive him in.'

'There's going to be a storm?' I asked.

'Why, yes!'

As if to confirm his words we heard a very distant, deep rumbling noise.

Consulting Miss Haldin by a glance, I saw her so reluctant to give up her quest that I asked the shopkeeper, in case Mr Razumov came home within half an hour, to beg him to remain downstairs in the shop. We would look in again presently.

For all answer he moved his head imperceptibly. The approval of Miss Haldin was expressed by her silence. We walked slowly down the street, away from the town; the low garden walls of the modest villas doomed to demolition were overhung by the boughs of trees and masses of foliage, lighted from below by gas lamps. The violent and monotonous noise of the icy waters of the Arve falling over a low dam swept towards us with a chilly draught of air across a great open space, where a double line of lamp-lights outlined a street as yet without houses. But on the other shore, overhung by the awful blackness of the thunder-cloud, a solitary dim light seemed to watch us with a weary stare. When we had strolled as far as the bridge, I said –

'We had better get back ...'

In the shop the sickly man was studying his smudgy newspaper, now spread out largely on the counter. He just raised his head when I looked in and shook it negatively, pursing up his lips. I rejoined Miss Haldin outside at once, and we moved off at a brisk pace. She remarked that she would send Anna with a note the first thing in the morning. I respected her taciturnity, silence being perhaps the best way to show my concern.

The semi-rural street we followed on our return changed gradually to the usual town thoroughfare, broad and deserted. We did not meet four people altogether, and the way seemed interminable, because my companion's natural anxiety had communicated itself sympathetically to me. At last we turned into the Boulevard des Philosophes, more wide, more empty, more dead – the very desolation of slumbering respectability. At the sight of the two lighted windows, very conspicuous from afar, I had the mental vision of Mrs Haldin in her armchair keeping a dreadful, tormenting vigil under the evil spell of an arbitrary rule: a victim of tyranny and revolution, a sight at once cruel and absurd.

III

'You will come in for a moment?' said Natalia Haldin.

I demurred on account of the late hour. 'You know mother likes you so much,' she insisted.

'I will just come in to hear how your mother is.'

She said, as if to herself, 'I don't even know whether she will believe that I could not find Mr Razumov, since she has taken it into her head that I am concealing something from her. You may be able to persuade her ...'

'Your mother may mistrust me too,' I observed.

'You! Why? What could you have to conceal from her? You are not a Russian nor a conspirator.'

I felt profoundly my European remoteness, and said nothing, but I made up my mind to play my part of helpless spectator to the end. The distant rolling of thunder in the valley of the Rhone was coming nearer to the sleeping town of prosaic virtues and universal hospitality. We crossed the street opposite the great dark gateway, and Miss Haldin rang at the door of the apartment. It was opened almost instantly, as if the elderly maid had been waiting in the ante-room for our return. Her flat physiognomy had an air of satisfaction. The gentleman was there, she declared, while closing the door.

Neither of us understood. Miss Haldin turned round brusquely to her. 'Who?'

'Herr Razumov,' she explained.

She had heard enough of our conversation before we left to know why her young mistress was going out. Therefore, when the gentleman gave his name at the door, she admitted him at once.

'No one could have foreseen that,' Miss Haldin murmured, with her serious grey eyes fixed upon mine. And, remembering the expression of the young man's face seen not much more than four hours ago, the look of a haunted somnambulist, I wondered with a sort of awe.

'You asked my mother first?' Miss Haldin inquired of the maid.

'No. I announced the gentleman,' she answered, surprised at our troubled faces.

'Still,' I said in an undertone, 'your mother was prepared.'

'Yes. But he has no idea ...'

It seemed to me she doubted his tact. To her question how long the gentleman had been with her mother, the maid told us that *der Herr* had been in the drawing-room no more than a short quarter of an hour.

She waited a moment, then withdrew, looking a little scared. Miss Haldin gazed at me in silence.

'As things have turned out,' I said, 'you happen to know exactly what your brother's friend has to tell your mother. And surely after that ...'

'Yes,' said Natalia Haldin slowly. 'I only wonder, as I was not

314

here when he came, if it wouldn't be better not to interrupt now.'

We remained silent, and I suppose we both strained our ears, but no sound reached us through the closed door. The features of Miss Haldin expressed a painful irresolution; she made a movement as if to go in, but checked herself. She had heard footsteps on the other side of the door. It came open, and Razumov, without pausing, stepped out into the ante-room. The fatigue of that day and the struggle with himself had changed him so much that I would have hesitated to recognize that face which, only a few hours before, when he brushed against me in front of the post office, had been startling enough but quite different. It had been not so lived in then, and its eyes not so sombre. They certainly looked more sane now, but there was upon them the shadow of something consciously evil.

I speak of that, because, at first, their glance fell on me, though without any sort of recognition or even comprehension. I was simply in the line of his stare. I don't know if he had heard the bell or expected to see anybody. He was going out, I believe, and I do not think that he saw Miss Haldin till she advanced towards him a step or two. He disregarded the hand she put out.

'It's you, Natalia Victorovna ... Perhaps you are surprised ... at this late hour. But, you see, I remembered our conversations in that garden. I thought really it was your wish that I should – without loss of time ... so I came. No other reason. Simply to tell ...'

He spoke with difficulty. I noticed that, and remembered his declaration to the man in the shop that he was going out because he 'needed air'. If that was his object, then it was clear that he had miserably failed. With downcast eyes and lowered head he made an effort to pick up the strangled phrase.

'To tell what I have heard myself only today – today ...'

Through the door he had not closed I had a view of the drawing-room. It was lighted only by a shaded lamp – Mrs Haldin's eyes could not support either gas or electricity. It was a comparatively big room, and in contrast with the strongly lighted ante-room its length was lost in semi-transparent gloom backed by heavy shadows; and on that ground I saw the motionless figure of Mrs

Haldin, inclined slightly forward, with a pale hand resting on the arm of the chair.

She did not move. With the window before her she had no longer that attitude suggesting expectation. The blind was down; and outside there was only the night sky harbouring a thunder-cloud, and the town indifferent and hospitable in its cold, almost scornful, toleration – a respectable town of refuge to which all these sorrows and hopes were nothing. Her white head was bowed.

The thought that the real drama of autocracy is not played on the great stage of politics came to me as, fated to be a spectator, I had this other glimpse behind the scenes, something more profound than the words and gestures of the public play. I had the certitude that this mother refused in her heart to give her son up after all. It was more than Rachel's inconsolable mourning,[19] it was something deeper, more inaccessible in its frightful tranquillity. Lost in the ill-defined mass of the high-backed chair, her white, inclined profile suggested the contemplation of something in her lap, as though a beloved head were resting there.

I had this glimpse behind the scenes, and then Miss Haldin, passing by the young man, shut the door. It was not done without hesitation. For a moment I thought that she would go to her mother, but she sent in only an anxious glance. Perhaps if Mrs Haldin had moved ... but no. There was in the immobility of that bloodless face the dreadful aloofness of suffering without remedy.

Meantime the young man kept his eyes fixed on the floor. The thought that he would have to repeat the story he had told already was intolerable to him. He had expected to find the two women together. And then, he had said to himself, it would be over for all time – for all time. 'It's lucky I don't believe in another world,' he had thought cynically.

Alone in his room after having posted his secret letter, he had regained a certain measure of composure by writing in his secret diary. He was aware of the danger of that strange self-indulgence. He alludes to it himself, but he could not refrain. It calmed him – it reconciled him to his existence. He sat there scribbling by the light of a solitary candle, till it occurred to him that having heard the explanation of Haldin's arrest, as put forward by Sophia Antonovna, it behoved him to tell these ladies himself. They were certain to hear the tale through some other channel. and then his abstention would look strange, not only to the mother and sister of Haldin, but to other people also. Having come to this conclusion, he did not discover in himself any marked reluctance to face the necessity, and very soon an anxiety to be done with it began to torment him. He looked at his watch. No; it was not absolutely too late.

The fifteen minutes with Mrs Haldin were like the revenge of the unknown: that white face, that weak, distinct voice; that head, at first turned to him eagerly, then, after a while. bowed again and motionless – in the dim, still light of the room in which his words which he tried to subdue resounded so loudly – had troubled him like some strange discovery. And there seemed to be a secret obstinacy in that sorrow, something he could not understand; at any rate, something he had not expected. Was it hostile? But it did not matter. Nothing could touch him now; in the eyes of the revolutionists there was now no shadow on his past. The phantom of Haldin had been indeed walked over, was left behind lying powerless and passive on the pavement covered with snow. And this was the phantom's mother consumed with grief and white as a ghost. He had felt a pitying surprise. But that, of course. was of no importance. Mothers did not matter. He could not shake off the poignant impression of that silent, quiet. white-haired woman, but a sort of sternness crept into his thoughts. These were the consequences. Well, what of it? 'Am I then on a bed of roses?' he had exclaimed to himself, sitting at some distance with his eyes fixed upon that figure of sorrow. He had said all he had to say to her. and when he had finished she had not uttered a word. She had turned away her head while he was speaking. The silence which had fallen on his last words had lasted for five minutes or more. What did it mean? Before its incomprehensible character he became conscious of anger in his stern mood, the old anger against Haldin reawakened by the contemplation of Haldin's mother. And was it not something like enviousness which gripped his heart. as if of a privilege denied to him alone of all the men that had ever passed through this world? It was the other who had attained to repose and yet continued to exist in the affection of that mourning old woman. in the thoughts of all these people posing for lovers of humanity. It was impossible to get rid of him. 'It's myself whom I have given up to destruction,' thought Razumov. 'He has induced me to do it. I can't shake him off.'

Alarmed by that discovery, he got up and strode out of the silent, dim room with its silent old woman in the chair, that mother! He never looked back. It was frankly a flight. But on opening the door he saw his retreat cut off. There was the sister. He had never forgotten the sister, only he had not expected to see her then – or ever any more, perhaps. Her presence in the ante-room was as unforeseen as the apparition of her brother had been. Razumov gave a start as though he had discovered himself cleverly trapped. He tried to smile, but could not manage it, and lowered his eyes. 'Must I repeat that silly story now?' he asked himself, and felt a sinking sensation. Nothing solid had passed his lips since the day before, but he was not in a state to analyse the origins of his weakness. He meant to take up his hat and depart with as few words as possible, but Miss Haldin's swift movement to shut the door took him by surprise. He half turned after her, but without raising his eyes, passively, just as a feather might stir in the disturbed air. The next moment she was back in the place she had started from, with another half-turn on his part, so that they came again into the same relative positions.

'Yes, yes,' she said hurriedly. 'I am very grateful to you, Kirylo Sidorovitch, for coming at once – like this . . . Only, I wish I had . . . Did mother tell you?'

'I wonder what she could have told me that I did not know before,' he said, obviously to himself, but perfectly audible. 'Because I always *did* know it,' he added louder, as if in despair.

He hung his head. He had such a strong sense of Natalia Haldin's presence that to look at her he felt would be a relief. It was she who had been haunting him now. He had suffered that persecution ever since she had suddenly appeared before him in the garden of the Villa Borel with an extended hand and the name of her brother on her lips . . . The ante-room had a row of books on the wall nearest to the outer door, while against the wall opposite there stood a small dark table and one chair. The paper, bearing a very faint design, was all but white. The light of an electric bulb high up under the ceiling searched that clear square box into its four bare corners, crudely, without shadows – a strange stage for an obscure drama.

'What do you mean?' asked Miss Haldin. 'What is it that you knew always?'

He raised his face, pale, full of unexpressed suffering. But that look in his eyes of dull, absent obstinacy, which struck, and surprised everybody he was talking to, began to pass away. It was as though he were coming to himself in the awakened consciousness of that marvellous harmony of feature, of lines, of glances, of voice, which made of the girl before him a being so rare, outside, and, as it were, above the common notion of beauty. He looked at her so long that she coloured slightly.

'What is it that you knew?' she repeated vaguely.

That time he managed a smile.

'Indeed, if it had not been for a word of greeting or two, I would doubt whether your mother was aware at all of my existence. You understand?'

Natalia Haldin nodded; her hands moved slightly by her side.

'Yes. Is it not heart-breaking? She has not shed a tear yet – not a single tear.'

'Not a tear! And you, Natalia Victorovna? You have been able to cry?'

'I have. And then I am young enough, Kirylo Sidorovitch, to believe in the future. But when I see my mother so terribly distracted, I almost forget everything. I ask myself whether one should feel proud – or only resigned. We had such a lot of people coming to see us. There were utter strangers who wrote asking for permission to call to present their respects. It was impossible to keep our door shut for ever. You know that Peter Ivanovitch himself ... Oh yes, there was much sympathy, but there were persons who exulted openly at that death. Then, when I was left alone with poor mother, all this seemed so wrong in spirit, something not worth the price she is paying for it. But directly I heard you were here in Geneva, Kirylo Sidorovitch, I felt that you were the only person who could assist me ...'

'In comforting a bereaved mother? Yes!' he broke in in a manner

319

which made her open her clear unsuspecting eyes. 'But there is a question of fitness. Has this occurred to you?'

There was a breathlessness in his utterance which contrasted with the monstrous hint of mockery in his intention.

'Why!' whispered Natalia Haldin with feeling. 'Who more fit than you?'

He had a convulsive movement of exasperation, but controlled himself.

'Indeed! Directly you heard that I was in Geneva, before even seeing me? It is another proof of that confidence which . . .'

All at once his tone changed, became more incisive and more detached.

'Men are poor creatures, Natalia Victorovna. They have no intuition of sentiment. In order to speak fittingly to a mother of her lost son one must have had some experience of the filial relation. It is not the case with me – if you must know the whole truth. Your hopes have to deal here with "a breast unwarmed by any affection", as the poet says . . . That does not mean it is insensible,' he added in a lower tone.

'I am certain your heart is not unfeeling,' said Miss Haldin softly.

'No. It is not as hard as a stone,' he went on in the same introspective voice, and looking as if his heart were lying as heavy as a stone in that unwarmed breast of which he spoke. 'No, not so hard. But how to prove what you give me credit for – ah! that's another question. No one has ever expected such a thing from me before. No one whom my tenderness would have been of any use to. And now you come. You! Now! No, Natalia Victorovna. It's too late. You come too late. You must expect nothing from me.'

She recoiled from him a little, though he had made no movement, as if she had seen some change in his face, charging his words with the significance of some hidden sentiment they shared together. To me, the silent spectator, they looked like two people becoming conscious of a spell which had been lying on them ever since they first set eyes on each other. Had either of them cast a glance then in my direction. I would have opened the door quietly and gone out. But neither did; and I remained, every fear of indiscretion lost in the sense of my enormous remoteness from their captivity within the sombre horizon of Russian problems, the boundary of their eyes, of their feelings – the prison of their souls.

Frank, courageous, Miss Haldin controlled her voice in the midst of her trouble.

'What can this mean?' she asked, as if speaking to herself.

'It may mean that you have given yourself up to vain imaginings while I have managed to remain amongst the truth of things and the realities of life – our Russian life – such as they are.'

'They are cruel,' she murmured.

'And ugly. Don't forget that – and ugly. Look where you like. Look near you, here abroad where you are, and then look back at home, whence you came.'

'One must look beyond the present.' Her tone had an ardent conviction.

'The blind can do that best. I have had the misfortune to be born clear-eyed. And if you only knew what strange things I have seen! What amazing and unexpected apparitions! ... But why talk of all this?'

'On the contrary, I want to talk of all this with you,' she protested with earnest serenity. The sombre humours of her brother's friend left her unaffected, as though that bitterness, that suppressed anger, were the signs of an indignant rectitude. She saw that he was not an ordinary person, and perhaps she did not want him to be other than he appeared to her trustful eyes. 'Yes, with you especially,' she insisted. 'With you of all the Russian people in the world . . .' A faint smile dwelt for a moment on her lips. 'I am like poor mother in a way. I too seem unable to give up our beloved dead, who, don't forget, was all in all to us. I don't want to abuse your sympathy, but you must understand that it is in you that we can find all that is left of his generous soul.'

I was looking at him; not a muscle of his face moved in the least. And yet, even at the time, I did not suspect him of insensibility. It was a sort of rapt thoughtfulness. Then he stirred slightly.

'You are going, Kirylo Sidorovitch?' she asked.

'I! Going? Where? Oh yes, but I must tell you first . . .' His voice was muffled and he forced himself to produce it with visible repugnance, as if speech were something disgusting or deadly. 'That story, you know – the story I heard this afternoon ...'

'I know the story already,' she said sadly.

'You know it! Have you correspondents in St Petersburg too?'

'No. It's Sophia Antonovna. I have seen her just now. She sends you her greetings. She is going away tomorrow.'

He had lowered at last his fascinated glance; she too was looking down, and standing thus before each other in the glaring light, between the four bare walls, they seemed brought out from the confused immensity of the Eastern borders to be exposed cruelly to the observation of my Western eyes. And I observed them. There was nothing else to do. My existence seemed so utterly forgotten by these two that I dared not now make a movement. And I thought to myself that, of course, they had to come together, the sister and the friend of that dead man. The ideas, the hopes, the aspirations, the cause of Freedom, expressed in their common affection for Victor Haldin, the moral victim of autocracy – all this must draw them to each other fatally. Her very ignorance and his loneliness to which he had alluded so strangely must work to that end. And, indeed, I saw that the work was done already. Of course. It was manifest that they must have been thinking of each other for a long time before they met. She had the letter from that beloved brother kindling her imagination by the severe praise attached to that one name; and for him to see that exceptional girl was enough. The only cause for surprise was his gloomy aloofness before her clearly expressed welcome. But he was young, and however austere and devoted to his revolutionary ideals, he was not blind. The period of reserve was over; he was coming forward in his own way. I could not mistake the significance of this late visit, for in what he had to say there was nothing urgent. The true cause dawned upon me: he had discovered that he needed her – and she was moved by the same feeling. It was the second time that I saw them together, and I knew that next time they met I would not be there, either remembered or forgotten. I would have virtually ceased to exist for both these young people.

I made this discovery in a very few moments. Meantime, Natalia Haldin was telling Razumov briefly of our peregrinations from one end of Geneva to the other. While speaking she raised her hands above her head to untie her veil, and that movement displayed for an instant the seductive grace of her youthful figure, clad in the simplest of mourning. In the transparent shadow the hat rim threw on her face her grey eyes had an enticing lustre. Her voice, with its unfeminine yet exquisite timbre, was steady, and she spoke quickly, frank, unembarrassed. As she justified her action by the mental state of her mother, a spasm of pain marred the generously confiding harmony of her features. I perceived that with his downcast eyes he had the air of a man who is listening to a strain of music rather than to articulated speech. And in the same way, after she had ceased, he seemed to listen yet, motionless, as if under the spell of suggestive sound. He came to himself, muttering –

'Yes, yes. She has not shed a tear. She did not seem to hear what I was saying. I might have told her anything. She looked as if no longer belonging to this world.'

Miss Haldin gave signs of profound distress. Her voice faltered. 'You don't know how bad it has come to be. She expects now to *see him*!' The veil dropped from her fingers and she clasped her hands in anguish. 'It shall end by her seeing him,' she cried.

Razumov raised his head sharply and attached on her a prolonged thoughtful glance.

'H'm. That's very possible,' he muttered in a peculiar tone, as if giving his opinion on a matter of fact. 'I wonder what ...' He checked himself.

'That would be the end. Her mind will be gone then, and her spirit will follow.'

Miss Haldin unclasped her hands and let them fall by her side.

'You think so?' he queried profoundly. Miss Haldin's lips were slightly parted. Something unexpected and unfathomable in that young man's character had fascinated her from the first. 'No! There's neither truth nor consolation to be got from the phantoms of the dead,' he added after a weighty pause. 'I might have told her something true; for instance, that your brother meant to save his life – to escape. There can be no doubt of that. But I did not.'

'You did not! But why?'

'I don't know. Other thoughts came into my head,' he answered. He seemed to me to be watching himself inwardly, as though he were trying to count his own heart-beats, while his eyes never for a moment left the face of the girl. 'You were not there,' he continued. 'I had made up my mind never to see you again.'

This seemed to take her breath away for a moment.

'You ... How is it possible?'

'You may well ask ... However, I think that I refrained from telling your mother from prudence. I might have assured her that in the last conversation he held as a free man he mentioned you both ...'

'That last conversation was with you,' she struck in her deep, moving voice. 'Some day you must ...'

'It was with me. Of you he said that you had trustful eyes. And why I have not been able to forget that phrase I don't know. It meant that there is in you no guile, no deception, no falsehood, no suspicion – nothing in your heart that could give you a conception of a living, acting, speaking lie, if ever it came in your way. That you are a predestined victim ... Ha! what a devilish suggestion!'

The convulsive, uncontrolled tone of the last words disclosed the precarious hold he had over himself. He was like a man defying his own dizziness in high places and tottering suddenly on the very edge of the precipice. Miss Haldin pressed her hand to her breast. The dropped black veil lay on the floor between them. Her movement steadied him. He looked intently on that hand till it descended slowly, and then raised again his eyes to her face. But he did not give her time to speak.

'No? You don't understand? Very well.' He had recovered his calm by a miracle of will. 'So you talked with Sophia Antonovna?'

'Yes. Sophia Antonovna told me ...' Miss Haldin stopped, wonder growing in her wide eyes.

'H'm. That's the respectable enemy,' he muttered, as though he were alone.

'The tone of her references to you was extremely friendly,' remarked Miss Haldin, after waiting for a while.

'Is that your impression? And she the most intelligent of the lot, too. Things then are going as well as possible. Everything conspires to ... Ah! these conspirators,' he said slowly, with an accent of scorn; 'they would get hold of you in no time! You know, Natalia

324

Victorovna, I have the greatest difficulty in saving myself from the superstition of an active Providence. It's irresistible ... The alternative, of course, would be the personal Devil of our simple ancestors. But, if so, he has overdone it altogether – the old Father of Lies – our national patron – our domestic god, whom we take with us when we go abroad. He has overdone it. It seems that I am not simple enough ... That's it! I ought to have known ... And I did know it,' he added in a tone of poignant distress which overcame my astonishment.

'This man is deranged,' I said to myself, very much frightened.

The next moment he gave me a very special impression beyond the range of commonplace definitions. It was as though he had stabbed himself outside and had come in there to show it: and more than that – as though he were turning the knife in the wound and watching the effect. That was the impression, rendered in physical terms. One could not defend oneself from a certain amount of pity. But it was for Miss Haldin, already so tried in her deepest affections, that I felt a serious concern. Her attitude, her face, expressed compassion struggling with doubt on the verge of terror.

'What is it, Kirylo Sidorovitch?' There was a hint of tenderness in that cry. He only stared at her in that complete surrender of all his faculties which in a happy lover would have had the name of ecstasy.

'Why are you looking at me like this, Kirylo Sidorovitch? I have approached you frankly. I need at this time to see clearly in myself ...' She ceased for a moment as if to give him an opportunity to utter at last some word worthy of her exalted trust in her brother's friend. His silence became impressive, like a sign of a momentous resolution.

In the end Miss Haldin went on, appealingly –

'I have waited for you anxiously. But now that you have been moved to come to us in your kindness, you alarm me. You speak obscurely. It seems as if you were keeping back something from me.'

'Tell me, Natalia Victorovna,' he was heard at last in a strange unringing voice, 'whom did you see in that place?'

She was startled, and as if deceived in her expectations.

'Where? In Peter Ivanovitch's rooms? There was Mr Laspara and three other people.'

'Ha! The vanguard – the forlorn hope of the great plot,' he commented to himself. 'Bearers of the spark to start an explosion which is meant to change fundamentally the lives of so many millions in order that Peter Ivanovitch should be the head of a State.'

'You are teasing me,' she said. 'Our dear one told me once to remember that men serve always something greater than themselves – the idea.'

'Our dear one,' he repeated slowly. The effort he made to appear unmoved absorbed all the force of his soul. He stood before her like a being with hardly a breath of life. His eyes, even as under great physical suffering, had lost all their fire. 'Ah! your brother . . . But on your lips, in your voice, it sounds . . . and indeed in you everything is divine . . . I wish I could know the innermost depths of your thoughts, of your feelings.'

'But why, Kirylo Sidorovitch?' she cried, alarmed by these words coming out of strangely lifeless lips.

'Have no fear. It is not to betray you. So you went there? . . . And Sophia Antonovna, what did she tell you, then?'

'She said very little, really. She knew that I should hear everything from you. She had not time for more than a few words.' Miss Haldin's voice dropped and she became silent for a moment. 'The man, it appears, has taken his life,' she said sadly.

'Tell me, Natalia Victorovna,' he asked after a pause, 'do you believe in remorse?'

'What a question!'

'What can *you* know of it?' he muttered thickly. 'It is not for such as you . . . What I meant to ask was whether you believed in the efficacy of remorse?'

She hesitated as though she had not understood, then her face lighted up.

'Yes,' she said firmly.

'So he is absolved. Moreover, that Ziemianitch was a brute, a drunken brute.'

A shudder passed through Natalia Haldin.

'But a man of the people,' Razumov went on, 'to whom they, the revolutionists, tell a tale of sublime hopes. Well, the people must be forgiven ... And you must not believe all you've heard from that source, either,' he added, with a sort of sinister reluctance.

'You are concealing something from me,' she exclaimed.

'Do you, Natalia Victorovna, believe in the duty of revenge?'

'Listen, Kirylo Sidorovitch. I believe that the future will be merciful to us all. Revolutionist and reactionary, victim and executioner, betrayer and betrayed, they shall all be pitied together when the light breaks on our black sky at last. Pitied and forgotten; for without that there can be no union and no love.'

'I hear. No revenge for you, then? Never? Not the least bit?' He smiled bitterly with his colourless lips. 'You yourself are like the very spirit of that merciful future. Strange that it does not make it easier ... No! But suppose that the real betrayer of your brother – Ziemianitch had a part in it too, but insignificant and quite involuntary – suppose that he was a young man, educated, an intellectual worker, thoughtful, a man your brother might have trusted lightly, perhaps, but still – suppose ... But there's a whole story there.'

'And you know the story! But why, then –'

'I have heard it. There is a staircase in it, and even phantoms, but that does not matter if a man always serves something greater than himself – the idea. I wonder who is the greatest victim in that tale?'

'In that tale!' Miss Haldin repeated. She seemed turned into stone.

'Do you know why I came to you? It is simply because there is no one anywhere in the whole great world I could go to. Do you understand what I say? Not one to go to. Do you conceive the desolation of the thought – no one – to – go – to?'

Utterly misled by her own enthusiastic interpretation of two lines in the letter of a visionary, under the spell of her own dread of lonely days, in their overshadowed world of angry strife, she was unable to see the truth struggling on his lips. What she was conscious of was the obscure form of his suffering. She was on the point of extending her hand to him impulsively when he spoke again.

'An hour after I saw you first I knew how it would be. The terrors of remorse, revenge, confession, anger, hate, fear, are like nothing to the atrocious temptation which you put in my way the day you

327

appeared before me with your voice, with your face, in the garden of that accursed villa.'

She looked utterly bewildered for a moment; then, with a sort of despairing insight went straight to the point.

'The story, Kirylo Sidorovitch, the story!'

'There is no more to tell!' He made a movement forward, and she actually put her hand on his shoulder to push him away; but her strength failed her, and he kept his ground, though trembling in every limb. 'It ends here – on this very spot.' He pressed a denunciatory finger to his breast with force, and became perfectly still.

I ran forward, snatching up the chair, and was in time to catch hold of Miss Haldin and lower her down. As she sank into it she swung half round on my arm, and remained averted from us both, drooping over the back. He looked at her with an appalling expressionless tranquillity. Incredulity, struggling with astonishment, anger, and disgust, deprived me for a time of the power of speech. Then I turned on him, whispering from very rage –

'This is monstrous. What are you staying for? Don't let her catch sight of you again. Go away! ...' He did not budge. 'Don't you understand that your presence is intolerable – even to me? If there's any sense of shame in you ...'

Slowly his sullen eyes moved in my direction. 'How did this old man come here?' he muttered, astounded.

Suddenly Miss Haldin sprang up from the chair, made a few steps, and tottered. Forgetting my indignation, and even the man himself, I hurried to her assistance. I took her by the arm, and she let me lead her into the drawing-room. Away from the lamp, in the deeper dusk of the distant end, the profile of Mrs Haldin, her hands, her whole figure had the stillness of a sombre painting. Miss Haldin stopped, and pointed mournfully at the tragic immobility of her mother, who seemed to watch a beloved head lying in her lap.

That gesture had an unequalled force of expression, so far-reaching in its human distress that one could not believe that it pointed out merely the ruthless working of political institutions. After assisting Miss Haldin to the sofa, I turned round to go back and shut the door. Framed in the opening, in the searching glare of the white ante-room, my eyes fell on Razumov, still there, standing before the empty chair, as if rooted for ever to the spot of his atrocious confession. A wonder came over me that the mysterious force which had torn it out of him had failed to destroy his life, to shatter his body. It was there unscathed. I stared at the broad line of his shoulders, his dark head, the amazing immobility of his limbs. At his feet the veil dropped by Miss Haldin looked intensely black in the white crudity of the light. He was gazing at it spell-bound. Next moment, stooping with an incredible, savage swiftness, he snatched it up and pressed it to his face with both hands. Something, extreme astonishment perhaps, dimmed my eyes, so that he seemed to vanish before he moved.

The slamming of the outer door restored my sight, and I went on contemplating the empty chair in the empty ante-room. The meaning of what I had seen reached my mind with a staggering shock. I seized Natalia Haldin by the shoulder.

'That miserable wretch has carried off your veil!' I cried, in the scared, deadened voice of an awful discovery. 'He ...'

The rest remained unspoken. I stepped back and looked down at her, in silent horror. Her hands were lying lifelessly, palms upwards, on her lap. She raised her grey eyes slowly. Shadows seemed to come and go in them as if the steady flame of her soul had been made to vacillate at last in the cross-currents of poisoned air from the corrupted dark immensity claiming her for its own, where virtues themselves fester into crimes in the cynicism of oppression and revolt.

'It is impossible to be more unhappy ...' The languid whisper of her voice struck me with dismay. 'It is impossible ... I feel my heart becoming like ice.'

IV

Razumov walked straight home on the wet glistening pavement. A heavy shower passed over him; distant lightning played faintly against the fronts of the dumb houses with the shuttered shops all along the Rue de Carouge; and now and then, after the faint flash, there was a faint, sleepy rumble: but the main forces of the thunderstorm remained massed down the Rhone valley as if loath to attack the respectable and passionless abode of democratic liberty, the serious-minded town of dreary hotels, tendering the same indifferent hospitality to tourists of all nations and to international conspirators of every shade.

The owner of the shop was making ready to close when Razumov entered and without a word extended his hand for the key of his room. On reaching it for him, from a shelf, the man was about to pass a small joke as to taking the air in a thunderstorm, but, after looking at the face of his lodger, he only observed, just to say something –

'You've got very wet.'

'Yes, I am washed clean,' muttered Razumov, who was dripping from head to foot, and passed through the inner door towards the staircase leading to his room.

He did not change his clothes, but, after lighting the candle, took off his watch and chain, laid them on the table, and sat down at once to write. The book of his compromising record was kept in a locked drawer, which he pulled out violently, and did not even trouble to push back afterwards.

In this queer pedantism of a man who had read, thought, lived, pen in hand, there is the sincerity of the attempt to grapple by the same means with another profounder knowledge. After some passages which have been already made use of in the building up of this narrative, or add nothing new to the psychological side of this disclosure (there is even one more allusion to the silver medal in this last entry), comes a page and a half of incoherent writing where his expression is baffled by the novelty and the mysteriousness of that side of our emotional life to which his solitary existence had been a stranger. Then only he begins to address directly the reader he had in his mind, trying to express in broken sentences, full of wonder and awe, the sovereign (he uses that very word) power of her person over his imagination, in which lay the dormant seed of her brother's words.

'. . . The most trustful eyes in the world – your brother said of you when he was as well as a dead man already. And when you stood before me with your hand extended, I remembered the very sound

330

of his voice, and I looked into your eyes – and that was enough. I knew that something had happened, but I did not know then what ... But don't be deceived, Natalia Victorovna. I believed that I had in my breast nothing but an inexhaustible fund of anger and hate for you both. I remembered that he had looked to you for the perpetuation of his visionary soul. He, this man who had robbed me of my hard-working, purposeful existence. I, too, had my guiding idea; and remember that, amongst us, it is more difficult to lead a life of toil and self-denial than to go out in the street and kill from conviction. But enough of that. Hate or no hate, I felt at once that, while shunning the sight of you, I could never succeed in driving away your image. I would say, addressing that dead man, "Is this the way you are going to haunt me?" It is only later on that I understood – only today, only a few hours ago. What could I have known of what was tearing me to pieces and dragging the secret for ever to my lips? You were appointed to undo the evil by making me betray myself back into truth and peace. You! And you have done it in the same way, too, in which he ruined me: by forcing upon me your confidence. Only what I detested him for, in you ended by appearing noble and exalted. But, I repeat, be not deceived. I was given up to evil. I exulted in having induced that silly innocent fool to steal his father's money. He was a fool, but not a thief. I made him one. It was necessary. I had to confirm myself in my contempt and hate for what I betrayed. I have suffered from as many vipers in my heart as any social democrat of them all – vanity, ambitions, jealousies, shameful desires, evil passions of envy and revenge. I had my security stolen from me, years of good work, my best hopes. Listen – now comes the true confession. The other was nothing. To save me, your trustful eyes had to entice my thought to the very edge of the blackest treachery. I could see them constantly looking at me with the confidence of your pure heart which had not been touched by evil things. Victor Haldin had stolen the truth of my life from me, who had nothing else in the world, and he boasted of living on through you on this earth where I had no place to lay my head. She will marry some day, he had said – and your eyes were trustful. And do you know what I said to myself? I shall steal his sister's soul from her. When we met that first morning in the gardens, and you

331

spoke to me confidingly in the generosity of your spirit, I was thinking, "Yes, he himself by talking of her trustful eyes has delivered her into my hands!" If you could have looked then into my heart, you would have cried out aloud with terror and disgust.

'Perhaps no one will believe the baseness of such an intention to be possible. It's certain that, when we parted that morning, I gloated over it. I brooded upon the best way. The old man you introduced me to insisted on walking with me. I don't know who he is. He talked of you, of your lonely, helpless state, and every word of that friend of yours was egging me on to the unpardonable sin of stealing a soul. Could he have been the devil himself in the shape of an old Englishman? Natalia Victorovna, I was possessed! I returned to look at you every day, and drink in your presence the poison of my infamous intention. But I foresaw difficulties. Then Sophia Anto-novna, of whom I was not thinking – I had forgotten her existence – appears suddenly with that tale from St Petersburg ... The only thing needed to make me safe – a trusted revolutionist for ever.

'It was as if Ziemianitch had hanged himself to help me on to further crime. The strength of falsehood seemed irresistible. These people stood doomed by the folly and the illusion that was in them – they being themselves the slaves of lies. Natalia Victorovna, I embraced the might of falsehood, I exulted in it – I gave myself up to it for a time. Who could have resisted! You yourself were the prize of it. I sat alone in my room, planning a life, the very thought of which makes me shudder now, like a believer who had been tempted to an atrocious sacrilege. But I brooded ardently over its images. The only thing was that there seemed to be no air in it. And also I was afraid of your mother. I never knew mine. I've never known any kind of love. There is something in the mere word ... Of you, I was not afraid – forgive me for telling you this. No, not of you. You were truth itself. You could not suspect me. As to your mother, you yourself feared already that her mind had given way from grief. Who could believe anything against me? Had not Ziem-ianitch hanged himself from remorse? I said to myself, "Let's put it to the test, and be done with it once for all." I trembled when I went in; but your mother hardly listened to what I was saying to her, and, in a little while, seemed to have forgotten my very existence. I sat

332

looking at her. There was no longer anything between you and me. You were defenceless – and soon, very soon, you would be alone ... I thought of you. Defenceless. For days you have talked with me – opening your heart. I remembered the shadow of your eyelashes over your grey trustful eyes. And your pure forehead! It is low like the forehead of statues – calm, unstained. It was as if your pure brow bore a light which fell on me, searched my heart and saved me from ignominy, from ultimate undoing. And it saved you too. Pardon my presumption. But there was that in your glances which seemed to tell me that you ... Your light! your truth! I felt that I must tell you that I had ended by loving you. And to tell you that I must first confess. Confess, go out – and perish.

'Suddenly you stood before me! You alone in all the world to whom I must confess. You fascinated me – you have freed me from the blindness of anger and hate – the truth shining in you drew the truth out of me. Now I have done it; and as I write here, I am in the depths of anguish, but there is air to breathe at last – air! And, by the by, that old man sprang up from somewhere as I was speaking to you, and raged at me like a disappointed devil. I suffer horribly, but I am not in despair. There is only one more thing to do for me. After that – if they let me – I shall go away and bury myself in obscure misery. In giving Victor Haldin up, it was myself, after all, whom I have betrayed most basely. You must believe what I say now, you can't refuse to believe this. Most basely. It is through you that I came to feel this so deeply. After all, it is they and not I who have the right on their side! – theirs is the strength of invisible powers. So be it. Only don't be deceived, Natalia Victorovna, I am not converted. Have I then the soul of a slave? No! I am independent – and therefore perdition is my lot.'

On these words, he stopped writing, shut the book, and wrapped it in the black veil he had carried off. He then ransacked the drawers for paper and string, made up a parcel which he addressed to Miss Haldin, Boulevard des Philosophes, and then flung the pen away from him into a distant corner.

This done, he sat down with the watch before him. He could have gone out at once, but the hour had not struck yet. The hour would be midnight. There was no reason for that choice except that the facts and the words of a certain evening in his past were timing his conduct in the present. The sudden power Natalia Haldin had gained over him he ascribed to the same cause. 'You don't walk with impunity over a phantom's breast,' he heard himself mutter. 'Thus he saves me,' he thought suddenly. 'He himself, the betrayed man.' The vivid image of Miss Haldin seemed to stand by him, watching him relentlessly. She was not disturbing. He had done with life, and his thought even in her presence tried to take an impartial survey. Now his scorn extended to himself. 'I had neither the simplicity nor the courage nor the self-possession to be a scoundrel, or an exceptionally able man. For who, with us in Russia, is to tell a scoundrel from an exceptionally able man? ...'

He was the puppet of his past, because at the very stroke of midnight he jumped up and ran swiftly downstairs as if confident that, by the power of destiny, the house door would fly open before the absolute necessity of his errand. And as a matter of fact, just as he got to the bottom of the stairs, it was opened for him by some people of the house coming home late – two men and a woman. He slipped out through them into the street, swept then by a fitful gust of wind. They were, of course, very much startled. A flash of lightning enabled them to observe him walking away quickly. One of the men shouted, and was starting in pursuit but the woman had recognized him. 'It's all right. It's only that young Russian from the third floor.' The darkness returned with a single clap of thunder, like a gun fired for a warning of his escape from the prison of lies.

He must have heard at some time or other and now remembered unconsciously that there was to be a gathering of revolutionists at the house of Julius Laspara that evening. At any rate, he made straight for the Laspara house, and found himself without surprise ringing at its street door, which, of course, was closed. By that time the thunderstorm had attacked in earnest. The steep incline of the street ran with water, the thick fall of rain enveloped him like a luminous veil in the play of lightning. He was perfectly calm, and, between the crashes, listened attentively to the delicate tinkling of the doorbell somewhere within the house.

There was some difficulty before he was admitted. His person was not known to that one of the guests who had volunteered to go downstairs and see what was the matter. Razumov argued with him patiently. There could be no harm in admitting a caller. He had something to communicate to the company upstairs.

'Something of importance?'

'That'll be for the hearers to judge.'

'Urgent?'

'Without a moment's delay.'

Meantime, one of the Laspara daughters descended the stairs, small lamp in hand, in a grimy and crumpled gown, which seemed to hang on her by a miracle, and looking more than ever like an old doll with a dusty brown wig, dragged from under a sofa. She recognized Razumov at once.

'How do you do? Of course you may come in.'

Following her light Razumov climbed two flights of stairs from the lower darkness. Leaving the lamp on a bracket on the landing, she opened a door, and went in, accompanied by the sceptical guest. Razumov entered last. He closed the door behind him, and stepping on one side, put his back against the wall.

The three little rooms *en suite*, with low, smoky ceilings and lit by paraffin lamps were crammed with people. Loud talking was going on in all three, and tea-glasses, full, half-full, and empty, stood everywhere, even on the floor. The other Laspara girl sat, dishevelled and languid, behind an enormous samovar. In the inner doorway Razumov had a glimpse of the protuberance of a large stomach, which he recognized. Only a few feet from him Julius Laspara was getting down hurriedly from his high stool.

The appearance of the midnight visitor caused no small sensation. Laspara is very summary in his version of that night's happenings. After some words of greeting, disregarded by Razumov, Laspara (ignoring purposely his guest's soaked condition and his extraordinary manner of presenting himself) mentioned something about writing an article. He was growing uneasy, and Razumov appeared absent-minded. 'I have written already all I shall ever write,' he said at last, with a little laugh.

The whole company's attention was riveted on the new-comer,

dripping with water, deadly pale, and keeping his position against the wall. Razumov put Laspara gently aside, as though he wished to be seen from head to foot by everybody. By then the buzz of conversations had died down completely, even in the most distant of the three rooms. The doorway facing Razumov became blocked by men and women, who craned their necks and certainly seemed to expect something startling to happen.

A squeaky, insolent declaration was heard from that group.

'I know this ridiculously conceited individual.'

'What individual?' asked Razumov, raising his bowed head, and searching with his eyes all the eyes fixed upon him. An intense surprised silence lasted for a time. 'If it's me . . .'

He stopped, thinking over the form of his confession, and found it suddenly, unavoidably suggested by the fateful evening of his life.

'I am come here,' he began, in a clear voice, 'to talk of an individual called Ziemianitch. Sophia Antonovna has informed me that she would make public a certain letter from St Petersburg . . .'

'Sophia Antonovna has left us early in the evening,' said Laspara. 'It's quite correct. Everybody here has heard . . .'

'Very well,' Razumov interrupted, with a shade of impatience, for his heart was beating strongly. Then mastering his voice so far that there was even a touch of irony in his clear, forcible enunciation –

'In justice to that individual, the much ill-used peasant, Ziemianitch, I now declare solemnly that the conclusions of that letter calumniate a man of the people – a bright Russian soul. Ziemianitch had nothing to do with the actual arrest of Victor Haldin.'

Razumov dwelt on the name heavily, and then waited till the faint, mournful murmur which greeted it had died out.

'Victor Victorovitch Haldin,' he began again, 'acting with, no doubt, noble-minded imprudence, took refuge with a certain student of whose opinions he knew nothing but what his own illusions suggested to his generous heart. It was an unwise display of confidence. But I am not here to appreciate the actions of Victor Haldin. Am I to tell you of the feelings of that student, sought out in his obscure solitude, and menaced by the complicity forced upon him? Am I to tell you what he did? It's a rather complicated story.

336

In the end the student went to General T— himself, and said, "I have the man who killed de P— locked up in my room, Victor Haldin – a student like myself." '

A great buzz arose, in which Razumov raised his voice.

'Observe – that man had certain honest ideals in view. But I didn't come here to explain him.'

'No. But you must explain how you know all this,' came in grave tones from somebody.

'A vile coward!' This simple cry vibrated with indignation. 'Name him!' shouted other voices.

'What are you clamouring for?' said Razumov disdainfully, in the profound silence which fell on the raising of his hand. 'Haven't you all understood that I am that man?'

Laspara went away brusquely from his side and climbed upon his stool. In the first forward surge of people towards him, Razumov expected to be torn to pieces, but they fell back without touching him, and nothing came of it but noise. It was bewildering. His head ached terribly. In the confused uproar he made out several times the name of Peter Ivanovitch, the word 'judgement', and the phrase, 'But this is a confession', uttered by somebody in a desperate shriek. In the midst of the tumult, a young man, younger than himself, approached him with blazing eyes.

'I must beg you,' he said, with venomous politeness, 'to be good enough not to move from this spot till you are told what you are to do.'

Razumov shrugged his shoulders.

'I came in voluntarily.'

'Maybe. But you won't go out till you are permitted,' retorted the other.

He beckoned with his hand, calling out, 'Louisa! Louisa! come here, please'; and, presently, one of the Laspara girls (they had been staring at Razumov from behind the samovar) came along, trailing a bedraggled tail of dirty flounces, and dragging with her a chair, which she set against the door, and, sitting down on it, crossed her legs. The young man thanked her effusively, and rejoined a group carrying on an animated discussion in low tones. Razumov lost himself for a moment.

337

A squeaky voice screamed, 'Confession or no confession, you are a police spy!'

The revolutionist Nikita had pushed his way in front of Razumov, and faced him with his big, livid cheeks, his heavy paunch, bull neck, and enormous hands. Razumov looked at the famous slayer of gendarmes in silent disgust.

'And what are you?' he said, very low, then shut his eyes, and rested the back of his head against the wall.

'It would be better for you to depart now.' Razumov heard a mild, sad voice, and opened his eyes. The gentle speaker was an elderly man, with a great brush of fine hair making a silvery halo all round his keen, intelligent face. 'Peter Ivanovitch shall be informed of your confession – and you shall be directed . . .'

Then, turning to Nikita, nicknamed Necator, standing by, he appealed to him in a murmur –

'What else can we do? After this piece of sincerity he cannot be dangerous any longer.'

The other muttered, 'Better make sure of that before we let him go. Leave that to me. I know how to deal with such gentlemen.'

He exchanged meaning glances with two or three men, who nodded slightly, then turning roughly to Razumov, 'You have heard? You are not wanted here. Why don't you get out?'

The Laspara girl on guard rose, and pulled the chair out of the way unemotionally. She gave a sleepy stare to Razumov, who started, looked round the room and passed slowly by her as if struck by some sudden thought.

'I beg you to observe,' he said, already on the landing, 'that I had only to hold my tongue. Today, of all days since I came amongst you, I was made safe, and today I made myself free from falsehood, from remorse – independent of every single human being on this earth.'

He turned his back on the room, and walked towards the stairs, but, at the violent crash of the door behind him, he looked over his shoulder and saw that Nikita, with three others, had followed him out. 'They are going to kill me, after all,' he thought.

Before he had time to turn round and confront them fairly, they set on him with a rush. He was driven headlong against the wall.

'I wonder how,' he completed his thought. Nikita cried, with a shrill laugh right in his face, 'We shall make you harmless. You wait a bit.'

Razumov did not struggle. The three men held him pinned against the wall, while Nikita, taking up a position a little on one side, deliberately swung off his enormous arm. Razumov, looking for a knife in his hand, saw it come at him open, unarmed, and received a tremendous blow on the side of his head over his ear. At the same time he heard a faint, dull detonating sound, as if someone had fired a pistol on the other side of the wall. A raging fury awoke in him at this outrage. The people in Laspara's rooms, holding their breath, listened to the desperate scuffling of four men all over the landing; thuds against the walls, a terrible crash against the very door, then all of them went down together with a violence which seemed to shake the whole house. Razumov, overpowered, breathless, crushed under the weight of his assailants, saw the monstrous Nikita squatting on his heels near his head, while the others held him down, kneeling on his chest, gripping his throat, lying across his legs.

'Turn his face the other way,' the paunchy terrorist directed, in an excited, gleeful squeak.

Razumov could struggle no longer. He was exhausted; he had to watch passively the heavy open hand of the brute descend again in a degrading blow over his other ear. It seemed to split his head in two, and all at once the men holding him became perfectly silent – soundless as shadows. In silence they pulled him brutally to his feet, rushed with him noiselessly down the staircase, and, opening the door, flung him out into the street.

He fell forward, and at once rolled over and over helplessly, going down the short slope together with the rush of running rain water. He came to rest in the roadway of the street at the bottom, lying on his back, with a great flash of lightning over his face – a vivid, silent flash of lightning which blinded him utterly. He picked himself up, and put his arm over his eyes to recover his sight. Not a sound reached him from anywhere, and he began to walk, staggering, down a long, empty street. The lightning waved and darted round him its silent flames, the water of the deluge fell, ran, leaped, drove

– noiseless like the drift of mist. In this unearthly stillness his footsteps fell silent on the pavement, while a dumb wind drove him on and on, like a lost mortal in a phantom world ravaged by a soundless thunderstorm. God only knows where his noiseless feet took him to that night, here and there, and back again without pause or rest. Of one place, at least, where they did lead him, we heard afterwards; and, in the morning, the driver of the first south-shore tramcar, clanging his bell desperately, saw a bedraggled, soaked man without a hat, and walking in the roadway unsteadily with his head down, step right in front of his car, and go under.

When they picked him up, with two broken limbs and a crushed side, Razumov had not lost consciousness. It was as though he had tumbled, smashing himself, into a world of mutes. Silent men, moving unheard, lifted him up, laid him on the sidewalk, gesticulating and grimacing round him their alarm, horror, and compassion. A red face with moustaches stooped close over him, lips moving, eyes rolling. Razumov tried hard to understand the reason of this dumb show. To those who stood around him, the features of that stranger, so grievously hurt, seemed composed in meditation. Afterwards his eyes sent out at them a look of fear and closed slowly. They stared at him. Razumov made an effort to remember some French words.

'*Je suis sourd,*'* he had time to utter feebly, before he fainted.

'He is deaf,' they exclaimed to each other. 'That's why he did not hear the car.'

They carried him off in that same car. Before it started on its journey, a woman in a shabby black dress, who had run out of the iron gate of some private grounds up the road, clambered on to the rear platform and would not be put off.

'I am a relation,' she insisted, in bad French. 'This young man is a Russian, and I am his relation.'

On this plea they let her have her way. She sat down calmly, and took his head on her lap; her scared faded eyes avoided looking at his deathlike face. At the corner of a street, on the other side of the town, a stretcher met the car. She followed it to the door of the

* 'I am deaf.'

hospital, where they let her come in and see him laid on a bed. Razumov's new-found relation never shed a tear, but the officials had some difficulty in inducing her to go away. The porter observed her lingering on the opposite pavement for a long time. Suddenly, as though she had remembered something, she ran off.

The ardent hater of all Finance ministers, the slave of Madame de S—, had made up her mind to offer her resignation as lady companion to the Egeria of Peter Ivanovitch. She had found work to do after her own heart.

But hours before, while the thunderstorm still raged in the night, there had been in the rooms of Julius Laspara a great sensation. The terrible Nikita, coming in from the landing, uplifted his squeaky voice in horrible glee before all the company –

'Razumov! Mr Razumov! The wonderful Razumov! He shall never be any use as a spy on any one. He won't talk, because he will never hear anything in his life – not a thing! I have burst the drums of his ears for him. Oh, you may trust me. I know the trick. Ha! Ha! Ha! I know the trick.'

V

It was nearly a fortnight after her mother's funeral that I saw Natalia Haldin for the last time.

In those silent, sombre days the doors of the *appartement* on the Boulevard des Philosophes were closed to everyone but myself. I believe I was of some use, if only in this, that I alone was aware of the incredible part of the situation. Miss Haldin nursed her mother alone to the last moment. If Razumov's visit had anything to do with Mrs Haldin's end (and I cannot help thinking that it hastened it considerably), it is because the man, trusted impulsively by the ill-fated Victor Haldin, had failed to gain the confidence of Victor Haldin's mother. What tale, precisely, he told her cannot be known – at any rate, I do not know it – but to me she seemed to die from the shock of an ultimate disappointment borne in silence. She had not believed him. Perhaps she could no longer believe any one, and consequently had nothing to say to any one – not even to her daughter. I suspect that Miss Haldin lived the heaviest hours of her life by that silent death-bed. I confess I was angry with the broken-hearted old woman passing away in the obstinacy of her mute distrust of her daughter.

When it was all over I stood aside. Miss Haldin had her compatriots round her then. A great number of them attended the funeral. I was there too, but afterwards managed to keep away from Miss Haldin, till I received a short note rewarding my self-denial. 'It is as you would have it. I am going back to Russia at once. My mind is made up. Come and see me.'

Verily, it was a reward of discretion. I went without delay to receive it. The *appartement* of the Boulevard des Philosophes presented the dreary signs of impending abandonment. It looked desolate and as if already empty to my eyes.

Standing, we exchanged a few words about her health, mine, remarks as to some people of the Russian colony, and then Natalia Haldin, establishing me on the sofa, began to talk openly of her future work, of her plans. It was all to be as I had wished it. And it was to be for life. We should never see each other again. Never!

I gathered this success to my breast. Natalia Haldin looked matured by her open and secret experiences. With her arms folded she walked up and down the whole length of the room, talking slowly, smooth-browed, with a resolute profile. She gave me a new view of herself, and I marvelled at that something grave and measured in her voice, in her movements, in her manner. It was the perfection of collected independence. The strength of her nature had come to surface because the obscure depths had been stirred.

'We two can talk of it now,' she observed, after a silence and stopping short before me. 'Have you been to inquire at the hospital lately?'

'Yes, I have.' And as she looked at me fixedly, 'He will live, the doctors say. But I thought that Tekla . . .'

'Tekla has not been near me for several days,' explained Miss Haldin quickly. 'As I never offered to go to the hospital with her, she thinks that I have no heart. She is disillusioned about me.'

And Miss Haldin smiled faintly.

'Yes. She sits with him as long and as often as they will let her,' I said. 'She says she must never abandon him – never as long as she lives. He'll need somebody – a hopeless cripple, and stone deaf with that.'

'Stone deaf? I didn't know,' murmured Natalia Haldin.

'He is. It seems strange. I am told there were no apparent injuries to the head. They say, too, that it is not very likely that he will live so very long for Tekla to take care of him.'

Miss Haldin shook her head.

'While there are travellers ready to fall by the way our Tekla will never be idle. She is a good Samaritan by an irresistible vocation. The revolutionists didn't understand her. Fancy a devoted creature like that being employed to carry about documents sewn in her dress, or made to write from dictation.'

'There is not much perspicacity in the world.'

No sooner uttered, I regretted that observation. Natalia Haldin, looking me straight in the face, assented by a slight movement of her head. She was not offended, but turning away began to pace the room again. To my Western eyes she seemed to be getting farther and farther from me, quite beyond my reach now, but undiminished in the increasing distance. I remained silent as though it were hopeless to raise my voice. The sound of hers, so close to me, made me start a little.

'Tekla saw him picked up after the accident. The good soul never explained to me really how it came about. She affirms that there was some understanding between them – some sort of compact – that in any sore need, in misfortune, or difficulty, or pain, he was to come to her.'

'Was there?' I said. 'It is lucky for him that there was, then. He'll need all the devotion of the good Samaritan.'

It was a fact that Tekla, looking out of her window at five in the morning, for some reason or other, had beheld Razumov in the grounds of the Château Borel, standing stockstill, bare-headed in the rain, at the foot of the terrace. She had screamed out to him, by name, to know what was the matter. He never even raised his head. By the time she had dressed herself sufficiently to run downstairs he was gone. She started in pursuit, and rushing out into the

343

road, came almost directly upon the arrested tramcar and the small knot of people picking up Razumov. That much Tekla had told me herself one afternoon we happened to meet at the door of the hospital, and without any kind of comment. But I did not want to meditate very long on the inwardness of this peculiar episode.

'Yes, Natalia Victorovna, he will need somebody when they dismiss him, on crutches and stone deaf from the hospital. But I do not think that when he rushed like an escaped madman into the grounds of the Château Borel it was to seek the help of that good Tekla.'

'No,' said Natalia, stopping short before me, 'perhaps not.' She sat down and leaned her head on her hand thoughtfully. The silence lasted for several minutes. During that time I remembered the evening of his atrocious confession – the plaint she seemed to have hardly enough life left in her to utter, 'It is impossible to be more unhappy ...' The recollection would have given me a shudder if I had not been lost in wonder at her force and her tranquillity. There was no longer any Natalia Haldin, because she had completely ceased to think of herself. It was a great victory, a characteristically Russian exploit in self-suppression.

She recalled me to myself by getting up suddenly like a person who has come to a decision. She walked to the writing-table, now stripped of all the small objects associated with her by daily use – a mere piece of dead furniture; but it contained something living, still, since she took from a recess a flat parcel which she brought to me.

'It's a book,' she said rather abruptly. 'It was sent to me wrapped up in my veil. I told you nothing at the time, but now I've decided to leave it with you. I have the right to do that. It was sent to me. It is mine. You may preserve it, or destroy it after you have read it. And while you read it, please remember that I *was* defenceless. And that he ...'

'Defenceless!' I repeated, surprised, looking hard at her.

'You'll find the very word written there,' she whispered. 'Well, it's true! I *was* defenceless – but perhaps you were able to see that for yourself.' Her face coloured, then went deadly pale. 'In justice to the man, I want you to remember that I was. Oh, I was, I was!'

I rose, a little shakily.

'I am not likely to forget anything you say at this our last parting.'

Her hand fell into mine.

'It's difficult to believe that it must be good-bye with us.'

She returned my pressure and our hands separated.

'Yes. I am leaving here tomorrow. My eyes are open at last and my hands are free now. As for the rest – which of us can fail to hear the stifled cry of our great distress? It may be nothing to the world.'

'The world is more conscious of your discordant voices,' I said. 'It is the way of the world.'

'Yes.' She bowed her head in assent, and hesitated for a moment. 'I must own to you that I shall never give up looking forward to the day when all discord shall be silenced. Try to imagine its dawn! The tempest of blows and of execrations is over; all is still; the new sun is rising, and the weary men united at last, taking count in their conscience of the ended contest, feel saddened by their victory, because so many ideas have perished for the triumph of one, so many beliefs have abandoned them without support. They feel alone on the earth and gather close together. Yes, there must be many bitter hours! But at last the anguish of hearts shall be extinguished in love.'

And on this last word of her wisdom, a word so sweet, so bitter, so cruel sometimes, I said good-bye to Natalia Haldin. It is hard to think I shall never look any more into the trustful eyes of that girl – wedded to an invincible belief in the advent of loving concord springing like a heavenly flower from the soil of men's earth, soaked in blood, torn by struggles, watered with tears.

It must be understood that at that time I didn't know anything of Mr Razumov's confession to the assembled revolutionists. Natalia Haldin might have guessed what was the 'one thing more' which remained for him to do; but this my Western eyes had failed to see.

Tekla, the ex-lady companion of Madame de S——, haunted his bedside at the hospital. We met once or twice at the door of that establishment, but on these occasions she was not communicative. She gave me news of Mr Razumov as concisely as possible. He was making a slow recovery, but would remain a hopeless cripple all his life. Personally, I never went near him: I never saw him again, after the awful evening when I stood by, a watchful but ignored spectator of his scene with Miss Haldin. He was in due course discharged from the hospital, and his 'relative' – so I was told – had carried him off somewhere.

My information was completed nearly two years later. The opportunity, certainly, was not of my seeking; it was quite accidentally that I met a much-trusted woman revolutionist at the house of a distinguished Russian gentleman of liberal convictions, who came to live in Geneva for a time.

He was quite a different sort of celebrity from Peter Ivanovitch – a dark-haired man with kind eyes, high-shouldered, courteous, and with something hushed and circumspect in his manner. He approached me, choosing the moment when there was no one near, followed by a grey-haired, alert lady in a crimson blouse.

'Our Sophia Antonovna wishes to be made known to you,' he addressed me, in his guarded voice. 'And so I leave you two to have a talk together.'

'I would never have intruded myself upon your notice,' the grey-haired lady began at once, 'if I had not been charged with a message for you.'

It was a message of a few friendly words from Natalia Haldin. Sophia Antonovna had just returned from a secret excursion into Russia, and had seen Miss Haldin. She lived in a town 'in the centre', sharing her compassionate labours between the horrors of over-crowded jails, and the heartrending misery of bereaved homes. She did not spare herself in good service, Sophia Antonovna assured me.

'She had a faithful soul, an undaunted spirit and an indefatigable body,' the woman revolutionist summed it all up, with a touch of enthusiasm.

A conversation thus engaged was not likely to drop from want of interest on my side. We went to sit apart in a corner where no one interrupted us. In the course of our talk about Miss Haldin, Sophia Antonovna remarked suddenly –

'I suppose you remember seeing me before? That evening when Natalia came to ask Peter Ivanovitch for the address of a certain Razumov, that young man who ...'

'I remember perfectly,' I said. When Sophia Antonovna learned that I had in my possession that young man's journal given me by Miss Haldin she became intensely interested. She did not conceal her curiosity to see the document.

I offered to show it to her, and she at once volunteered to call on me next day for that purpose.

She turned over the pages greedily for an hour or more, and then handed me the book with a faint sigh. While moving about Russia, she had seen Razumov too. He lived, not 'in the centre', but 'in the south'. She described to me a little two-roomed wooden house, in the suburb of some very small town, hiding within the high plank-fence of a yard overgrown with nettles. He was crippled, ill, getting weaker every day, and Tekla the Samaritan tended him un-weariedly with the pure joy of unselfish devotion. There was nothing in that task to become disillusioned about.

I did not hide from Sophia Antonovna my surprise that she should have visited Mr Razumov. I did not even understand the motive. But she informed me that she was not the only one.

'Some of *us* always go to see him when passing through. He is intelligent. He has ideas ... He talks well, too.'

Presently I heard for the first time of Razumov's public confession in Laspara's house. Sophia Antonovna gave me a detailed relation of what had occurred there. Razumov himself had told her all about it, most minutely.

Then, looking hard at me with her brilliant black eyes –

'There are evil moments in every life. A false suggestion enters one's brain, and then fear is born – fear of oneself, fear for oneself. Or else a false courage – who knows? Well, call it what you like; but tell me, how many of them would deliver themselves up deliberately to perdition (as he himself says in that book) rather than go on living, secretly debased in their own eyes? How many? ... And please mark this – he was safe when he did it. It was just when he believed himself safe and more – infinitely more – when the possi-bility of being loved by that admirable girl first dawned upon him, that he discovered that his bitterest railings, the worst wickedness, the devil work of his hate and pride, could never cover up the ignominy of the existence before him. There's character in such a discovery.'

I accepted her conclusion in silence. Who would care to question the grounds of forgiveness or compassion? However, it appeared later on, that there was some compunction, too, in the charity extended by the revolutionary world to Razumov the betrayer. Sophia Antonovna continued uneasily –

'And then, you know, he was the victim of an outrage. It was not authorized. Nothing was decided as to what was to be done with him. He had confessed voluntarily. And that Nikita who burst the drums of his ears purposely, out on the landing, you know, as if carried away by indignation – well, he has turned out to be a scoundrel of the worst kind – a traitor himself, a betrayer – a spy! Razumov told me he had charged him with it by a sort of inspiration . . .'

'I had a glimpse of that brute,' I said. 'How any of you could have been deceived for half a day passes my comprehension!'

She interrupted me.

'There! There! Don't talk of it. The first time I saw him, I, too, was appalled. They cried me down. We were always telling each other, "Oh! you mustn't mind his appearance." And then he was always ready to kill. There was no doubt of it. He killed – yes! in both camps. The fiend . . .'

Then Sophia Antonovna, after mastering the angry trembling of her lips, told me a very queer tale. It went that Councillor Mikulin, travelling in Germany (shortly after Razumov's disappearance from Geneva), happened to meet Peter Ivanovitch in a railway carriage. Being alone in the compartment, these two talked together half the night, and it was then that Mikulin the Police Chief gave a hint to the Arch-Revolutionist as to the true character of the arch-slayer of gendarmes. It looks as though Mikulin had wanted to get rid of that particular agent of his own! He might have grown tired of him, or frightened of him. It must also be said that Mikulin had inherited the sinister Nikita from his predecessor in office.

And this story, too, I received without comment in my character of a mute witness of things Russian, unrolling their Eastern logic under my Western eyes. But I permitted myself a question –

'Tell me, please, Sophia Antonovna, did Madame de S— leave all her fortune to Peter Ivanovitch?'

'Not a bit of it.' The woman revolutionist shrugged her shoulders in disgust. 'She died without making a will. A lot of nephews and nieces came down from St Petersburg, like a flock of vultures, and fought for her money amongst themselves. All beastly Kammer-herrs and Maids of Honour – abominable court flunkeys. Tfui!'

'One does not hear much of Peter Ivanovitch now,' I remarked, after a pause.

'Peter Ivanovitch,' said Sophia Antonovna gravely, 'has united himself to a peasant girl.'

I was truly astonished.

'What! On the Riviera?'

'What nonsense! Of course not.'

Sophia Antonovna's tone was slightly tart.

'Is he, then, living actually in Russia? It's a tremendous risk – isn't it?' I cried. 'And all for the sake of a peasant girl. Don't you think it's very wrong of him?'

Sophia Antonovna preserved a mysterious silence for a while, then made a statement.

'He just simply adores her.'

'Does he? Well, then, I hope that she won't hesitate to beat him.'

Sophia Antonovna got up and wished me good-bye, as though she had not heard a word of my impious hope; but, in the very doorway, where I attended her, she turned round for an instant, and declared in a firm voice –

'Peter Ivanovitch is an inspired man.'

THE END

NOTES

1. *Razum*: reason. Thus prudent, calculating, one who stands for rationalism. Likewise Razumikhin in Dostoyevsky's *Crime and Punishment*.

2. St Petersburg was founded in 1703 by Peter the Great, and was culturally the most Western and European of Russian cities.

3. Orthodox priests are allowed to marry.

4. Suggested to Conrad by Plehve, the Minister of the Interior, who was assassinated in 1904.

5. The Cossacks, a very independent people from the south-west of Russia, provided the Czar's crack mounted regiments.

6. Nicholas I (1796–1855). His regime was one of the most repressive of all, under which there was a complete censorship on the expression of opinion. It is said that in one year of his regime, there were more people employed in censorship than there were books published.

7. The Nertchinsk mines in Siberia were worked by convicts.

8. French was freely spoken by aristocratic and educated Russians.

9. A Tcherkess long coat was worn by the Cossacks.

10. Medusa's head was covered with hissing serpents instead of hair, and it was so fearful that everyone looking at it was turned to stone.

11. Various persons have been proposed as models for Peter Ivanovitch, among them Bakhunin, the anarchist, and Tolstoy.

12. Numa, the legendary second king of Rome who was famed for his wisdom and piety, was guided by the nymph Egeria about the forms of worship he should introduce for the Romans.

13. Alexander II (1818–81) made some moves, however modest, towards constitutional government and abolished serfdom.

350

He was assassinated in St Petersburg by a bomb thrown by a member of the populist group calling itself 'The Will of the People'.

14. Brutus was trained from an early age by his uncle Cato in the principles of the aristocratical party and later joined in the murder of Julius Caesar.

15. Giuseppe Mazzini (1805–72), Italian patriot and revolutionary, was exiled to France and Switzerland. He became a legend as the 'apostle' of the oppressed and as an arch-conspirator.

16. E. T. A. Hoffmann (1776–1822), German composer and writer whose tales were famous for their grotesque character.

17. Catherine II, the Great (1729–96), was sole ruler from 1762. A person of great intellectual and artistic ability, an enlightened despot of liberal ideas who put down all revolts and opposition very harshly, she had a scandalous reputation at court and was said to acquire supporters by seduction.

18. Jean-Jacques Rousseau (1712–78), one of the geniuses of French eighteenth-century literature, lived as a boy in Geneva. In much of his work he protested against existing society and promoted the cult of the 'noble savage'. In his major work of political philosophy, *Du Contrat Social* or *The Social Contract*, he argues that the sovereign power in the state should be the will of the people.

19. Matthew 2: 16–18:

Then Herod, when he saw that he was mocked of the wise men, was exceeding wroth, and sent forth, and slew all the male children that were in Bethlehem, and in all the borders thereof, from two years old and under, according to the time which he had carefully learned of the wise men.

Then was fulfilled that which was spoken by Jeremiah the prophet, saying,

'A voice was heard in Ramah,
Weeping and great mourning,
Rachel weeping for her children;
And she would not be comforted because they are not.'